OTHER BOOKS BY KIMBERLY MENOZZI

Ask Me if I'm Happy

Alternate Rialto

a novel

KIMBERLY MENOZZI

This novel is entirely a work of fiction. The names, characters, and incidents portrayed in it are the work of the author's imagination. Any resemblance to actual persons, living or dead, events or localities is entirely coincidental.

The right of Kimberly Menozzi to be identified as the Author of the Work has been asserted in accordance with the Copyright, Designs and Patents Act 1988.

No part of this publication may be reproduced, stored in a retrieval system, or transmitted, in any form or by any means, electronic, mechanical, photocopying, recording or otherwise without the prior written permission of the Author

ISBN: 0615816010
ISBN-13: 978-0615816012

For Alessandro, who answered the question correctly;

for the fangirls, of every age, all over the world;

and for the riders who leave everything on the road, every time they ride.

WW 108

Sei sempre con noi.

CONTENTS

Note from the Author

For the sake of the story, I have taken a few small creative liberties with the distances and geography of a number of locations, as well as with some details regarding the behind-the-scenes aspects of team life. No two cycling teams are exactly alike, however, and I promise that I have done as much research as possible to create a story both fans and non-fans of cycling will enjoy. Nevertheless, putting all of these elements together was bound to get a bit messy.

The teams and riders are all products of my imagination, some of them inspired by real teams and riders from all over the world. However, none of them are intended to depict any *actual* riders or teams in any way.

As for the race: it's important to note the Tour d'Europa is, of course, a figment of my imagination, and in this story's fictional world takes the place of the Tour de France. While cycling's Grand Tours (*il Giro d'Italia, le Tour de France* and *la Vuelta a España*) normally have twenty-one stages (plus or minus a time trial prologue), this fictional race has twenty-seven, hence its reputation as "The longest, hardest and most incredible cycling race in the world".

Thanks in advance for your understanding.

Stage One

(40 km - Individual Time Trial - Lisbon, Portugal)

Don't walk if you can stand. Don't stand if you can sit. Don't sit if you can lie down. The professional cyclist's mantra whirled around in my head until I could no longer be sure where it ended or began again.

At least I could do as instructed: I was flat on my back in bed, eyes closed, trying to ignore the way my stomach was twisting and turning. I wasn't sick, but it was going to be a struggle to maintain the poker face I'd need today.

I tried to shift my focus onto the time trial course I'd ride in a few hours. The recon ride with the group yesterday convinced me today's first stage was as good as mine. Barely forty kilometres long with only one climb through the heart of Sintra-Cascais Natural Park, then a winding descent on narrow switchback curves before the home stretch back toward Sintra itself.

My final, solo recon was in a couple of hours. I wanted to ride the route without distractions. I'd take it slow and easy, just enough to warm up and not expend too much energy before my afternoon start.

Refocusing again, I recalled yesterday's ride in detail: the bike as an extension of myself, the vibration of the road surface travelling through it. My reflexes and muscles twitched in anticipation of the increased effort of the climb and the slaloming descent on the other side, warm wind rushing past to cool the sweat standing on my skin. I grinned.

1

I've got the best fucking job in the world.

A tell-tale *snick* of a key card in the door's electronic lock pulled me back to full wakefulness. The door slammed open to the accompaniment of a fist pounding on the doorframe and a thunderous, demanding call:

"Renard! Brodowski! Wake up! *Sveglia! Réveillez! Zbudzić!*"

I glanced over at Romuald Brodowski, my roommate. Flat on his back he was, miraculously, still asleep.

He also sported a hard-on to shame even the most ambitious of men. His sheets made an impressive tent in the light from the hallway.

How the hell does he ride a bike with that thing?

Another pass from Jerzy Jankowski, our team manager/*directeur sportif*/Svengali, followed:

"Federico! Romuald! It's time!"

Jerzy moved down the corridor, banging open the doors of every room and shouting the names of my teammates as he had Rom's and mine. In the past, other occupants of the hotels had complained. This was a bad idea considering Jerzy's notorious temper, but few outside of the sport knew that. The team had been banned from five different hotels in France alone before the team sponsors had a talk with Jerzy (long-distance; they weren't crazy) and came up with a new plan.

Now, race organizers rented entire floors – sometimes entire bed-and-breakfasts or small hotels – to accommodate our riders and staff. This arrangement smacked of 'preferential treatment' to some of the other team organizations, and they were vocal about it, mocking all of *Alta VeloCidad* for being soft or for thinking we were somehow special.

Fuck it all.

I pulled my pillow out from under my head and ducked under it to block out the light and (as if it were remotely possible) to muffle Jerzy's shouting.

Besides, I knew what was coming next:

The nicknames.

"Ciccio! Robaczku! NOW!"

Once he'd reached this point, there was no going back. It was time to get up or risk an ice-water bath in bed. The bucket sloshed ominously while Jerzy stomped along the corridor, shouting out the nicknames for each member of the team.

Rom's nickname, Robaczku, supposedly means something like "Little Bug". No one has yet been able to clarify its origin for me.

My nickname is "Ciccio." In some regions of Italy, it's a term of endearment, which also means "chubby."

I hate it. Always have; always will. And that's precisely why Jerzy used it rather than "Chicco" – a proper nickname for "Federico." Subtle differences mean a lot.

Hearing it was motivation enough to get to my feet and shuffle to the toilet.

Before I reached the bathroom Jerzy poked his head into the room.

"*Enfin, tu t'es réveillé!*"

For some reason I'd been expecting Italian, not French, and it took me a moment to respond in my first mother tongue.

"*Oui... presque.*" I was barely awake in spite of the sonic barrage, and he knew it.

"*Est-il en place?*"

"*Certaines régions plus que d'autres, oui,*" I joked, regrettably aware some parts of my roommate were more awake than others.

Unamused, Jerzy grunted, shook his head and hit the light switch, bucket in hand. I went into the bathroom and closed the door.

At the same instant a flood of Polish expletives rushed out in Jerzy's voice, followed shortly thereafter by a splash and Romuald's simultaneous shriek of surprise.

I opened the bathroom door as Jerzy stalked out into the corridor and disappeared from sight. The now-empty bucket clanged hollowly from the direction of the ice machine at the end of the hall. I turned to find my team's *wunderkind* hill-climber dancing in place in the middle of our room, my dry bedcover wrapped around him for warmth.

He paused in his dance to look at me, his white-blond hair hanging limp and wet in his face, his eyes bright and alert. At least now the bedcover lay flat across his front.

"*Czy długo będziesz?*" he asked, pointing behind me.

I speak several languages – English, German, a smattering of Spanish, and I grew up speaking both French and Italian. Polish, however, hardly registers on my radar – with the exception of a few choice obscenities Jerzy had inadvertently taught us all.

I shrugged, not understanding, and ducked back inside to have my morning shower. One of my unofficial duties for the team was to get Rom speaking other languages. Though we'd roomed together for several months, he still spoke mostly Polish. He'd mastered food, drink, and rudimentary directions in a variety of languages, and that was about it. Oh, and swearing. He could curse in every language of the team (and there were plenty); in that regard, he was a prodigy.

I left the bathroom for Rom and got dressed. The process took much longer than normal, thanks to my compulsive handling of my mobile phone.

Put on underwear – check phone and make sure it's not on mute.

Put on sweatpants – check phone and make sure ringer is audible.

Put on t-shirt – check phone and make sure I didn't shut it off.

Put on socks and shoes – check where I put phone, to be sure I didn't lose it in the bedclothes.

Put on windbreaker and wristwatch – check phone and swear in frustration.

Where the hell was her call? Usually my fiancée, Solange, called early in the morning.

Today? Nothing. She hadn't called for a week.

I scrolled down to *Melo, Solange*, pressed "send," and waited.

And waited. The voicemail picked up, her stiff recitation of her name the only indication that the number was hers. I rang off without leaving a message. The others hadn't made a difference, anyway.

It was just as well. Jerzy was banging on doors again, summoning us to the dining hall. Rom and I fell into step behind our teammates on the worn hallway carpeting of our two-star hotel.

Heinrich Brunn was at the head of the group as usual. Without any breakfast in me, the sight of his back was enough to set my stomach on fire. I sensed Rom watching me and forced the scowl off my face, then rubbed my stomach, feigning hunger.

It was hard to keep my resentment to myself. Everyone on the team knew I was unhappy. I was sure Brunn knew it. Aside from Jerzy, Brunn knew me better than anyone else on the team did.

I'd been his domestique for three years, sacrificing my own strength and potential stage wins so that he, as team leader, could take the points, the titles – and often the entire competition. It was my job and I had done it without complaint, as Rom now did for me, because I knew my time would come.

Brunn had been in a major car accident in the off-season nearly four years ago, along with Jerzy and two other riders, one of whom died, the other rendered paraplegic. Both of Jerzy's legs had been broken. With a fractured pelvis, a cervical fracture and considerable damage to his knee, Brunn's initial diagnosis was that he'd never ride again. Then it was revised to say he'd never compete again. Then *that* changed to '*He'll never ride a Grand Tour*'.

Yet here we were, about to ride the biggest Grand Tour of all, the Tour d'Europa, and Brunn was our likely team leader. Again.

Instead of me.

The hotel staff paused in their duties, making no secret of the fact they were watching Brunn go by as our motley mob passed through the corridors. A few of them even applauded – quietly, timidly – and I knew that Brunn had assumed his trademark intimidating scowl.

In contrast, I flashed everyone we met the biggest smile I could manage. One or two of the staffers smiled back. A young chambermaid batted her eyelashes at me in a charming, flirtatious way and I had to resist looking back after passing her.

Jerzy's team rules dictated that women were strictly *verboten*. No fooling around of any sort was permitted until after the Tour. Not that anyone would be up to dealing with a woman after riding a bike over a mountain or across one hundred-plus kilometres, six days out of seven.

A second young lady offered me a suggestive smile and I was forced to recall the salacious cover story for *Grand Tours Magazine*, which had dubbed me "The Face of the Tour." Try and live with *that* hanging over your head.

Still, if it stole some of Brunn's thunder, it was all to the good.

I had been Jerzy's pride and joy for the last four years; the heir apparent to Brunn's title. But as soon as the German had announced an interest in riding again, I ceased to exist in Jerzy's eyes.

Nothing I'd achieved was as impressive as Brunn's remarkable comeback. Every last one of my accomplishments, my titles – everything I'd achieved in his absence was forgotten.

Don't get me wrong. Brunn *is* an incredible athlete – his showing in the Giro d'Italia was proof enough of that. Placing sixth after nearly four years away is outstanding for anyone – never mind that he'd recovered so quickly from his injuries.

The manic publicity after Brunn joined the team again was nothing short of incredible. It was fitting and he deserved it, but that didn't erase the fact that I'd been short-changed.

Until Brunn's decision to return to the sport, until he'd rejoined us, *I* had been Jerzy's focus. I'd been performing beyond my wildest dreams, riding extremely well, taking prizes and stages almost at will.

And now, it meant nothing.

In spite of Brunn's presence or Jerzy's focus on him, I was determined to do my best on this Tour. I was approaching the peak of my abilities and I was determined; my expectations for this year's Tour d'Europa were higher than ever.

There was nowhere to go but down.

Never mind that. I can ride the hell out of the descents.

For now I was reduced to refraining from shooting daggers from my eyes at Brunn while the team filed down to the dining hall for our first meeting of the day. Under Jerzy's curt direction, we sat at the "U"-shaped tables which had been placed so we could all see him clearly.

He paced between the prongs while we settled in, some of us stifling yawns and rubbing bleary eyes. We'd had the recon ride yesterday, gone over the itinerary of the entire Tour – all twenty-seven stages – and hashed out initial strategies last night. We'd finished around midnight.

Jerzy directed me to a chair close to Brunn and Rom took the seat next to me. At last our leader stopped pacing, bringing the group to a collective hush. He turned slowly, silently, until his gaze came to rest on Brunn, who sat at the apex of the "U" looking like a king at the table, presiding over the lot of us.

"Today will be a challenge for some of you," Jerzy began. "It's not an especially difficult route, but I still expect each and every one of you to give your best to this today. Ride with your heads as well as your legs. If I see any slacking off, I will bring the car up and personally give you the shove of a lifetime."

A murmur of chuckles passed through the group, but I don't think anyone doubted that he'd do it. We *knew* he would.

I watched Romuald in my peripheral vision when Jerzy repeated everything in Polish for his benefit. There was a distinct shine of hero-worship in Rom's eyes – and why not? In his time, Jerzy had been one of Poland's most celebrated cyclists.

Keeping one eye on the proceedings, I checked my phone. Australia was, what, eight or nine hours ahead of Lisbon? Surely Solange was done with her photo shoots by now. Finding nothing, I stuffed the phone back in my pocket.

"We've got to get some space between ourselves and *Maxxout*. If they get within sniffing distance of our asses, they'll fly right up 'em."

Silence filled the hall. We knew this was true, too. For every member of our team, Team *Maxxout* had an equal. Well, for nearly every member. The one notable exception had rejoined us this year.

"You've all been working hard. I've seen it. You all made me proud at the Giro this year. I expect the same fine work from you now." With this, Jerzy's gaze again went to Brunn, who gave a slight, modest nod. I bit my lip and tried to keep my expression blank.

"You already know what to expect from the route: one good climb in the middle and it's all downhill from there.

"You know your strengths and weaknesses as well as I do. This is *your* event, Ciccio. See that you do it justice."

I nodded, hoping the gesture looked nonchalant in spite of my surge of pride. I hated that such a small acknowledgement could make me feel so important, but being singled out like that – in spite of my all-rounder status – was recognition of my strength in time trials.

Not even Brunn – another all-rounder – could say that.

***

My husband Charles was still in the shower when I got out of bed. Our walking tour of Lisbon the previous night had exhausted me, but now I was awake and eager to start the day. In a few hours, we'd be in nearby Sintra, where the Tour d'Europa time trials would start and finish.

I sat at our hotel room's desk, took my digital camera out of its case and examined it, making sure everything functioned properly. I glanced over at the contraption now folded up into itself and sitting next to my backpack and sighed. Charles had been so pleased with himself when he'd given me the tripod, declaring it "a proper gift for a proper photographer". He clearly hadn't listened to a thing I'd said about what it would be like to take photos at a race. I'd only done a few – all of them local, amateur events – but I knew the last thing I'd need was something as complicated as that to deal with. And still, there it was. Maybe I could stash it in a suitcase, or "forget" it when we left for the stage start. If I didn't have it with me, I couldn't use it, right?

I went back to checking my cameras before Charles came out and stood behind me, drops of water falling from his hair onto the table.

"Do you mind, hon?" I asked over my shoulder. "You're going to get my lenses wet."

He *hmphed* in response and went to sit on the bed. I took off my eyeglasses and went to the window to open the curtains.

"What time does this race start anyway, Abigail?"

"One o'clock, but it's the time trial." I pulled the curtains apart and the tidy neighbourhood which housed our hotel came into view.

Charles shrugged, indifferent. "So?"

"It's only the first day. They'll leave one by one, circle through that huge park over on the coast and then come back."

He looked utterly uninterested but managed to keep from muttering anything under his breath. Needless to say, he didn't quite share my enthusiasm even though he'd given me this trip for our tenth anniversary: we were going to follow the entire Tour, stage by stage, from beginning to end.

When he'd given me the itinerary last September, then the plane tickets two months ago, I'd been thrilled speechless – both times. Now I realized my joy might have been a bit premature. Travelling around the continent with his moping mug in tow was going to be a stone drag if nothing changed.

Once I'd known this trip was a sure thing, I'd contacted a few sport magazines with a proposal for a photo journal called *The Tour d'Europa, Day by Day*. After a while I'd received a response from one saying they'd liked my portfolio and were interested. An added bonus: they'd agreed to reimburse me for equipment costs, as well.

My dream of selling my photographs was coming true.

I almost wished Charles would go home and leave me to it. I could surely find some English-speaking compatriots with whom I could enjoy myself, who would understand my interest and who wouldn't hope to see some crashes because they found them "quite entertaining."

"When it's over we'll go to the pub," I said and his face lit up.

"I saw one that looked promising a couple of blocks over," he said, genuinely interested for the first time. "It's made out to be a proper English pub, but we'll see."

"I guess we will." I put my glasses on again and turned my attention back to my cameras, my heart sinking ever-so-slightly in my chest.

*

Thanks to a paperwork mix-up, I didn't have my accreditation to shoot the race. The English-speaking official reassured me that I'd be able to collect my badge and vest at the press quarters in the morning before the next stage start. Undaunted, I made my way to the start line with Charles in tow. I'd have to try and grab the best shots I could from the sidelines.

If only Charles hadn't retrieved the bloody tripod when I'd left it behind in the room.

The crowd swarmed around us and I struggled to keep my camera up and properly focused on the top of the starting ramp. I took my time, using the tripod like a monopod and framing my shots with care. When each rider paused at the top of the ramp, I snapped a picture. When they began their descent, I snapped another. If I was lucky, I got another shot as they passed by.

In the interim between starts, I took "mood" shots: the crowd, the officials, details of the surrounding circus-like atmosphere. At the back of the ramp, a few cyclists waited for their start times. I aimed my lens behind the ramp and focused on one rider, cycling in slow circles, waiting for his turn to climb up to the starting house.

The scene reminded me of a race horse being paced before going into its post at the gate. There was something in the brightness of his team colours which cheered me.

An official signalled to the rider and he made a wide turn before dismounting to climb the ramp. After a few last-minute checks of his bike he was in position, poised and ready to descend onto the course.

"He looks mad enough to kill, doesn't he?" Charles laughed nervously, distracting me from the PA announcement of the rider's name. "I'd hate to be one of the blokes ahead of him."

I had to agree. A scowl of concentration twisted the handsome features beneath the space-age helmet and goggles. It was a chilling expression somewhere beyond determination, bordering on obsession.

A race official said something and the cyclist nodded, his gaze never leaving the road ahead of him. The countdown followed, the official's hand counting off the passing seconds as he called them out – *três, dois, um* – before snapping back as the electronic tone rang out. The rider shot down the ramp and up the street, a multicoloured blur disappearing into the distance.

The crowd cheered like mad. He was the last of his team to hit the tarmac and his reputation preceded him.

Exhilaration flooded through me, watching him go.

I checked the time and made a mental note to get to the finish and try to get a shot of him when he arrived. After detaching the camera from the tripod, I scrolled quickly through the shots stored in it. A bit of zooming showed his name on the display over the ramp: Federico Renard.

I nearly laughed, recalling the quasi-glamorous cover photo of him on the latest issue of *Grand Tours Magazine*. He looked quite different in real life.

"Come on." I put the tripod away before tugging Charles' sleeve to catch his attention again. "I have to get shots of the riders coming in."

He nodded, then followed reluctantly. His gaze strayed dolefully in the direction of the nearest pub as we passed it.

"Why don't you go and get yourself a drink?" I suggested. "I'll be fine by myself. You can even wait for me there, if you want."

"You're sure?" I hardly had a chance to nod before he hurried off.

Trying not to feel too relieved, I turned my attention back to the finish line. I snapped the next cyclist coming over the line and then the next, and the next.

I glanced in the direction of the pub, then back down the road. I took the tripod and rested it against a waste bin, then edged through the crowd to get some distance from the cumbersome object.

Around me the spectators waved flags and signs and cheered – not only for their favourites, but for every rider coming in. All at once, there were excited shouts and piercing whistles all around. Everyone turned to watch the giant screens on the sides of the road. Renard, the rider Charles thought looked so angry, had cleared the second checkpoint in record time. He was presently burning up the road on the descents out of the park, occasionally leaving the less-daring motorcycle cameramen behind. They weren't willing to take the curves at the same rate of speed.

Clearing a bend in the road to fly down to the straightaway beyond, Renard shot past a rider who'd left the start house a full two minutes ahead of him. The next switchbacks in the road made the crowd gasp, and my heart pounded so hard I could scarcely breathe. Finally he swept past yet another rider and out onto somewhat more open road.

The crowd tensed, watching along the road for him. On the screen another dramatic scene played out. Renard had now surpassed the time of his teammate and fan favourite, Heinrich Brunn – quite easily, by the look of it – and was making his way toward the finish. The seconds which separated them began to expand: Brunn's time was five seconds longer, ten, twenty. The standings on the screen shifted accordingly. Renard rose higher and higher, from fourth to third to second and then to a clear first-place finish.

My camera all but forgotten, I leaned over the barrier and watched eagerly for his arrival. I needn't have worried about missing him – the roar of the crowd swept along with him as he closed in on the finish line. The sound grew louder and louder still, every possible noisemaker being improvised and then employed. Cheers and shouts which bordered on screams, megaphones used to amplify shouts of joy, inflatable "thundersticks" *thwapped* together to produce manic, percussive sounds. People clapped their hands and banged on the barriers, jumping up and down.

And then, there he was. I gathered my senses and snapped photos of him approaching the line, one arm raised over his head in a show of jubilation, complete and utter joy on his face.

The chronometer overhead said it all: he'd arrived one full minute ahead of the fastest rider up to that point.

He rode straight into the waiting arms of his team handlers, his shoulders slumping as though he were melting into their hands. I caught glimpses of him collapsing onto the road, pawing at his helmet until someone helped him out of it, and then lying flat on the pavement past the fencing which kept the team buses and equipment away from the general public.

His chest heaved, expanding to twice its size as he gulped in breath after breath, his hands limp on his belly. He was still smiling.

Suddenly he was lost from my view. Only then did I realize I'd been snapping photos the whole time.

A touch on my shoulder shook me out of my trance. I looked up into blue eyes and it took a moment before I recognized my husband.

"What's all the excitement, then? And where's your tripod?"

"What? I—" I looked around with what I hoped looked like panic on my face. "Someone nicked it – I can't believe it! I had it just a while ago."

I raised my hand to my forehead and hoped he'd believe me.

For the moment, anyway, he seemed to. He looked around the crowd, quickly checking every hand in sight. I desperately hoped no-one was foolish enough to have one, and that he wouldn't start checking all the waste bins along the street.

That would be tough to explain.

***

Back at the hotel, I had two thorough goings-over at the same time. The team masseur worked his magic on my legs – cooling the fire smouldering beneath my skin – while Jerzy tore into me with a restraint I'd never seen before.

"Grandstanding," he growled, pacing the length of the room. "Shameless grandstanding, Ciccio. I don't approve of such things. It could have cost you time."

"But it didn't," I said, looking up at him from the massage table.

He whirled around and narrowed one eye at me, his signal that I should shut up if I intended to keep all my most precious body parts. The masseur kept his head down and continued working as though the threat weren't hanging in the air amongst us.

"It *could* have, is what I said. Save the shows for when you join the circus."

The blood drained from my face as shame filled it. He was right. Sure, I'd managed a phenomenal lead – fifty-five seconds ahead of Brunn, forty seconds ahead of Schlessinger and *Maxxout*, who would be marking my ass as a personal vendetta for sure – but starting tomorrow, the stages would be longer and harder, and I wouldn't be on my own.

"Work *with* the team, Ciccio, not against them."

I nodded, chastened. Jerzy remained at the foot of the table, behind the masseur, and glared at me before storming off. The masseur glanced up at me with a sympathetic look and I closed my eyes, exhausted.

A short while later Attilio "Attila" Castelli, our other climber, poked his head around the doorframe.

"*Ciao, Chicco. Come va?*"

"*Va bene*, Attila. Sorry I crushed your ass, today."

"*Ma, vaffanculo, amico mio.*" He gestured obscenely, then dragged a chair over to sit next to me."I've never seen them yank someone onto the bus for a piss so fast."

I shrugged, which wasn't easy to do lying down. "It's to be expected."

"Didn't it take the buzz off your ride? So to speak."

I shrugged again and the masseur started working on my other leg. "Not really. I must have made an impression." I listened carefully, trying to recognise the voices chatting in the corridor. "*Dimmi...* what has he said?"

My teammate lowered his head and shook it. He knew I meant Brunn, and he would be the one to know what Brunn thought. He'd been Brunn's domestique since he'd returned. "*Niente.* Nothing. It didn't bother him to get shoved down to fourth."

"*Beh*, never mind, then." I waved one hand airily before dropping it onto my stomach. "I guess it's better than having him pissed off."

"I'll see you at dinner tonight. Wear your helmet, just in case." He stood up as the masseur completed his work and towelled my legs dry. "By the way, rumour has it that a copy of *Grand Tours* popped up."

I groaned.

"Phil and James have it, so there's no way to get it away from them."

"I'll have to try."

Attilio paused in the doorway and gave me a wicked grin. "It's a *lovely* photo, by the way. 'The Face of the Tour'?"

"Fuck off," I said, half-grinning and chucking a towel at him.

He ducked my bad throw, raised one hand and disappeared, leaving me to contemplate the evening to come.

My desire to celebrate had evaporated.

***

After dinner at the pub and a short stroll around the neighbourhood, Charles and I returned to our room. He undressed in terse, jerky movements, scowling all the while.

It was my fault. I'd been antsy at the pub, eager to get back and have another look at the photos I'd taken in the afternoon. My heart raced while I looked over the shots of Renard's arrival. They'd turned out very well. Even the blurry ones weren't too bad.

"So how are they?" Charles asked from behind me.

"Pretty good, actually. There are some real possibilities in here. Especially of Renard."

"Which one's that?"

"The one who won today."

"Oh, right." He yawned and stretched, then started digging in his suitcase. "Well, I think I'm ready for bed. How about you?"

"Almost."

Charles disappeared into the bathroom, and I paused to examine one photo in particular. Renard lay on the pavement, looking limp as a rag while members of his team's staff surrounded him. I had a sudden, undeniable urge to reach out and touch him, to offer some sort of warmth amidst the seemingly clinical treatment of those observing him.

It was a silly thought but I couldn't help it. He seemed so alone in that crowd.

I shook my head, closed the file, shut the computer off, then went to close the curtains.

Before I put my nightgown on, Charles came out of the bathroom and stopped short.

"Abby, love… How tired are we?"

I considered this, then smiled. "I reckon I've got a bit more energy yet."

"Grand." He crossed the room and put his arms around me, his lips touching mine briefly. "It's time we celebrated our anniversary properly, isn't it?"

I nodded and let him lead me to the bed.
And so we celebrated.

Stage Two

(190 Km - Lisbon - Castro Verde, Portugal)

By ten a.m. the next day, winning the Royal seemed like a half-forgotten dream. Standing on the podium to receive the prizes – the flowers, the kisses from the podium girls and most important of all, the coveted royal-blue leader's jersey – had already taken on a nostalgic haze.

The team dinner had been a mild torture, with Phil and James reading the *Grand Tours* cover article, "The Face of the Tour," aloud in sing-song voices while the others (at least those with a sufficient grasp of English) laughed and egged them on.

"'He's half French, half Italian. He's young, comes from a privileged background and has a *hint* of scandal in his family tree'," James had read in waspish, gossipy tones while I'd cringed inside and tried to feign nonchalance.

"'He's a handsome fan favourite and he's dating a rising Top Model'," Phil continued, mimicking his best mate's tone in a posh accent. "'What more could he possibly want in life?'"

"'Oh, right; there's just that little matter of the Tour d'Europa. That should be quite the feather in the cap for –'"

"'The *Face* of the *Tour*!'" they'd simpered in chorus, to howls of laughter from the team. I'd given them an obscene gesture.

Well, perhaps the contents were harmless enough, but the unfortunate title gave me no end of grief. Then again, the perversely glowing terms used by the writer to describe my recent

17

career seemed like a terrible setup for failure. One small mercy was that at least he hadn't really delved into my family history. The thought of that was enough to make me sick.

It was bad enough to know the writer had rehashed my parents' meeting – media mogul proposes to dancer when they first meet – a favourite topic for gossip columns as it was. But in what was purportedly a *cycling* magazine, it was especially painful.

Throughout Phil and James' performance Jerzy had scowled down the length of the table at me whenever he wasn't chatting with Brunn.

The team's overall mood was celebratory. In the time trials, I'd taken first, Brunn fourth and Adrie Meijer had placed an astonishing eighth. Not a bad showing for the team, particularly considering *Maxxout* had only managed to place one rider, Jurgen Schlessinger, in the top ten ranking.

While I warmed up with my teammates on the stationary trainers alongside the team bus, I puzzled over the lack of communication from Solange. Still no calls in response to mine. No messages, either. An unpleasant voice in the back of my mind insisted something was going on: she'd never gone so long without contacting me before.

When I noticed Rom watching me with open curiosity, I returned my focus to what I was doing. I couldn't afford distraction.

I thought about the route ahead for that afternoon. I closed my eyes and visualized the profile: a few gently undulating hills but mostly flat, with one climb once we were well out of Lisbon. The whole course would run about two-hundred kilometres. Remembering the day before, my mood lightened.

I could do this. I knew it.

Supporters watched while we warmed up, taking photos, calling out good wishes to us. I turned up the volume on my mp3 player and let the percussive techno beat drive me on. I looked up only when my trainer nudged me and motioned for me to adjust my position on the bike.

Shit. Focus, Renard.

I let the music play and narrowed my world to the rhythm of my feet on the pedals and to keeping myself steady on the bike. I concentrated until I didn't hear the music anymore, just the thrumming of energy passing through me to power the bike. My legs pistoned smoothly and the hum of my rear wheel reassured me of my steady pace. The longer I went, the better I felt and the clearer my head became.

I'd climbed the hill yesterday with newfound ease. I'd never felt as comfortable before on an ascent. Sure, my training had shifted to improve my climbing ability. I'm too big – too bulky, that is, by cycling standards – and I was still far from a perfect climber. But if yesterday's effort meant anything, I'd clearly come a long way.

It was time to get on the bus for a quick shower and to suit up for the stage. My gear hung in its usual place on a hook near the back of the bus. There was, however, one significant difference: the Royal. The royal-blue jersey was the symbol of the race, the "trophy" most of us were killing ourselves – and each other – for. After winning yesterday it was mine, showing I was the leader – at least for now. I would continue to wear it until I lost first position in the General Classification.

I didn't intend to lose that position any time soon.

It wasn't as though I'd never won a race before, but this year success was more important than ever. My strong showing yesterday had put me in an advantageous position and confirmed my place as one of the favourites for the overall win. There was a downside, however: as long as I wore the Royal, I was not only the leader of the race but also the main target. Each of the riders on the other twenty-one teams would be gunning for me, aiming to reduce my lead and knock me back as far as possible.

Even worse, I suspected members of my own team might consider doing the same thing.

No matter what, the end of today's stage would belong to the sprinters – all the flat roads in the final kilometres were custom-made for them. The twins, Alvaro and Teodoro Mendoza, were *Alta VeloCidad's* sprinters. They were frothing at the mouth over the prospect of a stage win. As usual, they would conserve their energy within the peloton until the team led them out of the pack to the finish, where they would surge ahead to battle for the win. In the process, they would collect points for the team and a bit of glory for themselves. However, this meant a good deal of the work along the way would fall to the rest of us.

If things went as planned, I'd have the rest of the team's support and protection.

I resolved to wear the Royal on the final day of the Tour – on the ride in to Paris – even if it killed me. In this race, that was a distinct possibility, both literally and figuratively speaking.

I pulled on my jersey and zipped up, not allowing for more than a glance in the reflective surface of the darkened bus windows. A few of my teammates – Attilio, Phil and Rom – gave me a brief ovation, replete with whistles and catcalls, but the applause was genuine. I waved them off and opened the door to exit the bus, only to be greeted with a magnified version of my teammates' teasing appreciation.

The fans cheered and applauded while I went to my bike and examined it with the team mechanic one last time. One of the staff adjusted my radio, secured inside a pocket on the back of my bib shorts beneath my jersey. I taped in my earpiece and tried my microphone to be sure they worked properly, but it was almost impossible to tell, with the racket the supporters were making.

The call to the line followed soon after. I went to the head of the group, where Schlessinger and Gustafson waited, and gave them each a nod. Schlessinger disregarded me as expected. Gustafson offered his hand and I shook it. He'd said publicly that he'd been shocked to place third in the time trials, and he didn't expect to keep the position for long. Frankly, his surprise was no greater than anyone else's. He was a nice guy, and his warmth offset Schlessinger's usual frostiness.

While the race officials positioned their car to lead us out of the city, I took a good look around. A sea of video cameras surrounded us, projecting our images to the whole world. I imagined Solange watching, and laughed. Who was I kidding? She hadn't watched a single race of mine since the one where we'd met, two years before, when she'd been one a podium girl.

Focus, I thought, and willed everything around me to fade out to nothingness. Only Jerzy's voice in my earpiece and the lie of the road immediately before me were worth any notice. I ceased thinking of Solange or of anything that didn't involve me, my bike or the course ahead.

***

I'd tried repeatedly to convince Charles to wait for me at the hotel, but he'd refused. In light of our amorous undertakings the night before, my husband was particularly clingy in the midst of the crowd.

I ignored him as best I could and concentrated on getting ready.

I wanted to try for my shots unencumbered, but it didn't look like that would happen. Whenever I finally got them, my vest and badge wouldn't apply to both of us, and my accreditation for the race only covered me – I hadn't thought to declare Charles as an assistant. Then again, I hadn't expected us to be joined at the hip, either.

As a result, we stood at the barriers along the road, along with other spectators waiting for the stage to begin.

The riders wouldn't race within the city limits. They'd ride slowly together behind a car full of Tour officials until they reached a more open part of the road. Everything would get off to a proper start then, likely with a group breaking away from the pack to try and gain time, while the rest sat back and waited for their chances closer to the finish.

As for us, once the riders had gone past, we'd check out of the hotel, then drive our rental car to Castro Verde, where the stage ended. I'd take pictures of the finish, and in the morning I'd photograph the opening of the next stage.

This was the plan for the next few weeks, too.

A ripple of applause made its way toward us, reaching a peak when the peloton passed. I smiled as Renard went by, clad in the royal-blue jersey which marked him as the Tour's current leader. I framed him carefully and took several successive shots while he raised his hand and waved at the crowd on my side of the road. An obviously disgruntled Jürgen Schlessinger of Team *Maxxout* rode alongside him.

A flare of excitement flashed through me and I continued taking photos of the rest of the pack as it streamed by, southward bound.

The whole event didn't last long. Even with all the behind-the-scenes 'mood' shots I'd captured, Charles and I had only been out for a couple of hours.

"Finally," he said with a sigh. "Now let's get our bags before someone steals them, and find some lunch before the restaurants close for some bloody siesta or something."

"There's plenty of time." I checked my watch for good measure. "It's barely twelve-thirty."

He shrugged and turned in the direction of the hotel. "Let's go to that pub again. It's English-owned and they had a nice fry-up listed on the menu. Could be worth trying."

Turning my head so he couldn't see me roll my eyes, I packed up my things. "If you say so, hon."

"I do." He took me by the crook of my elbow and led me through the crowd. "I suppose this whole travel thing isn't so bad, once you find decent places to eat."

"There are lots of great restaurants in Lisbon, Charles. You have to be willing to try something different."

"And risk Montezuma's revenge? No thanks."

"That's what you call it in Mexico, I think," I offered in mild protest. A shake of his head dismissed me.

"It's all the same, darling. I don't doubt that some of this lot would do it on purpose."

"I think that's pretty unlikely. I mean, they'd lose business if that were the case."

"Not with the bloody Euro in the marketplace. Now they can do as they please without fear of losing their livelihood."

"You're talking like a businessman again. Couldn't we play happy tourists and have fun?"

He held the door of the pub open and I stepped reluctantly inside.

"Maybe later," he said. "Right now, I want my fry-up, all right?"

"All right. But I'm having the *cozido* this time."

"Suit yourself – and best of luck to you."

*

What followed wasn't as bad as it could have been, though I wasn't able to convince Charles of that. Several prolonged stops became necessary en route to Castro Verde, resulting in missing the end of the stage. We drove on to Córdoba, Spain, in silence.

As much as I hated missing the stage's end, my greater concern was that Charles would decide either to a) cancel the rest of the trip, or b) sue the pub for making him sick. Either one was possible.

I watched the coverage of the Tour that evening on the TV in our room, ignoring the Spanish commentary – easy enough as I didn't speak the language – and enjoyed the footage of Renard's arrival with Schlessinger close on his rear wheel.

Heinrich Brunn got more than his fair share of coverage, too. The press was fascinated by the man and his comeback bid. He remained in fourth place but, to judge by the excitement in the announcers' voices, he might as well have come in first.

The icy calm of his expression as he coasted over the line fascinated me. I could have captured it myself if I'd been there.

"Come on, Abby," Charles said from where he lay under the covers, "let's go to sleep."

I looked at my watch; it was only seven p.m.

"I'm hungry." I stood and got my handbag. "I'm going out for a bite. Do you want me to bring anything up for you?"

Charles groaned in reply and rolled over.

"Fair enough. I'll be back soon."

Key in hand, I eased the door shut and went down to the hotel restaurant. I'd forgotten that the Spanish tend to dine late, with dinner beginning around nine at night. Most of the restaurants, including the one in the hotel, weren't even open yet. I certainly didn't want pub fare so I headed along the street in search of something light.

In the main plaza people mingled and chatted around the fountain and in the cafés and pubs. Fathers played with their children or sat with their wives (or girlfriends) sharing coffee or sweets at the outside café tables.

I felt decidedly out of place, flying solo as I was.

I bought an iced lemonade and sat on a bench in the plaza, wishing I had my camera. What wonderful shots I was missing!

The last of the summer evening light gave the plaza a nostalgic feel. The sepia-toned light cast soft shadows with an almost liquid texture in the fading heat of the day.

Finishing my drink, I decided to go and get my camera. Maybe I could still get some good photos after all. I hurried up to our room and slipped inside quietly, hoping Charles was asleep and would stay that way.

No such luck.

"You're back," he said sleepily.

I stopped, putting my camera bag back on the table. "I decided to get some photos. It's a beautiful evening."

"No, no... Why don't you come to bed? You can get your little snaps in the morning."

I wanted to protest but I was in no mood to argue. Instead, I went to the window and pulled the curtains closed on the plaza.

My 'little snaps' would have to wait.

***

Night had settled over the countryside and most of us on the team bus were calming down at last.

Most of us, but by no means all.

Teodoro was still crowing about his sprint victory of the afternoon – he'd led Alvaro by precisely .75 seconds at the finish, and it was clear he didn't intend to let it rest. Alvaro, in turn, kept reminding his brother that he had not only placed higher in the time trials, but he had also been *born* first, and Teodoro would forever be five minutes behind him in this life.

More banter was exchanged at top volume in Spanish down the phone to their family. Spirits were understandably high, and no one on the team begrudged them their fun. The twins had crossed the line in first and third position, with Eddie Coleridge of *BigUk* between them.

I looked up from my magazine – *not* a copy of *The Rag Which Shall Not Be Named*. Adrie Meijer, our Dutch lead-out rider, grasped the overhead rail and leaned toward the window next to where I'd stretched out to read. A motorway sign for Sevilla flashed past. Adrie sat across from me, still watching through the window at the lights of the city aglow in the distance.

"Confidentially speaking? Spain sucks."

"Why do you say that?" I asked, genuinely curious.

Adrie shrugged and shook his head, his crooked nose looking even more bizarrely twisted beneath the lighting over his seat. "I don't know. I've been in this country more times than I can count and I've never come to like it at all. Some of the cities are nice, I guess, but on the whole? The place leaves me cold."

"Where would you rather ride, then?"

He made a dismissive gesture with one hand and slumped in his seat, crossing his legs loosely. "It's not even about riding. When I ride, it doesn't matter where I am, except if it's going up or down, and how fast, or if the road is good." Adrie looked directly at me for the first time. "You know that, Chicco."

I nodded. It was the same for all of us – if we were riding a race not suited to our strengths, we focused on surviving and that was it. Surviving was sometimes easier said than done.

"So if it's not about riding, then…?"

Adrie shrugged. "I don't like the weather, the food, the hotels… The people are nice. They're certainly lively."

As if to make the point, Teodoro hooted in delight somewhere behind us. Laughing, Adrie took my magazine from me and flipped lazily through it.

"How are you feeling about tomorrow?" he asked. "Lots of climbs coming."

I nodded and stretched, then got up to go the fridge behind us. "I'm feeling pretty good, so far. Tomorrow I might vomit, but we'll see when we get there." I gestured toward the open fridge with my bottle of water and Adrie shook his head. As I went back to my seat, Brunn and Jerzy hunched over the itinerary for the next stage, with Romuald and Phil leaning over the seats ahead of them to see, too. Attilio and James watched from across the aisle, their full attention on the road book.

Maybe I'd vomit sooner rather than later.

Sinking back into my chair, I pulled out my own copy of the road book, ignoring the little powwow at the head of the bus. The next stage looked tough. It was only the third stage and already we were reaching some potentially painful climbs. It would be a real test of my climbing ability, and I wasn't looking forward to it.

Today had been nothing compared to what lay ahead.

"I can't wait to get to the hotel." Adrie stifled a yawn behind his hand. "I just want to get as much sleep as I can. Tomorrow's going to be misery."

"I don't envy you dragging Alvaro and Teodoro up those hills."

Adrie shook his head, waggling one finger as he did so. "I won't be dragging anyone except myself before the end. James and Phil are doing that heavy lifting. I'll be hanging at the back of the bunch until we get outside Granada. *Then* I'll worry about the Terror Twins."

He paused, briefly rose up in his seat to watch Brunn and Jerzy, then sank down again to face me. "Today's press was a pain, too."

I shrugged, feigning indifference, and picked my magazine off the floor when Adrie dropped it. "I've dealt with worse." I glanced ahead at Brunn, relieved to find he and Jerzy were still deeply ingrained in their studies. "But if I get one more question about Brunn I'm going to lose my lunch."

Adrie smiled, nodding. "I know it's no consolation, but we're all getting asked about him. Not as much as you, but you'd think there wasn't anything else to write about."

"At least I haven't heard any more of that 'Face' nonsense – that is, not from anyone besides Phil and James."

"That really got under your skin, didn't it?"

"Yeah, I suppose it did. Between the title and the cover... Jesus! Don't I have enough trouble being taken seriously?"

"You shouldn't let it bother you. Only the dilettantes read it, anyway."

I laughed. "I don't want *anyone* thinking I'm literally 'The Face of the Tour'. Besides, do you really want *this* –" I pointed to my face, "representing your chosen field?"

Adrie cocked an eyebrow and then shook his head. "You poor little fucker; I should be so lucky. Most of the people cheering you outside the bus this morning were chicks. Thank God for Jerzy's rules, else you might be up to your neck in barely-legal pussy."

I laughed again but the expression on his face showed he hadn't made a joke.

"You didn't notice?" he asked, amazed. "Really?"

"Does it matter? Anyway, I'm engaged. And then there's Jerzy's rule, like you said."

Serguei "Goosh" Pavlichenko, this tour's team intern, popped his head up over the seat in front of me. "You are *not* serious."

"Not you, too," I groaned and he and Adrie exchanged looks.

"Get your camera, Goosh. He needs to see that pic."

"What pic?" I asked, but already Goosh had vaulted over the seat to get his bag from the gear locker.

"Here." He switched the camera on and scrolled through a few photos before handing it over. "You have to see this."

Adrie was already smirking in anticipation, and I delayed looking at the photo as long as I could. Although I was curious, a larger part of me didn't want to know. On the tiny screen of the camera was a cluster of girls, holding up a banner.

"Zoom is there." Goosh pointed to the button on the upper right.

I pressed it once, twice, and the image closed in on the writing on the banner. My heart sank into my stomach. How in Hell had I missed that?

"*Go Foxy Fede!*" it read; "*Ride hard, Renard!*"

26

I was on the fast track to being a laughing stock, for sure.

***

I lay quietly while my eyes adjusted to the light seeping through the small gap in the curtains. My camera bag rested on the table near the door, my laptop was closed atop the desk near the window. The clothes I'd worn that day were folded and waiting to go into the plastic laundry bag the hotel had provided. I'd pack them away in the morning before we left Córdoba for Granada.

The sounds in the plaza had faded away, but Charles' soft snoring beside me continued. If I hadn't been so afraid he'd wake after I'd gone, I'd have returned to the plaza to get the photos I'd wanted.

Now it was late but I still couldn't sleep. I had no idea what time it was; I couldn't bear to look at the clock. I turned over and watched Charles for a while, his dark curls making a small halo on his pillow, his face slack in sleep. Maybe it was because I couldn't see well enough to discern the grey in his hair, or maybe it was because sleep relaxed his squared, serious features, but he looked younger than usual. Almost as young as when we'd met ten years ago.

Work had aged him. Commuting to London daily by train, staying there overnight when meetings ran too long, was stressful. Then again, I suppose running a company is generally a stressful job. With each passing year, though, he seemed to change a little more. He'd become more conservative, less interested in the outside world, more hesitant to do spontaneous things.

With one exception. Not that it was spontaneous, exactly, since he brought it up every so often. He seemed to think repetition would change my mind. He was reliable as clockwork, chiming in whenever things had gone a bit, well, *stale*. If only in his opinion.

I shivered a little and pulled the blanket up over my shoulder. I wasn't sure what was worse – that he'd mentioned it again today? Or that now it didn't bother me as much?

Yes, I'd kicked up a fuss in my own head, but I hadn't even bothered to *tell* him I was angry. Maybe he thought he'd begun to persuade me? That maybe I was on my way to saying "By all means, let's do!" Could it be that I really was?

But I wasn't. I'd meant what I'd said that morning, and every other time he'd brought it up. There was no way I could do what he'd suggested, unless I didn't love him anymore.

And even then, he'd never know. If I didn't love him, I'd never stay with him.

Would I?

Stage Three

(165 km – Córdoba – Granada, Spain)

With each crank of the pedals, liquid fire ran through my legs. My skin burned in the late afternoon heat radiating from the tarmac. A grimace carved itself into my face, a death's-head grin for exquisite suffering under the summer sun.

Up ahead, a motorcycle swayed to and fro, going slowly up the steep incline so the camera operator on board could keep filming. In its wake the crowd on either side of the road spilled toward us, swallowing us up in a constantly shifting, screaming mass of humanity – all of whom were too close for comfort.

All the usual chaos of a mountain stage on the Tour d'Europa.

The peloton had broken apart prior to the climb, with the leaders and the better climbers forging well ahead of the pack. The blur of colour and noise on either side of my head was lost to my tunnel vision and the sounds inside it.

"You're doing fine, Ciccio." The voice in my earpiece was Michael, our *directeur sportif*'s-second-in command. "Once this climb is done it's straight down to the bottom for the stretch to Granada."

That we were doing well wasn't news to me. That it wasn't Jerzy's voice in my ear, however, was. Brunn had caught up with me after we'd cleared the previous, rather dodgy, descent, where I'd thought he was well behind me. Now he was recovering on my rear wheel and Rom and Attila were doggedly leading us up the hardest climb of today's stage.

I still had no intention of letting Brunn ride my slipstream all the way into Granada. His job – at least for now – was to help protect *me* and keep the Royal in my possession as long as possible.

Right now the greater threat was Schlessinger, coming up slowly alongside me. *Maxxout*'s blue-green team colours stood out even in the confusion of the crowd surrounding us. I refused to look his way, knowing his smug expression awaited me.

There was a *basso profundo* shout from somewhere in the crowd as Schlessinger made a subtle gesture in my direction – something between a wave and an obscenity – and then he crept upward, first aligning himself with his support and then slyly sidling next to Rom.

I ducked to avoid a carelessly-handled German flag, and heard yet another guttural shout, this time cheering Brunn on. There was no point in responding, no sense in coming any further out of my trance. Some of these people cheered for all of us, which gave the riders the will to dig deeper and make the climb. Others were oblivious to the mayhem they caused while they mugged for the television cameras, and frankly, for the most part, so were we.

I focused on the feel of my bike beneath me, the forward motion no longer quite as fluid as I'd have liked. My subconscious screamed bloody murder at me for each second I lost while I made my way up.

Schlessinger drew around Rom and continued the ascent, and I dropped my head. A pair of kilometres and we'd clear the top. All we had to do now was maintain the pace and, like Michael had said, we'd make up time on the long descent into Granada. The grade of ascent had increased until I was on the front edge of my saddle or standing on the pedals to grind out every turn to propel myself upward.

When I looked up again, Schlessinger was standing on his pedals, cranking for all he was worth. The smarmy bastard had launched an attack, and hard.

All at once, Rom gave an incomprehensible shout and followed suit. The little fool was giving chase!

Such a move made absolutely no sense from a team standpoint. Had I missed something? Had Jerzy told him to chase Schlessinger?

Distantly, Brunn swore and we watched as Attila gritted his

teeth and chased after Rom.

We had no choice but to follow. We'd lost our lead man and now Brunn was the only one left to pull me up the climb.

The sudden thunderous shout in my earpiece was proof enough that Rom had bolted on his own. I ducked instinctively at the sound and Rom wobbled the least little bit before he settled back into a cadence we could all follow. Soon enough we were all in a line: Attila, Rom, Brunn and me. Phil and James had fallen back ages ago, along with Adrie, to carry Alvaro and Teodoro up. They needed to conserve their energy for the final sprint.

Careful not to touch wheels, I kept my gaze on either Rom's back or the now not-so-distant horizon. I was champing at the bit to surmount the summit and begin my descent.

Let Brunn *try* to follow me down this one.

We crested the summit and the plain stretched out at the foot of the mountain, fading into the heat haze enveloping the panorama. Jerzy spoke at last: "Brunn, go with Ciccio."

Fuck.

Then I was over the top and beginning my descent with Brunn on my rear wheel and the wind slapping me full in the face. The first switchback was visible in the near distance. Schlessinger's back tyre wobbled; he overcorrected, taking the curve with too great an arc, and a flash of elation shot through me.

I broke into a greedy grin and reset my focus, aiming downhill while pedalling at speed. The blue-green blur that was Schlessinger was more a target than a competitor.

Approaching the curve, I tucked in low and my fingers tensed the slightest bit on the brakes. I was pedalling again before I'd cleared the full arc, still grinning at the thought of Schlessinger's over-cautious approach.

From behind me came a single, sharp yelp of laughter and I spared a quick glance to spy Brunn's delighted expression before the straightaway banked hard to the left on the next switchback.

We slalomed downward, gaining speed with each straightaway and slowing just enough to keep from slipping out of control at the apex of each curve. Schlessinger, aware of our approach, was working much too hard to gain distance. In the past he'd had a bad crash on a segment exactly like this, and was ill-prepared for us to challenge him here.

He was only a few meters ahead, once again taking the curve

too slowly. Brunn and I exchanged a glance before I moved to take the inside of the turn and he dropped behind me again.

With a few more pedal strokes I was alongside Schlessinger, grinning like a madman.

The sight of me next to him spurred him onward. He shouted something in German and Brunn shouted something back in a light, almost playful tone. Schlessinger scowled back at him and bore down harder still, pulling ahead until the next switchback rushed toward us.

He was too close to me as we made the turn. Brunn shouted something else, a command this time. I held back and let Schlessinger go, a rush of fresh heat in my veins propelling me forward on the straightaway.

On the next turn, he wasn't as brave. I slipped to the inside again and cut close enough to the edge of the road to hear the whisper of the weeds on the rocky outcropping brushing against my jersey.

Schlessinger obligingly and sensibly let me pass. Brunn followed close behind me.

Now the real race could begin.

***

I tried to hide my resentment, but it wasn't easy. Charles had dragged his feet and delayed our departure long enough to ensure we'd miss the beginning of the stage in Córdoba.

I had no proof he'd done it on purpose, but I certainly had reason to suspect. He'd said he was feeling better, had even heaped a pile of pastries on his plate at breakfast, but when the time came to pack our bags in the car and get going, he suddenly felt lethargic and locked himself in the bathroom along with a copy of the *Times* he'd bought at the hotel newsstand.

With this rather significant shift in our schedule, the decision was made to go straight to Granada. *Fine. I'll get some photos of the city before the end of the race.* No sooner had we passed Sevilla than Charles' mobile started ringing. He answered with a too-chummy "Hello, who's this?"

As if he didn't know. As if he hadn't been getting calls from work for the last three days.

I watched out the window while he drove at varying speeds,

conditioned by the turns of the conversation, rather than those of the road we were on. When a lay-by presented itself, he pulled in quickly and snapped his fingers at me, unwilling to interrupt the conversation long enough to actually *ask* me to find his notepad in the backseat of the car. Instead, a series of wild, vague gestures served to communicate his need to me.

Frowning, I turned in my seat to start digging in his briefcase, realizing that this was how he'd managed to get such a long holiday; he'd made himself available to his co-workers for the duration of our trip. So much for getting away from it all.

At last he finished making notes and exhorted his associate for doing the right thing by calling him.

"No, never fear – we weren't doing anything important. No, just going to see the finish of this bike race today, that's all. Yeah, I don't know; me, I'd prefer a good football match. Anyway, *she* seems to enjoy it."

Too-hearty laughter followed this last, and my cheeks burned red-hot. He rang off and continued to make notes for a few minutes, oblivious to me or the fact we were sitting in a car without the air conditioning on, in full sun, alongside the motorway.

"You know," I began quietly, "if you're not enjoying this trip, you could always go home."

After a while he looked up at me, his expression vague. "What's that, then?"

I took a deep breath and plucked at my blouse where it had stuck to me. "Nothing. Are we ready to go?"

"Not yet. I should make this call," he said, already dialling.

"Can't you call from Granada? We could at least be in a nice, cool hotel."

Charles cocked one eyebrow at me. "Abby, sweetie, this is important. If I don't do this right away, who knows what might come up next?" He pressed *send* with his thumb and then made another notation on his notepad. "Is that Edgar? Edgar, this is Charles White..."

I opened the car door and got out. A warm breeze, enhanced by the rush of air from cars and trucks passing on the motorway, did little to cool my temper.

At this rate, we'd never make it to Granada in time, either. I'd have missed a full day of the race, and there went my project. How was I supposed to do a photo journal called *The Tour d'Europa; Day by Day* if I missed a day? If we missed one, he'd ensure we'd miss another, and then another.

I leaned against the guardrail at the edge of the lay-by and watched him through the window of the car. He nodded and made notes, occasionally looking round and shaking his head as though in disbelief of where he was.

"Join the club," I muttered, turning my face up to the sunshine. *I might as well get a tan if I'm stuck out here.*

The repetitive *whoosh* of passing cars lulled me into a stupor beneath the sun. My skirt swayed in the breeze, my ponytail swung to and fro against my neck. The light behind my closed eyelids took on a purple-pink hue.

I imagined the shots I was missing. With luck, Renard would win the jersey again and I would catch him crossing the line. I enjoyed how animated he was when he won, the genuine delight which negated the exhaustion on his face. I wondered if I could ask some of the riders to let me do *before* and *after* photos of them, to show the stresses and tolls a single stage could take.

I considered how I could go about making the contacts I'd need to arrange that. Who would I need to talk to?

The car horn blared, startling me out of my daydreams.

"Abby, darling, do come on; we're running late as it is."

I straightened up and crossed to the car. "Silly me," I muttered, opening the door.

***

The plain stretched out before us, lost in an endless heat haze. As the road levelled out, I shook my legs without dislodging from the pedals to shake out the lactic acid building up in them. Brunn and I were still speeding along, but now that Schlessinger had been swallowed up by the next chase group, it was only a matter of time before we were caught, too.

Catching Schlessinger had been remarkably satisfying, and hearing that he'd dropped well back in the chase group was even more so. Brunn moved ahead of me and I rode in his slipstream, letting him pull me along. The final sixteen kilometres to Granada would go quickly if we continued in his steady cadence.

"The chase group is almost to you," Michael said, and I stole a quick look behind us. Sure enough, the chase group – a cluster of riders separated from the peloton on the way up the climb – was closing in on us. The remainder of the peloton – mostly composed of sprinters and a few of the weaker or newer riders – was still making the final descent.

It was difficult to be certain, but I didn't spot Schlessinger at the head of the group. Surely he hadn't dropped back further?

"Keep it up. You're doing great."

I switched on the microphone under the front of my jersey at my shoulder. "How are the twins managing back there?"

"They're fine. Adrie had a flat and is catching up."

Brunn looked back at me. He nodded and smiled, an expression which never failed to look off-kilter on his face, and went back to pounding out his tempo on the pedals.

Soon enough the chase group reached us. Rom drew up next to Brunn and me, looking like the world's smallest, most awkward camel, and handed over several bottles of water, pulling them out from inside the back of his jersey, one by one.

Since we'd cleared the last mountain, the headwind had picked up considerably, slowing our progress further as it shifted to blow across the roadway. Attila fell in line behind me, and more riders followed. Before long, we streamed out into an echelon across the width of the road, every rider keeping in the slipstream of the one ahead of him. We traded off at regular intervals to take the lead for a while and pull the others along. The regularity was impressive, if imperfect.

"Keep your pace steady, Ciccio; there's plenty of time," Brunn said to me as he passed, signalling to Marco Lombardi from *Speed Zone Italia* that he should come up to him.

Marco passed me, shrugging, and rode alongside Brunn for a while to chat. I couldn't help bridling a bit at being talked to like that. How many times had I dragged *him* along the last kilometres of a stage? I knew not to push too hard, not to get ahead of myself and wear myself out, and he also knew that everyone riding with us would hear him speaking to me like I was some inexperienced stagionaire.

Focus, I told myself. *Deal with that later.*

"Eleven kilometres to go," said the voice in my ear. "We'll start setting up soon. Get yourself in a good position, Ciccio."

As long as I stayed safe, I'd keep my grip on the Royal for another day.

The wind picked up. The Sierra Nevada loomed on the horizon, beyond Granada. I recognized it only as a target to be reached. The chatter around me died down as the tension grew.

Resting was over – it was time for one last push to the finish.

The caginess of the other riders was palpable. Each and every rider was listening to his *directeur sportif,* waiting for the order to break away, to lead our sprinters in (if they were in any condition to try for the finish), or whatever other tactic had been deemed appropriate to the game plan.

Phil and James took their places ahead of Alvaro and Teodoro while Adrie, Brunn and I took a final pull at the front. All eyes were on the leaders, and I could have sworn their eyes were burning holes in my back.

We kept leading the bunch, gradually increasing speed until we were pouring it on, hurtling along the straight stretch of road toward Granada. My pedalling was fluid, my breathing smooth and regular, the only sounds were the wind rushing past my ears and the steady *schirr* of the bikes surrounding me.

That's when everything happened.

First my wheel gave a tell-tale wobble and I slowed in spite of myself.

At that same instant, Schlessinger – being either exceptionally observant or stupendously blessed with good timing – shot out of the group and made for Granada, never looking back.

Brunn gave a growling, angry shout and took off after him. He'd catch him up to pull him back with a reminder that it's bad form to attack the leader when he's dealing with a mechanical issue.

I switched on my microphone, called out "Puncture!" and raised my hand in the air to signal to my team mechanic. Biting back curses while the peloton swept past me, I waited for the car to pull alongside.

Merde! There was absolutely no time to lose, and here I was, losing it.

Rom had slowed to a halt a little further down the road to wait for me, so he could take me to the peloton again.

The mechanic jumped out before the team car had stopped, his hands already working the locks of the bike rack on the roof. Instead of changing the wheel he got a new bike on the road before he pushed me out for a rolling start.

I made it up to Rom, who was already standing on the pedals

and cranking full-tilt. I would have screamed if I could spare the breath for it. We'd catch the group, but could we catch Schlessinger?

Jerzy shouted in my ear – incoherent German I couldn't be bothered to translate on the fly, so I knew it was meant for Brunn, not me – my heart pounded harder than ever, my breath dragged and rasped in my lungs.

God, had the day been this hot all along?

Now that my rhythm had been wrecked, there weren't enough curses in all the languages I knew – combined – to give voice to my frustration.

Now? This had to happen NOW?

I raged in my head but did my damnedest not to break on the surface. I might be tempted to destroy the hotel room later, or bust something up on the team bus, but I'd be damned before I'd let Schlessinger know he'd got the best of me.

Rom glanced back at me, a manic expression plastered on his face. Was he actually enjoying all of this?

How was it that I was starting to feel the same?

The answer came to me once we'd worked our way through the peloton and emerged at the head of it. The breakaway group was about to be caught, and Schlessinger was part of it.

My elation faded at once.

Where the fuck was Brunn?

***

We only just made it into Granada before the end of the race. I changed quickly into my walking shorts and left Charles unpacking at the hotel before hurrying to the finish line, camera in hand, still hoping to salvage something of the day. The crowd was raucous and I knew something huge was happening. Fuming over my continued lack of credentials, I pushed through the crowd, trying to get close to the road.

Thanks to a generous group of Germans, I managed to squeeze up to the barriers where I could hold my camera out and snag some shots. I managed a few as the breakaway group crossed the line, fighting for the stage win in a bunch sprint.

The chanting began soon after the sprint ended. It started out at a moderate tempo, accentuated by handclaps: "Brunn! Brunn!

Brunn! Brunn!"

I looked up at the screens showing an overhead shot of the final stretch into Granada. Five cyclists – two of them in *Alta VeloCidad*'s violet and grey colours, one in *Maxxout*'s blue-green, one in the red and blue of *Ligne Infinie* and Renard in the distinct Royal jersey – had broken away from the peloton and were bearing down on the finish with all their might.

One in particular was swiftly pulling ahead.

At this, the chanting grew louder, and one of the Germans next to me began to pound out a steadily intensifying rhythm on the barrier ahead of us. With every thunderous *whap* of his hand on the plastic banner taped over the railing, my heart sank lower into my stomach.

"BRUNN! BRUNN! BRUNN! BRUNN!"

I looked up at the times on the screen above the road. Brunn had broken away from Renard and Schlessinger. As I watched the broadcast, the other rider in *Alta VeloCidad*'s colours dropped back, head hung low, slowing while he drifted to the side of the course to wait for the peloton to pick him up. Renard's domestique was exhausted, unable to help him anymore.

In spite of the late afternoon heat, my arms were covered in gooseflesh.

No…Please, no.

I didn't know why I wanted so much for Renard to win, but I did. I wanted it with all my heart.

As one, the crowd turned their attention away from the screen to watch Brunn's actual arrival. His name was no longer being chanted, the crowd was screaming it, the noise riotous and manic until my heart raced so hard I could barely keep my camera in hand. I managed to lean out across the barrier to capture his arrival. I squeezed the release and the shutter obligingly snapped shot after shot in quick succession as Brunn lifted his hands from the handlebars of the bike and waved to the tumultuous crowd, long before he crossed the line.

More manic shouting followed, and I turned my camera – already shooting – down the final stretch. The remainder of the peloton swept into view, a sea of bright colours rushing down the boulevard. The fans on either side of the road waved their flags, banners and signs while Renard and Schlessinger battled ahead of the group.

As they approached the last hundred meters, the whole mass of humanity appeared to undulate toward the finish, a rising wave threatening to crest too soon.

Shoulder to shoulder, the two riders stood and danced on the pedals, their bikes rocking to and fro beneath them so violently I was certain one would surely knock the other to the tarmac. The fierce, determined grimace on Renard's face was equalled by Schlessinger's as they barrelled toward the finish, neither one acknowledging the other, save for their speed.

Schlessinger pulled ahead and powered past the line, Renard lagging seconds behind, and I feared I'd go deaf from the clamouring of the crowd.

Weak, dizzy and close to tears, I clung to the barrier and let my breath out in a rush, before catching shots of the peloton flashing past. I couldn't explain it in a million years, and I was grateful Charles wasn't with me.

The rush ebbed out of my limbs, leaving them heavy and dull, and all I wanted was to sit down somewhere and have something to drink. I also wanted to look over my shots and consider whether any were keepers or not – though surely the shots of Renard and Schlessinger when they'd approached the line would be, bittersweet though they were.

Renard still had the Royal, but his grip had loosened. Schlessinger had gained a little time, but Brunn had made phenomenal gains in this stage. I was stunned. I'd never seen a rider attack his own teammate like that – especially not when that teammate was wearing the Royal. It was simply unheard of.

TV crews converged on Brunn and Renard separately. I watched the screen as they closed in tight to record Renard's exhausted dismount and weary stagger into his handler's care.

I pushed through the crowd, heading for the podium to photograph the awarding of the prizes for the day's standings. I still felt a small glimmer of hope that Renard would make better time and increase his lead, but I knew it wasn't likely. More mountain stages were ahead and he'd acknowledged his difficulties in those a long time ago.

I fussed with my bag, digging out a zoom lens. One man in the press pit at the foot of the podium saw me and tilted his head, indicating I should come closer.

"*Parlez-vous français?*" he asked, and I shook my head and

shrugged in response.

There was no way I was going to try to say so much as "*Non*," and risk screwing up.

"English?" he asked, and I nodded. "You can come on this side of the barrier if you want. There's room."

"Ah, thanks," I said and feeling braver, added "*Merci*."

Laughing, he grasped the barrier and pulled, giving me enough space to slip through the gap. He turned back to face the podium and I resumed fiddling with my camera, blushing furiously.

I was in a fog. I took shots of Brunn, the stage winner, as he was presented with his prizes and a kiss on each cheek by the two podium girls.

I was really only waiting for one shot. Then I would pack up and go back to the hotel to go over my meagre collection for the day.

Renard came out onto the podium and the cheering and whooping was generous, indeed. However, it was nothing compared to Brunn's reception at the finish line before. My heart went out to the younger champion and I snapped as many shots of him as I could.

One in particular stood out for me – Renard's hands raised over his head, the new Royal neatly zipped over his team jersey, flowers and stuffed mascot (a multicoloured caterpillar dressed in a miniature royal blue jersey) held aloft. The smile on his face belied the anger in his eyes, and I wondered how many people could see this, how many casual fans understood what had happened.

But who was I to think *I* did? And what difference did it make, anyway?

Stage Four

(206 km – Granada – Lorca, Spain)

I was still seething when I woke up. I lay in bed staring up at the softening shadows on the ceiling, picturing Brunn's attack again and again.

Brunn hadn't gained very much time, but he was still a stronger climber than me. Even though I'd ridden part of today's route before – the road into Lorca had been covered in a Vuelta when I'd first joined the team – I knew his superiority could lead to future attacks on the hills and mountains ahead.

I considered the reality of losing the Royal. I'd already become accustomed to waking up and putting on that colour instead of the team's purple and grey and now it was at risk of slipping out of my hands.

All because I'd had a flat tire at the worst possible moment, and my teammate had attacked, thanks to what Jerzy claimed had been a "simple miscommunication".

Yeah. Sure.

I turned onto my side and tried to sleep, ignoring the time on the digital clock on the bedside table. I was too wound up, but if I didn't rest I'd ride this stage with all the finesse of a trained circus bear. One of the first things I'd learned under Jerzy's tutelage, years ago, was how to fall asleep on demand. The skill comes in handy after late nights or long transfers, when an early morning is on the next day's schedule. Over time, I'd learned how to manage at least a

41

few hours of real sleep, no matter what.

Not now, though. I'd been trying so hard to sleep I was more awake than before. I got out of bed. Rom wouldn't wake until Jerzy's sonic barrage.

While I showered I turned my thoughts away from the race and drifted to Solange. Her silence made no sense. Surely nothing was wrong, or her mother would have called me. In the steam after my shower, a shiver ran down my spine. A few morbid scenarios played out in my head while I shaved at the sink – a car accident in the Australian outback leaving her waiting for help that didn't come; a photographer taking a sinister shine to her and murdering her during a shoot; she'd met some other guy –

My blade went awry with that last thought. "*Putain!*" I cursed as a few drops of blood plopped into the foamy water in the sink.

I didn't believe that, did I? Solange had never given me the slightest indication she might stray. The last time we were together, at my home outside Paris, we'd been talking about where to have the wedding. (A mansion near Torino had caught her eye. I'd fancied the idea of a ride in the mountains surrounding it, but I didn't tell *her* that.)

We'd spent the better part of two weeks together, and the only time we'd been apart was when I'd taken training rides, or she'd gone shopping. The rest of the time we'd stayed in bed together, strolled through town or looked at real estate ads for a house to buy after the wedding.

Was it possible I'd missed something important or done something stupid to scare her off?

Well, sure it was *possible*, but was it likely?

Jerzy's banging and crashing on the other side of the bathroom door ended my ruminations. I stepped out as he was leaving and he paused to look me over.

"Were you suiciding in there, boy?" he asked, arching one eyebrow.

"What?"

He reached out, flicked my neck with one fingertip and showed me the bright trace of blood on it.

"Go clean that up. Or better yet, stay in here a while longer and come out like that. We'll tell the guys *I* did it to you."

"I'll clean up. I don't want to be responsible for anyone pissing himself this early in the morning."

Jerzy barked laughter and went back out into the hall.

When I looked at myself in the mirror again, I startled. The blood wasn't just on my neck, but had trickled down onto my chest in a long, steady thread. I grabbed a washcloth, ran it under the tap, then cleaned the mess away. After digging around in my shaving kit, I found my styptic pen and applied it to the cut.

I knew it would hurt like a bitch once I started sweating on the ride.

Beh, there's nothing like a little pain to motivate you, I suppose.

***

"We're going to be late if you don't hurry," I urged, trying not to hover.

Charles rolled his eyes, still fastening his shoelaces.

Remembering the shots he'd cost me the day before, my blood was up in an instant. "You don't have to come, if you don't want to. Why don't you just stay here anyway? I'll manage fine on my own."

"No, I'll come along. Give me a second, will you? Your boyfriend won't be going anywhere, don't worry."

I swallowed the retort which sprang to my lips. His little digs about Renard were getting on my nerves. He insisted on calling the cyclist my "boyfriend" at every opportunity and I'd had about enough.

"Honestly, Charles. Anyone would think you were jealous."

He snorted laughter and stood up, brushing imaginary lint off his jeans. I noted the perfect crease and wondered why he couldn't even relax in casual clothing.

And then I wondered why it hadn't bothered me, before.

"Jealous?" he muttered, gathering his wallet and keys. "Jealous of whom? Scrawny boys who shave their legs? Jesus, Abby; you should know me better than that."

"I guess so…"

"Besides, if you think you can have a pull, by all means, do."

"I didn't say anything at all like that," I huffed, my stomach turning. He was quite clever, I suppose, being able to twist any topic round to *that* one again.

Another call had come for him before I'd arrived back at the hotel room, last night. I'd overheard him speaking with someone in decidedly unprofessional tones before I'd unlocked the door.

Nothing, to the best of my knowledge, had happened between them yet. I'd seen her number on his mobile from time to time. And yes, I checked it. Whenever a call came and he rushed off to take it elsewhere, or when he ended a call because I'd come into the room, I made a point of checking.

It wasn't jealousy which motivated me. I wanted to *know*. I didn't want to be in the dark about these things. I needed to be sure to protect myself, in case he'd acted on his urges without my knowledge.

Now he'd begun to talk openly about being, well, *open*.

As in the two of us seeing other people.

His rationalization was something only he could invent: if we saw other people, he wouldn't be so worried about me being at home alone for stretches of time when he was in London. Of course, he didn't mention if he wanted to act on his own cosy impulses with *her*. At this point, I wasn't even sure who she was. Was she a secretary? A co-worker? Maybe she was a client who was especially grateful for his business?

Still, I was fairly confident he hadn't acted on anything yet, though I wasn't sure how much longer he'd resist her charms, whatever they might be.

Before my imagination could run away with me, I turned my attention back to my camera bag and double-checked that I had everything I needed. I hefted my bag onto my shoulder and crossed to the door, my room key in my pocket and my backpack slung over my other shoulder.

Charles gave a low chuckle. "You look like a pack mule."

"I don't hear you offering to help, darling," I smiled, and continued on my way.

He blew out a sigh and followed me. At least he was clever enough to know he'd stepped in it.

I made my way to the trailer in the plaza where the press credentials were issued. Charles waited outside while I stood in line to speak to the English press official. At last it was my turn and the clerk slid my ID badge and a resealable plastic packet containing three day-glo vests across the table to me.

"Do you have an assistant?" he asked. "I can issue you an ID for them if you do." I said nothing. I hadn't expected this question, or the opportunity to drag Charles along with me to the photographers pit.

I glanced out the open door on the other side of the trailer before answering. "No," I said, shaking my head. "I don't."

He nodded and made a note in his paperwork, I signed off and went on my way.

"So, you got them," Charles said, sounding half-interested at best. I nodded and fumbled a vest out of the packet, then managed to put it on without any help from my distracted husband.

"I'm going over there, to the start line. I can go through the barriers, but I'm afraid you can't."

"No worries. I'll go as far as I can and wait for you."

"Okay." I hoped my lack of enthusiasm didn't show as we headed that way.

Along the start line, the crowd was packed quite tightly. Charles followed in my wake, my bright vest encouraging people to let us through with minimal fuss.

After I crossed the barrier, leaving Charles on the other side, I took quick stock of my equipment. I set up my second camera with a shorter range lens so I could use it when the cyclists lined up prior to the start.

I took a few shots while the riders came to the line, admiring the brilliant colours of their kits against the mix of dun-coloured classical architecture and modern buildings. I zoomed in on a few faces here and there and snapped away, capturing any number of different emotions: anxiety, eagerness, resignation. Some of the cyclists were eager to go, it was clear – the wiry climbers were eyeing the Sierra Nevada in the distance and all but licking their lips in anticipation.

Other riders, not so much.

Watching them line up, a peculiar sadness struck me. Renard's fierce expression showed his determination, but his downward slide might well continue. Brunn had received such a hero's reception the night before, the younger rider must be disheartened.

However tenuous Renard's hold on the Royal, with luck he'd still be the one wearing it tomorrow.

I waited for Renard to look in my direction. He was speaking to Brunn, whose expression was distant and cool. Schlessinger, also at the head of the group, wore his resentment plainly. His promising break for the finish had not only been thwarted by Brunn's powerful chase, but by Renard's subsequent counterattack and recapturing. I could only imagine how frustrating it must have been for him to gain only a few precious seconds after working so hard.

I pressed the shutter on the camera. I was immediately pleased with the result – I couldn't have had a better shot if I'd posed him myself. His dark eyes were wide and determined, with a little of his dark hair showing from beneath his helmet. The straps framed his face perfectly and made it seem longer and sharper than usual. He looked especially predatory; more vulpine than ever.

In short, his resemblance to his namesake – the fox – was quite apt.

My stomach did a little flip-flop at the thought. I turned my focus to Brunn, waiting for those ice-cold eyes to stray my way. I caught him instead in profile – proud, dangerous and resolute. His blue eyes seemed to flash in the morning sun, the bronze of his skin all the more impressive in contrast.

Schlessinger came into frame and I followed him, panning out a bit to capture him with more of the peloton in the background. His dirty-blond hair stuck out here and there from beneath and through the vents of his helmet, his strong, stubborn jaw protruding with a hint of petulance. I'd seen him at the hotel restaurant the night before, laughing and joking with his teammates, and I'd thought him quite handsome when he smiled.

Now there was little, if any, resemblance to the man I'd seen then.

His demeanour was quiet and calculating, eyeing the other leaders as though sizing them up yet again. He wouldn't be caught out another time.

I certainly didn't envy the other cyclists today. Renard, least of all.

*

I squeezed through a gap in the barriers at the finish in Lorca, still amazed at the access my press pass and vest granted me. The bright safety green glowed in the late afternoon sunlight, making a slight halo effect around me, clashing with the vests of the other photographers clad in green and yellow and orange vests of their own.

It was strange to move freely among them, photographers whose work I had admired for years. There were only a handful of women there, and I had to hunt to spot them, camouflaged as they were in cycling caps, plain t-shirts and jeans or cargo shorts. Seeing this made Charles' criticism of my functional and comfortable – if not particularly stylish – clothing sting a little less.

In the lingering heat of the day, time passed slowly. We milled around within the lines taped down on the road to indicate where we should stand while the crowds gathered on the other side of the barriers. Some of the photographers shared in-jokes or chatted about photos they'd taken earlier in the day. Others kept a keen eye trained on the road, occasionally raising their cameras to frame a shot they didn't take.

The sky grew dark, the clouds gathering for a late-afternoon shower. Photographers instinctively covered their precious cameras and other equipment as thunder rumbled and rain began to fall. I couldn't speak for the others, but I was slightly relieved. In the muggy mid-afternoon heat, the rain brought some relief after standing out on the tarmac for so long. The rainfall was short, but intense, over almost as quickly as it had begun, leaving shallow puddles to reflect the re-emerging sunlight.

As the helicopters hovered overhead, harbouring the arrival of the riders, more photographers assembled until the lines of our designated box seemed completely arbitrary. A final few arrived at a dead run, one of them vaulting the barrier to take a place directly in front of me.

"Hey!" I jostled him out of my way, gesturing angrily toward the road and the line at my feet. He shook his head and made as though to take the spot again, before another man reached out for his arm and tugged him roughly to one side. I glanced over to find my supporter was the French photographer who had sneaked me inside the barriers a couple of days ago. He smiled warmly and gave me a wink and I couldn't help smiling in return.

The crowd noise ratcheted up a notch – or ten – and all of the photographers took their positions. Some lay on the ground sniper-style while others, like me, knelt precariously in a line, aiming our cameras down the final stretch. The rest stood waiting, ready to jump or shift as necessary to capture their shots.

A rising roar of excitement rolled toward us, chasing the bunch sprint as it thundered our way. The battle for the stage win was fierce, and even though I'd photographed a few finishes already, this was the first time I'd seen one from this point of view: through my lens, it seemed that they were barrelling straight toward me with no sign of slowing. Several riders skidded through the water still on the road, losing control of their bikes before they could slow down.

One moment I was taking photos of riders crossing the finish line, the next I was backing up and stumbling over the feet of one photographer and being knocked to the ground by the elbow of another.

I landed hard, breath *woosh*ing out of my lungs even as I held my camera aloft in an attempt to protect it. I was aware of equipment scattered around me – lenses, battery packs, memory cards – some of it mine, some of it theirs. Then the base of a crowd-control barrier was at my back, the sharp metal edge of one foot biting into me.

Winded, I lay on the pavement, my eyes closed, one hand clutching my side as though I could press the pain so deep I wouldn't feel it any more. I was dizzy; taking quick, short breaths had pushed me to the point of hyperventilation.

A moment later the sun broke through the cloud, warming my face before shadow settled over me.

***

In spite of the warning over the race radio, I was still surprised when I rolled across the line and saw most of the photographers pulling themselves together. One of them was still on the ground, bloodied and clearly hurt, already under the care of the race medics, as was the rider who'd hit him. More members of the media filmed the scene, scrumming for the best shots of the post-crash chaos.

As I passed, I noticed another photographer who hadn't gotten up yet. She lay curled up next to the barrier, camera still in hand, surrounded by the scattered tools of her trade.

I don't know why I went back. Maybe it was because she was a woman, or because no-one seemed to notice her there, off to one side. Whatever the reason, I circled back and got off my bike, resting it on the pavement before I knelt next to her.

My soigneur jogged up and took my bike in hand, watching with concern. "Renard, what are you doing?"

"*Etes-vous bien?*" I asked her, ignoring him. She blinked up at me, dazed, uncomprehending.

"Eh?"

Merde. Spanish, then? But she didn't look Spanish. My lips refused to form the question in any language, and I had no idea which one she spoke, anyway.

"*Anglais?*" I asked, hoping for the best. "English?"

Relief flooded her face and she nodded.

"Are you okay?" I reached down and took her hand in mine and she winced, still holding her side with her other hand.

I couldn't help thinking she was really quite attractive in spite of having been roughed up.

When her dark eyes met mine the whole world tilted out from under my feet. I wanted to attribute it to the cessation of the adrenaline that had kept me going during the race, but I couldn't.

I knew better than that.

I kept holding her hand in mine, and without looking away, I waved my free hand to draw the attention of one of the paramedics. In the meantime, the photographer drew herself up to a sitting position, using me for leverage.

"Are you okay?" I repeated and she nodded.

"I think so." She took a deep breath, pushed her hair back from her face with her free hand and looked at me again. "Yeah, I'm okay. I just got knocked silly." Her grip on my hand tightened for an instant and then relaxed.

"Don't worry, I've got you," I said, reassuring her. "The paramedics will check you out soon," I added, my mind still reeling. I wasn't sure why I was there but I wanted to stay with her as long as I could.

"Thank you."

A moment later, a medic pushed me aside and began asking the photographer questions, her gloved hands moving gently to check for injuries.

"She speaks English," I said and the medic nodded, not taking her eyes off her new patient. I hesitated, waiting until my soigneur tapped me on the shoulder to indicate we should go.

"Your name?" the medic asked her.

"Abigail," she said, and our eyes met one last time. "My name is Abigail."

My soigneur helped me back onto my bike so he could steer me through the crowd toward the presentation area. Once there, I could hardly lift my limbs to assist the crew and wound up slumped in a folding chair, dehydrated, exhausted and done-in.

But victorious.

I was smiling now. In the final kilometres Schlessinger had looked daggers through me so hard I swear I had wounds in my back; Brunn had been harder to read. Schlessinger had had his own troubles and slipped back to third, and there was no question he was unhappy about that development. Now Brunn was in second place.

Fuck them. I still had the Royal.

My wheezing laughter came from about a million miles away while the team doctor gave me a quick once-over and the soigneur gave me a swift rub-down. I had about twenty minutes before the Piss Patrol would come calling.

I laughed again and took comfort in the fact I sounded stronger. I breathed deep, leaned back and dumped a bottle of water over my head, the lukewarm contents refreshing in the muggy late afternoon heat. I drank the next bottle they handed me without even looking at it, knowing from the weight of it in my hand it was a recovery drink.

Slowly, I began to feel like myself again.

"Time to hit the head," said the soigneur. "They want you on the test bus."

I nodded and he extended his hand and hauled me up to my feet. A Tour chaperone stood waiting nearby, ready to escort us.

We started walking. The chaperone went ahead of us, fending off the press unless I chose to talk to them.

I didn't.

I only wanted to get everything over with; to have a piss on the record and a change of kit before the presentation ceremony. A round of interviews would follow at the hotel, and then a meeting, and then a massage before dinner, and then...

Every muscle in my body ached and cried out for rest, but sleep was still a long way off. I looked forward to it greedily.

I caught a glimpse of myself in the window of the doping control trailer as I climbed aboard, and I hesitated, surprised by the manic expression on my face. What a day it had been – and the way I looked, the testers would be convinced I was on *something*.

Victory *is* sweet, but what no one ever tells you is that it makes you higher than a fucking kite.

*

Clad in my new Royal, I stepped down from the podium and made my way behind the grandstand, heading for the gauntlet of endless post-race interviews that follow every stage. The media were busy with Brunn and Schlessinger as well as with a few other riders of interest; today's stage winner, an American sprinter on the *MassMiler* team named Gerard Putnam, was among them. I wanted nothing more than to skip this part and go straight to the team bus.

Naturally, there was no chance of that. The soigneur steered me in the usual direction, and I glimpsed Jerzy speaking with one of the satellite channel sport shows. Jerzy gave me a quick nod, which I returned, and then I was swept into my first interview.

The line seemed endless; the longer it took, the more I wished for it to be over. In reality, there were only maybe ten people to talk to, all of them asking the same questions or variations thereof in different languages. I made the switches from English to French to Italian to German and then to Spanish, hoping I wasn't making any glaring errors in the process. As tired as I was, it was hard to be sure.

Finally, I reached the end of the line, a mass of spectators and fans of varying degrees, some manic, some merely curious, some who were along for the hell of it. I dutifully signed autograph after autograph, one after another, and posed with a few fans for photos as they leaned over the barriers to do so.

I started thinking about the photographer at the finish line. I hoped she was okay. I wanted to know more about her, and kept remembering how her dark, expressive eyes had looked into mine.

I don't believe in fairy tales. It's important to make that clear. Castles don't impress me, and princesses and princes are nothing special in Europe. I've lived here all my life and I've never had a magic spell cast over me.

In that moment, however, I was convinced that was what had happened.

She was no princess, no member of royalty, just a woman who happened to be involved in some tangential way to my profession.

All she'd wanted was a photograph, but it had put her in the right place at the wrong time.

Her voice echoed softly in my mind as I gave answers to the usual questions. I wished I'd stayed longer with her. I wished I could explain – if only to myself – what I was feeling.

It didn't matter. Desire has its own language, and needs no words to have a voice.

"Abigail," she had said, and it had seemed like she was speaking directly to me. "My name is Abigail."

Stage Five

(230 km – Sagunto – Reus, Spain)

While Charles drove us to Valencia, I feigned sleep. In spite of my clean bill of health he'd been extremely upset after I'd been released by the paramedics. A few bumps and bruises were the extent of my injuries. I'd been lucky compared to the other photographer and the rider who had hit him. Still, it was the first real interest my husband had shown in anything related to the Tour since we'd begun the trip.

In the car, I listened while he spoke on the mobile, chatting obliquely with someone – but not, I don't think, his most secret someone. The conversation seemed work-related, going off on small tangents here and there.

I wished sincerely, heatedly, that it were her on the phone. Then my persistent reflections on Renard wouldn't have seemed so excessive, or so unfair.

I kept seeing his eyes – exquisitely dark, the lashes ridiculously long and feminine – their expression wide and startled as they gazed straight into mine. The crowd around us had become distant and unreal as he crouched down in front of me, his hand holding mine as though he'd never let go.

Again and again, I recalled that falling sensation sweeping over me, feeling it just as I had then. I could still feel his hand, the humid warmth wrapped around mine.

Then he'd stood up, urged on along his way by his soigneur. His eyes had met mine again, appearing to search my face for something while the paramedics checked me over.

My first, foolish thought was that he'd been memorizing me.

*

When I awoke in our hotel in Valencia the next morning, stiff and achy from my fall the day before, my first thought was nevertheless of Renard. Now that some time had passed – only a few hours, but that was enough – I had to acknowledge the fact something more had happened to me.

Yet surely I was overreacting.

I lay next to Charles, listening to him sleep, hearing the steady rhythm of his breathing which I knew so well. No matter what I did, my thoughts turned to the man who'd been the focus of my photographic efforts in the Tour. Perhaps it was natural to feel this kind of attachment?

God, how attractive he was! Up close there had been no denying it – in spite of my dazed state of mind.

I shook my head and turned toward my pillow to block out the first signs of daylight outside. I needed to put the man out of my mind. It was useless to turn him into some sort of teen idol in my head – doing that might skew my work and ruin the project.

Charles coughed softly and turned away from me. I moved to lie on my back, resolutely keeping my eyes closed. My heart sped up and I clutched my hands into fists, trying to erase the sensation of Renard's hand holding mine.

This is ridiculous.

I got out of bed and went into the bathroom, running the shower until the room filled with steam. I showered quickly, flinching when I touched my bruises with the shower pouf, running a comb through my hair under the spray to untangle the tats and gnarls from my restless sleep. When I stepped out again, clear-headed and relaxed, I wanted nothing but more sleep.

There wasn't time. We needed to be packed and ready to begin the drive to Barcelona as soon as the last cyclists rolled out.

I'll sleep in the car.

Dressed in my cotton robe, I sat on the edge of the bed to continue drying my hair with a towel, bending at the waist to comb out the worst of the stubborn tangles. Charles sat up behind me and stretched lazily before disappearing into the bathroom without a word.

Lost in my thoughts, I didn't notice he'd come back until he sat next to me on the bed.

"Abby?" he said, in a tone I knew too well. He didn't even wait for my response but pulled me up to give me a kiss on the cheek, turning my face to his with his fingertips.

We kissed in silence, his hand moving down to slip one finger into the loose knot in the belt of my robe. He pulled it open and then nudged me to lie back on the bed, which I did in spite of my desire to do otherwise.

Sleep called to me and I forced my eyes to stay open while Charles undressed me, exposing me to the cool air of our room. I tried not to pull away when he inadvertently pressed a bruise or stretched the taut skin around a cut. Oblivious, he kissed me again, his hand heavy on my breast, cupping, squeezing as he shifted position and prepared to join me.

I sighed and he did too, misunderstanding.

"Charles," I began, and he shook his head.

"Won't take long," he murmured against my neck. "We'll be there in plenty of time."

It was *not* what I wanted to hear. I nodded and closed my eyes.

And then I wasn't with him anymore.

I gasped in surprise, my eyes springing open to stare at the light fixture overhead and the tangled shadows it threw along the length of the ceiling.

"Abby," he soothed, never stopping, and I closed my eyes again, giving in.

Just this once. Just this once, I'll let myself pretend and then I'll move on.

And so I clutched Renard to myself, felt him moving with me, inside me, and I ached so deeply I wanted to cry. It was his rhythm countering my own, his body on mine, his kisses moving over my skin while Charles' lips were miles away from me.

I rocked my hips hard against him, sucking in another gasp of air as I tried to push the ache away, seeking more of him, needing more than I would ever find.

Oblivious to the drama playing out in my mind, Charles forged ahead, his quiet, urgent sounds of effort never quite reaching my ears. As always.

My voice shaping itself around a different name, I choked back my cry. I drove myself against him, eyes shut tight, trying to remember every last detail.

The way Renard had smelled was what sent me over. That faintly metallic tang of his sweat and the lower, animal musk beneath was all I needed.

I arched against Charles, grinding myself hard against him and exhaling a deep, wordless cry. After a few, stuttering shudders he froze in my arms before sinking down onto me. There was a short silence before he pulled away.

We dressed and packed our things.

I wondered if he understood it wouldn't happen again.

***

I wanted to assume my fatigue from the stage was what left me so out of sorts. I wanted to believe that, because it was crazy to attribute the sense of headiness to a woman whom I'd barely met.

Then again, perhaps there *was* something to that. Even after a few hours on the bus I was still distracted, and I didn't sleep well after we'd arrived around midnight. Jerzy had given me a wary look in the morning when he'd come in to wake Rom and me, and even as we'd warmed up and headed out to the line, I'd felt his eyes on me. His gaze was heavier than usual, as he assessed my performance and considered whether I was in shape for the stage.

The last time he'd watched me so intently was years ago, when I was an inexperienced kid. I'd gone on a team training ride with a low-grade fever. The fever had climbed steadily until I'd passed out in the saddle and the ride had culminated in one hell of a fall. I still have the scar on my hip where I shredded myself on the asphalt.

I'm not sure who Jerzy had been angrier with that day: me, or himself. I didn't want a second dose of that anger, either. He'd berated me with a thousand furious epithets in the ambulance, in every language I knew and a quite a few I didn't, and all I could think at the time was, *I'm off the team. I'm off the team.*

I wasn't, though. Instead I had to recuperate for a few days, get over the 'flu, and then I was back on the bike again and all was right with the world.

Now, however, I watched the crowd. My gaze skimmed over the people armed with cameras of all sorts and shapes and sizes before I realized I was looking for someone in particular.

Abigail.

My name is Abigail.

I forced myself to quit watching the spectators, putting my attention instead on the road ahead of me. I took off my sunglasses and rubbed my eyes; the tightness around them was worrying, but I resolved to put it out of my mind.

Christ, I was a mess. Today was bound to be a disaster. There were no hard climbs in the mountains, but feeling like this, even the long coastal ride to Barcelona could take the Royal off my back – and if that happened, it would most likely go to Brunn.

As hard as I was trying, I couldn't manage to resign myself to that. But what choice did I have? I was exhausted, and I was still scanning the crowd for the woman from the day before.

For Abigail, my mind corrected, and I longed to shrug it off.

This was nuts, it was madness, pure insanity – and yet I kept hearing her say her name, kept wishing I'd listened for her surname, kept wanting a chance to talk to her and find out who she was.

We were only minutes away from rolling out to begin the stage.

I closed my eyes and leaned back, my bike upright between my thighs while I made a surprisingly satisfying, vertebrae-popping stretch. Part of me wanted to go have a good long lie-down. Part of me wanted to get going and get this finished. Not the stage, but the whole damned Tour.

If I did have to surrender the Royal, I wanted to do it as quickly and painlessly as possible. There was no point in dragging out the agony.

Finally, the convertible carrying the Tour officials pulled ahead of the start line. We all watched expectantly as the guest of honour – some Spanish actor I didn't recognize – saluted his home city and unfurled a Tour banner and waved it over his head. Pockets of excitement erupted on either side of the road, and the head of the Tour proceedings blew his whistle. The car moved forward and we followed close behind.

Cheers went up all around us as we rode off at a measured pace. The push wouldn't come for a little while yet – this was the neutralized section which began every stage. Soon enough, though, once we were out of the city limits and the roads were a little more open, the car would pull away at speed and the official would announce the start through his bullhorn, blow the whistle again and a few members of the pack would break away in a bid for fame at the drop of the flag.

Then it would be up to the rest of us to decide if they were worth chasing down or not. Usually, they weren't, especially not so early in the day. Depending on who was in the group and what the strategy of the day happened to be, sometimes we let them go. They'd wear themselves out well ahead of time and by the end of the day they wouldn't matter.

Sometimes, though, we *had* to chase them down, no matter how early it was. If any of the riders in the breakaway had any chance at overall victory and got too far ahead, it could prove disastrous for the main contenders.

I hoped *Maxxout* wouldn't get any bright ideas. If Schlessinger gained and overtook both Brunn and me, I didn't think I had the strength to pull him back this time.

The thought of the Royal on his back was marginally more unpleasant than thinking of it on Brunn's. At least with Brunn it would stay with my own team. Small consolation, sure, but I'd take it if I had to.

"Eh, Ciccio?" Brunn called out, pulling up alongside me. "Is everything all right?"

I shrugged and took a drink from my water bottle, to have something to do. "Sure, I'm fine. Why?"

"You don't seem all *there*, today. *Était hier si difficile pour vous?*"

There was a hint of teasing in his tone, which threw me. Brunn? Making jokes?

"*Pas plus que pour vous,*" I said, and grinned.

Adrie rode up alongside me, grinning. "*Hou vol,* Ciccio. It's not so bad, today."

We slowly picked up the pace in anticipation of the real start of the race, chatting all the while. It felt like I was among friends again. Unfortunately, it also felt like I was sliding back into my old role as Brunn's helper. I had the uncanny feeling that's where I would be again soon – if not at the end of this stage, then at the end of another.

A slow burn in my stomach nauseated me, but Brunn didn't notice my smile fading away. His gaze was fixed on the car ahead of us, the official turning to face the peloton with bullhorn in hand.

The tension ratcheted up all around me, every one of us wondering the same thing: Who would break away first, and who would drag them back?

And then the flag waved, a muffled announcement lost in the grunts of effort and the whirr of shifting gears and shouts while riders jockeyed for position to break away.

The race was on.

***

We hardly spoke for the rest of the day. I couldn't shake my sense of guilt. Every glance Charles sent my way seemed loaded with distrust.

Or I was reading too much into everything? It wouldn't surprise me if I had been.

The strangest part was the sensation of having actually *been* with Renard. My overactive imagination had outdone itself, and I sincerely regretted permitting myself that indulgence in fantasy.

I had never done it before, and on the drive along the coast toward Barcelona, I made a quiet vow never to do it again. How did my girlfriends fantasize about movie stars or models or the guy on the train or whatever and not come away feeling like they'd actually done the deed?

Charles' phone chirped and he took it out of his pocket to see who was calling. After a sidelong glance at me, he pressed a button and tucked the phone away again. I glanced at him in turn, then focused my attention on the passing scenery.

Maybe that's *how*, I thought, knowing the call had to be from his "friend" back in London. *He probably does a little fantasizing of his own, too.*

I closed my eyes, blocking out the view of the Mediterranean peeking through the orchards along the coastline. The sun beat down on us in spite of the weather reports predicting rainfall in the next few days. I had a feeling the rain would arrive in the mountains near Andorra.

I longed for sleep to take me out of the tedium of driving in the near-silence Charles preferred. The radio was on, an English pop song playing so softly I could barely hear the music. The air conditioning was on low and a light layer of perspiration lingered beneath the summer-weight blouse and shorts I wore.

The phone chirped again and Charles repeated the process, checking the caller's ID and then switching it over to voice mail before putting the phone away.

I looked at him again and he shrugged in a gesture of indifference.

"Work," he mumbled. He reached out and turned up the volume on the radio, just a little, before resuming his steely stare out the windscreen at the *Autopista del Mediterráneo* rolling beneath our wheels.

How could he possibly think I wouldn't find it suspicious that he wasn't talking to whoever it was calling him? He'd taken nearly every call from work since we'd been on this trip, so why stop now?

The music played on, the thrumming of the wheels over the tarmac hypnotic, lulling me into a doze. I'd never understood how Charles could stay awake with that sound as his only accompaniment on the road, but he could. I needed music when I drove, when I went over my photographs – anytime I wasn't actually talking to someone. Unless, of course, Charles was there. Then the silence got between us.

Just like now.

Another chirp from his phone sounded and I sat up from the slouch I'd assumed in the interim. I watched him out of the corner of my eye as he examined the number and went to silence the ringer.

"Answer it," I said quietly. "Go ahead and answer her, or she'll call all the way to Barcelona." I turned my gaze out the side window, to the blue of the water at the horizon sending up sparkles under the sunlight.

He watched me, the phone continuing to chirp politely, muffled somewhat by his hand until it stopped altogether.

"Hello?" he answered, a questioning tone to his voice. "Could I call you back later? I'm en route to Barcelona…"

I closed my eyes against the landscape flashing past, shut out the water and the flecks of silver dancing across it and hid from my reflection in the window, visible only because I was up close to it. The stinging behind my eyes crested and faded, the tears drying before they were shed.

I'd hoped so much that he'd ignore the call.

***

Rom was fighting to get me to the head of the pack, in the throes of the final kilometres on the broken-heart-shaped perimeter road around Reus. Attilio did the same for Brunn, growing more aggressive as the stretch of roadway straightened out in front of us and the peloton surged forward as a whole.

There was some confusion at the long oval roundabout, and a few riders in the back of the peloton went down. More footage for the fans of crashes, then. After some tight curves, the road rounded gently to the left and we continued jostling for position, trying to reassure ourselves of maintaining our standings. It was unlikely that Schlessinger would try anything today – strategically speaking, the climb into Andorra was his best bet for a Royal finish – so it was all a matter of maintaining the status quo.

Rom, doggedly forging ahead of me to open a slot in the pack so we could advance, threw me a look somewhere between amusement and agony. Tomorrow he'd be happy – the mountain stage would be brutal for some of us but he'd be on his preferred turf – though he was suffering now. He never coped well with the monotony of flat stages.

Brunn and I were riding at speed amongst the peloton, but the group containing the sprinters was well ahead of us, gunning for the finish at the end of this flat stage. From Valencia to Torreblanca, Alvaro had sparred with Teodoro, promising his own victory to even the score with his brother. Teodoro had instead assured us all of his own imminent victory, going so far as to predict a one-second gap at the finish.

Braggadocio, all of it – but the good-natured teasing between the brothers was enough to entertain the rest of us for the length of the stage.

A burst of shrieking and screaming across the team's radio frequency was difficult to comprehend. Either Jerzy had slipped over the edge into insanity, or somewhere closer to the line, one or more of my teammates had made a tactical mistake.

Brunn glanced at me, his expression inscrutable, save for a flicker of concern in his eyes before he turned back to the matter at hand.

Listening to the invective spewing over the airwaves, I had the feeling things weren't exactly going according to plan at the finish.

We pressed forward, the final roundabout looming ahead when Attilio gave a shout and bumped shoulders with another rider who was riding too close as the curve tightened.

Rom broke through the last few cyclists blocking us and I followed close on his wheel, the two of us making our way up to the head of the pack to lead the group through the roundabout and down the short final stretch.

We breezed our way down Avinguda de Sant Jordi, avoiding the concrete lip of the island separating the lanes of the road, but other riders weren't so lucky, judging from the shouts of the crowd and the *skree* of titanium on pavement which followed the final turn.

Rom fell back behind me in short order and Brunn was soon at my shoulder, a slight grin on his face the only indication that he was pleased with how things had gone. As far as I could tell, there wasn't even a hint of curiosity regarding Jerzy's previous rant, not one iota of concern for Alvaro or Teodoro or for how they'd fared.

We'd find out soon enough.

In the meantime, for the riders who'd remained upright, it was a brisk finish. A few of the other riders picked themselves up and finished the stage with no problem. Only a handful of riders were unable to ride across the line, mostly from mechanical difficulties.

As for me, a strong sense of relief took hold once I was solidly across the finish line. The Royal was still mine, and I'd wear it into Andorra, regardless of whether I'd keep it once we got there.

As I made my way back to the team area to get ready for the presentation ceremony, the source of Jerzy's dismay was made clear. Alvaro and Teodoro had gone very, very wrong and lost the sprint – which, by all estimations, had been theirs to take.

To my amazement, Jerzy hadn't quite exploded yet. We were, however, fifty miles outside Barcelona, and it looked like it was going to be a very, very long ride.

***

The end of the race was rather quiet, compared to how the other stages had gone. Only the sprint, with its disastrous turn of events for *Alta VeloCidad*, proved noteworthy. I was lucky enough to get photos of it all: from Putnam storming the line to Renard's arrival a short while later, to the last, lingering arrivals after the crash in the final turn.

Wishful thinking had me almost convinced he'd seen me shortly after he'd crossed the line. I tried my best to shake the sensation –

foolish as it was – and concentrated on snapping shots of the last of the peloton as they straggled across the finish line, the walking wounded, sometimes in a literal sense. I wondered at the sense of pride which could compel these athletes to soldier on this way, in some cases broken, bleeding and not lightly injured.

Then I wondered if I was much different, since I'd been doing the same in my own way.

Charles had driven us to Barcelona, and I'd driven myself back to Reus, alone. I was grateful to spend the drive, and then my dinner that night, that way as well.

I supposed he was in the hotel room, eating room service and talking with her on the phone, since I'd decided to leave him to it in the end. It was preferable to hearing the constant ringing of the phone, or to watching his guilt emerge each time it rang.

Honestly, if I'd had a choice, I would have preferred to stay alone in the hotel.

As the situation stood, I didn't have a choice, and it probably didn't matter. If I let myself consider it realistically, the idea of completing the Tour alone was too intimidating.

I lingered at the finish for a while after the end of the race. I grabbed shots of the chaperones who ran from place to place, some of them escorting riders, some of them running official errands; the fans, excitedly discussing the events of the race; the clean-up crews getting to work as soon as possible.

I belatedly made my way to the press pit in front of the podium and held my camera up over the crowd to capture a few more atmospheric shots before the presentations. I managed a few tight shots of the competitors receiving their jerseys, my spirits lifted somewhat by the cheering and applause of the crowd.

I did my best to remain professional as Renard stepped out to receive his Royal for the stage. A strange melancholy came over me as he stepped off the podium and shook hands with the town officials and other guests, before making his way backstage.

Remembering his expression when he'd checked on me after the crash, I slowly melted a little inside. Ridiculous. A schoolgirl's crush, and I was – what? – at least ten years older than he was. At *least*.

I made a mental note to look up his birthdate online when I got back to the hotel. Or maybe I'd look it up on my netbook from the bar before I went up to the room. I didn't really feel like enduring any snide comments from Charles when I returned to Barcelona.

Then again, maybe he wouldn't be making them anymore, now that I'd called him on his "phone mate" and everything.

Drifting back to my car, I paused as a shiver ran along my spine in a light, tingling caress. The hairs on the back of my neck stood up and I turned toward the Village, where the remainder of the crowd milled around outside the team areas.

There was no-one there, but I would have sworn I'd felt his gaze on me, if only for a split second. I clucked my tongue dismissively. *I'm getting dotty in my old age*, I reckoned, and resumed my walk to the car.

When the feeling came again, I took out my camera, aimed it over my shoulder, and clicked the shutter. I'd examine the shot when I got to Barcelona.

***

As a rule, Jerzy's rantings were ballistic. In a confined space, such as the team bus, they could be positively nuclear.

My only relief was that I wasn't the target.

En route to Barcelona, Alvaro and Teodoro (along with their lead-out crew of James, Phil and Adrie) were sequestered in the "crash pad" in the back of the bus. The area where we usually slept on longer trips was now where Jerzy was ripping them apart for their error at the end of today's stage.

They hadn't given sufficient attention to the rider in their slipstream during the crucial final meters of the race, and had been drafted and subsequently pipped at the line by Gerard Putnam of *MassMiler*, who had managed to eke out a stage win with his sprint.

Glancing back at Jerzy as he paced, I believed steam was coming out of his ears, but it was how the light hit his close-cropped hair.

James sat on the edge of the big bench, his head hung low, only chancing a glance at Jerzy as he moved away. He caught my eye and his expression was one of purest misery. He'd fucked up and he knew it.

And so did Jerzy.

"It was stupid! Careless! What the fuck were you thinking?"

"Jer-" Alvaro didn't get the chance to finish.

"Where was your focus? On your stupid jokes with your

brother? When you race you aren't brothers, do you understand? You are *teammates*. You are riders, nothing more!"

A torrent of rather colourful Spanish followed, and Teodoro, seated next to James, winced.

Adrie was reflected in the back window of the bus even though he stood out of my sight. When Jerzy turned on James, Adrie's arms were folded across his chest in the posture of someone about to be sick.

"Sloppy! I should send Goosh out there tomorrow in your place, if I only could. He'd do a better job, if that's the best you can do. You had it! You fucking had it, and then you let the American get it? The *American*? It's his first fucking Tour and your third, and you *still* let him by? You fucking Brits are *useless*!"

I couldn't bear to watch any more but I couldn't avoid hearing it.

"Did you see how he was riding?" Adrie shouted back, and the murmur of conversation in the main cabin of the bus silenced. "It was too dangerous to hold the line, Jerzy. If James hadn't let him go, he'd have taken the whole lot of us out! The pack was too goddamn tight!"

"I watched the video, Adrie. I watched it. Where the fuck was your defence?"

"I shouldered as hard as I could, and he came back with more," Adrie answered calmly. "That little fucker is crazy. The finish was suicidal in that last turn – you saw how many got taken out by the kerb – and, frankly, I thought I'd like to end the stage without a busted collarbone or a broken neck."

Another silence, this time including the group at the back of the bus. Only Brunn had ever been so bold with Jerzy in the past, and *he* got a special pass by being his best friend.

"Very well, then. You have a strategy meeting in the morning. Seven a.m. If you're even a minute late, I dock the day's pay."

"But it's not even a sprint sta –"

Jerzy wheeled around in the doorway, levelling a finger in Alvaro's direction. "That's where you're wrong. There are plus points for the sprinters all along the route, and now you're the one who's riding for them. Minus the bonuses. At least you'll get the *glory* when we ride into Andorra, right?"

With that, Jerzy stormed out and made his way to the head of the bus, where he took his usual seat behind the driver and got out his portable DVD player. After a few minutes, Brunn joined him, and the low buzz of their conversation while they reviewed the video of the day's stage almost covered the sound of Alvaro punching the stuffing out of a pillow in the back, until Adrie shut the door.

Stage Six

(210 km – Barcelona, Spain – Andorra)

In the intense afternoon heat, the climb seemed endless. Chatter amongst the riders quieted and then finally stopped altogether as the route trended slowly upward.

The mountains had lined the horizon all day and now they were all I could see, seeming to close in while I dragged myself toward the summit of the penultimate climb. The ascent grew steeper still, clawing the breath from my lungs in hot, ragged pulls through the heat-shimmer off the tarmac in the midsummer afternoon.

I dreamed of rain, but none was expected. There was no breeze. The crowds of obscenely exuberant spectators lining the roadway blocked it from us. My sweat cooled in the currents created by my forward motion, or slowly evaporated through the layers of spandex I wore. It pooled in the small of my back and under the receiver taped to my ear, loosening the adhesive to a sticky drag along my lobe. With every movement the radio slid along my back over the sheen of perspiration. Unzipping my jersey did little to alleviate the heat. The fabric hung limp, absorbing my sweat, adding to the weight I was hauling up the mountain.

A faint, metallic scent hovered in the air over the peloton, a humid, elemental odour of exertion and willpower. It lingered in the dryness of my mouth between swallows from my water bottle. It rose out of me with every crank of the pedals as I maintained my place in the group, ascending the Pyrenean slope.

After hours in the saddle, with exhaustion rearing its head, I began to slide backward, into the heart of the peloton. Rom did all he could, but I couldn't keep up.

The group I rode in had thinned out to a long, straggling line. Someone called out my name a moment before a spectator's hand rested on my back, pushing me forward in a gesture of assistance. I wanted to resist their help and swat them away, but I didn't.

Attilio and Brunn rode ahead, maintaining their pace in a generous bid to keep me in the running, but I knew there was no real hope. Not today.

Schlessinger and his domestique, a scrawny little powerhouse named Lorenzo Motta, were right behind us. I knew they wouldn't be there for long; if my rival intended to make a grab for the Royal, it would be today. This was his clearest chance and he'd be a fool not to take it.

Even as the thought occurred to me, Motta and Schlessinger seemed to float past, their ascent on the steep grade appearing as smooth as if they were gliding *down*hill, instead. I watched, stunned as Schlessinger glared back at me over his shoulder and then broke into a wide grin.

"How's the girlfriend, Ciccio?" he called before the crowd swallowed him up, their shouts and cheers drowning out anything else he had to say.

My puzzled reaction was not the one he'd sought. His scowl returned and he put his back to me, continuing to power his way uphill. Brunn followed him slowly, Attilio carrying him along, and both of them spared me brief, sympathetic glances as they went.

What the hell is going on here?

I pushed myself harder, striving for a summit barely visible over the churning crowds. Brunn was already gone, and Rom doggedly led me through the chaos as we climbed toward the top. Brunn would catch Schlessinger, I was sure of it. On the final ascent, they'd race to the top for the mountain finish, and Brunn would keep him at bay.

He had to, or the Royal would be out of *Alta VeloCidad*'s hands. Neither of us wanted *that*, even if I didn't want Brunn to have it.

I caught a glimpse of Schlessinger as he disappeared over the summit. Several agonizing moments later, Brunn left Attilio behind and did the same. The image of Brunn's purple-and-silver team colours winking out of existence, burned into my brain.

When at last I crested the top, Brunn was giving chase below. Schlessinger was working damned hard to lose him on the descent, but it was clear he still lacked the confidence to use the sharp curves of the steep downward slope to his advantage.

From a distance, Brunn and Schlessinger appeared as two tawny, golden beasts of speed, hurtling downhill until one – Brunn – swatted casually with one great paw, and just like that, it was over.

Not literally, of course, but once Brunn had passed Schlessinger and the final ascent had begun, the end of the stage was clear. All the same, I rode as hard and fast as I possibly could, to no avail. It made no difference how swiftly I descended, leaving Rom and the others behind. The next climb took me out in spite of my best efforts.

I'd lost the Royal.

To Brunn.

***

The first riders ascended the final climb with some difficulty, reaching the slight plateau and straightaway with a suspenseful slowness. I was disappointed to see the Royal wasn't amongst the brilliant colours flaring against the dark of the tarmac.

I snapped several shots of Heinrich Brunn crossing the line, a desperately disillusioned Jürgen Schlessinger in frame over his shoulder. Both of them wore fixed grimaces of effort, but the expression in Schlessinger's eyes was something on the edge of sheer defeat.

My heart went out to him. From what we'd seen on the giant screens along the finish, it had been a mighty struggle for him. Brunn had gained the win in the final lengths on the ascent while making the whole thing look positively effortless. That surely added insult to injury for the younger German rider.

More riders passed, and still Renard hadn't shown. I turned to the screen and saw the shot filmed by the helicopter hovering a short distance away: Renard was nearly to the plateau, but it was a fight he seemed to be riding to a draw. His domestique, Romuald Brodowski, was working hard to pull Renard up to the finish.

When they came into view, I focused where the road levelled

beneath them. Was it my imagination, or did Brodowski look particularly frustrated? From his previous performances in the mountains, I knew he was an excellent climber, and this chore had to drain all the enjoyment of the stage from him. Still, he did his job admirably, and managed to get them both across the line in time for Renard to stay in top five classification.

Nevertheless, one full minute had passed since Brunn's arrival.

I captured them crossing the line, slowly riding to their handlers. Renard's shoulders were slumped in exhaustion, and this time there was neither a giddy, delirious grin or expression of victory to buoy the fatigue. I kept taking photos of the arrivals, but I couldn't resist trying to aim the camera to catch Renard as he slid to the ground with his back against the barriers, unable to face the people around him.

I photographed more late arrivals, my mind drifting to Renard, forcing me to turn and watch him through the lens, snagging a few photos in the process. Finally the group of sprinters arrived *en masse*, barely within the maximum time allowed, and when I turned back Renard was gone. He'd been spirited away, presumably to the team bus and his post-stage cool down.

Disappointed, I packed up most of my gear before heading toward the podium for the presentations. Making my way through the crowd, I noticed that some of the faces were now familiar to me. Some were photographers – professionals or amateurs, like me – others were devoted fans, I guessed, following the Tour as it snaked its way across the Continent. We exchanged nods or tilts of the head whenever we caught one another's eye, silently acknowledging the sense of recognition and community growing amongst us.

The heat was incredible, made even worse by the press of bodies beneath the late-afternoon sun. At last I found a spot where I could set up in the photographers' pit. The Frenchman I'd met a few days before – the one who'd backed me up when I'd tussled with the other photographer at the finish line – saw me. He smiled and indicated I could set up in the gap next to him, so I did.

I dutifully snapped away as the stage winner received his prizes on the podium. Brunn followed shortly thereafter. All the while, I pictured Renard crossing the line. It wasn't losing the Royal – the margin wasn't yet so great he couldn't reclaim it after the mountain stages were finished. No, something else was at work beneath the façade he presented to the public.

I shook my head. What the hell was wrong with me? Did I really think I was so attuned to him? Based on what? A one-minute meeting and a lovemaking fantasy, which I had to admit was a rather one-sided deal.

But my instincts had been correct in Reus, hadn't they? When I'd checked my photos afterward, I'd found him in the crowd at the team buses in the final photo I'd snapped over my shoulder before going home. Not that it meant he'd been watching me or anything, but couldn't my awareness of him mean –

No. It was a stupid fantasy and nothing more, but at least it made time spent at the hotel bearable.

Charles' silent resentment was hard to take, but his absence at the race had been a relief. I hated to admit it, but there it was: I was more relaxed without him around. Without his grousing, his pronounced disinterest – and yes, his constant phone calls from "work" – it was so much easier to focus on what I was doing. There was no need to worry about him being happy, particularly knowing nothing I did, shy of sending him to the nearest pub, would please him.

I had the uncanny feeling tonight would be like last night, and I would spend the better part of it alone again. I had already decided where I would pass the time, and was already considering what I might have for dinner. Charles had told me, not long after lunch and after he'd already taken two calls, he would have to take care of some work and thus wouldn't be able to have dinner with me.

"Since these bloody Spaniards can't eat at a proper time," he'd complained, "I suppose I'll have to have room service instead of waiting until eleven bloody p.m."

"This is Andorra," I'd said in response, putting my bag on my shoulder. "We're not even in Spain anymore."

"Well, then. Maybe there's hope for a meal at a proper time?" His gaze met mine evenly, and I waited for him to continue. "But I'll still be working tonight, Abby."

"Okay." With that, I'd picked up my other bag and gone out.

And now I was sitting in the bar I'd planned to go to all day, alternating my drinks between mineral water and white wine while examining my photos and waiting for a response to the e-mail I'd sent my publisher.

All in all, it was *not* how I'd imagined following the Tour would go.

***

A hush briefly falling as soon as I entered the team's section of the hotel restaurant was my first sign that something was up. It was too short to be anything of consequence but I knew I hadn't imagined it when Rom didn't meet my eyes. Attilio also shifted uncomfortably in his seat, doubtless feeling guilty for having got Brunn so far ahead of me.

As for the new race leader, Brunn went back to talking privately with Jerzy, barely glancing in my direction. I resisted a scowl and went to the last available seat at the table along the wall, where the bulk of my teammates and the rest of the crew sat.

With everyone politely averting his gaze from me, I knew I reeked with the stench of failure.

I picked up the manila envelope which rested on my chair and examined it, confused. There was no return address, no postmark – no stamp or postage at all, for that matter – just my name written in clear block letters across the front.

"What's this?" I asked, holding the envelope up for my nearest seatmates to see. I got a shrugging chorus in response and everyone went back to their conversations.

I shook my head and bent back the metal tabs of the seal to open the envelope. The contents slid out onto my plate: an issue of *Avant-Mode*, a French women's fashion magazine. I smiled, seeing it.

Ah, it's from Solange. She must be in this one.

I disregarded the lack of postage or return address in an instant, and picked up the magazine to fan through the pages, distractedly seeking her picture.

"Solange?" Rom asked from across the table, and now it was my turn to shrug. I hadn't seen her anywhere when I'd flipped through, and now I paged through more carefully.

I stopped dead when I found her.

I'd never seen Solange like that in a photograph. She stood with her legs spread wide, her bathing suit bottom little more than a sheer strip of fabric over her shaved pussy, her hands behind her back holding what looked like some sort of whip or riding crop. Her bare breasts were thrust toward the viewer, her hair wild around her face, her red, glistening lips open and expectant.

I stared, stunned. *I'd* seen that expression on her face before, but none of my *teammates* ever had. Until now.

What the fuck *is* this advertising, anyway?

It wasn't until the appreciative whistles and applause broke out from the others that I realized I was holding the magazine out and away from me like a loathsome, living thing. And most of the team had taken a good, long look at my fiancée in all her glory.

"*That's* your Solange?" Goosh asked in something like amazement.

My first instinct was to deny it. This was not the woman I'd flirted with on the podium a couple of years ago, whose kisses had lingered enough to be outside the professional limits, whom I'd asked to marry me after nearly a year of dating.

This wasn't the woman I'd made love to a few weeks ago, before she'd travelled to Australia for another project to pad her portfolio. Lots of presentations and art modelling, she'd said. Maybe some television work, too.

This wasn't the woman for whose call I was waiting so eagerly. She wasn't this brazen, this coarse – she wasn't this *vulgar*.

And yes, it was her. I knew because I knew the face she was making in this photo. I knew every curve of her body, digitally altered or no, and I found in that picture allusions to the passion she'd shared with me. In strictest confidence, I'd thought at the time. Now I wasn't so sure.

James grabbed the magazine away from me, held it up to examine it more closely, and the rude comments soon followed.

"I wouldn't mind keeping her company for an hour or so – do you reckon she looks lonely?"

"D'you mind if I take her up to my room, Ciccio? You know, just for a little while."

"I knew she was pretty, but I had no idea she was this *hot*, mate. Cor..."

"I've never met someone before who's had a piece of ass like that. What's she like, then? Y'know, what's she *like*?"

"Oi, and what *does* she like? I need to fuel my imagination for tonight..." Phil added with a laugh, making a rude gesture.

I kept my mouth shut, refusing to rise to the bait, but they continued, growing coarser as the night went on. It wasn't until Phil made a show of stuffing the magazine under his shirt and sneaking toward the door of the restaurant with one hand on his crotch that I finally spoke up.

"For fuck's sake, all of you – she's my *fiancée*! How about a little respect?" I snatched the magazine away from Phil and stormed out, making my way to my room. My ears and face burned red-hot, not cooling for a long while even after I'd flopped down on my bed and examined the magazine again.

There were more photos on the next pages. How I'd missed them – how my teammates had missed them – was beyond me. Nonetheless, I counted my blessings that they hadn't spotted the more provocative and quasi-grotesque poses.

I smoothed out the offending pages and stared hard at them, hating that I must have sounded like a foolish old prig downstairs. Still, what did they expect? She *was* my fiancée, and that they'd talked about her like that… Then again, to them – most of them, anyway, since Brunn, Rom and Adrie hadn't taken part – this wasn't anyone who actually *existed*. Solange was someone they'd only met briefly, if at all, and here she was merely an image on the pages of this magazine.

Frankly, she had started to feel equally remote to me.

I dug my mobile out of my pocket and scrolled down to her name, hitting the *send* button to make the call. I didn't care what time it was in Sydney now. Maybe if she were sleeping, she'd wake up and answer.

She didn't. The phone rang until the voice mail picked up, and I hesitated before leaving a brief message.

"It's me. *Ciao*."

I hung up.

The more I looked at the photo in the magazine, the less it resembled Solange. Soon all I saw were the full breasts and the dampened, barely-there swimsuit bottom, which more than hinted at what lay beneath as it clung suggestively to her.

I hadn't seen her in so long. I'd almost forgotten what her hair smelled like, or her skin, or her –

The rattle of a key in the lock brought me out of my reveries, and I rolled onto my side, away from the door before Rom could see the state I was in.

Jesus, I was as bad as the rest of them! At least I could go by memory, since I'd actually been with her.

Rom said nothing. He merely picked up his MP3 player and fell onto his bed, bouncing slightly so the mattress gave a few weary squeaks beneath him. He plugged in his earphones and read over the itinerary for tomorrow's rest day.

We were due for a training ride in the morning, some interviews and photos to follow, and then a little free time in the evening. Until today, I'd looked forward to the break. Now, with Solange's soft-porn spread and the loss of the Royal still fresh in my mind, I couldn't even consider a day without a stage as anything but a long, slow torture.

"For fuck's sake," I muttered, getting up to go to the bathroom. "What *else* is going to go wrong?"

I should have known better than to ask.

***

I didn't want to see Charles and delayed going back to the hotel room as long as I could. I went down to the hotel bar and restaurant and settled into a corner booth to set up my computer. It was early so the restaurant was still quite empty.

I planned on leaving once the crowds started coming in. By that time, Charles would surely be done with his "work" and I could go to bed right away. At least, I hoped so.

I transferred photos from my camera to the computer hard drive, and then to the portable external hard drive for additional backup. I couldn't be too careful.

When the file transfers were finished, I put on my eyeglasses to study the photos of the day. The heaviness in my chest persisted as I examined the photos of Brunn on the podium.

There was no sense denying to myself that I had a personal favourite in this Tour. It was possible – if not particularly probable – that Renard could regain his position at the top. The fact that his teammate had the Royal now was a significant victory.

I clicked through the slideshow on my screen until I found a photo of Renard from that afternoon. It was – even if I did say so myself – a remarkable shot: he was striving for the finish, his face a mask of pain and determination, the muscles of his legs and arms standing out in relief beneath his skin. The background was the indistinct jumble of the crowd with their signs and flags and replica jerseys – the multicoloured rainbow making Renard – in his Royal jersey atop the blue bike – stand out even more.

I was drawn to the expression on his face: such agony, such anguish was written there that my heart twisted in empathy. It was a photograph of someone losing their hard-fought dream in spite of giving all they had to hold on to it.

I was starting to understand exactly how he felt.

*

"You've been drinking...?" Charles put his cell phone on the bedside table and gave me a quizzical look.

"Not much. Just a little wine with dinner. You know, as you do." I shrugged and went through my suitcase, digging out my nightgown and slippers.

"Are you upset about something?"

The disingenuousness of the question was insulting.

"Charles, how do you play at ignorance so well?"

"Come on, Abby." He stood and came over to my side of the bed to stare down at me while I changed clothes.

"You can't honestly be this oblivious." I looked up and met his eyes, daring him to pretend further.

He didn't.

Instead, he returned to his side of the bed. After a moment's silence, he sank down onto the bed and sighed. "This is why I thought we should consider..."

"I've already told you why I don't want that." I got under the coverlet, and Charles kept his back to me.

"I'd feel better, Abby, if you had someone with you when I'm away."

Bullshit.

"No, you'd feel better if I said *you* could have someone with you when you're away. That's what this is all about."

"No, it isn't."

"For all I know, you already have."

"Abby..."

I turned onto my side and resisted the urge to sigh, too.

"I didn't want you to feel this way about it," he said.

"How else would I feel? You're talking about taking a *lover.*" I turned to face him and found him staring at the carpet, shaking his head. "And me, giving you the okay."

"No, I'm not."

My throat tightened and I got out of bed. I stood up straight and smoothed down my nightgown, trying to keep my hand from shaking. I held up the other hand and started counting off: "You put down the phone when I come in the room, you stay late at work even if you don't have to, and you get more phone calls than you need from work…"

"That's not proof of anything, Abby. Circumstantial at best."

"Give me time…" I gathered my clothes and piled them into the laundry bag. "I'm sure I'll dig up ample evidence soon enough."

Charles said nothing but exhaled softly behind me. I got back into bed and pulled the blanket up to my shoulder after putting my back to him. Silence stretched out between us until he switched off the light and lay down.

"I haven't done anything," he said after a while.

"Yet," I said, curling up and wincing in spite of myself

I didn't want to be like this. I didn't want things to go this way, but it was taking all my control to keep from shouting at him. I was tired of his 'suggestions'; tired of hearing how an open relationship could work for us; tired of knowing he was unhappy enough to consider this, but not unhappy enough to abandon the whole thing.

Most of all, I was tired of not being tired enough to make the break on my own.

Rest Day One

(Andorra)

I woke to the sound of rain pattering on the window, which wasn't the best precursor to a training ride. A glance in Rom's direction showed me he was greeting the day in his usual manner. It was just another day.

No, check that: it was a rest day. That meant a *ride*, not a race. There would also be interviews with members of the international press in the morning and evening, perhaps a few photos, and then the team strategy meeting to follow. Lunch and dinner would fit in there somewhere.

And then, maybe, some free time. I planned on making phone calls; as many as it took to find out what was going on with Solange. The photo shoot – the one in the magazine last night – was done months ago. That fact had only occurred to me in the small hours of the morning.

This meant she'd lied to me when she said the photographer, Conway something-or-other, didn't do those sorts of shoots and she'd never do that sort of work anyway.

In spite of everything, I still hoped she'd call me first.

When I joined the team in the dining hall, Phil and Attilio were chuckling in the midst of the group. My paranoia was strong enough I was convinced they were laughing at me. It was stupid and I knew it.

Rom and Jerzy chatted in the breakfast line, the unfamiliar

cadence of their shared language blending in the murmur of conversation surrounding me. Even though I didn't speak Polish, I still tried to pick out familiar words or phrases.

Unless they started cursing I wasn't likely to comprehend much of what they said to one another. While Jerzy might burst into vibrant invective, there was no way Rom would speak to his idol like that.

The rain slackened to a drizzle by the time breakfast was over. After a ride in the team van, the riders assembled under the awning pulled out from the bus. We wouldn't ride the planned recon after all. If there wasn't a stage to race, we wouldn't take the chance of riding in this weather. The risk of a fall or illness in these conditions was too great.

The routine of warming up was soothing. Making sure everything was operating properly, hearing the reassuring *click* of my shoe attaching to the pedal, finding my rhythm on the stationary bike – all of this gave me a sense of rightness in the world. If only for a short while.

The teasing from my mates resumed. The comments about Solange began gently at first, then grew cruder and more probing before Jerzy barked orders and cut them short.

Put it out of your mind. Focus.

I put my head down, trying to ignore the humid air and cold breezes which found their way inside my warm up gear. I shivered and wiped my sweat away.

In spite of the effort of training, no matter how loud I turned up the volume of the music in my earphones, my thoughts turned back to Solange.

And, in spite of Jerzy's previous orders, James and Phil were at it again.

Perhaps I should be proud to have a girlfriend who made me the envy of my teammates. Maybe I should be flaunting the fact I had a woman like her, using those photos to make them all jealous and wish they were me.

I couldn't do that. I could do anything like that to my Sunny. And in spite of the lurid poses and barely-there costumes, she was still my sweet sunshine, just as she'd been since we met.

Wasn't she?

*

In the team van, returning to the hotel, the teasing kicked in again, and I endured it as best I could. Attilio wasn't as aggressive as before; as one of my oldest friends on the team, he knew when I was reaching my limits. James and Phil, not so much. Their good-natured banter pressed every button with stunning precision.

"Say, Ciccio?" James called after me as we climbed out of the van and crossed under the canopy in front of the hotel.

"Yeah?" My response came out somewhere between a grunt and a sigh.

"I was wondering if I could borrow your magazine sometime. Those of us presently unattached tend to get a little lonely, eh? D'you reckon she'd be amenable to a little – ahem – *company*?"

"All right; that's *it*!" Heat rushed to my face as I turned on James. "Fucking drop it! Give it a fucking rest and show the woman some respect already!"

Startled, he took a couple of paces back, his hands raised to fend me off. "Whoa, mate, steady on... I was playing around."

"She's not just some piece of ass, you know."

"I know, I know –"

Phil cut in between us, a goofy smile on his face. "Ciccio, mate – calm down, yeah?"

"I will not! Not until you all lay off Sunny!"

I became aware of Adrie behind me, his usual calm presence raising my hackles even before he spoke.

"You're overreacting, Chicco."

"Am I?" I spun around to face him. "She's my *fiancée*, isn't she?"

"It's just a *photo* – no big deal."

My stomach did a long, slow roll over itself as I considered this. Easy enough for him to say, wasn't it?

"You know, I suppose you're right." I shook my head and turned to go. "By the way..."

"Yes?"

I faced him again. "D'you have any pictures of your wife?"

His eyes widened, then narrowed, his jaw setting in a stern line. "Excuse me?"

"Aw, come on, Adrie. It's no big deal, right? Like James said, we get a little lonely, from time to time. Some of us like a little variety, too –"

His hand shot out so fast I hardly saw it coming, his grasp on the neck of my jersey threatening to rip the fabric. I tried to pull away but his hold was too strong.

"*Stomme eikel!* Don't alienate everyone, *Ciccio*," he said, taking obvious care to use my team nickname and not my personal one. "Not unless you don't really *want* to get within shouting distance of the Royal again. We can *all* see to that."

Before I could respond, Jerzy's hand landed on Adrie's and parted us with a rough shake, keeping a strong grip on me. Epithets streamed out of our team manager until he found a common language for both Adrie and myself and focused on it.

It took all my willpower to keep from trying to slap his hand away or to shout the worst, most blasphemous phrases I could think of in return for his abuse. My childish fit of temper faded as Jerzy turned me loose and spun me away from my teammate, propelling me out of the lobby and toward the stairwell.

"Your rooms, idiots!" he shouted, and the rest of the team flinched, hesitating before they dispersed. Jerzy had only been addressing Adrie and me, anyway. I took the stairs two at a time, slammed through the door of my room at the end of the hall and went straight into the bathroom. I fumbled clumsily with my kit, flinging everything into the corner without a second thought before giving the shower handle an angry twist to start the water. I stepped under the spray and exhaled, trying to compose myself.

Why was I running so hot today?

When I reached for the shampoo, I found my hands clenched in fists, my muscles trembling. I had to rectify this – and soon – or else I'd burn out before the Tour was half over.

I considered how it would feel to punch the tile wall of the shower stall, imagined how the ceramic might fracture under the bones of my hand, even as my bones likely did the same.

Being unable to ride, for that ridiculous reason, would be even more humiliating. To miss out because I'd had an injury unrelated to racing, caused by my own stupid temper? What a way to go down in history.

In spite of the heat of the water, an icy calm descended over me.

I had to focus.

I had to plan.

I had to win.

That was all I had to do.

*

I played it cool as I stepped out onto the patio of the hotel restaurant. A murmur of conversation followed as I walked over to take my seat, the eyes of my teammates tracking me every step of the way.

I picked at a salad to start, my interest in the meal fading fast. There was too much effort involved in trying to wrap my head around the events of the last twenty-four hours.

Why hadn't Solange told me she'd done that sort of photo shoot? Why hasn't she answered or returned my calls? How did I manage to lose the Royal so soon?

Okay, so some questions had simpler answers than others.

All the same, I had never felt so low.

Adrie settled into a chair nearby, giving me a brief, annoyed glance before turning his attention to his tablemates.

Rom sat down, bottles of water in both hands before he slid one over to me. He looked at me quizzically until I picked mine up and took a grateful sip.

A short while later one of the team staff came out with an armful of letters and packages and began handing them out. As he approached my table, he sorted out a smallish box and put it down in front of me. "All the way from Sydney," he said with a grin before moving on to the next group.

No sooner had I picked it up than Phil and James had seated themselves at my table, Attilio and Goosh close behind.

"What the fuck, guys?" I protested, not yet opening the package.

"Can't we see?"

I sighed, begrudgingly and perversely pleased by their attention, but still dreading any repeats of the night before. "It's personal," I said, splitting the tape and pulling it back.

"Oh, come on..." Phil wheedled, and James rose from his seat to stand next to me.

"I've got my fingers crossed for something special," Attilio joked, and James made a show of crossing his fingers.

"Pretty panties, pretty panties, pretty panties..." James chanted, his crossed fingers raised up to either side of his face.

I shook my head, resigned myself to their company and

continued opening the package. Once I'd opened the flaps of the box, I froze. Crumpled paper filled the empty space on the edges of the interior of the box.

A few pages from a magazine were folded around a smaller box. I took the pages out and unfolded them to find photos of Solange once again. This time, however, she was dressed in a floor-length evening gown as she clutched the arm of a man I'd never seen before. He certainly wasn't *me*, anyway.

On the next page was Solange with the same man, her arms wrapped around his neck while she kissed him passionately in front of a crowd at some sort of event. At the bottom of the page I found his name alongside hers: Daniel Conway, fashion photographer.

I reached into the box again, my hands numb, feeling as though I'd been doused with the icy water from Jerzy's bucket. I no longer heard James chanting, no longer felt the jovial curiosity of my teammates clustered closely around me.

My fingers closed around the only other object in the box, the soft velvet sliding slightly underneath my shaking fingertips. I hoped the guys couldn't tell.

I put the cardboard box back on the table, clutching the velvet box in my other hand.

"Oh, fuck..." Attilio let out a slow, stunned breath. My heart beat too hard, my mouth tasted too dry. My hands scarcely remained under my control.

I lifted the box up and pulled it close to my chest, slowly prying the halves apart for a glimpse of what was inside.

Not that I didn't know.

A faint sparkle as the diamond caught the light, and I snapped it shut.

The sunset cast the patio in shades of red, or my temper coloured my vision. All the guys withdrew, not all at once, but fast enough to make it obvious they knew, too.

I opened the box and closed it, resisting the urge to grab my phone and call her yet again to demand an answer. I wanted to know when she'd made this decision, and what had prompted it.

Why tell me this way? Why tell me now? Couldn't you have waited until the Tour was over?

The faint creak of the hinge sounded again and again as I opened and closed the box repeatedly. I watched the flash of the diamond I'd spent most of my winnings on wink in and out of view.

I glanced toward Adrie and found pity written clearly on his face. I stood and walked away from the tables where my team sat, the world vague and unclear all around me.

My hands kept worrying the velvet ring box, and I compulsively stole glimpses inside while I walked to the railing. Finally I tore my gaze away from the object in my hands to stand and look out at the panorama, still trying to comprehend what this meant.

Footsteps on the stone flooring behind me broke through my confusion. I turned to face Adrie and found him looking at the box. To my surprise, it was open. Again.

I put my back to the railing as a breeze swept up over the balcony. The wind pushed my hair off the nape of my neck, like Solange's touch once had.

It seemed as though a hand grasped my heart to crush and twist it before pulling it out of me. Adrie still said nothing. I swallowed hard, willing my chest to stop hurting, my hands to close the fucking box.

Without thinking, I spun around and hurled the box as hard as I could, the tiny black object sailing out over the mountainside to disappear into the valley below.

I stalked off the patio, not making eye contact with anyone as I exited the lobby and left the hotel behind. I didn't want to talk. I didn't want to think.

All I wanted was to forget, and there was only one way I could think of to do that.

I needed a bar, preferably a quiet one, and some solitude.

Mostly I needed alcohol, as much as possible.

The race be damned.

*

That Jerzy didn't send anyone out after me was probably a sign. Word would have spread quickly amongst my teammates who were there, and then on up to the management. The thought of all of them knowing about Solange made me physically ill.

On the street in front of the hotel there were only a few touristy types wandering about. I briefly hoped they weren't there for the next morning's stage. Ducking into the first available pub seemed the most logical thing to do, until I considered fans might be there, too.

I skirted the block apprehensively, trying not to skulk, knowing anything I did could inadvertently draw attention. With a profound sense of relief I found a small pub a few storefronts down and slipped inside. My eyes were slow to adjust to the diffused lighting, but once I could see, I was reassured by the sparse patronage. Granted, it was still early in the evening and the crowds wouldn't be coming in until the dinner hour, but that might well provide me plenty of time to accomplish my goal.

Not that I was so sure of what I wanted, any more. I wanted to forget about Solange, at least for a little while, but now the idea of fucking off the race wasn't nearly so appealing as it had been before.

Finishing with the Royal would be the perfect way to show her she hadn't got to me.

My stomach gave a slow twist around the salad I'd managed to force down at the hotel, an acidic reminder that I'd yet to eat a proper meal this evening. I walked further into the pub, seeking a quiet corner where I might weigh my options over a few drinks and a sandwich. Starting with the drinks.

After turning a corner I stopped short, seeing a familiar but wholly unexpected face, illuminated by the light of a tiny laptop computer. I stepped back behind a tall potted plant, the broad leaves providing the perfect cover for me to study her, to be sure I wasn't mistaken. Seated as she was in a booth in the corner, a single glass of wine on the table next to her computer, she was obviously alone. And it was definitely *her*.

Abigail. The photographer who'd been hurt at the finish in Lorca.

All the drama with Solange had pushed Abigail out of my mind for a while, but this glimpse of her was all it took to bring her front and centre.

My hand trembled where it rested on the wall. Making a fist, I willed myself to remain steady. A fleeting, desperate image of going to her and giving her the deepest, most passionate kiss I'd ever given faded swiftly before my shaking ceased.

I'm losing my mind. I'm too stressed. It's crazy to be thinking like this.
And yet...

I was stunned to find myself standing next to her table, my

hands in my pockets in an attempt to look casual. "Abigail?" I queried, as though I weren't positive it was her. As though I hadn't memorized her face the first time I'd seen it, or sought a glimpse of her in the crowds before and after the start of the last two stages.

As though she hadn't lingered in the back of my mind ever since I'd knelt next to her and held her hand at the finish line.

My mind went blank when her eyes met mine. The lack of comprehension written in her face gave my heart a small, sympathetic turn and brought a smile to my face. Behind her dark-framed eyeglasses, her gaze darted to my right and my left, flicked back to her computer screen and then returned to scrutinize me warily.

"You really shouldn't look at a screen like that without better lighting around you," I said. "It's bad for your eyes." I was amazed: I almost sounded like I was thinking clearly.

"Yeah, I know," she said, her voice low in deference to the relative quiet of the pub, and then she tapped her eyeglasses. "I guess that's why I need these." Two heartbeats later, she added, "You remember me."

That it was a statement and not a question made me feel weak for some reason.

"Of course I remember you." I wondered if she understood the depths of honesty in my words.

She continued looking up at me, her lips parted slightly in a slack expression of surprise. At last she sat up straight and looked around, slightly flustered.

"So, um..." She gestured offhandedly to the seat across from her before removing her glasses to tuck them away in her handbag. "Would you like to sit down?"

"Ah, yes, thanks." I sat, hoping not to look too eager. Once more, I went hopelessly blank. I couldn't think of anything to say to her.

Before it was too noticeable, a server came over to her – *our* – table and waited patiently for me to order something.

"*Una cervesa, per favor,*" I said and he disappeared into the darkness from which he'd emerged, presumably to retrieve my drink.

"You speak Spanish?" she asked.

"That was Catalan," I said, and instantly felt bad for correcting her. "I hope it was, anyway." I trailed off, grateful the dim lighting would hide my flush of embarrassment.

"So, you speak Catalan?"

"Just enough to order drinks. And to get myself into trouble."

"Wow... I've been speaking miserable high-school Spanish the whole time I've been here." She shook her head. The movement was mesmerizing.

The server returned and I mumbled my thanks as he placed my glass on a coaster and turned away.

"I'm sure most people do that, actually. I wouldn't worry about it. How are you doing, by the way? I mean, after the crash and all."

"Well, I'm doing better. Still bruised, still scraped up, but it wasn't too bad, so..." Her shy smile made my heart jump and then plunge into my stomach.

Was I crazy? Sitting here with her where anyone could see us, and then word might get back to –

Oh, right. Solange. Why was I worrying about *her*? For that matter, why wasn't that dagger still twisting my innards?

Abigail reached to close her computer. I leaned forward, my hand resting over hers before I had a chance to stop it.

Her eyes widened in mild surprise and I withdrew my hand. What the hell was I doing?

"What are you working on?" I asked, indicating the laptop with my retreating hand and then folding my numb fingers around my glass.

Suddenly she was blushing, her eyes evading mine by returning to the glow of the screen. "Oh, I was just... Nothing."

"Nothing?" A smile crept onto my face and settled in. "Are you sure? That's a lot of equipment for doing nothing."

She blushed again. I was delighted to see it.

"Well, okay. It's not 'nothing,' exactly. It's my work."

I nodded as if I understood, though nothing could have been further from the truth. Then again, I was having difficulty focusing on anything. Her accent intrigued me, a curious blend of British and what I presumed to be an American twang of some sort, unfamiliar as it was. She could have told me the sky was made of orange juice and I would have nodded along, in order to keep her talking.

"I mean," she continued, her gaze still avoiding mine, sweeping over the table, "I was reviewing some of my photos."

"Oh, right, your photos."

"Yeah." She nodded, more confident. "I've been shooting the Tour. The starts and, uh, the finishes, mostly."

The way she'd stumbled over "finishes" gave me a fleeting pain. My last finish hadn't exactly been my best.

"Could I see what you were working on?" I'd had no idea I was going to say it until the words were out there, lingering between us over the table. Besides, did I *really* want to see visual proof of me losing the Royal?

It was too late now, regardless.

"Um… If you really want to."

Again without thinking, I slid out of the booth and went over to her side, even as she half-turned the tiny computer toward me. An awkward hesitation followed: should I sit back in the booth I'd just vacated, or sit next to her even though she hadn't exactly invited me?

Beh. In for a penny, in for a pound, as the Brits say.

I slid in beside her when she made room for me and turned the computer back toward us. Blessedly, my ego was momentarily spared: the image on the screen was not of me but of Schlessinger and Brunn's finish. It was a fantastic shot, and when she stroked the key to advance to the next picture, I knew it wasn't a fluke. The second picture was of the peloton arriving, a crisp, brilliant capture of the colours and expressions of every rider in the foreground. Everything else was blurred, giving the impression of movement.

I watched the screen while she continued clicking through the pictures, one by one. Finally she reached one and clicked swiftly past it, before the image had time to register in my mind.

"Wait, wait… Go back? I didn't see that one." I glanced over at her, my eyes adjusting from the bright glow of the screen to the ambient light it created, and found her finger trembling where it hovered over the keypad.

She pressed the key and I turned back to the screen to find a photo of myself after the initial time trial, lying on the ground, surrounded by the team staff and doctor. It was quite close up – enough to make me self-conscious.

"The time trial," she said, and I turned to face her. "It's one of my favourites."

"Why is that?" I asked, looking back at the photo.

She shrugged, her arm brushing mine as she did so. I realized she was leaning in to look at the photo, too, and I shifted my shoulder so we were almost facing each other, our necks craned to study the screen.

"You looked... I don't know... so vulnerable. I wanted to help you, some–" Falling silent, she turned away from me. An indescribable pull in my chest, next to my heart forced me to smile. I made a point of keeping my gaze on the screen.

"Thanks," I said quietly, when she turned back toward me. I cleared my throat and clicked through a few more photos on my own while she folded her hands in her lap. "I suppose this explains why I couldn't find you again – you're hidden behind a camera all the time."

My cell phone rang in my pocket. For a single, foolish moment, I hoped it was Solange.

It wasn't.

"*Dov'è sei, Ciccio?*" Jerzy asked. "The meeting is about to start."

I glanced at my watch, surprised to see how late it was. "Jerzy, *non ti preoccupare...*" I explained hastily. "I'm not far from the hotel."

"Get *here*, now." He hung up, and already I was sliding out of the booth.

"I'm sorry, Abigail, but I have to go."

"Oh, all right," she said, her voice a little too light. I fought the urge to imagine she was disappointed by my departure.

"Thanks for showing me your photos. You're really –" I wanted to say *amazing, great, incredible,* anything besides what was proper to say. "You're really *good.* I'd like to see more of your work, sometime."

"I'd like that, too." She fidgeted, her hands unsettled. "Could I ask a favour?"

"Of course," I said, sitting beside her again. "What is it?"

"Could I take a picture of you?"

"What, now?"

She nodded in response, one hand drifting toward her handbag. "Not for my project; for me."

"Oh. Okay, sure."

Her smile blossomed, surprisingly bright, causing another hitch in my chest. Now I *knew* I was losing my mind.

Otherwise, if I didn't know any better, as I put my arm around her shoulders and she held the camera out and aimed it toward us, I'd have thought I was falling for her.

Stage Seven

(205 km – Pal, Andorra – Col du Tourmalet, France)

"What the bloody hell is that racket, anyway?" Charles rolled out of bed and stuffed his feet into his slippers before shuffling to the door of our hotel room.

The distant sounds of doors being slammed and someone shouting gradually got through to my foggy brain. My sleep fug faded and I sat up in bed while Charles peered out our door.

"Can you see anything?"

"Nothing. Obviously it's on another floor." He closed the door and stood in the middle of the room, listening keenly for the next salvo.

And there it was – another door downstairs banged open and someone was yelling incoherently, for some unfathomable reason.

Charles put his suitcase on the luggage rack and opened it. He huffed a disapproving breath while hastily selecting a pair of trousers and a shirt.

"What are you doing?"

"No consideration," he grumbled, ignoring my question. "No thought at all for any other people in this hotel. Bloody rude, if you ask me, carrying on like that."

"What are you *doing*?"

"I'm going to tell that inconsiderate arse to keep it down, as there are other people in this building who have paid for the privilege of getting a few hours of sleep."

91

Another door banged. This time it seemed to come from directly below us. A booming shout was followed by a startled-sounding shriek.

"Just our luck – we've been booked in a place full of kids on holiday."

"'Kids'?" I echoed.

"Teenagers, most likely. Or a bunch having a prowl before heading back to Uni. Whatever, I don't care. I don't appreciate them waking us up like this."

"What if they're not kids? Do you want to take a chance on–"

"Should I stay up *here*, then, and cower under the covers? I don't think so. You might want to stay here, though." He paused, seemed to consider something, then sat on the bed, slipping his shirt over his shoulders. "Perhaps I'll go down and talk to the manager on duty. That might put things right."

"You could *call*," I suggested, not fancying the idea of him getting himself into some sort of scuffle with a rowdy bunch of twenty-somethings. "Why not just do that?"

"No, darling, I'm sorry. I think it's best if I go in person." With this, he finished buttoning his shirt and bent to fasten his shoelaces. "It makes a stronger impression." He stood and grabbed his room key and mobile phone off the bedside table. "I'll call you if there's any problem, okay?"

"Sure." I nodded, wondering why he'd need his mobile phone to call me from the lobby.

And then he was heading out of the room, another echo of a slamming door sounding before our door closed behind him. The shouting and banging stopped and my mind drifted elsewhere in the regained silence of the morning. I sank back down into the pillows and pulled the blanket up over my shoulder, thinking to the night before, in the pub.

With Renard.

I still couldn't believe he'd been there, or that he'd remembered me from Lorca and had stopped to speak with me. It was unreal to think he'd sat and admired my photos, or that we'd chatted amiably as though we'd known each other for some time.

But the proof was right there in my handbag, on my little hobby camera. By some miracle I'd found the nerve to ask for a photo with him.

After he'd left the pub, I'd sat there for an age looking at the picture. I put it in a separate file on the computer and looked at it on the screen in a haze of disbelief.

He was everything I'd thought he'd be: handsome, charming, relaxed and comfortable with himself. Even now I silently prayed that he hadn't noticed how nervous I'd been when he approached me, or when he sat next to me in the booth.

I covered my face with my hands, unable to keep myself from recalling the soft, spicy scent of his cologne, or his warmth when we'd sat so close together. My stomach did a little flip way down low, and my throat tightened.

Reaching out for Charles' pillow, I pulled it close and inhaled deeply, drawing his scent deep into my lungs. Still I fancied that I could smell Renard's cologne, and I closed my eyes against the sudden burn behind them.

I didn't want this. I *really* didn't.

How stupid was I? Forty years old and crushing on some good-looking guy like a teenager! No wonder those 'boyfriend' taunts irritated me so much – they rang too true.

"I never had a boyfriend like *him*, though," I said to the empty room, and laughed a little. That felt good; laughing made me feel a little less like I might be losing my mind in a mid-life hormonal surge.

That innocent encounter at the pub had been enough to keep me from reaching a deep sleep for most of the night. When I'd slept, I'd dreamed of him – nothing out of bounds, just reliving the conversation we'd had, again and again.

At the sound of footsteps in the corridor I released the pillow and rolled back onto my side. I tried to push away the memories: of my dream, of the pub, of whatever it was we'd talked about...

Renard's response to what I'd said about the photo after the time trial continued to echo in the back of my mind. The softness of his voice, the simplicity of what he'd said; was it crazy for me to put so much weight on a single "Thanks"?

Why did it have to mean so much to me?

Charles' key in the lock seemed to shake loose another memory, and I shivered pleasantly in spite of myself, clutching the covers closer as I remembered what Renard had said next:

"I suppose this explains why I couldn't find you again."

***

Phil's shrieking from down the hall was motivation enough to propel me out of bed in spite of the ungodly hour. Today's stage would take us over the Pyrenees into France – onto the Col du Tourmalet, to be exact – and the word as of last night was that I had a large contingent of fans awaiting me there.

Because of this, I was even more concerned about a poor performance that day. It would be especially embarrassing to lose a substantial amount of time while returning to my home country.

Don't think about that. I stared at myself in the mirror while the water ran into the sink, the rising steam slowly obscuring my image. I hadn't slept well, and it showed.

In spite of the shadows under my eyes and hangdog look, I didn't feel tired. There was no sign of the bone-weariness I should have from a long night spent tossing and turning. Maybe I hadn't actually done that? The hours since I'd left the pub had a slightly unreal quality about them, like events remembered from a dream. Even the team meeting had a hazy quality about it. I could recall in detail everything we'd discussed and all the strategy we'd worked out, but there was a sepia tone surrounding it all.

After we'd retired to our rooms, I'd drifted between thoughts of Solange and Abigail the whole night long. Thoughts of either one were torture of a sort; one bitter, one sweet.

"*Mamma mia*, I'm ridiculous..." I muttered, cupping my hands under the stream from the spigot. I'd lost one woman and here I was, considering another.

I hated to think my feelings might be nothing more than a rebound, but the timing was suspicious. Hadn't I received Solange's package literally *minutes* before I'd found Abigail in the pub? Didn't that prove I'd been looking for a way to nurse my wounded pride? I might have joined any woman open to sharing my company.

Or maybe not. I'd been seeking Abigail in the crowds ever since I'd talked to her.

I continued washing, my thoughts returning to the subject in spite of myself.

If I *was* attracted to Abigail, so what? There was no guarantee she'd feel the same – the point was moot. I hadn't got her number, I hadn't given her mine. I had no way to find her, no matter how much I wanted to. I didn't even know her last *name.*

I'm such an idiot. Why didn't I ask?

I recalled the glint of gold on her ring finger, a small diamond which flashed in the light over the table in the pub.

Married. I was getting all worked up over a *married* woman.

A married woman I'd never see again, in all likelihood.

I paused and regarded my reflection again. What was it she had said about the photo of me after the time trial? It was one of her favourites, and…?

You looked…so vulnerable. I wanted to help you…

My chest surrendered to the same pull at the memory of her words as when she'd said them the night before. She'd wanted to help me.

Who knew? Maybe she already had.

***

"Well, that explains everything." Charles dumped his room key on the desk and frowned down at me. Noting the almost accusatory expression on his face, I waited for him to go on. He didn't.

"Okay, then…" I sat up in bed, pulling the sheets around me to stave off the chill of the air conditioning. "What explains everything?"

"That entire racket was from some bloody cycling team."

My heart jumped into my throat, a hint of guilt following it. It was ludicrous, yes, but my first thought was that I actually *was* somehow responsible. I bit my tongue, wondering if he knew which team it was.

It doesn't matter, so don't ask.

"I don't know about you, but since I'm awake, I think I'll go down for breakfast shortly. I have a lot of work to do today." He turned and picked up his briefcase from the floor, opening it on the desk.

I nodded, already sliding out from under the covers. "I might try to go down to the start line early, too."

Charles didn't answer. His attention was focused on a document he was holding up to read in the sunlight coming through a gap in the curtains.

I went into the bathroom, shivering when my bare feet settled on the cold floor tiles. Even the shower knobs were cold to the touch when I turned them to start the water flowing.

Suddenly my stomach fluttered and I put my hand over it, as

though I could still the sensation that way.

What had all the noise this morning been about? Why would a team make such a nuisance of themselves at such an early hour? Was it rambunctious behaviour on the part of younger members? Some sort of initiation? Were all teams like that?

I shook my head and moved under the hot stream of the shower. Hopefully Charles' travel agent hadn't booked us into any more hotels where teams might be staying, if this was normal behaviour for them.

A phone call or two might give us some answers in that regard, but did I want him to raise a fuss over it? It was unlikely we'd find another decent place to stay on such short notice – and surely most hotels had been booked well in advance.

I knew better than to suggest any small bed-and-breakfasts or renting a room from a resident of the towns hosting the Tour. The prices would be too high for what we would get, and Charles wouldn't want to stay anywhere that wasn't top of the line.

The door opened, bringing a rush of cool air into the steamy confines of the bathroom.

"I spoke with the manager on the phone. He's offering us the deluxe breakfast for free."

"That's nice," I said, rinsing soap off my goose-fleshed skin while wishing he'd close the door.

"We'll go down as soon as you're ready."

The door shut with a soft *whump*, sending another rush of cool air over the top of the shower stall. I increased the hot water until the chill wore off.

If nothing else, Charles could certainly get results when he wanted to.

***

The team met in the lobby before going out to the patio restaurant for our buffet breakfast. The air was still cool, but the sun was already reaching around the hotel to light the dining area and warm it up.

No one had said anything to me about Solange. Not yet.

If nothing had been said by now, nothing would be. I took some consolation from that.

Then again, most of us had a lot on our plates already, with the mountains ahead. It was going to be a long and potentially difficult ride but I wasn't dreading it nearly as much as before.

I got into the buffet line and made my selections, and Attila joined me shortly afterward. Adrie stepped up behind him and nodded to me. I returned the gesture.

Just like that, our disagreement from the day before was forgotten.

It was reassuring to be in Adrie's good graces. He had always been the team's mentor; when Jerzy was too intimidating or when Michael was unavailable, Adrie was there for you. You had to work really hard to upset him or offend him – but I had managed to do exactly that.

Jerzy stood chatting with the team doctor and the dietician at the end of the buffet line. In spite of the nonchalance they projected, the three of them were making sure each and every rider got enough to eat before he set out that day. Since all of us had slightly different requirements, this form of dining had its pitfalls.

It was one of Jerzy's tests. If any one of us went off our plan, he'd note it and bring it to our attention in front of everyone.

He didn't believe in the riders having someone handle each individual meal for them, the way some teams did. This was as much our responsibility as anyone else's, and it was part of our job.

Because no matter what some people would have you believe, being a cyclist is really that: a *job*. An exciting and fun job, yes, but still a job. Jerzy wouldn't stand for any of us behaving like spoiled dilettantes, demanding special treatment or refusing to pull our own weight. All of his demands, his disciplines and his eccentricities made him look like a madman at times, but there was a method to that madness, and we respected him for it.

This was why everyone wanted to ride for him, why *Alta VeloCidad* was the team every young rider aspired to join and why bitter rivalries could erupt between long-time friends if one made it on board and the other didn't.

This was my experience, anyway, having been the lucky one. My luck was the reason I hated my achievements being overshadowed by ridiculous things like the gossipy article in *Grand Tours Magazine*, or the "Foxy Fede" label recently assigned to me by female fans.

Most guys would have loved it, I knew, but not me. It was all one huge lodestone I had to wear around my neck every time I got on the bike, even if my teammates had (mostly) stopped mentioning it years ago.

Jerzy signalled it was time to go. Our bus and team cars waited in front of the hotel, and we passed through the formal dining room on our way out to the lobby.

Somehow I managed not to trip over my own feet at the sight of her. She sat alone at a table, her room key next to her coffee cup, watching us go by. An expression between shock and amusement was etched onto her face. As I passed her, I raised my fingertips in what I hoped was a subtle gesture of recognition. Her smile broadened and I felt lighter at the sight of it.

At least I didn't do anything stupid, although in retrospect that gesture might have seemed a bit too cavalier. Could she tell I wanted to sit down with her and talk again? Was it obvious that the only thing keeping me from doing that was the day's stage?

I tried to gauge whether I had time to run back and get her name and phone number, if maybe I could find out if she would be staying in the same hotel as the team, tonight.

No chance of that. Jerzy was waving us out of the lobby with his usual impatience, the team bus rumbling beneath the hotel canopy in front.

I had a job to do, and I needed to wrap my head around that fact soon, before I fucked everything up.

***

Good as his word, as soon as I'd finished my shower and dressed, Charles and I went down to breakfast. The manager greeted us warmly, extending one hand to indicate the way to our table, and offered yet more apologies as we took our seats.

"And you mustn't worry," the manager said, holding out my chair for me. "The matter of this morning has been addressed by the staff. The, ah, *clientele* who were the source of the disruption have asked us to apologize on their behalf as well. They have offered to pay a portion of your bill to make amends."

Charles gave me an insufferably smug look before he turned to the manager again. "*Gracias, Signor.* We appreciate your endeavours to make up for the oversight."

I held back a groan. As if the manager could have controlled this? Or guessed it would happen?

A few more minutes of chit-chat and the manager excused

himself to return to the front desk. I couldn't help wondering what my husband must have threatened the hotel with to get such a response.

"Oh, no. I've left my mobile in the room." Charles patted his trouser pockets and stood next to our table, looking around.

"Oh, leave it. I mean, we're only going to eat breakfast. Surely you could just return any missed calls?"

He hesitated, his hands momentarily frozen over his pockets. I understood at once the source of his agitation. He was expecting a call.

Scratch that. He was expecting *her* call.

"Fine," I said, pretending not to notice. "Go on up. I'll take my time over the menu."

Another hesitation, and then he was walking away from our table with obvious restraint.

I wasn't sure how to feel. Charles had never before been quite so transparent. Part of me was hurt by this, and yet part of me was relieved. Of course, now I had my own mental diversion, and while it wasn't exactly the same it did seem to ease the pain a bit.

I scarcely had time to consider this before a group of men passed through the dining room and headed toward the exit. Stunned, I sat and watched them file by, ticking their names off a mental list: Meijer, Browdowski, Mendoza, Mendoza...

How was it possible we'd stayed in the same hotel and I hadn't even known it?

So much for any 'psychic connections,' then. I had to smile at my silliness, and that was when Renard passed by me, one hand raised in a subtle greeting. My smile stayed in place even as my heartbeat sped up and my hands shook on my lap.

He smiled and continued out to the lobby. He glanced back at me before stepping through the doorway. The team bus presumably was the source of the rumbling outside.

If we ever meet again, I have got to ask him what was going on this morning.

The idea of that being my lead-off question in our next conversation made me laugh out loud.

"What's so funny?" Charles asked, taking his seat and picking up his breakfast menu.

"Oh, nothing," I said, shaking my head. "A random, little thought."

He nodded and continued perusing the menu. "I wonder what the closest thing is they've got to a proper fry-up? I'm starving."

I shrugged and turned my attention back to my own menu. "I honestly don't know."

***

Bad luck and more bad luck: that's what greeted us on the road all the way into France. Cheering fans were all I had to keep me from falling hard into my own personal darkness on the final downhill, as I watched Schlessinger sail along without a care in the world.

Okay, that's not *quite* how it was.

He fought like a lunatic for every hundredth of a second he gained across the Pyrenees. It was a battle worthy of the history books – though only time will tell if that's the case.

Brunn held on as long as he could, with much gnashing of teeth and displays of machismo such as I'd never seen from him. His legendary cool evaporated in the summer heat before Schlessinger's onslaught, and everyone watched, amazed as Brunn fell behind second by incredible second.

In the meantime, Rom's ambition grew exponentially. In light of the unforeseen implosion of our supposed team leader, the wiry Pole remained undaunted.

A glance in my domestique's direction proved even more alarming. The boy was gazing so lustfully at the top of the mountain, I wondered if he saw a sign at the summit with '*Free pussy to the first five finishers!*' writ large in neon letters.

There was a climb to be made, honour to be claimed atop the Col du Tourmalet, and all at once Rom seemed determined to be the one to do it. He said something into his team radio and he was off, doggedly pursuing Schlessinger, oblivious to the apoplectic fit the rest of us suddenly endured.

I wondered if the team doctor would have to work on Jerzy, instead of one of us.

It was down to Brunn, Attila and me to pull Rom back and bring Phil and James along if we could. Adrie was at the back of the main group, hauling Teodoro and Alvaro up the previous ascent. The better the team did as a whole, the less painful the results for all of us would be.

Attila gave me a strained, slightly panicked look and I surged ahead, pounding out my anger and frustration in pursuit of my domestique, who had apparently lost his mind. Jerzy's screaming continued unabated, and an amazed realization dawned on me.

Rom, ignoring his idol? So blatantly? Impossible.

"His radio's broken," I gasped into my mic. "What else could it be?"

"I don't give a fuck if his *head's* broken," Jerzy cried. "Get him back!"

We all moved forward, grinding out our own energy reserves. My heart was thudding, yet sank ever deeper into my stomach.

The Royal was lost to us now. It had slipped out of *Alta VeloCidad's* grasp and into *Maxxxout's*. The psychological blows are often the hardest to overcome, and the inexplicable nature of this one made it all the more devastating.

The climbs had taken out more promising riders than myself, and by some miracle, I had managed to hold on to more of my time than I'd dreamed possible. It was as though my fingernails were scraping over the surface of the standings, threatening to tear out as I dug in deep.

If *Alta VeloCidad* were going to stay in the top rankings, we had a lot of work to do. I was determined to hold on – even if Rom's miscommunications and foolhardy impulsiveness made it more difficult.

After dinner and a thorough thrashing at the team meeting, we were granted a bit of precious free time. I seized it with both hands, bolting for the hotel bar. I wouldn't drink any alcohol this time – not with a stage the next morning.

It wasn't long until I realized watching for Abigail was the real reason I had hurried there. I didn't need to sit around with a decoy drink in my hand – I needed to rest, to relax and put the stage behind me.

Even more than that, I wanted to see her again. I wanted to see the photos she'd taken that day, even though the day hadn't been particularly worth remembering. I wanted...

I wanted. Simple as that. I wanted *her*, even if all I could get was a little of her time at the end of the day.

I left the pub without ordering anything. If she wasn't there, I had no interest in the place. I went outside and looked up and down the street, noting the other hotels there. An absurd urge to see if she was in one of them rose, only to be quashed by the fact I *still* didn't know her last name.

"*Quel crétin,*" I muttered, shaking my head and turning to go back inside. What kind of idiot doesn't ask a woman for her last *name?*

Stage Eight

(175km – Pau – Toulouse, France)

The barrage of phone calls began before we'd left the room for breakfast. For a wonder, Charles actually looked apologetic as he answered each one. He followed me down to the hotel restaurant without delay. Of course, this meant most of the time he was having a one-sided conversation, but once we were seated he switched the phone off and put it in his trouser pocket.

I managed not to stare at the spot next to his plate where the phone usually rested.

"Lovely day, isn't it?" He looked out the window beside us, toward the trees at the edge of the hotel property. "Perhaps we should consider coming back here next year for a decent holiday."

Who are you, and what have you done with my husband?

"That would be nice. Maybe next summer?"

He nodded, his expression blank, his gaze still distant. "Yes. Next summer. Once you've got this out of your system." His brow creased with concern. "They won't be here again next year, will they?"

"Who won't?"

"These cycling types." He waved his hand dismissively. I turned and saw one of the teams gathered on the lawn, taking breakfast in the cool morning air. "Will they be coming here again?"

"I don't know. The route won't be announced for a couple of months, but I doubt they'll be back so quickly." I picked up the list of available selections on the buffet table and read it over. "They make fresh crepes on request," I noted, trying to talk away the sinking feeling in my chest.

"We'll hold off on any plans, then." Charles faced me, smiled, and studied his own copy of the list. "Ah, the crepes do sound good, don't they?"

As he continued reading, I watched him over the top of my list. His blue eyes darted back and forth over the page, squinting since he was reading without his glasses. On impulse, I reached across the table and brushed back a stray lock of his hair from his forehead.

His hand rose in turn, touching mine gently to push it away. I wasn't sure how to take the rebuff – it hadn't been obvious enough to make me feel self-conscious, but he hadn't seemed to want my attention, either.

When he glanced around at the other patrons in the restaurant, I understood. His usual aversion to public displays of affection included such gestures.

God, how long has it been since he's held my hand in public?

Suddenly, it was what I wanted from him more than anything else in the world: his hand to hold mine without shying away, his kiss on my cheek, for him to give me a hug in public. I didn't think any of this was too much to ask, especially since he'd once done all of this without hesitation.

He'd been shy then, too. He was six years older than me, and after we'd dated a while he confessed he'd been afraid to ask me out for that reason.

The distance between us hadn't come until we bought the house in Hampshire, and he'd begun his long daily commutes to London. After a couple of years he staying overnight in the city on a regular basis, and at the time I'd thought nothing of it.

No, my doubts on that front were a more recent development.

The worst thing was, it took so little to think we could regain what we'd had before. Never mind it had been an eternity since we'd shared a completely carefree weekend together, much less a full holiday.

It was all there, resting uneasily in my memory: our first holiday in Cornwall – not so far from home, but it could have been a million miles away for all the time we spent together uninterrupted. It had been blissfully romantic, and he'd done much, much more than hold my hand in public. He'd done it all: soft kisses, holding me close, telling me he loved me loud enough for other people to hear.

We'd met at a fancy dress party of a mutual family friend, and I had been (rather disastrously) dressed as Tinkerbell in a short, sparkly green dress, white tights and a set of fairy wings. My little blonde wig had refused to stay on all night long, and Charles had caught it when my date (dressed as a very masculine Peter Pan) knocked it off my head while drunkenly attempting to fly.

Charles was dressed as a pirate, and my date thought it the height of hilarity to challenge him to a duel. ("Aha! Hook!" my date had cried, and flung himself at Charles while the rest of the room screamed in laughter.) Never mind Charles was a full head taller and armed with his plastic sword, which he used to swat my date away.

Mortified, I'd rushed out of the party, and Charles pursued me, calling out "*Arrêter, ma petite fée verte!*"

"What does that mean?" I'd said, stopping short and letting him catch up to me.

"I hope it means 'Stop, my little green fairy'," he'd said, giving me back my wig. "But with my French, well..." We chatted a bit before I got in my car and left, not caring if my date got a ride home or not.

Next thing I knew, Charles was in my photo lab's storefront, dropping off rolls of film. It took me weeks to understand he wasn't just developing photos.

"What was he on about?" I'd asked my co-worker after one particularly painful exchange in which Charles had stammered his way through the purchase of several more blank rolls of film.

Marcia, my co-worker and roommate, had sighed, shaken her head, and explained the obvious to me.

On our first proper date, he called me his little green fairy again, and in the twists and turns of conversation, he mentioned that absinthe had once been called the same: "*la fée verte*," to be exact. As it turned out, it was almost all the French he freely claimed to understand.

That was a million years ago. Or seven, at least. It was hard to remember. Now he was so work-obsessed, so dedicated to his job, so bloody focused he hardly seemed like the man who had brought roll after roll of film – some of them blank! – to the photo lab and ineptly chatted me up.

I wondered why he was so cheerful in spite of his calls that morning. Usually one or two calls were enough to send him into a dark mood for much of the day. The pressure to get to the office usually prevailed until I either sent him away or we found ourselves arguing over some petty issue.

Charles looked up at me and smiled and the sunlight streaming in the window faded. The light and warmth returned an instant later but it was too late to warm the small chill which had settled over my heart. Again, my eyes stung with unshed tears and I blinked them away, rubbing one finger in the corner of my eyelid afterward to wipe away the small tear which threatened to fall.

***

The mood in the team meeting that morning was restrained, but I didn't trust it to remain that way. Jerzy's glares across the table did little to settle my nerves. Brunn brooded at one corner of the table. Attilio sat as far away as he could without being too obvious.

Schlessinger had rattled Brunn's cage, all right; now we all knew he was as vulnerable as the rest of us. This hadn't gone over well. They'd spent quite a while the night before going over tactics and strategies to understand what had gone wrong.

In retrospect, the benevolence of being granted a few free hours the night before now made sense. It had been our last chance at that kind of freedom.

"No way should that stage have taken us out. You've all been letting things slide, acting on your own, not following orders." Jerzy turned his cold gaze to Rom, who ducked his head. No English was necessary to know he'd screwed up. "*This* is what happens. As of today, you get one hour of free time after dinner. That's all."

Adrie's scowl behind Jerzy's back didn't go unnoticed by the rest of the team, but no-one would rat him out. Any rider with a family, or at least a girlfriend, was bound to resent still more limits on our free time.

Adrie calmly cleared his throat, and Jerzy turned to face him. James tensed next to me, and Alvaro, seated next to Adrie, shifted his seat away to one side after a skyward glance.

"You have something to add, Major?"

106

"What about our families? An hour a day is hardly enough time to spend with my wife and my daughters, and you know there will be days we don't see them at all."

Silence spooled out in the meeting room, and I wondered if anyone else had neglected to breathe, like me. I drew a long, quiet breath, waiting for Jerzy's response.

"I'm being generous. I could make it one hour a *week*," he said, and turned again to face the rest of us. "You all need discipline; that's clear. You should be supporting the team leaders, and instead, you fell apart!"

I couldn't help bristling. *Leaders?* I wanted to shout. *That's the whole fucking problem!*

"As far as families go – I don't want to keep anyone away from theirs. If you want to be with your family, go." He gestured toward the door and Adrie dropped his gaze to the table. "If you stay, you need to remember this: I am your father, your brother, your best friend – even your mother! I *am* your family. This *team* is your family. You depend on them, and they depend on you."

The composure with which he spoke was chilling. This was not ranting Jerzy, not blustering or manic Jerzy.

This was Jerzy at his angriest, and I'd never been more aware of walking on a knife-edge. No one spoke, whispered or so much as coughed in the silence that followed.

"Get out to the bus. Now."

Jerzy stalked away, and we all stood, not a chair scraping across the tiled floor before we filed out as quietly as possible.

I was already calculating how to make the most of my hour. If I left dinner early – if it was permitted – I might be able to find out where Abigail was.

It was a slim chance at best, but it was better than being cooped up with these guys.

***

'Working', again. At least, that's what he claimed. Unaccustomed to feeling so paranoid, I didn't know what to think. Maybe Charles *was* working, at least part of the time. I had little proof otherwise, but it seemed clear to me he was hiding something.

Nevertheless, once again I was sitting alone in a pub, examining my photos while I ate a light supper and nursed a glass of wine. I was considering a glass of something stronger when the shuffle of footsteps nearby ended abruptly.

No. It can't be.

I raised my eyes from the computer screen and let them adjust, grinning before I actually saw Renard standing there. A rush of giddy pleasure swept through me, and I knew I wouldn't be able to speak if I tried.

My silence didn't seem to bother him. He glanced around and gestured to the seat opposite me, and I nodded and shrugged, hoping to appear nonchalant.

"*Quelle coïncidence,*" he said, the French phrase close enough to English for me to understand. "Working again?"

I nodded. "Atmosphere shots, mostly. I'll be at the start line tomorrow, though."

"I won't," he muttered, and I looked at the computer when the server came over to take Renard's order. *Alta VeloCidad* had had a rough day, and I was sure he must be licking some wounds over it.

A change of topic was in order, then.

"Could I ask you something?"

"Certainly." He folded his arms atop the table and leaned forward to show I had his attention. "What is it?"

I slid my netbook to one side and leaned toward him, too. "What was all that racket about, this morning in the hotel?"

He looked mildly chagrined, one hand rising to cover his embarrassed grin. "I'm sorry about that."

"I've never heard anything like it," I said, finding it difficult not to copy his pose. "What was going on? Was there a fight or something?"

"Oh, no. No, that's just Jerzy – our team manager. He has a special, ah… *routine*, for waking us in the mornings."

"Evidently."

"Normally we don't stay in hotels with other guests."

"I can see why. My husband was very upset and complained to the management."

An expression of disappointment flickered across his face. The server returned with a bottled water and a glass, placed the glass on a coaster and then asked Renard something in French as she poured, her voice too soft for me to hear. He answered her as quietly and took a large drink from his glass, his eyes downcast.

"You can give him my apologies, if you like," he said, not

looking at me.

I laughed and shook my head. "He'd never believe me if I tried to."

"What, that I apologized?"

"No, that I sat here with you as if we knew each other or something. He'd never believe it. *I* hardly believe it."

"We *do* know each other, don't we? You're Abigail. I'm Federico."

"Acquaintances at best." I shook my head. I didn't want to delude myself into believing anything too far-fetched, even if he *was* encouraging it.

"Yes, but…. It has to start somewhere, doesn't it?"

"What does?"

He licked his lips, took another drink and set his glass back on its coaster with exaggerated care.

"Friendship," he said with an air of finality, his gaze meeting and holding mine. "Don't you think these coincidences are enough to show maybe we could be friends?"

Or something else altogether, if your eyes are saying what I think they are.

I pushed the idea aside to focus on the inherent sweetness of what he'd said. Friendship *was* a lovely option, wasn't it?

"Well, going back to the hotel thing…" I began, not really wanting to return to the topic.

"Hmm?"

"Where is the team staying tonight? That is to say, I doubt we're in the same place again, but it's probably a good idea to be sure."

He laughed, nodded, and I understood he wanted to put me at ease. In that moment he ceased to be "Renard" in my mind and became "Federico" instead.

That's one step closer to something, *but what?*

Friendship?

***

I had a foolish hope when she asked me about the team's hotel. I knew better than to pin anything on such a question – hadn't she already mentioned her husband? Hadn't I already noticed her rings?

Then again, he wasn't *with* her. She was sitting alone in a pub, again, and she had welcomed my company with no hesitation. Maybe there wasn't really a husband. Maybe she was being careful;

a single woman in a pub might attract unwanted attention otherwise.

"We're staying in a place a few blocks down," I kept my hands busy turning my glass round and around on its paper coaster. "There's only enough room for the team and some of the staff there. The rest are staying in a nicer place in the city centre."

"I guess the key question here is: 'Where is Jerzy' – did I say that right? – 'staying?'"

I couldn't help laughing. Both her question and her pronunciation of Jerzy's name were fair, but the earnestness in her face was endearing.

"He and his bucket are both with us. The city of Toulouse is safe for another night."

Now she laughed, her eyes narrowing in puzzlement. "'Bucket'? What are you talking about?"

"You don't know about the bucket? But this is the stuff of legend!"

She shook her head and sat back, taking a drink from her glass of wine. "I guess I'm still new to this side of things. I have no idea what you're referring to."

And so I told her about the banging of doors, the shouting of nicknames, and the last resort for delayed responses: the bucket of ice water. Her eyes widened with disbelief with each detail, and I struggled not to exaggerate in order to keep her enthralled with the bizarre practices of my team's manager.

Keep it to the truth, and that's all, I cautioned myself. *No sense in getting into bad habits.*

"Nicknames? How do you mean?"

"Every rider on the team has a nickname. Well, *almost* every rider," I corrected myself, thinking of Brunn. "It's meant to show us life on the team is different from life off it. Serguei is 'Goosh,' Adrie is 'Major,' Attilio is 'Attila' and so on."

"So, what's yours?"

"My what?" I asked, stalling for time. I regretted my decision to be honest.

"Your nickname."

I cleared my throat. "Ciccio," I muttered, looking away and trying not to frown.

"Does that mean anything in particular?"

"I think the English translation would be something like, ah…

'Fatty', perhaps, or maybe…'Chubby'." Colour rose to my cheeks, an old habit which refused to die when this subject came up.

"I don't understand. Why is *that* your nickname?"

"With the team," I hastened to stress the point. "*Only* with the team."

"Okay. But why?"

"Because I tend to be too big." I patted my stomach and then tapped the side of my now less-appetizing glass of beer before I pushed it away. "I have to really work hard on my self-control. I've always had this problem – even before I joined the team. So, I'm 'Ciccio'."

"It's kind of cute. It sounds like something you'd say about a baby."

"I hate it."

"Sorry." She spoke softly, with a hint of amusement in her voice.

"No, *I'm* sorry. It's not your fault."

I became aware of a soft beeping before she hurriedly turned to dig in her purse. "Excuse me," she said, pulling out her phone to read the screen. Her expression turned to disappointment as she put it away. "I'm sorry, I have to go. I didn't realize it was so late."

I glanced at my watch and was surprised to find it was nearly eleven o'clock. If I didn't leave soon, I'd miss my own curfew.

Abigail's hands moved with remarkable efficiency, putting away her computer and all its peripheral objects with a minimum of fuss. From time to time she glanced in my direction apologetically. When at last she'd finished packing up, she slid to the edge of her booth seat.

"I'm glad you found me," she said, seeming on the verge of saying something more. I tried to ignore the brief flash of her diamond ring in the light of the lamp over the table when she reached to put the strap of her computer bag over one shoulder.

"I am, too."

"Maybe we'll bump into each other in Montpellier?" she offered hopefully.

I nodded. I wanted to ask her last name, for all the good it might do me, but couldn't form the words.

Her phone beeped again, once, from the depths of her bag and she stood and offered her hand to me. "Thanks for the chat," she said, and I took her hand in mine, still without speaking.

I wanted to kiss her fingers, not in some gallant, seductive gesture, but to press my lips to her fingers and memorize the way they felt. I wanted to kiss the palm of her hand, to breathe in her scent.

Her hesitation made me wonder if she'd seen this in my eyes.

"*Ciao...*" I managed at last, and she slowly took her hand out of mine, leaving me feeling adrift in the midst of the pub as she smiled and walked away.

I have no idea how long I sat there, feeling the warmth of her touch fading from my hand. Suddenly, the sound of footsteps approached, and I looked up to find her holding several sheets of paper out to me.

"Okay, tell me quickly – are *any* of these your team hotels?"

Her face was flushed. I slid over and made room for her to sit in the booth next to me and glanced over the papers she'd brought.

Jesus, this is her entire travel itinerary.

I scanned the names of the hotels listed, seeing but not really reading them. I didn't know in advance where the team was staying, not in most cases, anyway. I was about to explain this when her phone rang. It was a melody this time, not the beeping chime of an arriving message, and she stood up to walk a few paces away to answer.

Taking advantage of her distraction, I tried to pay more attention to the hotel names. It might be useful to know where *she* would be, I mused, remembering my impulse to seek her out the night before.

"Uh-huh? Okay. Um... Right. I know. I'll do that. Bye." Abigail stepped back to me, looking flustered. "Now I really do have to go. I'm sorry to bother you."

"No bother," I said sincerely.

She smiled again, and elation replaced any disappointment I still felt at her pending departure. "Montpellier, then? Fingers crossed?"

I nodded and raised my hand, fingers duly crossed. "Here's hoping."

She rushed away and I leaned out of the booth so I could watch her go. She had nice legs in spite of the scratches from her fall in Lorca, and I liked the way her walking shorts fit her full bottom.

When I sat back again, I realized she'd left her itinerary on the table in her hurry to depart. I glanced back toward the exit, ready to call her name, but she was gone.

I sifted through the pages, reading the names of hotel after hotel, some of them familiar, most I was sure I'd never seen before. When I came to the first page again, even though it reinforced her marital status, it told me exactly what I wanted to know: the rooms in each hotel were reserved for Charles and Abigail White.

Stage Nine

(220 km - Toulouse - Montpellier, France)

The day's stage started well. We began outside Toulouse, rolling out under clear skies and warm sun. It was a mild day, perfect for a gentle ride, pleasant for a long, flat stage. There wasn't a breakaway worth worrying about, just a few eager youngsters looking to make a name for themselves and their sponsors by gaining a stage win.

In spite of the easy ride, Schlessinger kept close to me and to Brunn. The Royal wasn't far out of reach, and he made it clear he was determined to keep his enemies as near as possible. He wasn't about to allow us to gain a single second.

Outside Carcassonne, the young guns in the breakaway pulled further ahead, their lead stretching from two minutes to five, then to seven. Brunn and I rode in the main group, and soon we moved ahead with Attilio and Rom, taking our turn to lead.

For a short while, Brunn and I rode shoulder to shoulder, an unspoken truce between us. He asked whether I was still considering moving to Italy, and if so, where? I said I hadn't changed my mind, but was undecided about where exactly I wanted to go.

Behind me, Schlessinger barked a short, disdainful laugh and pulled alongside. I paid no attention to him, allowing him to take his turn at the head of the group without comment.

Brunn looked back at me, shrugged, and took his turn at the

head of the bunch again.

"You never did answer my question, Ciccio," Schlessinger said, dropping behind me.

"Which question was that?" I filled my voice with as much bored disinterest as I could.

"How's your girlfriend?"

A ripple of chuckles went through the group around me, but I pretended not to notice. Word had gotten around. Now I understood who had sent the magazine.

I took a long drink from my water bottle, then meticulously replaced it in its cage. It was my turn to lead again, and I did, noting Brunn's questioningly-raised eyebrow as he faded back.

I waited until my turn was over, and then Schlessinger's, before responding.

"She's fine. I wish her the best."

He laughed again, but said nothing more. I fell into the rhythm of the ride and the kilometres rolled past. Around the halfway point, we reached the feed zone and the peloton slowed as we approached the soigneurs along the side of the road. We snatched our musettes of food and drink from their outstretched hands and then slung them over our shoulders.

Relaxed and easy. There was no doubt in my mind that something had to change. Something was bound to go wrong.

I sat up and put my protein gels in the back pocket of my jersey. Riding hands-free, I unwrapped the protein bar and held it in my teeth before I flung my empty water bottle off to one side, making sure to arc it high to land it in the ditch, and not the road. I replaced that bottle with the fresh one from the bag.

Rom pulled up to me and we traded a few things out with each other. His cranberry bar for my apple-banana one, and so on. At last I wadded up my bag and gave it to him; he stuffed it into his bag and then tossed the lot along the road. I caught a glimpse of a fan running over to pick it up and smiled.

At least we weren't littering.

***

After the stage start, I returned to our hotel room. I paused outside the door, wanting to be sure I wasn't about to interrupt Charles' inevitable phone call. Once inside, I was surprised to find him standing silently at the window, admiring the city panorama.

"D'you know that you can see the race from here?" he asked.

I shook my head and stepped up to the window. There wasn't much left of the start line now. In the time it had taken for me to walk back, a good deal of the circus atmosphere had already been packed away to leap-frog to another town on the route. Much of the travelling cycling village had been dismantled and hauled away, too.

Charles turned to face me, a bemused almost-smile on his lips.

"Could you do me a favour?"

"Sure." I looked up at him, curious. "What is it?"

"Could you explain to me what it is you enjoy about this?" He tilted his head toward the window, indicating the distant start line. "Why is it so important to you? It's not like you ride a bike or anything."

I shrugged and looked out at the slowly vanishing multi-coloured chaos in the square. "I don't know. It's a sport, isn't it? Why do you like football so much? Aside from goofing about a bit with a ball now and then, you don't play but you're fanatical about Chelsea. Why is that?"

"No fair, answering a question with a question."

"Why not?"

"Stop it." He grinned in spite of himself.

"Why?" I asked, grinning too.

"God, I've missed that smile," he said with a wistfulness so genuine I wanted to cry. I tried to keep smiling, instead.

"I smile," I said softly, facing him again. "I do."

"Not for me, you don't. I hardly see it unless you're talking about your photos or this race or some such thing."

"Those things make me happy."

"But I *don't*." It was a statement, not a question. And it was a statement made so simply it stunned me.

"You *could*." I blinked, trying to chase the threat of tears away. It didn't work. "I don't reckon it'd take much."

"I seem to be making you miserable on this trip. You spend hours in the pub…"

"You're on the phone."

"You could stay with me, here in the room."

"But you're working. I'm working, too. And you could always come with *me*, you know. Make your calls from there."

"I need the landline," he said, shrugging off my suggestion. He sighed softly and went to sit at the small table by the other window. "I really need to be home, anyway. For the sake of convenience."

"I thought we were supposed to be on holiday. Or at least that *you* were treating it like that." I sat opposite him. "You never told me you'd be working the whole time."

Charles rubbed his eyes then lowered his hand to the tabletop. "Abby…"

I stiffened. What on earth was coming, now?

He took a deep breath and looked out the window again. "I should go home."

"Why?" My heart pounded so hard it hurt. Was he going to tell me about the other woman? Was he going to ask for a divorce? Should I be feeling so *eager* to hear, one way or the other?

"Work, darling. Always for work."

I sat in silence for an eternity before a question finally formed.

"When were you thinking of going?"

"We'll leave from Torino."

"'We' will?"

"Of course, 'we'. I couldn't possibly leave you here alone, following that bunch of miscreants –"

"I'm not going home. Not until the Tour is over."

"Abby, be reasonable –"

"I *am*. If you need to go home, then go home, but I'm not going with you. I'm following this through, all the way to Paris."

He sighed again and I resisted the urge to stand and slap him. "Abby, Abby… Of all the things to see through, you pick *this*?"

For a moment, I hated him. The moment passed, but it passed slowly.

***

Lying in the darkness, I couldn't get that glimpse of Abigail out of my head. I was certain it was her I'd seen going alone into the restaurant of the hotel across the street. Now, I'd recognize her anywhere.

If I hadn't put her itinerary away, I could read it and see if she was staying there. I'd nearly memorized the names of her hotels by now. I spent more time studying that list than I did reading the road book of the stage routes.

I recalled watching her leave the pub the night before; the sweet, rounded shape of her bottom in her walking shorts was a particularly pleasant memory. Even when I tried to push the image away, I savoured it a little longer, a smile creeping onto my face.

We'd caught the breakaway well before the finish today. Jakub Moravec, a twenty-two-year-old neo-pro, won the stage, and there hadn't been any change of note to the overall standings. I'd expected to fall asleep with a sense of a job well done, that night.

Instead, Rom continued snoring on the bed across the room from mine, and I sat up to put my back against my headboard, my eyes adjusting to the dark. According to the clock on the bedside table it was only ten-thirty. I was growing more restless with every passing minute.

I've had enough.

I got up and dressed in the dark, putting on the clothes I'd abandoned to the foot of my bed a short while before. I didn't care if they were rumpled; if anything, I hoped that would somehow make me less conspicuous.

Hopefully there wasn't a dress code at the restaurant.

A little voice in the back of my mind ranted incoherently. I resented that my voice of reason had to sound so much like Jerzy, and I quashed it as best I could before slipping into the trainers I'd dumped next to the door on my way into the room.

Rom snorted softly behind me and I moved closer to the bathroom door, ready to feign a visit in case he should wake up. He didn't. I turned on the light and the ventilation fan in the bathroom and closed the door, hoping the sound would convince him I was in there, if he woke after I left.

I picked up my room key and put it in my pocket, eased the door open and slipped out into the corridor. I took a quick look around and then shut the door as quietly as possible.

No sign of Jerzy, or Michael, or anyone else from the team. Good.

Giddy anticipation had me shaking where I stood. That little voice spoke up again, telling me to go back in and go to bed – or turn on the light and read – but this sneaking-out business was a fool's errand. Was I crazy? I was bound to get caught. Wasn't Jerzy half-Polish, half-Bloodhound? He'd grab me before I got to the end of the corridor.

But he didn't.

Before you get downstairs, then. He'll be on the elevator.

I'll take the stairs.

He'll be there!

He wasn't.

My confidence grew with every step I took. By the time I passed through the lobby, a sense of invincibility had begun to sink in. Over the years, I'd been convinced that Jerzy had some sort of sixth sense. He'd caught so many of my teammates when they'd misbehaved. Why the devil wasn't he down here now, dragging me back upstairs and threatening to break my legs or something?

Because I am doing what I am supposed *to be doing.* Not even the desk clerks saw me go by on my way to the front doors.

I stepped out and watched the entrance of the restaurant across the street. I was sure that were I to start walking across the street without so much as a glance in either direction no harm would come to me.

Still, I checked. No point in pushing my luck and getting mown down by a bus.

Once I'd crossed I glanced back at my own hotel, fully expecting to see Jerzy scowling from a window. Or perhaps waiting at the front door with a hangman's noose in his hand. Or the bucket.

I shivered a little, unable to stop, and went inside.

Abigail wasn't there. I searched as discreetly as I could, but found no sign of her. Feeling foolish for taking such a risk, I made my way out of the restaurant only to find I'd taken the wrong exit door and gone into the lobby of the hotel which housed it.

Disoriented, I paused, trying to understand which way I needed to go. What had I been thinking, anyway? How long did I think she'd linger over her dinner? At least a couple of hours had passed since I'd spotted her going in.

I had barely reached the front doors when they swung open to admit a flood of guests and their luggage. I stepped to one side and stumbled into someone coming out from a door behind me.

I spun around to offer apologies and stopped short.

"Federico?"

Abigail.

One little voice in my head groaned in dismay while the other cheered triumphantly.

Now if I could just string a few sensible words together so she wouldn't think I was an idiot, all would be well.

***

"Abigail," he said, a smile spreading across his face and lighting his eyes. "You're *here*."

He looked at me with such sincere surprise, I almost laughed. Of course, he couldn't have been much more surprised than *I* was to find him there.

Maybe if he hadn't seemed so happy to see me, things would have gone differently. I would have excused myself and he likely would have done the same. Or maybe we'd have exchanged pleasantries and small talk, and then gone our separate ways. I certainly wouldn't have permitted myself to believe, even for a second, he'd come there to find me. My ego wasn't big enough to believe that.

But faced with such a genuine smile, what else could I think? I knew I wasn't imagining the relief in his expression once the surprise had faded away.

There was something else I couldn't pin down, something in his face which made me think this meeting was no coincidence.

Not this time.

"Yes, *we* are." I was careful to use the plural, if only to remind myself of the fact that Charles was on the phone upstairs. "It's wonderful to see you. I didn't think your team was staying here."

"No, no – we're across the street." Federico gestured toward the front doors, and I nodded, recalling the team bus parked on a side street earlier that evening. "I thought I saw you come in here a while ago, so I…" He trailed off, his tanned face reddening slightly.

My breath caught in my throat and I did my damnedest not to show it. I waited for my heart to start again while a single foolish thought flitted through my mind in the interim: *I could die happy, knowing this.*

He'd come looking for me. God, how ridiculously romantic was *that?*

Ever the realist, I decided to press my luck. I didn't want to drift off into some ridiculous daydream about his intentions.

"You didn't come here to look for me," I said, opting not to phrase it as a question.

"Yes, I did."

I swallowed hard, not caring if he heard it, though it wasn't likely he would in the noise of the arriving guests.

English isn't his first language, right? Surely he misunderstood what I said, or meant, or –

"I'm glad I found you, Abigail."

"Abby," I said, my lips forming my own name in spite of the fact I couldn't feel them, any more. "My friends call me Abby."

That smile again – innocent, not sly or seductive – and I couldn't pull my gaze away. I was aware of heat rising to my cheeks. And a few other places, as well.

My heart pounded. The din of rushing blood in my ears and the rattling of suitcases as they were pulled through the lobby behind me had rendered me nearly deaf.

When he rested his hand on my arm, below the short sleeve of my t-shirt, I snapped out of my daze.

"Abby." My name sounded awkward as he used it for the first time. "Could I buy you a coffee, or something? I'd like to see more of your photos, if I may." His eyes flicked in the direction of my computer bag, and I looked too, uncomprehending.

"Oh," I said, half-laughing as I understood at last. "Of course. We could go in the restaurant here, or in the bar in the back. I think they might have some booths free."

"Perfect." We started across the foyer, his hand rising to touch the back of my arm. It was an innocent, gentlemanly gesture, nothing more, but it sent a small shock through me.

It was unnecessary for me to be escorted the fifteen paces to the restaurant. I didn't need his guidance to get there, and yet, had he taken my hand in his, I would have let him.

We passed through the double doors and turned to walk down the corridor to the bar. Windows on either side of us faced both the lobby and the restaurant and left me feeling exposed. I kept waiting for someone to jump to their feet, pound on the window and point at me, shouting "Married! She's married, and not to him!"

Even more, I expected someone to recognize *him*, to ask for an autograph or snap a picture. Was it really possible for him to be here, now, and no one know who he was?

Then again, he wasn't in the team colours. His long, baggy cargo shorts and tennis shirt (in tan and white, respectively) were about as far as possible from *Alta VeloCidad*'s skin-tight violet and grey Lycra.

If not for the lightening of his skin around his eyes and the back of his jaw, it would have been difficult to peg him as a cyclist at all. That is, until we sat down to order our drinks, and I caught a glimpse of his leg bobbing restlessly under the table.

I'd noticed it before, of course. Everyone knows professional cyclists shave their legs. It struck me anew then, sitting across from him, as a strong, compelling desire to touch his leg and feel its apparent smoothness came over me.

We placed our drink orders and I took out my tiny laptop and switched it on to pull up the shots from that day. I turned it around to face him as the server brought our coffees and set them down in front of us.

"Wow." He leaned toward the computer and narrowed his eyes, studying one photo intently. "Where were you this morning? I don't remember this..."

"Which one is it?"

He turned the computer around so I could see, and I nodded, smiling. "Oh, yeah. I managed to shimmy a little way up a light post to grab that one."

"Shimmy?"

"I climbed it," I explained, taking a sip from my coffee, and he nodded his understanding as he chuckled softly.

"Very enterprising." He turned the computer toward him again. A few clicks more and he laughed quietly. "I need a copy of this one, so I can show it to James – what a face he's pulling here!"

"Which-?" I began, and he was already turning it for me to see. "Oh, yeah. That *was* a good one, wasn't it?" I laughed too, and Federico turned the computer around again.

He continued tapping away at the key to advance the photo slide show, occasionally shaking his head, sometimes smiling. He stopped suddenly, his eyes narrowing. He tapped the key again and leaned in to examine the image more closely.

"What is it?" I asked, apprehensive.

Federico shook his head. "It's nothing. It just looked like... Nothing." He sat back and shrugged. "It was the angle of the shot."

I tugged at the tiny computer so it faced the wall of the booth, evenly angled between us. Schlessinger was at the finish on the screen, and I studied it before I looked across the table at Federico. "What should I be noticing here?"

"Like I said, it's the angle."

"Was something wrong?"

"No, it's..." Federico tapped a key and went back to another, almost identical, shot of Schlessinger. "Okay; there are certain standards for the bikes we race, right? Here," he indicated a segment of the bike with one long index finger, "it looks like he's using a modification which isn't permitted. But in *this* shot," he added, advancing to the photo from before, "it's clear that wasn't the case."

"Oh, I see. I think." I dug in my handbag and got my eyeglasses out, then leaned awkwardly over the table to see better.

His gaze shifted from the computer screen to me and back again, before he slid out of his booth seat. He moved to my side of the table and turned the computer to face us both.

"See? Just the angle. He didn't do anything wrong."

"Would you have said anything if he had?" I asked, sitting back and looking at him. He stiffened next to me.

"Why would I?"

I shrugged, took off my glasses and put them away. "I don't know. I get the impression you don't like each other very much."

Federico tapped the key until the shots of Schlessinger were past, but said nothing.

"I'm sorry," I said, breaking the silence after a few moments. "I shouldn't have said that. I run off at the mouth sometimes."

"No. It's a good observation."

He was about to say something more, but glanced at his watch and took a sharp, alarmed breath. Gulping down the last of his coffee, he slid out of the booth again.

"I'm sorry, Abigail – Abby – but I have to go. I've missed my, erm, curfew."

I looked at the time in the corner of the computer screen and saw it was a few minutes after midnight. He counted out a few euros and left them on the table beneath his emptied cup.

His expression proved he had more to say to me, but he was already primed to bolt for the door.

"I'm sorry I kept you so late –"

"No, no – it's my fault, but... I really hope I see you again, Abby," he affirmed with my name and then raised one hand shyly. "Abby," he repeated, and hurried out.

I watched him go, then turned back to the computer, a light melancholy coming over me. What had I said to upset him? Was my comment about Schlessinger the reason he left?

My fingers skimmed the keys, not typing, feeling the cool plastic under my fingertips. Finally, I double-clicked on my internet connection and pulled up my internet browser. If I'd offended him, I wanted to know how.

***

My heart was beating triple-time as I hurried across the street back to my hotel. I put my hand in my pocket around the key card there, then took it out and grasped it tight. After a quick scan of the lobby, I went straight to the stairwell and unlocked the door with my key card, taking the stairs two at a time, bounding up them as quietly as I could.

When I reached my floor, I paused, forcing myself to take slow, deep breaths until I could hear the air-conditioning hum echoing around me.

I opened the door and poked my head out, harbouring a momentary, insane longing for a mirror so I could check around the corners. No sign of Jerzy. He wasn't lurking behind the decorative ficus, nor was he standing by the door to my room. The corridor was empty.

Easing the stairwell door shut behind me, I took a few tentative steps toward my room, the key card against my palm now slicked with sweat.

More silence. Only silence. Even the quiet padding of my trainers across the carpeted floor barely registered. A sudden, blatting fart – reminiscent of an angry duck's *quack!* – made me jump as I passed James and Phil's room.

I bit down on my lower lip, hard, to stop the laughter which threatened to erupt. I had to be crazy. This was the biggest risk I'd ever taken – no race even *compared* to this. I knew as well as anyone that Jerzy's wrath wasn't something to be trifled with – contract or no contract, if he wanted you off the team, you were *gone*.

And here I'd acted against his explicitly-expressed wishes. I'd broken one of his biggest rules and defied the team curfew.

When I opened my door, I glanced down the corridor half-expecting Jerzy to appear from nowhere. When I stood in my room in the dark, I still expected the same.

Rom's stuttering snore proved he was alone in the room. I

turned off the light and the fan in the bathroom and waited for my eyes to adjust before making my way to my bed.

I undressed and got under the covers, my heart slowing to a reasonable pace, my muscles slowly relaxing from the unexpected adrenalin rush. I'd done it: I'd actually gotten away with sneaking out.

I wanted to think about Abigail, about sitting next to her, how nice she'd smelled, how soft the skin on the back of her arm was. I did think about these things, but then my thoughts turned to her question about Schlessinger, and the pleasant memories faded.

Just as they always did whenever I remembered losing my best friend.

Stage Ten

(200 km – Orange – Grenoble, France)

First thing in the morning, Charles was on the phone, booking a flight out of Torino. I lay in bed with my back to him, listening, hoping he wasn't booking a ticket for me as well.

"Yes, that's right. Two seats on..."

I shut my eyes tight and wondered if the sound of my gritting teeth was audible to him.

Clearly, I had a choice. I could tell him I wasn't going back with him, or I could ask him one last time not to leave, to stay with me until the end of the Tour.

I wasn't entirely sure which one was the better option.

The hell of the whole thing was, he hadn't always been this way. This arrogance and complete disregard for my feelings or wishes was fairly new. The more time we'd spent apart, with him working in the city and me running our house in the country, the worse things had become. I had repeatedly offered to move closer to London, thinking that would be enough to give us a chance to spend time together and repair the rift growing between us.

He always refused. In my naiveté, I'd allowed myself to believe he'd wanted me to be happy in the house I'd loved on first sight. Now I knew I'd been fooling myself. In recent months, whenever he noticed me looking at real estate sites or ads, examining properties closer to the city, he became edgy and anxious, if not hostile.

Yet it wasn't easy to say he didn't want me anymore. In some ways it seemed like he still did.

I wished I could see things his way. If nothing else, my crush on Renard showed that I was attracted to other men besides my husband, that I could at least *imagine* being with someone else. That had been inconceivable before. However, a fantasy was one thing; to actually go against my marriage vows was something else entirely. Regardless of whether or not my husband gave me permission – or worse yet, was actively *encouraging* me – to do so.

Perhaps my best choice, in the short term, was to let him go ahead and have a mistress. In the meantime, I could set myself up and prepare for the inevitable separation and divorce and stop being concerned with the 'whys' and 'whens'.

I felt hollow at the thought. Could I really be that pragmatic? Could I really let him go so easily? Living alone was something I could handle – I was already doing so – but truly making the break?

Charles replaced the receiver in the cradle of the phone and I pulled the covers up over my shoulder. I listened as he crossed to the window, heard the *shick* of the curtains opening and the soft patter of rain against the windowpane.

"Abby, you need to get up. We'll want to leave as soon as possible this morning."

I ducked under the covers. He was right. The stage was starting in Orange today. It wasn't likely we'd arrive early enough to beat most of the crowds. Perhaps I'd have to shoot further along the route instead?

I shook my head. He'd already refused to drive ahead of the race to let me snag pictures anywhere other than the starts and finishes. Today's logistics made it even more unlikely that Charles would agree to any changes in our planned itinerary.

With a groan, I extracted myself from the covers and shuffled across the room. My lack of sleep the night before might be a problem. Charles laughed softly behind me.

"What?" I asked, allowing myself a smile at the sound of his gentle mirth.

"You're becoming an old fart like me, darling. The late nights aren't agreeing with you as much as they used to, eh?"

"I guess not." I nodded, stepping onto the cool, tiled floor of the bathroom. "Maybe I need to get back into the habit?"

"Maybe."

He stood in the doorway while I took off my nightgown. His gaze slid over me, steady, assessing, while I turned on the water in the tub and pulled the lever to send the water up to the showerhead. I stood straight and faced him, making no attempt to hide myself. Why should I? He'd seen everything a thousand times before, and he'd shown his appreciation a few days ago.

And yet... The desire to cover myself up, a perversely demure impulse, flitted through me. The words were there, on the tip of my tongue, waiting to be spoken.

Who are you? Where did you come from? Why did you go?

And the worst, most painful question of all came as he turned away, half-smiling.

What did I do wrong?

***

I held my position on Brunn's side for much of the day. The stage was easier than I'd thought it would be, after I had awakened still feeling the thrill of sneaking out the night before. Part of me kept waiting for Jerzy to ask some leading questions to trip me up.

Now I sailed along, content to concentrate on the ride while keeping my expression neutral and hiding the smug smile which kept creeping onto my face.

Foxing Jerzy wasn't all that had me so giddy. Lingering at the back of my mind, always, was Abby. Even now, I savoured using her nickname, mentally rolling it around my tongue when everyone held steady in their positions and the tempo of the race lagged.

I'd gotten the name of her hotel from her itinerary and looked the place up on the Internet while on the team bus that morning. I already had a pretty good idea where it was; all that was left was finding out if the lay of the land would work in my favour again.

I had a feeling it might.

Rom glanced over at me and I nodded in his direction. I trusted that my excursion last night wouldn't have caused him any trouble, but for an instant I wasn't so sure.

The climb started in earnest. Conversation faded out as riders saved their breath for the growing effort. Rom and Attilio took their customary positions, aiding Brunn and me, and Schlessinger was close behind, with Motta pulling him along.

The mood wasn't as tense as it would get toward the end of the stage. Grenoble was still a distant dream as we left the valley floor and began the series of switchback roads which would see us up and over the mountain. The sprinters wouldn't make the climbs with any speed. The straights into Grenoble on the other side would be left to the rest of us instead.

I wondered how Schlessinger thought he might fare on the descents this time. Would he manage his nerves better this time around? In the team meeting that morning, Jerzy had alluded to the descents as being of key importance to the overall contenders. My sense of invincibility returned as I worked my way up the ascent. I was climbing stupendously well.

I couldn't deny the feeling which had wrapped itself around me this morning. I was smiling again.

The day came into sharp focus: the green of the mountains, the white peaks in the distance, the deep grey of the tarmac rolling beneath our wheels all had a clarity which I would have sworn wasn't there before. The air was crisp, magnifying the approaching summit until it seemed close enough to grasp and pull myself up with it.

In the back of my mind was her voice, whispering her name to me.

She was in Grenoble by now. She was waiting.

I had to reach *her*. Forget everything else.

And if I happened to snatch a little time and close the gap a bit? If I happened to get a bit closer to the Royal in the process? All the better.

***

Watching the screen, I could hardly keep the smile from my face. Ripples of excitement threaded through the crowd, spates of applause and cheering erupting as the crowd were caught up in the events broadcast overhead.

Federico had managed a brilliant climb on the final ascent — attacking much sooner than anyone had anticipated and then seeing it through. After the frequently heart-stopping descent down the other side, he'd led Brunn and several of the stronger climbers in the peloton to form a breakaway group. They led by more than a minute, and looked stronger with every passing second.

He'd made it look absolutely effortless. Was *this* the same cyclist who had been fighting his way through the climbs in Andalusia and the Pyrenees?

On the drive to Grenoble, I'd read a few articles about Renard I'd found online. He'd given no small amount of dedication to improving his climbing without losing his time trial skills. He'd become a genuine all-rounder, now. I felt a proprietary surge of pride on his behalf. Not that I'd had anything to do with it.

Beside me, Charles impatiently fanned himself with a copy of the *Times*.

"Your boyfriend is doing pretty well today."

I blushed furiously and hoped he wouldn't notice. "Back to that again, are we?" I asked, fussing with my camera bag so he wouldn't be able to read my expression.

"Well, you *do* seem to have an interest there. I've seen those photos, you know. You have more of him than of the others."

"I do not." My protest was weak, to say the least. "I take photos of all the riders, but he was the leader most of the first week. That's all."

Charles shrugged and stood up. "I'm off for some shade. Would you like anything?"

"No, I'm all right," I said, raising my bottle of water as though in salute. "But, thanks anyway."

He looked around the bleachers where we were. They were filling swiftly as the end of the race drew closer.

"Perhaps I'll go back to the hotel. I don't fancy fighting my way back up here."

"Okay. I'll see you there for dinner?"

"Why not? See you then." He touched my shoulder and then made his way down the stairs without as much as a backwards glance. It didn't bother me very much.

I still hadn't said anything about the fact I wouldn't be on the flight home. I'd rehearsed my spiel a thousand times on the drive to Grenoble, when I wasn't trying to read on the computer without getting carsick – but I still hadn't spoken up.

I'm waiting for the right time, that's all.
Bullshit.

No matter what I said, or did, there was no way this wouldn't be a problem. Charles would go home even if I stayed behind. I knew how I *should* have felt: I *should* have been angry, hurt, or maybe even on the verge of despair, but I wasn't.

And that disturbed me.

What kind of wife doesn't care if her husband is leaving her a thousand miles behind? Okay, maybe not a *thousand* miles, but still – I should be ready to stand up and fight. Especially if he might well be going to see his mistress?

Then again, hadn't I wished that I were by myself almost from the start? Hadn't I thought I'd be better off alone?

Brilliant, that. A woman travelling through Europe alone.

There were three more weeks of racing. Could I really do this on my own? And if I did, what would I be going home to? In a way, it was almost better not knowing. At least then I could imagine whatever I wanted, and deal with the reality later.

I understood it was a foolish way to address the situation, but it was already too late. No matter when I told him (Tomorrow? The day after? The day he left?), there was no way to know how he'd react.

We'd have to hash this out eventually, but I was reluctant to set it all in motion.

I could go home with him and be done with it.

No, that would never do. I'd hate myself forever. How many of my dreams had to die to find the dream I wanted most? I'd postponed having children when his career made it clear I'd be raising them alone, and now it was nearly too late. I'd passed up owning a photo lab in our small town because *he* thought it was too risky and besides, "The chemist has that covered." Artistic photography? Too arty-farty and I'd need a proper patron in order to make it work. "And what would you photograph, anyway? Backsides and landscapes?"

He'd methodically shot down each and every dream with stunning accuracy. I still didn't understand why he'd gone along with the Tour project. Maybe because the magazine had liked my demo shots and put up some funding for this project? Or maybe because his job had been pushing him to take a holiday in the first place?

Most likely he'd thought I'd get bored and abandon it, just like I'd done with past projects: furniture refinishing, an attempt at watercolour paintings of landscapes, volunteering at the local crafts club.

This was different. My passion was reborn, but he couldn't see it.

He couldn't see the changes in me. I reckon we'd grown too far apart for him to see me clearly any more.

**

The evening seemed like it would never end. The high of the stage win had all of us buoyed beyond belief, and the usual crush of reporters afterward added to the rush. On the descent and on the straights into Grenoble, *Alta VeloCidad* had made serious gains – not enough to get the Royal back, but enough to get within shouting distance.

Schlessinger hadn't been so lucky, remaining with the main group. The breakaway pack led the way into the city forty-five seconds ahead of the rest.

Specifically, ahead of Schlessinger.

Dinner that evening proved a more relaxed affair than the night before. Jerzy was in an especially good mood. No doubt he believed his free-time restriction had had the desired effect on the team.

In my room, I grew agitated, waiting. There was no way to keep myself occupied enough to ignore time as it passed. I pretended to read over the route map for the next day while Rom listened to his MP3 player and drifted off. After several false alarms where he awoke with a start and settled back in again, he finally drifted off and sank into a sound sleep.

His snoring was going full gas as I slipped out of bed and put on my shoes. My biggest concern that evening had been that all the excitement of the post-stage interviews and photos might have my roommate so keyed up he'd never relax. I'd worried for nothing.

I opted to retry my gambit with the light and fan in the bathroom. It worked before, hadn't it? But if I used it too much, my roommate might think I had some sort of gastro-intestinal issue which only struck during the night. I'd have to think of another decoy for next time.

I put on a sponsor-logoed baseball cap, pocketed my room key and stepped outside. After a glance down the length of the corridor, I walked as calmly as I could toward the stairs. If anyone saw me, I'd say I'd forgotten something on the bus and was going down to get it. I'd left my camera down there, just in case, to make the story more convincing if I needed it.

I didn't.

I managed to get out of my hotel and caught a passing taxi without incident. How had I gone from having such shit luck to all this good fortune?

Don't question it; go along while it lasts.

The façade of her hotel blended in with the rest of the business-zone surroundings. If not for the flags of different countries hanging outside, I'd have thought nothing of it and passed it by.

Disappointingly, the restaurant and bar were closed, thanks to the renovations underway. I went back outside and stood, hands in pockets, deciding my next move. Catch another cab to the hotel and get back into bed, then?

No cabs were in sight, so I sighed and trudged along the empty sidewalk for several blocks toward the team hotel. I couldn't shake the feeling she'd managed to ditch me.

I passed a café/Internet point and paused in front of the neon-lit window. The faces of numerous teenagers and twenty-somethings were illuminated by the glow of their computer screens along the bar facing the street. All of them seemed to be looking past me – or through me, for that matter – oblivious to anything else.

I wished I had her e-mail address so I could write her and ask to plan a meeting in Courmayeur. It would be much, much better than taking these risks on the chance I might see her.

Why hadn't I asked for her mobile number? She obviously had one.

I resolved to go back to the hotel and stop by the bus on my way in. If Horst, the driver, was still there I could duck in and grab my camera and take it up to the room. It made a good cover story for going in or out.

Before I turned away from the mesmerized faces in the window, I glimpsed a familiar pair of khaki walking shorts heading for the back of the café. On impulse, I went inside and ordered a coffee at the bar, then went in the direction she'd gone.

"Abby? Hi."

Smiling, I removed my cap and slid into the booth opposite her. She smiled back, but it was a shy gesture this time. There was no artifice, no attempt to lure me, but I had been lured all the same.

Without a word, Abby turned the computer around so I could see the picture on the screen. Her hand seemed to be shaking the tiniest bit. I focused on the image: me, arriving with the breakaway group I'd led into Grenoble.

"You were in absolutely *exceptional* form today," she said, and it took real effort for me to wipe the beaming grin off my face.

"Thanks," I managed, sitting back as the server brought my coffee. "It was a good day."

Fuck that, it was a miraculous *day, start to finish.*

"A 'good' day?" she echoed, then shook her head. "You're too modest, Federico. I watched the final ascent on the screens here at the finish – I had no idea you could climb like that. I mean, after last week, when you seemed to be struggling so hard?"

I nodded again, trying to shrug it off. It had been an amazingly fortunate turn of events, both for me and for the team. Tomorrow's climbs would cross the border into Italy, and I'd given Schlessinger something to chew on.

"I was due for some good luck, I guess."

"'Luck', nothing. You've been working on your climbing in the off-season. It's paid off."

My finger drifted over the touch pad on the computer, sliding the cursor here and there across the screen. "I don't know how to explain it, really." I moved the cursor up to her browser's address bar. "It all came together at once. I had to go with it."

"Your interview with *InfoCycle* this evening was pretty interesting." I looked up at her and she blushed a little, adding, "It was on the feed by the press tent."

"Oh." I turned my attention back to the computer and clicked on the address bar, which obligingly unfurled to show me where she'd recently been.

A photo search, a Wikipedia lookup, and…

Fuck.

I closed the address bar and went back to the photos, resisting the frown which threatened to replace the smile I'd worn all afternoon.

"Sorry." Her voice was soft, nearly lost in the ambient chatter and music of the pub.

"For what?" I asked, making a final attempt to avoid what was surely the next topic of conversation.

"I heard what happened with Solange. Her pictures are all over the internet now."

I had no idea what she was talking about. Did she mean the

AvantMode – pardon the unfortunate choice of word – spread?

Abby blushed again, deeper this time.

"I saw the photos of her with that Conway person. They were on the entertainment news on TV, too."

"They were?"

"Yes. Some sort of art show or premiere or something? I hadn't heard anything about that until today. You're taking it rather well, though."

"Well, you know," I said, trying to stall for time and still sound coherent, "I wish her the best. Really, I do. She'd never have been happy with me, anyway."

As soon as I said it, I realized it was true. Solange hated cycling – she hated most sports – and she had admitted it to me once her gig as a Tour d'Europa podium girl was over. It wouldn't have done for the public to know that the smiling girl in the royal blue dress, giving kisses to each cyclist on the podium, thought the sport was boring and the competitors were egotistical bastards (her words, not mine).

"How can you say that? You shouldn't be so hard on yourself."

"I'm not." A small chuckle wormed its way out of me. "Honestly. It's very kind of you to defend me, though. Even if it *is* against myself."

"Well, you seem like a decent enough person. I mean, you're nice, you're accessible, you're attra-" She stopped short. I'd already understood what she meant to say and the deepening flush in her cheeks only confirmed it.

"Maybe I'm not so nice, Abby."

"What do you mean?" Without looking up at me she turned the computer so she could see the screen.

"The fact I've hardly thought about her the last couple of days should mean something, shouldn't it?"

Her eyes met mine. "You've been racing. That's reason enough."

"Not the only reason."

Silence stretched out between us, filled by the murmur of conversation surrounding our booth. I tried to read her face, but no emotion registered in her expression.

I took a slow sip of my coffee and looked around at the other patrons of the coffee bar. None of them seemed to be paying us any undue attention.

Abby watched me intently. It was our first meeting all over again; I couldn't look away from her, and I didn't want to. An immediate, undeniable desire filled me: I wanted to lie down beside her and watch her sleep. I didn't just want to make love to her – I wanted to hear her breathe in the darkness and to wake up beside her at first light. I wanted to know she'd be there for every stage of the Tour – that if I called her, she'd answer.

I wanted everything Solange had ever denied me. Since those ties had already been cut, all that was left was to cast them off.

The last of them slipped away as I reached out and took Abby's hand in mine on the table. She flinched, barely considerable as a gesture, but it was there nonetheless. I held her hand loosely in my own until she squeezed my fingers lightly in hers and withdrew.

I knew it was time to go. I wanted to ask for her mobile number; the words were on my lips, but the look in her eyes kept me from saying them. It wasn't the right moment, no matter how much I wanted it to be.

"Courmayeur?" I said instead, standing.

She nodded. "Courmayeur," she echoed and I turned to go.

More than anything, I hated to be the one leaving.

*****

As soon as he was out the door, I clicked on one of the pages I'd bookmarked. A short article written by a fan of Schlessinger's, it covered much of his earliest career, but contained several mentions of Renard. Thankfully, not all of them were as disparaging as the others.

Having met after the creation of the Renard Media *team, Schlessinger and Renard became fast friends. According to some sources, the two most promising members of the junior team were practically inseparable, and looked to make a powerful one-two punch within the team dynamic as they matured. Renard's remarkable time-trial skills and Schlessinger's power as a climber made the youthful duo a force to be reckoned with from the start.*

But the sudden end of sponsorship from Renard Media in 2001 threw the team's future into chaos. When no new sponsor appeared, Jerzy Jankowski had to move on. After Team Mechanizmo *expressed interest in Jankowski, he insisted on bringing along several riders, including his protégés Schlessinger and Renard.* Mechanizmo *balked at taking on so many new cyclists and whittled Jankowski's imports down. He chose Renard, citing his promise as an all-*

rounder with proper development, along with his impressive time-trial skills. Schlessinger moved on to work first with Team Lontano *for several years, and then went on to* Maxxout, *where he has been riding with considerable success for the last three years.*

I stopped reading and sat back to consider this. I sipped at my now nearly cold cappuccino and scrolled back up the page.

'*Having met after the creation of the* Renard Media *team, Schlessinger and Renard became fast friends.*'

The *Renard Media* team? I didn't remember any team by that name. Was the name a coincidence? I did a quick search and found a few transcriptions of articles online, draining my cup in the meantime.

Renard Media was one of the largest entertainment complexes in France, but the cycling team had only existed for a few years, from 1998 to 2001. Federico's father owned *Renard Media*, and according to more than one article, he had bought the remains of the ailing *Exigency* cycling team, pouring enough money into it to bring it up to speed again. Jerzy had signed on as manager and Renard Senior allowed him to use his unorthodox methods to whip the team into proper shape.

It intrigued me that Federico's father had bought a team when his son was barely old enough to join one. This explained the snide tones in other articles I'd read. Many insinuated that preferential treatment – not talent – had earned Federico his place on the team at that time.

Obviously, he's proved them all wrong, hasn't he?

I smiled, considering this.

Citing lack of a co-sponsor, *Renard Media* dropped their sponsorship shortly after Federico made headlines with surprising wins in several races of note. This was particularly puzzling, in my opinion. Why cease sponsoring the team your own son rides for when he's making a name for himself?

There was speculation that Jerzy's desire to bring Federico along with him had more to do with avoiding the 'questionable practices' – i.e., doping – undertaken in the junior levels than with advancing the boy to professional-level racing.

So was it a business decision, or a protective measure on Jerzy's behalf?

Either way, it had been the right choice. Federico flourished in the company of Jerzy and his newfound teammates in what became the core of today's *Alta VeloCidad* team. Further tutelage had come from Adrie Meijer and, in the following years, Heinrich Brunn.

Was it so simple? Why would the dissolution of the team and/or Jerzy's taking Renard along with him cause such a rift? Teammates went their separate ways all the time. The open hostility of Schlessinger toward Federico, and Federico's stoic face in response to his former friend said there were volumes more behind the story I'd read.

I had to wonder what could make friends turn against each other so completely.

Stage Eleven

(170 km – Grenoble, France – Courmayeur, Italy)

I finished my breakfast without tasting any of it, eating out of necessity rather than hunger. For the same reason, I kept the food down instead of being sick – I needed the energy for the ride. I plodded through the warm-up, dragging my focus back to the task at hand, to the stage that morning.

But nothing changed.

I still couldn't believe it. In the hours since the breakfast meeting, nothing had changed, in spite of the fact that, deep down, I hoped something would.

Jerzy made the announcement to the team at breakfast, and then to the media afterward in a brief pre-warm-up press conference: As of that morning Brunn was officially the team's leader.

The press hadn't been allowed to ask us anything – not that I would ever say what I was thinking. I was numb and furious at the same time, raging inside. Judging by the lack of concern and attention from my teammates, only Brunn suspected. After so many years working together he knew me too well. His silence on the matter spoke volumes.

Everyone said Jerzy's reasoning was solid: Brunn was closer to the Royal time-wise, and it made sense to get him there again. The team could do this if we worked together.

Never mind the success of the team time trial in two days would depend greatly on *me*. Jerzy had made that clear this morning. He'd said it with an air of fatherly indulgence, like I should be grateful to be granted such a responsibility.

Of course I'd be leading the team in the time trial – it went without saying! I'd bring Brunn down the mountain today, and then I'd drag him the seventy-five fucking kilometres from Torino to Casale Monferrato two days from now.

Knowing he'd be sitting on my wheel most of the day did little to improve my mood. I scowled at the thought and worked to make my expression neutral. It took more effort than I cared to admit.

I caught Attilio's eye when I dismounted my stationary bike. He turned his gaze back to the ground in front of him and continued pedalling, pretending he hadn't been watching me at all. He and Rom would be in charge of getting Brunn over the peaks into Courmayeur. I would be the safest wheel for him to follow down into the valley.

It would be a difficult ride. I stood to lose a fair amount of time if I messed about. As long as I made it with the lead group to the final ascent, I'd do what I had to. After that, all bets were off when we crested the final summit.

Fuck it. I'll beat him all the way down the mountain. I can always ride for another team next year.

I chatted with supporters and the team staff, checked my bike and prepped my gear and kept reminding myself not to get bogged down inside my own head. Worse things had happened, worse things would still happen.

Years ago I'd been convinced my career was over before it had even begun, when my father had pulled funding from the team. At the time it had seemed like the end of the world. Jerzy's confidence in me back then had gone a long way, carrying me over to the new team amidst loads of scepticism.

The Rich Kid. Daddy's Pretty Boy. Spoiled Brat.

I'd proved my abilities on the bike time and again. Some fans still refused to believe I was winning on my own, or that I had achieved my success honestly while riding clean. I worked harder at riding than I had at anything else in my life.

To those people, I would always be *Daddy's Pretty Boy*, being handed everything on a silver platter. I was still the rider singled out by gossip magazines and telecasts for the women I'd dated, or who my parents were. I was still the rich kid with the former-showgirl mother and media-empire-owner father.

Or, more recently, *The Face of the Tour*.

The back of my neck broke out in a light sweat, my stomach churning. I hurried onto the bus to shut myself in the tiny bathroom. I closed the lid of the toilet and sat down, my head in my hands.

This is ridiculous. I've got to get past this.

I took several long, slow breaths – which wasn't easy, considering Teodoro must have been the last one in there – and forced the tunnel vision away. I wasn't ill. I was panicking, and for what?

'Fanculo, I mouthed at the floor. *Joder! Fuck!*

I continued in every language I knew and a few I wasn't too sure about.

After a few minutes, my head cleared and I straightened up again. This was going to be a long day, but I would get through it.

And in Courmayeur, however I had to do it, I would find Abby. I closed my eyes, took another breath, and stood. It was almost time to sign in; I needed to make a point of showing *The Face of the Tour* before then.

***

I got ready to go, while Charles whistled happily to himself and packed his things yet again.

"It's just a few hours to get into Courmayeur," he said when I protested his *laissez-faire* approach to packing. His good cheer grated on my nerves. "We'll be there in plenty of time for you to get your piccies, darling. Don't fret."

I swallowed my retort, which would have dubbed him a condescending prick, and gathered my camera bags. "Fine, but if you make me run late –"

"I won't, Abby; Scout's honour." He held up his hand in the salute and gave me the smile which always wobbled dangerously close to a smirk. "I wouldn't ruin the last day of your race, would I?"

Why not? You had no problem ruining the others...

"I'll be back in a while." I hoisted my bag onto my shoulder and went out the door without another word.

Insufferable. Obnoxious. Hateful.

As I made my way toward the start line I mined my vocabulary for words to describe him. Only pejorative terms came to mind. Unsure how I'd got there, I found myself sitting on a bench in the park, away from the cycling village and from most of the crowds.

My chest tightened, my throat constricted; I struggled to breathe. When at last I managed a deep, sure breath, I let out a sharp sob which I tried to muffle behind my hand.

Done, done… I am done with this. For now and for good.

I sobbed again, leaning forward to rest my elbows on my knees. My camera bag slid forward off my shoulder to land with a muted *plop* on the grass. I wanted to follow it, to curl up on grass still damp from the morning dew in the shade. I wanted to cry until I got it all out.

In two days, I'm going to leave my husband. Rather, he's going to leave me, and I'm not going after him.

Why had I held on for so long? Was I really so afraid of becoming another statistic, like my mother and father? Was I so afraid of failing I'd prefer to stick with something which hadn't worked for years?

For some reason this made me cry more. I didn't cry out loud, but I wondered if I'd be able to stem the tide of my tears in time to make the start line.

I wiped my face with the sleeve of my shirt and sat up, listening to the voice over the PA system calling the riders to the line.

Shit.

I pulled my things together and calmed myself, standing on still-shaky legs.

I can do this.

I walked resolutely through the crowd, pushed toward the barriers and snapped away, catching the riders chatting and joking, with an air of impatience which hovered over them all like a cloud of insects.

The agitation was palpable, sinking slowly into me from above. My hands started to shake and I wanted the race to get *started* already.

I panned to and fro, snapping photos more or less randomly. I didn't recognize Federico, and scanned past him only to return an instant later.

The good cheer I recalled in his expression from the night before was gone. His jaw was tense, his eyes narrowed. He watched the front of the group, waiting for the start.

I stopped to watch him. The world seemed unfocused, the ground shifting beneath my feet, and I closed my eyes, wishing I'd slept better the night before. When I opened my eyes again, he turned toward me – by chance, nothing more – and spotted me.

His expression underwent a sea change: his jaw relaxed, the line of tension faded, his eyes widened. A smile tugged at his mouth as the rollout got underway.

A brief wave in my direction and then he grasped his handlebars and rolled out with the group, his attention diverted to more immediate concerns.

He had a stage to ride – perhaps even to win.

The urge to cry grasped me again, icy fingers clutching at my midsection while I resumed taking photos of the passing cyclists.

I can do this. Even though I still wasn't quite sure what 'this' was, exactly.

***

I did my job and nothing more. *Alta VeloCidad* made up most of the first chase group out of the valley, and we paced ourselves, unconcerned about Schlessinger up ahead. Rom and Attila hauled us along the rising grade, and when we crested the summit, I threw a glance behind me to be sure Brunn was there. He gave me a nod and tucked in tight as the road sloped downward.

And then we flew.

The final descent before the straightaway into Courmayeur was full of switchbacks, some so tight it seemed my front wheel would lock with the back before I'd got around the curve. With every crank of the pedals, with every turn of the wheels, we reeled Schlessinger in. His reluctance on descents like this was his Achille's heel.

I was sure he'd push himself today, that he'd do whatever he could to maintain his lead. I grimly wished he'd hit the deck; nothing too serious of course, just a tangle bad enough to spook him and shake him up, maybe enough to make him wait for the team mechanic's car to arrive for some minor repair.

Suddenly I was aware that I'd nearly left Brunn behind.

The temptation was almost too much. If I powered on, I could overtake Schlessinger here when he was weakest, and prove I was the stronger rider, the surer bet in this race. Brunn was doing phenomenally well but was he really strong enough to keep it up?

I reconsidered.

If I overtook Schlessinger and gunned it for Courmayeur, I'd have to do it on my own. I wasn't crazy enough to think I could do that. Schlessinger had support; for that matter, Brunn would, too. I wouldn't. If I went on the attack, Jerzy wouldn't allow anyone to help me.

Gritting my teeth, I let my momentum slacken enough for Brunn to catch up to me.

Fuck. Fuck-fuck-fuck!

At the last sharp turn before the final descent to the valley road, my teammate regained what distance I'd put between us. The road straightened out and Schlessinger's bright colours flashed up ahead. Brunn looked over at me and pulled ahead to take a turn in the lead.

As hot as the day was, his gaze chilled me. With a single short glimpse, it was as though he'd read my mind, seen all the plotting and planning which hadn't come to fruition. As if he'd read it all in my drawing ahead and dropping back.

Unreadable as ever, he moved forward and I planted myself on his wheel, ready to take over when we got closer to Courmayeur, if only long enough to launch him forward.

Just like always.

*

Jerzy's joy after the finish was undeniable. As we'd planned, Brunn had gained a few more time on the stretch into Courmayeur, placing himself within shouting distance of the Royal once again. All of Schlessinger's effort on the climb and the descent had been cancelled out.

Knowing tomorrow was a rest day to recuperate before the team time trial in Torino, Jerzy stunned us all with his announcement on the bus to the hotel.

"Since you've all worked so hard and done what you're supposed to, I've decided to give you three hours tonight. Lights out won't be until midnight."

With that, he left us in stunned silence and went to sit at the front of the bus with Brunn, where they analysed video of the day's race.

My stomach burned while I watched the two of them put their heads together in deep discussion. All around me, the murmur of conversation rose to animated anticipation of a night out. I was certain I wouldn't be able to find Abby this time, considering the direction my luck seemed to be taking.

We were staying in Courmayeur for two nights, driving down to Torino the morning of the time trial. It was the closest thing to rest we'd be able to achieve before the next stretch of the Tour.

The team was consigned to two different hotels – one small and traditional, the other slightly larger and more modern. The bulk of the team was housed in the modern facility, most of the management in the smaller one.

When we filed off the bus and into the lobby, I went to the desk for my room key. As always, I would share with Rom, who followed in my wake like some sort of overgrown blond puppy.

I grabbed him by the shoulders and playfully pushed him up to the desk ahead of me. Rom needed to practice his Italian, anyway. He took one look at the pretty receptionist helping us and went dumb, blushing furiously.

"*Lui è timido,*" I explained to her over his shoulder. "He's shy." I prodded him in the back so he thumped against the high desk.

The girl asked for his name and after what felt like an eternity he answered her question in heavily-accented Italian. She smiled, began typing, and I turned my attention to the lobby.

The décor was simple: traditional Alpine, in spite of the rather modern façade outside. I liked it. A strange feeling came over me, a sense of gestalt, of purpose. I couldn't understand it at first, but it was the best I'd felt all day.

I wasn't at all surprised when I spotted her seated near the dining hall. Only then did I recall I'd seen the name of this hotel on her itinerary.

We were staying two nights in the same hotel. At once, everything felt absolutely *right*.

***

I was thankful Charles had gone up to the room to do some work, particularly since one of the teams was staying at our hotel. He hadn't made a fuss because they would be on the bottom floors and we were staying on the top floor.

The riders came into the lobby while I sat in one of the overstuffed chairs by the dining hall entrance, passing time before I went up to dress for dinner. I put away my computer, resisting the urge to go up to Federico and…do what? Throw my arms around him and kiss him? Ask him to take me away?

I shook my head and laughed. *Ridiculous. I'm absolutely ridiculous.*

When I got up to leave, he turned around and spotted me as though he'd expected me to be there all along.

I stopped short, his gaze holding mine from across the lobby. In spite of the chaos of a couple dozen people checking in, the lobby seemed silent and still. He broke eye contact with me only to face the receptionist and take the key card she'd slid across the desk to him. Then he pushed past his teammates in order to come over and join me.

I stopped breathing until he stepped up to me, smiling his usual sweet, warm smile.

"*Ciao*, Abby. *Come stai?*"

"Eh?"

"How are you?" he asked, laughing. Then, before I could answer: "I'm glad to see you here."

"You are?"

"I was hoping maybe, er… I was hoping you might join me for a drink tonight."

"Um…" Dumbstruck, I stared at him. Had he asked me out on a *date?*

After a moment he laughed nervously and glanced around, making sure none of his teammates had overheard his invitation to me. No chance of that, with all the commotion they were making.

I could swear his cheeks reddened, now.

"You're staying here too?" I said, instantly feeling stupid. "Of course you are. You got your key. Sorry."

He said nothing, just smiled at me.

"So? What do you think?"

"About?" I was confused.

"A drink? You and me? We could meet down here after dinner, perhaps around nine? Or ten?"

"That's a late night for you, isn't it?"

"It's a rest day tomorrow." He shrugged.

"Oh, right. I knew that." Why did I feel defensive? And why did this invitation feel so provocative?

A silence, then: "Please?"

How could I say 'no' to that? I nodded and said "Nine o'clock," and left the lobby as quickly as I could, hopefully without being too obvious. With every step I took, I wondered:

What the hell have I done?

***

Throughout dinner, while my teammates joked and chatted, I thought of her – only of her. It felt wonderful and wretched at the same time.

I wondered if she might bring her husband along, and if she did, what would he make of that?

True to her word, she was outside the hotel pub at nine o'clock. Before she saw me, I stepped back behind one of the decorative posts in the lobby to watch her. The pale pink of her button-down blouse and the grey of her knee-length skirt stood out against the alpine wood grain which surrounded her. It seemed like she glowed beneath the hidden track lighting. The shine of her sleek ponytail was mesmerizing.

A breeze from the air conditioning nudged the fringe around her face. Strands of hair too short to pull back curled around her ears and she tucked them back impatiently, glancing at the thin gold watch on her wrist.

She startled a little when she looked up and saw me. The truth was, I was nervous as hell myself. I wanted to shake the day off like so much road grime and lose myself in conversation with her, at least for a little while.

As I stepped aside and held the door for her, the same nervousness as I'd had on my first date ever.

The pub was practically empty and I wasn't really surprised. The team made up the majority of the patronage of the hotel, and most of them were either with their families or attending the festivities in the city centre.

The server led us to a circular booth in one corner. I liked the enforced privacy of the set-up right away. Between the high edges of the booth seat, the plentiful greenery scattered around the top and the low lighting in the pub, there was little chance of someone spotting us.

Abby ordered a white wine and the server looked expectantly at me.

"*Una birra, per favore,*" I said, figuring today I'd earned at least a beer.

We sat in silence, which gave me a chance to consider a few things. First, there was the fact I'd repeatedly run into Abigail in the pubs. The second thing was that I always found her alone, in spite of her claim she was married. I'd yet to see this phantom husband, though she said he'd somehow played a part in her photographing the Tour.

Any mention of her husband saddened her – that much was clear. When we discussed the stage, or I told her about events on the road, her mood improved. Every time she laughed – or merely smiled – she drew me in deeper.

This is bad. Very, very bad.

My heart clenched tight with understanding: married woman or no, I wanted her. Never mind the Solange debacle. Never mind her mythical Charles, wherever he was. I wanted Abigail White, and I couldn't have her.

"Federico? What are you thinking?"

I had to laugh. Why do women always ask that? If men were ever honest enough to answer with the truth, women would never come near us again.

"What's so funny?" she asked. "Tell me."

"You really don't want to know."

"Sure I do."

Her eyes searched mine, and I had no choice but to be honest. Maybe it would be best if she *did* go away.

"For a while I was thinking about the next stage," I said. "Then I thought about how I keep finding you alone in these places. Then I wondered where your husband *really* is. And then...?" I shrugged, hoping to make light of my next thought. "I started thinking how much I want to kiss you."

I looked down at my drink, not wanting to see her disappointment. I'd had enough of that in the past week to last me a lifetime.

***

150

I stared at his profile in the low light, afraid to believe. "Really?" was all I could manage.

Still not looking at me, he gave me a half-nod and took another drink of his beer. "Really."

To say I was surprised would have been an understatement of staggering proportions. After the reality sank in, I stifled the temptation to dismiss his confession. I knew somehow he'd meant it sincerely.

That he'd doubted me about Charles was actually rather amusing.

"Okay," I said, amazing myself.

He faced me slowly. "Okay?"

I nodded, hoping it looked confident and worldly, rather than as over-anxious as it felt.

When his eyes met mine again, the world shifted wildly beneath me. Denying I wanted this wouldn't change anything. It was better to give up trying to control things and let events follow their natural course.

I waited for him to say something more. The silence wasn't quite uncomfortable, but it stretched taut between us.

The dull ache from afternoon returned. Right up until then, I'd still believed my fancies about him were ridiculous, fantastic conjurings to pass the time in Charles' poor company.

I'd never wanted someone so much in my life; to feel this way toward a man I hardly knew was incomprehensible.

I wanted to press my fingers to my temples to still my thoughts. Instead, I slid my hands under my thighs and wondered that they'd gone cold.

Federico slid closer, the leather upholstery of the curved booth lending the movement a familiar, slippery sound. A blush crept up to warm my face as he leaned in. Up close, his handsome features held a few flaws; a small scar on his cheekbone under one eye, another on his chin, a small mole on his right cheek. My heart skipped, and he hesitated. I wondered if my heartbeat had betrayed me.

But I'm married! This is cheating, isn't it? And Charles is upstairs!

And he was; on the phone with *her*, no doubt talking about his return to London in a couple of days.

"Abby...?" Federico murmured, his voice so soft I leaned

toward him instinctively, expecting him to share some secret. But what could compare to what he'd already told me?

I was trembling. Too many thoughts were running through my mind to keep them all contained, and it took more effort than I'd expected not to run away with them.

Reaching up, he rested his fingertips against the back of my jaw, his thumb curled beneath my chin. My eyes closed against the fresh dizziness which swept over me as he tilted my face upward. His lips brushed over mine, so lightly his warmth seemed a figment of my imagination. The next kiss was scarcely more than gossamer tracing the shape of my mouth, until his lips pulled oh-so-gently at mine and lingered there for an eternity or so before withdrawing.

He pressed closer and his mouth sought mine again. His lips pressed and parted mine gently but firmly. My world became the hint of the beer he'd had a short while ago, my lips warmed beneath his and the fleeting soft, wet touch of the tip of his tongue to my own which made me shiver eagerly inside.

When we parted, he rested his forehead against mine. My blush burned as he exhaled a quiet, satisfied sigh. I opened my eyes and he drew away, his eyelids fluttering open.

I wanted to close my eyes again, childishly thinking the act could somehow hide me, but I didn't. Instead his gaze penetrated mine, his eyes reading my own until I was certain he saw every thought I'd had about him since we'd met. His silence left me feeling exposed and vulnerable as though I'd stripped down in front of him and begged him to take me there and then.

If he didn't quit looking at me that way, it was possible I would.

***

I was stunned. She wanted this, too. She'd admitted it easily, freely, but she was holding something else back. Even as I moved closer to her, I was afraid of frightening her away. If she rejected me now the humiliation wouldn't be the worst thing. At least there wouldn't be any witnesses.

I held back at first. I just wanted to know what her lips felt like, how her breath tasted.

She had the most kissable lips I'd ever encountered: petal soft, even when she returned my kiss.

My control slipped – I'd only meant to kiss her once. Instead I

152

came back again and found her even more willing than before. She opened up to me slowly, her tongue teasing mine and sending a shockwave through me at the contact. I touched her face, needing to centre myself, an anchor before I could be swept away.

Her soft sigh warmed my lips and I kissed her again, and again, wishing this moment could last, somehow defying fate and time and everything else against us.

A married woman. I'd thought I'd feel guilty, or get some illicit thrill from kissing a married woman, but I didn't. She was just Abby, just a woman, but she was the only thing I wanted in that moment and from that moment on.

It was all I could do to force myself to stop. It was difficult because of how good, how *right* those kisses felt. When I pulled away from her I was sure I'd never feel that *rightness* again.

At least, not until I kissed her again. I couldn't do that now; the timing was all wrong. I touched her face, loving the warmth and the curve of her cheek, how her dark eyes seemed to draw me in so she could whisper every secret she'd ever kept.

God, how I wanted to hear her whisper to me, to feel her lips brush my ear as she shared confidences in the dark, the warmth of her body beneath mine...

A glimmer of regret grew inside me, stronger and stronger. I didn't want to go back to my room and leave her there alone. I didn't want to spend another minute of my life not knowing what it was like to make love with her.

I wanted that more than anything else. Nothing else mattered at all. No race, no team – nothing.

That little voice in my head moaned in protest – *too soon, not now!* – but it was too late.

I breathed in deep, hoping to clear my head, but it only made me more aware of *her*: her presence, her warmth, her scent. Her perfume – soft and subtle –beckoned me closer. The desire to press close to breathe the scent off her skin, to touch her and see if warmth made the scent stronger, muddled my thinking even further.

In an instant she appeared in my mind's eye: smiling, naked, welcoming... I shivered from the intensity of the image and had to calm down again.

I withdrew my hand, aware of the way my fingers ached to feel the softness of her hair tangled around them. I wanted her more than I'd have thought possible – and knowing I couldn't do anything about it was maddening. If her flushed face and heavy gaze meant anything, the feeling was mutual.

If I pressed for more, I'd have it. But there were still a few problems:

She was still married (though this wasn't the barrier it should have been).

I was due back upstairs soon.

And, finally, Jerzy would kill me and kick me off the team, in that order. Any such behaviour would mean instant termination. That was his rule.

Even if I *did* somehow, miraculously get away with it, chances were it would wreck my performance in the race.

Any way I looked at it, I was fucked.

***

His gaze remained locked onto mine, until the need either to throw myself into his arms at last, or to flee, arose. If only for practicality's sake, I chose the latter option.

"I should—"

"-should go."

We spoke at the same time, and it seemed more embarrassing than anything else.

"I'm sorry, Abby, but my free time is over, and if I'm late, well…" Federico drew his finger along his throat in the classic gesture and I nodded.

"Of course. I should get back upstairs, too. Charles should be done by now."

"What is he doing?"

"Work," I answered, too quickly.

Nodding, Federico slid out of the booth to stand up. "Abby, about, um… About this…?"

"Don't worry," I said, sliding out to stand, also. "Our little secret, okay?"

He smiled and I melted inside. "Okay. It's not that I'd mind, it's—"

"I know."

He nodded again. "Ah, hah… Still, you know…I'd like… I'd like to see you – to talk, I mean – if we could."

I nodded too. He turned to go, but stopped short.

"At the finishes," he said. "I'll watch for you there. That's the place I always see you."

And with that, I realized he really had been watching for me.

Rest Day Two

(Courmayeur, Italy)

I didn't sleep.

I lay in bed, eyes closed, remembering Federico's kisses. Those memories were better than any dream I could conjure, sweeter than any rest I might find in the night. I should have known enough to expect the downside of it: remembering those kisses made me want him even more.

I was exhilarated and embarrassed, proud and ashamed. For the first time in my life, I'd kissed a man who wasn't my husband. And that man who wasn't my husband had been compelled to kiss *me*.

Also a first; I *wanted* someone who wasn't my husband. The mix of excitement and fear was intoxicating. Was this something I could handle?

I kept feeling the brush of his stubble over my lips; not quite rough, almost soft to the touch from a few days' growth. I touched my fingertips to my mouth, wishing that his kisses hadn't been so... what?

Gentle. I wish they hadn't been so gentle.

I had nothing to show for what felt like so significant an event. No tenderness in my lips, no visible marks – nothing. I'd tried not to look guilty when I'd returned to the room and found Charles already in bed, reading over some paperwork. Apparently I'd done a good enough job, because he didn't react in the least.

He didn't even ask where I'd been, what I'd been doing. My absence for the better part of two hours didn't even warrant an inquiry in passing.

So why did I still feel such guilt? Was it because it had happened, or because I wanted it to happen again?

The hours passed. While Charles slept, my mind drifted to the booth in the pub downstairs. I quashed the desire to get up and get dressed, to go down to the pub and see if Federico was still there. It was nonsense and I knew it. He'd been the first to leave, to be sure he didn't slip up and break curfew.

Did that mean he'd wanted to stay with me, but feared we'd be drawn together again and linger too long that way? The idea gave me a pleasant shiver and warmed me at the same time.

Maybe it meant he hadn't trusted himself to resist much longer.

I smiled, and the 'what-ifs' started in earnest:

What if we had the chance to be alone?

What if we kissed again?

What if Charles found out about this?

That darkened my mood. That was what Charles wanted, wasn't it: for me to take a lover so he could, too, guilt-free? He'd suggested in the past that I should take a lover for a night or more, and even give him the details afterwards.

To be fair, he'd only said that last part once or twice, but inevitably that was the part I'd never forget. The other part, about taking a lover, he'd mentioned more recently. Or, rather, he'd *hinted* at it. He was an expert at saying volumes without saying precisely what he meant. Charles could twist words so skilfully I found myself agreeing to things I'd never meant to in a million years, confessing things I'd never done nor had ever wanted to do.

That was probably half the reason I'd married him in the first place – he'd set his sights on me, and made short work of the whole deal.

At this thought a wave of nausea swept over me. I went swiftly into the bathroom, thinking I was about to be sick.

Was I really so weak-willed that he could have *conned* me into marriage? Surely not. I'd resisted his attempts to sway me into an open marriage all this time, after all…

I thought of Federico again, of how I'd felt in the pub, and of how I'd felt while trying to sleep.

Oh, God, no…

Was *that* all this really was? Was Charles somehow manipulating me into this?

"Get a grip," I muttered to myself, moving to the sink on shaky legs to splash some water on my face until the panic receded. I wanted Federico because I wanted *Federico*. Open and shut, case closed, full stop. I returned to bed, slipped under the covers and lay on my side, focusing on the window and the shape of the light illuminating the curtains.

Knowing Federico was there, only a couple of storeys below, made it difficult to rest. *Is he sleeping deeply, or is his sleep restless too? Is he thinking of me at all, right now?*

Probably not. He has more important things to concern himself wi—

I cut off the thought and sighed quietly. I burrowed a little deeper under the covers before Charles rolled over and, still asleep, slipped his arm around my waist. I froze, waiting to be sure he wasn't waking up, and then I tried to empty my mind of any thought. I needed rest. I needed sleep.

I'd deal with everything in the morning. In the meantime, I'd try to dream about those kisses so I could feel them all over again.

*

I paused, my hand still on the doorknob, my heart in my throat. He obviously hadn't heard me come in from my solo excursion in Courmayeur.

"Don't worry, Jennifer darling, I'll be home tomorrow evening. No, of course I won't be out to see you. I have to go home with Abby first." He paused then, which gave me time to put it together.

Jennifer. That must be Jennifer Goodrich, that lawyer for the company.

"I'll be in the office on Monday, as always, okay? We'll have lunch, catch up."

And then, lest I might still try to make this an innocent conversation: "You said you *liked* things this way. We will, I promise. Soon. We'll be together, the two of us, very soon."

Easing back out of the room, I closed the door quietly. Shaking, I leaned against the wall, pressing my shoulders to the wallpaper in order to keep my feet. I needed something to help steady me, and the wall would have to do. The fact it made my bruises on my back hurt helped keep me centred, too.

Still, my knees were like water, wobbling dangerously beneath me, threatening to give way.

I'd been right all along. If they hadn't made love yet, it was obviously on the "to-do" list.

Any guilt over my kiss with Federico the night before dissolved in the span of a few long breaths drawn while I regained my equilibrium. I'd done nothing wrong. Nothing wrong at all, compared to what my husband had done. Would do. Was, in fact, still *doing.*

Now I had to go into that room and pretend I hadn't overheard. I had to pretend there was nothing bothering me, even though it was already eating away at my insides, bit by precious bit.

But why should I pretend? Why not confront him, tell him what I knew?

Simple. If I do that, he'll find a way to convince me I'm wrong. He'll convince me I've misconstrued everything. I don't want to play these mind games any more.

I wished suddenly, passionately, that I knew which room Federico was staying in. Was he in the hotel, now, or out training? Did I want him for revenge, or for comfort, or both?

I can't really be considering this, can I?

But why not? I'm pretty sure he wants to.

Not for the first time, I cursed my luck. The timing was off. It still didn't feel quite right. Would it be so bad to go along, see what happened?

Talk about getting ahead of myself.

I shook my head and straightened, feeling strangely detached from my movements. I knew, somehow, when I came back to myself again, it would be a shock. I was certain of it.

Key in hand, I took a deep breath, paused, and this time I made no effort to hide my entrance. I banged the door open with my hip as I entered so Charles would know I was coming in.

"I wondered when you'd get back up here. Were you able to find a restaurant for dinner tonight?"

I bit back a smart retort. "Yes, I did. It's a couple of blocks away. The hotel staff highly recommended it."

It was so much easier to do than I'd expected, I had to wonder if the rest of it would be, too.

*

The restaurant was modest by every standard: inexpensive, understated decor, and good – though not outstanding – food. The meal had been pleasant, if unremarkable, and our conversation light and carefree.

At least, as long as I didn't let my thoughts drift to Charles' phone call from that afternoon.

It was impossible not to, however, when the familiar chime of his phone told him he had a text message. Without completely taking the phone out of his pocket, Charles read the display while I continued spooning the crème brûlée from the dish in front of me.

He turned an eye toward my efforts, half-grinning. "Why do you always eat it like that?"

"Like what?"

"You scoop the crème out from under the crust. Why?"

"I like it best that way. I save the crunchy part for last. It's like eating sugar glass, or something."

With that, I tapped the crust to break it. I put some in my mouth and let it dissolve.

Shaking his head, Charles put his phone back in his pocket.

"Don't you need to answer that?" I asked, knowing I'd never convince him the question was asked innocently.

"No, I don't. Let's enjoy our meal."

"Our meal is almost over."

"There's still coffee yet. Perhaps a digestive?"

As if on cue, the server appeared to clear our plates and offer the coffee service. Without asking me, Charles ordered for both of us and the server disappeared to fill the order.

I said nothing. It really wasn't worth it.

"Abby, I—"

His phone rang softly from the depths of his pocket. A call this time, not a text.

I stared down at the tablecloth, at the small, pale violet blotches from the drops of wine which had dribbled down the side of my glass to pool in a thin arc at the base.

He answered his phone, stood and walked away. I presumed he went somewhere quieter for his conversation. Quieter, and farther away from me.

After a few moments he returned, discomfited. "I have to go back to the room. They need me to fax something I was—"

"Just go," I said, resigned. "I'll be back in a while."

For once, he didn't stay to argue, or to protest. He gave me his credit card and wound his way toward the door through the maze of tables. The server returned shortly afterward, placed the coffees on the table and departed without a word.

I drank both my coffee and Charles', the shots of espresso hot, black and bitter on my tongue, like all the words I longed to say.

Tomorrow. The thought hovered bleakly in the back of my mind while I stood and picked up the credit card and the bill. I crossed to the cash register near the front door, paid, and signed.

In the few blocks between the restaurant and the hotel, there were several chocolatiers. After passing all of them by, I doubled back and made a purchase in the second shop: several pieces of chocolate including one block of dark, milk and white chocolate, all in a row.

I walked back to the hotel, the bag in my hand, already daydreaming their taste. I had no idea why I'd bought it, but I hadn't been able to resist the idea of sweetness after the coffee at the restaurant.

The lobby of the hotel was surprisingly quiet. Only the sound of activity in the dining hall and the meeting rooms out of sight kept the place from feeling eerily abandoned.

I dug in my handbag for my room key while I walked toward the elevator, trying not to drop my bag. I considered throwing the sweets away. I couldn't imagine actually eating them once I'd gotten upstairs.

Changing direction, I went toward the front desk to look for a wastebasket.

"Abby!"

My heartbeat sped up at the sound of his voice. I stopped in the middle of the lobby and turned to face Federico as he crossed the floor to me in a few long, easy strides. He looked younger than he had last night, but it wasn't his attire. The light blue short-sleeve oxford and sand-coloured hiking shorts weren't especially youthful.

"Hi," I said, trying to sound casual and knowing I'd never manage it if I tried to use his name. "How are you?"

"I'm great." The eagerness of his smile was positively charming. "How are *you*?"

"Good, good…" I lied, gripping the bag in an effort to keep my hand from shaking. He'd shaved since last night. *That* was what seemed so different. "You're making the most of your rest day?"

He shrugged, then scratched his chin and fussed with the sunglasses resting on top of his head. "Yes, and now I've got some free time."

"Isn't that what a rest day is for: free time?"

I thought of his kisses last night, of the friction of his three-days-growth against my lips. A light warmth rose in my cheeks.

Still grinning, Federico shook his head. "No, we've spent the day in meetings, training, doing interviews – that sort of thing. Rest days are more stressful than riding, in some ways. Tomorrow, I'll have to find my legs again."

"Oh, I didn't think about that." I realized we were walking toward the elevators again. "I was going to—" I began, and then cut myself short. "Never mind. It's not important."

"I'm sorry. Am I keeping you from an appointment?"

"No, not at all. Like you, I've got some free time now."

"Have you had dinner? I've already eaten, but I'd be happy to take you –"

"Yeah, I'm afraid I did." I grinned sheepishly and held up the white bag. "I even got myself some, uh, dessert." Horrified, I realized I'd nearly said "extra dessert".

He grinned. "What did you get?"

"Chocolate, from a little shop about three blocks from here."

His expression changed, suddenly wistful. "That's my favourite thing in the world," he said longingly. "I haven't had a good chocolate in forever."

"Would you like one? I have plenty." The rich, milky aroma rose from the bag as I opened it and offered it to him.

Federico glanced around nervously before plucking a single bonbon out and popping it into his mouth, whole. His eyes closed and his expression became nothing short of blissful.

"That's better than cocaine," he murmured, and I smelled the chocolate on his breath. "At least, from what I'm told."

I laughed and he smiled again. "Do you want another one?" I proffered the bag once more and he shook his head with what appeared to be genuine regret before I put the candy away in my handbag.

"I'd better not. Do you want to go to the pub? We could have a drink and talk."

"I think it'll be a bit crowded. Things are pretty lively tonight."

"Oh. I have an idea, then." He led me along a corridor, turning a couple of corners before stopping to open a door. "What about this?" he asked, reaching to hit a switch that turned on half the lights in the room. The door swung shut behind us with a soft, pneumatic *hiss* and we stood in the middle of the "U" shape the tables made. Pens and notepads, all of them bearing the *Alta VeloCidad* logo, were still on some of the tables.

"This is where we've been most of the day," he said. "I don't think there'll be anyone in here until the morning."

Although there was plenty of room, we stood close together and his hand brushed mine. I recalled an illustration from a children's book: Hansel and Gretel in a forest clearing, the trail of breadcrumbs they'd left behind already long gone.

Will I be able to find my way back?

"I don't know," I said, my stomach doing a little flip. "This feels like trespassing, somehow."

"It's okay, really."

He stepped away and I went to the bottom of the 'U' to pull myself up and sit on the table. Federico turned and, without looking at me, began straightening the pens and pads of paper on the tables around the room. His sudden agitation was unnerving.

"Federico, please sit down. You're starting to make me nervous." I laughed lightly, hoping he wouldn't continue fidgeting.

He gave me a shy grin, ran a hand through his hair and then sat next to me on the table at what I judged to be a respectful distance. My eyes were drawn to his sharp tan line on his legs, and I couldn't help smiling. The shift from dark to light couldn't have been more precise if it had been painted on his skin.

"Wow. You guys really *do* get dark out there, don't you?" I laughed again, trying not to permit the next logical thought, about how pale he must be elsewhere.

"Yes, we do. Some of us tan more than others." To my surprise, Federico hiked up his pant leg further so I could see the pale pink of an old scar cutting a diagonal path from the darker skin to the lighter skin of his thigh. His arm was as dark as his leg but his hand was a shade darker than his upper thigh.

That's from wearing the gloves.

"I really should spend some time at the beach. Maybe I could even out a bit more, if I found the time to relax in the sun."

"That sounds like a really good idea." In the glow of the overhead fluorescents, the lighter stripe of skin along his jaw stood out from the rest of his face. I could see where he'd shaved his beard, the faint imprint from his sunglasses, even a strip of lighter skin right below his hairline on his forehead from his helmet.

Suddenly Federico was tugging at his sleeve, pulling it upward so I could see the abrupt tan line there, too. The difference between his tanned skin and the lighter skin on his upper shoulder was as remarkable as on his legs; it was as though he wore a clean white t-shirt beneath the short-sleeved oxford.

I laughed in spite of myself, and his grin widened.

"Wait – look at this."

To my surprise he started unbuttoning his shirt. Before I could panic, he turned toward me with a few buttons undone to show me the varying shades on his neck and upper chest, underneath the fine, dark hair there.

"Eh?" he queried, grinning, as I noted the demarcation beneath his Adam's apple. "That's from zipping up all the way," he explained. "This one," he continued, indicating the next darkest patch which ended in a wide 'V', "is from unzipping about halfway on a hot day. And this one," he said, pointing with his middle finger, "is from unzipping completely, like in the mountain stages."

I couldn't help laughing a little.

"It takes ages to even these things out," he said with an air of resigned amusement. "Not that I've been able to. I usually fade in the winter, unless the team goes to Australia or something."

At this, he fell silent. I wondered if he was thinking of Solange and her very public betrayal in Sydney a week before.

"Oh, wait," he said, undoing his shirt completely. "There's this, too." He took his left arm out of the sleeve and pointed to a stripe which ran from his shoulder to the top of his biceps. "I wore a sleeveless jersey sometimes while training last spring. I've had this ever since."

His tan resembled the stripes on the tricolour bar of chocolate I'd purchased that evening, and I barely stopped myself from saying so.

Without thinking, I reached out to touch his arm, as if checking to see if the colour might smear. I half-expected it would, the lines were so perfect. What I didn't expect was how strange it would feel to touch him. Yes, we'd kissed the night before in the pub, but this gesture was even more intimate. The warmth and smoothness of his skin under my fingertips surpassed my expectations, exciting me more than I cared to admit.

I wondered if the line on his throat felt the same, or the faded downward arrow on his chest. He was broader in the chest than most of the other cyclists I'd seen, his build less slender. He seemed more like an adult, not as boyish as the others.

"Abby?" he asked softly, and I drew my gaze up from his heart, now beneath my hand. I'd been tracing each and every line on his skin all along.

"What's this?" I asked, touching my fingertip to the pendant on the slim silver chain around his neck.

"That's the Madonna del Ghisallo; the patron saint of cyclists." He half-smiled and I drew my hand away. "My mother gave it to me when I started riding professionally."

"I didn't know you were Catholic."

"I'm not. My mother is."

As he pulled his shirt back on, his eyes met mine, and when he moved closer, it was the kiss in the pub all over again. I wasn't resisting, and I wasn't seeking. I simply wanted to let it happen, to see *what* would happen, and most of all, I wanted to *know*.

He reached to rest his fingertips on the sensitive skin behind my ear. The hairs on my neck stood on end in both anticipation and a hint of guilt.

Charles was upstairs – in all likelihood on the phone with Goodrich. Because he'd left me alone in the restaurant earlier this evening, he had no idea where I was or who I was with.

All this left my mind as soon as Federico's lips met mine in a light, teasing caress. He withdrew, giving me ample time to pull away and bring an end to his gentle advances.

I didn't want to.

"Abby..." There was a hint of hopefulness in his voice as he pressed closer.

He shivered beneath my touch as my fingers strayed down his throat and chest to linger over his belly. He moved closer to press against me and deepen our kiss. I returned each kiss he gave, letting him go deeper, harder.

Too aware of his body, I moved my hand away, but he grabbed it to place it over his belly again. I slid my palm up and over his chest, my touch lingering to tease his nipple erect.

He moved closer still, his skin warm in the cool air of the room. It was too difficult to think clearly, but stopping was impossible. I might not get another chance like this. I sank into his kisses, relishing the wet heat of his mouth on mine.

I was aware of the room tilting, spinning around me. His kisses moved smoothly from my mouth to my neck, the tender pull of his lips on my skin sending shivers throughout my body.

I breathed in deep, taking in as much of his warm, spicy musk as I could. He reached up to unfasten the buttons of my camp shirt and slipped his hand underneath, cupping my breast through the spaghetti-strap tank top I wore.

My sigh escaped before I could stop it, and then his mouth was on mine, kissing me with an even greater urgency than before. I returned every kiss, every touch, flooded with a hunger I hadn't felt in years.

This was what I'd lost. I'd long since forgotten this desire for another human being, wishing I could have his body moving against mine, his weight pressing me into a mattress in one of the rooms upstairs. I longed for him to be with me, inside me, filling me.

Federico slid off the table to stand close in front of me and drew his hands up along my leg, his fingertips lingering as they traced up from my calves to my outer thighs, then slid slowly underneath my skirt, pushing it upward.

He gently pulled me forward to the edge of the table, and I wrapped my legs around his. Eager heat rushed through me as I flattened my palms against his back, beneath the shirt still draped loosely over him. Federico pressed against me and drew a shaky breath a moment later when I caressed him through his trousers.

I hesitated, frozen, until he kissed me again and I stroked him with the same rhythm as our kisses.

His breath caught again and he exhaled slowly, shifting his body so my reach was less awkward. He filled my hand perfectly and all I was aware of was his warmth, the soft strength of his lips, the hard length of him in my hand beneath his clothes.

He pushed my skirt up out of the way and eased his hand between us, and then –

We were apart again, my head whirling from his sudden and unexpected departure. My hands were already smoothing down my skirt, straightening my shirt, checking my hair.

Federico's face was flush with frustration. He glanced at me, an edge of panic in his eye before he turned to look toward the doorway. He reached back and clutched my hand in his, a brief, steadying gesture.

The door of the conference room *hiss*ed open. Federico pulled at my hand, indicating I should stand up. Without his help, I couldn't have done it.

"It's Rom," he murmured to me out of the corner of his mouth, and I nodded my understanding.

The younger man's bright blue eyes regarded us with obvious surprise as they shifted from Federico to me and back again.

"*Jesteście ty zwariowany? Co jesteście ty robienie?*" he said, and I looked at Federico, who was already leading me to the door.

"*Ti prego, Rom; non parlarti di questo con Jerzy*," Federico answered.

I didn't have to understand Italian to know Federico was asking Rom not to tell someone.

Rom blinked in surprise and shook his head fervently. "*No, non parlerò con Jerzy…*" He waved Federico away, his expression shifting from open anxiety to puzzlement as we walked past. "*Powinieneś był wiedzieć jak się zachować,*" he muttered.

Federico led me down the corridor, heading for the elevator. "I'm sorry about this," he said, pressing the call button. "I'm afraid I let things get a bit out of control."

"Please, don't apologize. It was my fault, too."

"No, Abby; it was me. I shouldn't have done that. I just…" He fell silent as the elevator doors slid open and an elderly couple stepped out. They smiled at us and he returned the gesture before indicating I should get in first. Once the doors slid shut again he took a deep breath and continued speaking. "I just wanted to be alone with you."

My smile felt watery on my lips, somehow shaky, too full of emotion to trust. "I did, too."

He nodded and pressed the button for his floor. "There's something I need to give you. It's in my room, but it won't take a minute."

I stifled the urge to answer with "I sure hope it takes longer than *that*" and instead said "What's that, then?"

The elevator doors opened and we stepped out onto a floor buzzing with activity. Loud laughter, music and the unmistakable sound of video games came from different rooms along the corridor as he directed me to a closed door about halfway down.

Before he'd even turned on the lights, I noticed the

unmistakable *maleness* which seemed to permeate the air inside the L-shaped room. It was, I had to concede, not an entirely unpleasant sensation, but it was rather foreign to me.

I was used to Charles' scents – his cologne, his shampoo and soap, his after-shave, even his dirty laundry. None of those was anything like this. This was youth and energy and, yes, some of the natural messiness of men travelling together. It was a disorder which wasn't exactly offensive or off-putting, but...different.

"Sorry about the mess," he said, sincerely apologetic. Obviously maid service had come and gone – the beds were neatly-made, the curtains open to show the view of the street and of Mont Blanc looming in the distance – but the possessions of the room's occupants were still scattered across every available surface.

He switched on the lamp on the bedside table while I waited, then turned and piled some things into a carry-on bag.

"I, uh, should give you this." He took some folded sheets of paper out of the front pocket of his carry-on bag and faced me again. "Your itinerary," he said, holding them out.

"I wondered what I'd done with those. Charles and I had a little row about my misplacing them." *Why did I tell him that?* The last thing he needed to hear about was Charles.

"You left them in the pub," he said, fussing with the mess atop the desk. "I kept forgetting to tell you I had them. Sorry."

"Stop apologizing. It's not necessary." I glanced around the room once more then turned toward the door. "So, I suppose this is 'good night', then?" I asked quietly, trying my best to keep my disappointment out of my voice.

He took a deep breath, nodding. "I'm afraid so. I could see you to your floor, if you like."

"Sure, why not?" Imagining Charles seeing me with him, I couldn't resist the smile tugging at my mouth. I pushed the elevator call button and we stood silently together in the din of the corridor.

In the elevator, there was only the hum of the machinery as we rose to the fifth floor. Federico stood near me, his hand at the small of my back as though he feared losing contact with me. My heartbeat pounded against my ribcage until it seemed it might break.

We had been so close...

The doors opened onto my floor and I stepped out, expecting him to stay on the elevator and bid me a quick farewell. Instead he followed me, keeping a half-step behind while I walked to my room. When we passed the stairwell, he pulled me inside and closed the door.

The whitewashed brick and concrete wall was cool at my back before he slipped his arms around me and held me to himself, heatedly kissing me. I wrapped my arms around his neck certain I'd do anything – absolutely anything – he asked of me then. If he wanted a quick coupling here amidst the smells of damp, concrete dust and the stale smoke of furtively-smoked cigarettes, then so be it. I wanted what he wanted, even if it was a one-time thing.

"Abby," he murmured against my neck, then kissed me again, his intended words forgotten.

I touched his face, his hair, his shoulders and back – I wanted to memorize everything about him, if I could.

"Abby," he said again, a little more clearly this time, a little more focused even as his hands slid down to my hips and gripped them. "I want you to promise me something."

"What is it?"

He framed my face in his hands and kissed me again before replying.

"I want you to call me if you need me. Any time, before or after the stage. Will you do that?"

"Of course, but I don't have your number."

"You do, *amore* – I already gave it to you."

Another kiss.

"When did you give it to me? You didn't."

"I did." He patted my handbag and gave me yet another kiss I wished were endless.

At last we parted, and he went to the top of the stairs leading down. "When you get to your room each night, message me with the room number. If you need me, call me. If I can, I'll come to you. If I can't, we'll talk on the phone."

My heart leapt at his words. I wished I could snatch them out of the air and hold them to myself.

"That's the most romantic thing anyone has ever said to me, Federico."

"Chicco," he said quietly. "Call me Chicco – that's what my friends call me." He grinned, and I knew he was remembering the night in the pub.

"Okay, Chicco," I said, seeing it as "kee-ko" in my mind's eye.

"*Au revoir*, Abby," he said, his accent giving my name a peculiar little turn.

I smiled too, finally catching my breath again.

He hurried down the stairs and out of sight. I leaned against the wall until his footsteps faded and the sound of a heavy door opening and shutting rose up to me. In the half-light of the stairwell, I rummaged in my bag and took out the itinerary of my trip, quickly scanning it.

Scrawled in unfamiliar script across the blank bottom half of the last page was a mobile phone number and a short message:

"I made a copy."

Stage Twelve

(Team Time Trial - 75 km Torino - Casale Monferrato, Italy)

I was honestly amazed I hadn't been caught out. Rom hadn't said anything and Jerzy hadn't caught wind of my indiscretion the night before. I couldn't help thinking it was another chink in the armour of our team manager.

After I'd left Abby behind in the stairwell, I'd come back to the room and gone straight to the shower, determined to find some relief. After a lukewarm dousing I calmed down, but my mind never strayed far from her. I had trouble sleeping. Constant thoughts of her kisses, her softness – and then her scent beneath my lips, the heat of her body against mine being so abruptly taken away – kept me in a state of frustration.

I had to take matters into my own hands before I could relax and sleep. Once I had, I slept better than at any time since the start of the Tour.

The bus moved out for Torino and I was hit by a sense of regret. Not for what I'd done in the room alone, but for what I'd done with Abby. I'd pushed for too much, too fast. While she seemed willing enough at the time, I had to wonder if she'd really wanted it.

Come on. She had to know what might happen when we were alone.

From the moment we were alone in the conference room – a completely insane act, in retrospect – the idea had lurked at the back of my mind. While I wasn't stupid or egotistical enough to think that paparazzi were lurking around every corner, waiting for me to emerge with a new woman, it would be foolish to think – should a photographer spy me with someone new – it wouldn't be recorded and reported in short order.

Better to keep it private, as long as possible; besides that, she said she was married, and her husband was here with her. There was no point in pretending the tabloids wouldn't have a field day with *that*.

I couldn't stay away from her. I'd asked her there, we'd talked for a while and then I was kissing her and yes, she was kissing me back. And more.

I'd never kissed a married woman, before. I don't think I've ever wanted to. Whenever she was close to me, I couldn't focus on anything else. I wanted to bury my face in her hair and smell her; to taste her skin, her mouth and the palms of her hands. I wanted to spend hours exploring her body, getting to know every inch of her, to learn what I could do to make her sigh or laugh or call my name in a way she'd never done for anyone else.

I hadn't planned on showing her my tan lines, which must have seemed like a rather unsubtle invitation. Her touch had driven me mad, the way she'd traced each outline on my body. Was it any wonder I'd tried? When she'd been there with me, with her mouth on mine, it all seemed possible.

The way she'd returned each kiss, the way she let me go deeper, harder, felt like a premonition of what could follow, given time.

Then she'd driven me crazy with her touch, pushed things just that much farther than I'd expected to go. But then she kept stroking me, kept kissing me, and I knew it was what she wanted too.

Wasn't it?

As disappointing as it was, she was definitely married. The delicate tickle of the fine hairs along her thigh had been all the proof I needed of this. No unmarried woman would go to her lover's room without having shaved.

At least, I didn't think so.

Or maybe it only meant that she'd had no intention of going any further than that.

I supposed I'd find out soon enough. When the stage was over, we'd be in Casale Monferrato, and maybe I'd hear from her again. If I *did* see her again, I resolved to apologize again for my

into my stomach.

Start the car. Get the air going and cool down before you get a heatstroke or something.

Belatedly, my hand obeyed the order, clumsily jabbing the key towards the ignition even though I was looking right at it. I hung my head and closed eyelids of sandpaper, feeling like I'd been crying for days.

If I didn't get going soon, security would arrive to usher me along.

I pressed my other hand, the one without the keys, to my forehead. My touch was cool – almost chilly, actually.

That sensation was enough to get me moving.

I slid the key into the ignition and started the car. The smooth rumble of the engine, somehow distant and near at the same time, reassured me as did the sensation of the car idling around me.

I can do this. I will do this.

I must do this.

If only to show Charles I could follow through with a project.

My dry lips ached but my smile still felt good to me. I called the hotel and the English-speaking clerk gave me my room number after reassuring me it was still available. I rang off, consulted my directions and programmed my destination into the GPS on the dashboard. Finally, I took a deep breath and eased out into the traffic passing slowly in front of the departures area.

If Charles thought I'd wait around to see whether he'd change *his* mind, he was sorely mistaken. With a little luck, I'd make it to Torino for the start of the time trials. Otherwise, I'd head out to Casale Monferrato for the finishes, after grabbing a few shots along the route.

The traffic paused at a roundabout where a lorry had stalled, blocking the way. I pulled out my mobile and tapped out a few digits into an SMS:

4. 0. 5.

Without having to look, I scrolled down the list of contacts and tapped the first listing, then hit *send* with a shaking hand. I didn't need to send any other information.

He already had a copy.

***

The noise was unbelievable. When we entered the final stretch into Casale Monferrato, the cheering was so loud the sound was a physical thing, buffeting us from either side.

The world was a stream of colours surrounding me, flowing past without anything standing distinct or clear, with one exception: the banner of the finish line looming in the distance, a brilliant blue herald above the blurred confusion.

I lowered my head, prepared for my final pull. Jerzy had been clear: he wanted me to lead this charge, and I knew I had performed to my utmost abilities. We'd arrived in what looked like record time. Was it too much to hope for? A team stage win *and* the Royal ours once again?

But we weren't finished yet.

We slipped through the rotation again, just a few pedal strokes for each one of us – Attilio had dropped off the group as we'd come out of a gentle ascent in Cinzano, apparently for a technical problem – and now Teodoro showed sudden signs of difficulty.

A sharp gesture from Brunn, and then we all advanced, pushing harder to make up for the loss.

We had seven men left, and the finish was *there*.

Right there.

The meters flashed past and we moved as one, a clockwork mechanism, shedding Teodoro off the back as we had shed the minutes off our time en route to the finish.

It was time for the final push.

The cheering grew louder – I wouldn't have believed it possible, but it did – and as the finish line swept past, the sound was like being caught in a nuclear blast. The whooshing *roar* rolled toward us as we slowed into the waiting hands of the team handlers, and almost as one we turned to view the time on the readout by the line.

Our average speed: 58 kilometres per hour.

Our time: One hour, eighteen minutes, 45 seconds.

***

Although I'd captured as many shots as I could of the other teams too, I knew I was taking more of *Alta VeloCidad*. I was mesmerized by the synchronicity of their efforts, by the grimaces of pain and determination they wore as they barrelled down the final stretch

180

toward the finish, the pandemonium of the crowd as they passed and cleared the line, marking them with the fastest time of the day by far.

With only one more team to go, they'd probably won for the day unless *Maxxout* managed a miracle. Their gains had put Brunn over the top.

In spite of my weary sadness over Charles' departure, a little shiver of anticipation slid down my spine. I kept shooting, my camera clicking and whirring dutifully all the while.

While I watched from a distance, carefully zooming to capture the expressions of all the riders as they were congratulated and steered away to cool off and clean up, he did what I'd hoped for.

Federico pulled off his helmet and turned around in a tight circle, scanning the crowd. Through my lens, it looked as though he was scowling, challenging all comers, until he stopped abruptly and a warm, sunny smile broke on his lips.

He raised one hand and waved, and a collection of fangirls behind me started jumping up and down, squealing and tittering at a gesture they'd thought was meant for them. Maybe it really was – it was impossible to know for sure.

I couldn't help grinning in return, zooming in to capture his expression. The warmth in his smile, in his eyes, flooded me with warmth of my own, and I savoured the feeling even as he was led away to clean up and await *Maxxout*'s arrival.

Not that their approach was any sort of threat. They hadn't cleared the checkpoints in anything close to *Alta VeloCidad*'s time.

I checked my watch, cast a glance toward the screens, and turned my camera back down the stretch in anticipation of the next team's approach. A few minutes later, my mobile buzzed in my shorts pocket, startling me.

"Okay." I read, and breathed a sigh.

"Message received and understood," I murmured to myself, sighing with relief.

*

That evening, the soft knock at my door was almost too quiet to hear. Perhaps if I hadn't been listening so intently, I would have missed it. As it was, I crossed the room, silently, and peered out the peephole with exaggerated caution.

Federico stood quietly in the corridor, glancing about with an air of anxiety. Opening the door, I stepped aside after he turned to face me, the corners of his mouth quirking upward the least little bit.

"*Ciao*," he said softly. He brushed my arm as he passed.

"*Ciao*," I echoed, the word feeling impossibly foreign on my lips. After hearing Charles' associates use it so often it still struck me as ridiculously pompous.

Well, I'm in Italy now. No harm in using it here.

"So-"

"Well-"

We started and stopped speaking at the same time, then shared a nervous laugh. He gestured for me to continue but I shook my head. The words balancing on the tip of my tongue weren't anything I really needed to share. Not now, anyway.

"Please," I said, "why don't you go first?"

"All right, then…" Federico rubbed his hands together – or rather, he rubbed his fingers together, his palms held awkwardly away from each other. "There's something I should tell you, Abby, about last night."

"Okay." My heart suddenly revved to a hundred miles an hour as I sat on the tiny sofa next to the window. *This can't possibly be good.*

"The thing is," he began, crossing from the wardrobe in the corner to the head of the bed, and then back again, "I feel terrible about what happened."

"You do?" I said, if only to fill the silence which followed while he searched for what he wanted to say.

"*Sì, sì*, I do. Very much so. It was unfair of me to put you in such a position, er, so to speak." He continued pacing. "I got carried away, you know? And I didn't mean to make you think you had to, or, uh, that it was all I want from you, because I want more – I mean, I don't just want that, but I, uh…"

By this point he'd turned such a deep red I feared he might overheat or turn purple, or something. I giggled in spite of myself and he stopped in his tracks, a stricken expression on his face.

I patted the seat next to me on the sofa. "Federico, sit down please?"

He did, rather reluctantly, and kept his gaze trained on the carpet. I resisted the urge to pat his knee as I would a child's.

"You need to listen to me, okay?" He nodded guiltily. "Nothing happened last night that I didn't *want* to. Was I resisting anything we did? Did I try to fight you off?"

He shook his head, chancing a glance at me before staring down at the carpet again.

"I didn't think so. And Heaven knows I don't want to send you any sort of mixed signals, Chicco, so let me be perfectly clear about that."

He faced me at last, now grinning broadly. "You called me 'Chicco'."

"I know. I like it."

"I like *you*."

The sweetness and sincerity with which he said it twisted my heart a little. *What on earth am I getting into here?* I wondered as he framed my face in his hands. When he drew me closer for a short, tender kiss my heart twisted again.

Talk about mixed signals. I don't even know what I want from this.

"Something is wrong, isn't it?" he asked as we parted. It was my turn to look away.

"I'm not sure, to be honest."

The little sofa creaked as he shifted position and wrapped his arm around me as naturally as though he'd been doing it for years.

"*Dimmi*, Abby. Tell me."

My heart started racing again and I was sure he could feel it, pressed against his side as I was. My whole body was thumping in time to the accelerated beat while his hand stroked my arm in counterpoint to the rhythm.

"Well, I..." I sighed, took a deep breath and started again. "Charles went home today."

In spite of the fact he stiffened somewhat at what I'd said, he continued stroking my arm. "He did?"

I nodded. "He didn't even..." I tried, but I couldn't form the words, even though I wanted to tell him. Even if it hurt, and I was sure it would.

"*What* didn't he do, Abby?" His voice was soft, reassuring, while his fingers continued their soothing caress on my arm.

"Say goodbye," I whispered. "He didn't try to convince me to leave with him, and then he didn't say goodbye."

His fingers ceased their repetitive stroking and rose to my hair, gently brushing it away from my face, pushing it behind my ear.

Then he leaned in and gave me a soft kiss on the temple.

"I know it's probably bad form to tell your lover about your husband – I'm new at this and I'm not sure of the rules." I laughed, hoping to lighten the mood. "But I needed to tell you, to tell someone who, oh, I don't know..."

"Someone who cares," Federico murmured, his lips still against my temple. "You wanted to tell someone who cares about you."

I didn't trust myself to speak, so I nodded.

"Why did he go home?"

I shook my head. "He said it was for work, but I don't think so. I overheard him talking to his lov—" I choked on the word, then gathered myself and forced it out. "His lover. I overheard him talking to his lover on the phone. As far as I can tell, he's gone back to be with her."

***

I was stunned at the stupidity of the man. Any man who had a woman like Abigail and threw her aside for someone else was obviously an idiot. While I stood to benefit from his foolish mistakes it pained me to gain anything at the cost of her happiness, however briefly.

The sooner she understood she deserved better than an overeducated idiot, the better. Not that I was any more deserving of her.

"Now it's your turn," I said. She looked up at me, puzzled.

"My turn to *what*?" There was an edge to her voice I didn't like.

"To *listen*."

"Oh."

I took her hands in mine, ever mindful of the time. I had to be back at the hotel before eleven or Jerzy would have my head.

"Abby..." I met her gaze and held it as best I could, ducking my head when she did so she couldn't evade me. "I will only say these things now, okay, but I will say them. Your husband is a *fool*; he does not now, nor has he *ever* deserved you."

I tightened my grip on her hands when she moved to pull away.

"But the most important thing for you to know is this: his leaving is not because of *you*. It is not because of anything you have or haven't done."

"He wanted me to—"

"I don't care. It doesn't matter. He is a stupid, stupid man, and now he has gone to meet his lover and left his wife alone with a man who would do anything to be with her."

Perhaps it was wrong, perhaps the time wasn't quite right, but I kissed her anyway. She kissed me in return, one arm around my neck, the other wrapped tight around me until I pulled her over to rest on my lap, snug against the arm of the sofa.

She gave me a thousand little kisses, her small hands touching my face, my hair, as they had the night before. Every soft pull of her lips on my skin sent a shock through me. In spite of myself, I started weighing my options.

For the most part, it would be a flat stage tomorrow. Today had been draining, but perhaps not too much so.

Theoretically speaking, sex before a stage was a bad idea.

It was, therefore, solidly on Jerzy's "Forbidden" list, and according to some, justifiably so.

But with her lips on mine, her round bottom nestling on my lap, her breasts pressed against me…

Merde… In spite of everything, she was too vulnerable. This was genuinely taking advantage, and I couldn't live with myself if I took things any further.

Well, maybe I could… No. No.

The small *beeps* of my watch alarm put an end to any further contemplation, whether of the situation or of her shapely form on my lap.

I had to go back to the hotel.

My watch kept *beep*-ing, but we kept kissing; in fact she kissed me harder and harder, fogging my mind until the alarm faded away into near-nothingness. I had to try to still her, my hands framing her face again to draw her gently away from me so I could speak.

"Abby, *amore*, I really have to go."

"Your curfew?" she asked, and I nodded before she kissed me again, heatedly, her effort bringing a dull pain with it.

Mon dieu, she's rubbed my lips raw.

My arms were wrapped around her again, tighter than before, and as though out of my control, my hand crept up to her breast –

Stop before it's too late…

Either way, this is going to hurt.

"Abby," I repeated, making a greater effort this time to ignore her flushed cheeks, the heat of her skin beneath my hand on her back – *and how did that get there, anyway?* – trying to will away my erection which was now straining against my trousers in search of her warmth and softness. "I don't want to go," I said, meaning it more than she'd ever comprehend, "but I really do have to."

She nodded – slowly, reluctantly – and slid off my lap and onto the sofa. It was excruciating but sweet torture. I did my best not to show it, but I'm sure she knew.

How could she not?

"Did you mean those things you said, Chicco?"

Gah! Women! Then again, to be fair, if any woman had a reason to doubt…

"Of course I did. I *do*."

She gave me a tentative, trusting smile, and I thought my heart might break.

"Call me tomorrow night," I said, once I thought I was in good enough condition to walk back to the hotel at last.

"I will."

"I don't want to go now."

"I know."

I stood up, put my back to her to adjust myself both physically and mentally, then bent and gave her a final kiss.

My hand rose to her hair and stroked the tousled waves as I lingered for a dangerously long time. If she had asked me directly – if she had *asked* me to stay with her, to be with her that night, I'd have done it no matter what.

Instead she pressed her cheek to my hand, sighing, and a minute later I was walking down a quiet hotel corridor alone.

Again.

Stage Thirteen

(168 km – Casale Monferrato – Dongo, Italy)

The breakaway came three kilometres out, and the small group maintained their distance for nearly the entire 168-kilometres from Casale Monferrato up to Dongo, on Lake Como. None of the riders in that group were any threat at all, and so the contenders and their teams let them go on their merry way. There was no sense wearing ourselves out clawing back a bunch whose times had them foundering at the bottom of the classification.

Before we reached Como itself, the road was quite flat, but the light and intermittent rains gave us some trouble, resulting in a few small crashes on the plain. When the roads began to undulate around the lakeshore, we climbed through a tunnel to open air high above the water. The sheer drop on the right offered a view that, under any other circumstances, would have commanded my full attention, even on a dreary and overcast day like today. I made a pledge to myself to come back and ride this route again one day, whether as a training ride or a pleasure outing.

Whenever the peloton would pick up speed, it seemed the road would narrow drastically, the buildings closing in to scarcely more than a passenger car's width across. Forced to slow all at once, there was much jockeying for position and shouting as riders rounded curves to find themselves faced with much less road than they'd had seconds before.

In spite of this, it was an easy ride – just the thing we needed after the effort we'd expended in the time trial yesterday. Exactly what I needed after a nearly sleepless night spent thinking about Abby and what we were – or, rather, *weren't* – doing.

I'd hated leaving her alone so suddenly last night, but what could I do? The team's small celebrations wouldn't hide the fact I'd disappeared from the hotel – not for long. The sense of good fortune which had surrounded me the first times I'd sneaked out, the sense of being able to do no wrong, eluded me now.

I was hopeful for its return, though. Perhaps more than common sense should allow.

With the Royal covered by his rain jacket, Brunn rode at the head of the peloton for now, leading the team as we took a turn at the front.

The kilometres passed, our destination drawing ever closer. We didn't catch the breakaway group. The sprinters would still fight for the finish, battling for the Points jersey.

Unless one of the contenders took a notion to gain some extra time – and in this weather it was unlikely – we'd finish as a loose group and all of us would take the same time for the day, maintaining our current standings.

I glanced at the notes taped on the top tube of my bike. We'd entered San Vito, so we were nearly at the finish.

The road wound gently along the lakeside and the sprinters and their lead-out men started jostling for position. While the group didn't slow on the still-drying roads, no one wanted to get in the middle of the fight for the perfect line.

The sounds of the crowds along the marina as we entered Dongo filtered through our own noisy efforts, the inevitable increase of speed toward the finish like a contagion sweeping over us all. We swept past the signs for the last two kilometres as weak sunlight broke through the clouds, casting a shimmer on the pavement ahead.

Ever mindful of the standing puddles of wet still on the road, I led Brunn to the front of the pack, both of us hanging back safely within the group while the sprint trains found their lines. For us, it was more important to lead the group once the sprint was underway. If there were going to be any more crashes, they were more likely to happen in the back of the group.

All of the riders tensed as we waited for the final burst of speed of the sprint. Every man sought to hold his line, morbidly aware of the possibility of getting caught up in someone else's bad judgement.

One kilometre to go, and then they were off, charging into the distance, bumping shoulders when someone got too close, standing on the pedals and riding for all they were worth. The roar of the crowds rose sharply as the sprinters, by now lost to our sight, shot round the curve and into the final straightaway.

By the time we'd cleared the final curve, the excitement of the fans was obvious. I knew we hadn't taken the sprint, there was no sound of celebration on my earpiece, nor was there any sound of disappointment.

Very strange.

***

I made it to the finish line shortly before the sprinters came through. I'd never heard of Mirko Molteni, the short, stocky rider who was first across the line. Judging from the exultations of a great deal of the crowd, he was a local favourite. I was happy to snap his joyous expression as he crossed the line with his arms upraised and tears streaming down his face.

Right behind him the other sprinters bore down on the finish. Marcus Tanner of *Big UK* led the charge and Alvaro Mendoza of *Alta VeloCidad* was right in there, too. Mendoza lacked the power to hold Tanner's wheel. I didn't envy Mendoza his reception at the meeting afterwards, if anything Federico had told me about Jerzy's temper held true.

Shortly thereafter, the peloton swept past. I spotted Federico in the rush of bodies and Brunn's scowl registered in the split-second I'd had to recognize him. It was over. I went to the podium for my shots of the stage winners and of Brunn getting the Royal yet again.

I caught more emotional snapshots of the boy who'd come in first – the woman embracing him was almost certainly his mother, the older gentleman standing off to one side, beaming, was surely his father.

I made my way to the podium press area and set up in the pit. My French friend was nowhere to be seen. No matter. I was already thinking about tonight, Federico, and what might happen if

189

we met again.

I wasn't sure what I was hoping for. I hadn't sent him my room number yet – my things were still in my car, waiting for me to go to check in – and there was no absolute certainty I'd see him anyway. Besides, what would we do if we met up?

Talk, of course. We always talk. And kiss, and… well.

Recalling the night before, I could still feel the sensation of his arms around me, his mouth opening to mine and how bold I'd been, how hard I'd kissed him, and –

Go on, you know you want to think about it.

I could still feel how *excited* he'd become, how hard he'd been, how urgently he'd pressed against me with obvious need.

He'd wanted me every bit as much as I'd wanted him. I never would have believed it in a million years, but now I'd had plenty of evidence.

The heat in my face intensified, even as a different heat pooled low in my belly, stirring pleasantly. I glanced at the spectators surrounding me, their eyes trained on the podium. When young Molteni stepped out, sections of the crowd went absolutely mad. He still looked very emotional as he raised his arms high, nodded, smiled and then bent to accept first his prize from the official and then the kisses from the podium girls.

Another gesture of triumph, and I zoomed in to find his eyes filled with tears, even though he lifted his chin and smiled his biggest smile yet. Next to me, a cluster of young girls squealed and jumped up and down, shouting his name, but it was clear he couldn't hear them above the crowd.

As I packed my things, the crowds drifted away, either toward the Tour village or into town. Soon there would be the traffic jam of people leaving on the lakeside road in either direction, some continuing to the next town the Tour would depart from – Chiavenna, several kilometres up the road, toward Switzerland – or heading back to Como and points south.

I only wanted to get to my hotel, find my room number and send it to Federico. No sense in actually starting to *expect* him to arrive, only to be disappointed later.

One of the clasps on my camera bag refused to close. I fussed with it fruitlessly until someone reached out and pushed it from a different angle, sliding the sticky plastic tab shut with apparent ease. Startled, I looked up and found my photographer acquaintance smiling at me.

"Oh, um… *Merci*," I said, and he grinned at me.

"I wondered where you'd gone when I didn't see you around, this morning."

"Yeah, I was running behind."

He nodded and then extended one hand to me. "I'm Pascal, by the way," he said, taking my belatedly-offered hand in his. "And you are…?"

"Abigail."

With one gentle shake of my hand he released me, and I exhaled a quiet sigh of relief. At least he hadn't tried to kiss it or anything.

"Abigail. Would you like to have a coffee?"

"Um, no, thanks… I'm, uh, married." I raised my hand to show him my rings, and he chuckled softly.

"It's only a coffee."

"I'm sorry, but I can't. I have to get back to my hotel." I pulled the strap of my camera bag higher on my shoulder and turned to go.

"Which hotel?" he asked, and damned if I didn't nearly tell him.

Instead, I gave him a smile and walked away, hearing his chuckle behind me as I went. Again, that sense of satisfaction rose. I hoped I'd handled things well. I needed to check in to my room.

I had a message to send.

***

As we coasted over the line, aiming toward the chaperones and staff awaiting us, Brunn's jaw was tight, his eyes searching the familiar faces in the crowd. He dismounted and handed the bike off to one of our mechanics before disappearing with a soigneur to clean up for the podium.

Michael continued shouting orders and I detected a hint of tension in the air while the rest of us made our way through the press crush on our way to a rubdown, a shower and a quick recovery meal.

After tending to our most immediate needs and changing into fresh clothes on the bus, most of us collapsed into our seats to rest. We'd stay the night somewhere close to Dongo tonight and drive to Chiavenna in the morning.

I settled into my seat and felt a vibration in the pocket of my windbreaker. I grinned and took out my mobile – my personal phone, not the team-issued phone – to read my new message:

2. 1. 7.

My grin broadened, widening enough to earn me a curious glance from Adrie as he dropped onto the seat opposite me with an audible *whumph*.

"Good news, Chicco?"

I shrugged and then nodded. "Yeah, I guess so." I memorized the number, closed the message and put the phone away. There was weary, post-race analysis amongst my teammates until Teodoro turned on the TV and found a newscast about the race. He raised the volume high enough that my first thought was to ask him to turn it down.

My second thought was arguably more practical.

I gestured to Adrie, motioning for him to sit in the seat next to mine. He did so, taking his seat more gracefully this time, still with that curious expression on his face.

"What's going on?" He stretched out and propped his feet up on the seat across from him.

"Nothing special," I had a sudden urge to stall. I hadn't expected to be so nervous about actually asking him about this. "Could I ask you a personal question?" I managed at last, and he raised one eyebrow.

"What kind of personal question?"

"A *personal* question."

His light growth of beard rasped under one big hand as he rubbed his jaw, considering. I sincerely hoped he wasn't going to hold my foolishness from a few days ago against me.

"Come on, let's talk back in the crash pad," he said, standing up. "I can't hear myself think up here," he added jokingly, raising his voice over the television. Teodoro waved him off and Attilio laughed loudly as we made our way to the back of the bus.

Adrie slid the door closed behind us and I sat on one of the sides of the padded bench which lined the back walls of the bus in a horseshoe shape.

"So, what is it, Chicco? What's troubling you?"

"Well, it's not that something's troubling me, Major. I'm just, erm, curious about something and I hoped you might be able to tell me."

He made a 'go on' gesture with one hand and I swallowed hard before I spoke again.

"You know how Jerzy has that rule, right? The one about, ah… sex."

Adrie sat on a corner portion of the bench, resting his legs along one long cushion. "Uh-huh?"

"I was wondering if you, um… Do you know if it's really true?"

"If what is true?"

"Does it mess with your riding? Sex, I mean." Heat rushed to my face. I sounded like a fumbling virgin.

Adrie blew out a soft breath, nodding to himself as though pondering one of the great truths of life itself. "It depends."

When he added nothing else to this, I was compelled to prod him along. "On *what*, exactly?"

"What sort of sex? I mean, are we talking about fucking, or what?"

"You tell *me*."

He half-laughed and stretched lazily. "Well, Jerzy's rules are sacrosanct. I mean, his methods are pretty well proven."

"Yeah, but –"

He raised one hand to silence me. "I can tell you this: if we're talking about hand jobs or blow jobs, there's no problem. Hell, I'm sure every bastard on this bus has rubbed one out before a race at least once." He paused, then added, "Once this *week*. Hell, *today*."

We laughed, and I hoped he couldn't detect the guilt in my laughter. He kept his gaze judiciously averted, focusing instead on the ceiling.

"Tell you the truth," he began, lowering his voice so I had to lean closer to hear, "if I'm able to have time with Danielle, we do more than that. Sometimes. Usually it's just that, but sometimes, when the babies fall asleep early…" He shrugged, letting his words trail off.

"But it *doesn't* affect your riding, then?"

"We don't go at it all night. A quick fuck isn't much different from jerking off. If you're not trying to keep her coming all bloody night, then, no, it's not a problem – but I wouldn't want to get caught out by Jerzy. He's got a point about them being a distraction, though. It's hard enough to maintain focus on the road when you're *not* worrying about that."

I nodded, saying nothing, and he turned to look at me.

"Is, uh… Is there someone you've got your eye on, Chicco?"

It felt like a betrayal to say it, but I did, anyway. "No, not really. I've been thinking about it all, lately. Maybe it was part of why Solange…" I let my words trail off and shrugged again, a ball of ice expanding in my stomach. I'd never thought about it before, but now a small part of that puzzle had fallen into place.

"You'd do well to forget all about her."

"I know, I know."

"Women like her are a dime a dozen. No offence, but you should have known better than to get involved with her in the first place."

I said nothing, my thoughts taking a sour turn. Adrie sat up and moved closer to me, his attitude strangely paternal.

"Here's my advice on the matter, and you can take it or leave it, okay?"

I nodded again.

"If you fancy one of the podium girls, make a play for her when the Tour's nearly over. Fuck her brains out when the Tour's done and move on. You'll feel better for it."

"Why a podium girl? Why not someone else?"

Adrie's crooked grin beneath his crooked nose pulled a grin from me in spite of myself.

"It wouldn't be a revenge fuck, otherwise. You need one of those, at the very least. Whoever you're with next is going to be your rebound, anyway. Might as well make it short and sweet to begin with, eh?"

He gave my shoulder two hard, friendly slaps of his heavy hand then stood up. I stayed seated, my heart pounding.

He's got to be wrong about that, right? Abby's not a rebound, *is she?*

"Come on," Adrie said, stretching until his spine *crack*ed. "Let's get back up there and find out what's going on. We should have been on our way to the hotel by now."

***

Federico stood in my doorway, his expression troubled. I stepped aside and he entered the room, walked straight to the bed and sat down without a word.

My mind started racing, reviewing everything from the night before, any bad news which might have come since we'd parted company. He'd seemed in reasonably good spirits after the race.

"Chicco?" I tried using his nickname in hopes of seeing him smile.

No response.

"What's going on? What's happened?"

"*Rien*," he said, then shook his head and looked at me, dazed, a waking sleepwalker. "I mean, ah…" His brow furrowed as though he sought words too difficult to say. "Nothing. Nothing happened."

I sat beside him on the bed, keeping a little distance between us so he wouldn't feel pressured.

"Are you okay?"

"I'm fine." He nodded belatedly, making the gesture seem out of sync with the sentiment. "Could I lie down, though?"

"Of course." I stood and gestured for him to stretch out.

It's really difficult to think of a six-foot-something tall man as small, but that was how he seemed. I considered how childlike he'd seemed the night before, and how fragile his emotions appeared now. Was this the age gap talking, or was I really seeing him like this?

"Abby?"

"Yes?" I was mortified to realize I was about to ask if he wanted a glass of water, as my mother always had when I was small and worried about some intangible horror I couldn't put into words.

"Would you lie down with me? Next to me?"

"Sure, if that's what you want."

Mentally switching gears so fast I could almost hear them grinding, I went to the other side of the bed and lay down beside him. He was positively rigid, and I flashed back to the party game I'd played with my girlfriends growing up: *Light as a feather, stiff as a board*, we'd chant, trying to lift the girl who'd volunteered to be the 'liftee' with our fingertips.

Federico and I lay side by side, looking up at the ceiling. I was desperate to ask him what was going on, what had upset him.

Before I could ask, he spoke on his own.

"Jerzy had a…problem, today."

"What kind of problem?"

Silence spooled out instead of a reply, and I bit my tongue, determined to wait.

"His heart, they think. He's in hospital overnight, tonight."

I turned to face him. "I'm so sorry to hear that, Federico."

"Chicco," he corrected, the corners of his mouth twitching upward.

"Chicco," I echoed with a hint of a smile. "Will he be okay, do they think?"

He shrugged then looked over at me. "They think so."

"Well, that's good, then."

Federico reached out for me and I went to him, sliding carefully into his arms. In light of his news, I didn't want to seem too eager, although, selfishly, I was. He rolled onto his side to embrace me, his arms wrapping snug around me, holding me firmly to him.

I pressed my face to his chest to breathe in his scent, still so exotic to me. Warm spice mingled with clean cotton; a light, sporty scent beneath it all.

He slowly began to stroke my hair before his fingertips slid down my jaw to my chin, tilting my face up to his with unexpected tenderness. A lump formed in my throat until I couldn't speak. Something in his eyes stilled my voice as he gazed down at me, the bedside lamp lighting his dark hair from behind like a halo. He pressed closer, bringing his mouth to mine in a light, teasing kiss which left me wanting when we parted but remained side by side.

"Abby..."

"Yes?"

"This is what I want. For now."

"What do you mean?"

"*This*." He swept one hand over the two of us. "This is what I want. It's all I want."

"Oh."

"Is that all right with you?"

I smiled at him in spite of my confusion. "Yes, Chicco, of course."

Such relief flooded his features at my answer I was momentarily filled with a sort of pity for him. Had he really believed I'd say *no*?

"I'm going to close my eyes, Abby. Just for a little while. Don't worry, I'll wake up before it's time to go."

As though I'd want him to leave soon?

He gathered me to himself, his chest to my back, and curled up with his arm around my waist, his breath tickling my neck. The tension slipped out of him, exhaled away on each breath until they were slow and deep and steady.

He slept. I didn't.

Stage Fourteen

(185 km - Chiavenna, Italy - Altstätten, Switzerland)

The trip to Chiavenna was filled with solemn silence. Even James and Phil were subdued, and I wished they would do something to break the tension.

The official word from the team physician was that Jerzy would be fine, although the hospital's diagnosis of an angina attack was alarming. We all knew it didn't bode well for someone with Jerzy's temperament, but we thought he'd be back to work – riding in the team car, planning strategy and so on – in a day or so.

Brunn and Michael led the team meeting, detailing the day's stage, encouraging us to work at getting over the mountains. Not that any member of the team didn't know what to do. Pointless routine prevailed, along with a sense of being cast adrift in the absence of our fearsome leader.

Brunn was wearing the Royal, and for the first time in what felt like forever, jealousy nagged me. I wanted it back. It wouldn't happen today, but if I could make good gains once we were over the mountains...

I read over the stage profile, noting the height and length of the day's climbs. Up and over the Alps once again, this time into Switzerland. The city of Chur, where the route came out of the mountains, was where things could get *really* interesting. I mulled over the possibilities until we arrived in Chiavenna.

Confidence swept through me, but I wouldn't be able to take Brunn on until later. Much later.

I tried to clear my head while I warmed up. The press had gotten wind of Jerzy's condition and flocked to see how the team were "holding up." It was hard not to be annoyed – it wasn't like he had *died* or something, for fuck's sake.

What if he did die? I wondered. *Who would take over the team? Would we be as good?*

It wasn't until Brunn gave one particularly pushy reporter a piece of his mind – to my surprise, he echoed my angry sentiments almost exactly – that Michael called an end to the interviews.

I considered that this must be especially hard on Brunn. Jerzy wasn't just his manager, coach or *directeur sportif* – he was his best friend.

We'd never talked about the car accident they'd been in. Jerzy had been driving, Brunn a passenger along with Denis Kohl and Alan Shaughnessy, two young new additions to the team. Kohl's death and Shaughnessy's paralysis had been fodder for tragedy fetishists worldwide at the time, and I knew they'd start digging it up all over again, if they were this fervent about a blip in Jerzy's health.

The call to the line couldn't come quickly enough for any of us.

***

It was shortly past midnight when Federico had gone, but I'd stayed awake for a long while after, watching the digits on the alarm clock flick slowly by, minute by minute. I'd started missing him before his side of the bed had even grown cold.

Eventually I'd slipped under the covers, trying not to think of his hand on my belly, his face pressed to my neck, his body nestled against mine. There was precious little about the embrace which had been sexual, yet I still felt as though he'd managed to somehow possess me and claim me for his own in those simple, familiar gestures.

I wanted to feel all these things again. I wanted him to claim me for real, in whatever manner he needed to do it.

Sleep came eventually, but there was an ache in his absence I'd never anticipated. Every dream was about him, reliving every touch, every kiss we'd already shared, and imagining new ones. I made love to him again and again, both of us seeking to please each other in ways we hadn't yet really done.

When I awoke, it was only seven a.m. I got out of bed, showered, dressed and packed my things, feeling all the while as though I'd forgotten something important. Remnants of my dreams lingered, frustratingly and determinedly unfocused, beckoning me back to bed to dwell on images already fading from memory.

I wished they wouldn't. Until something actually happened between us, until we actually made love, this would be all I had. I'd already betrayed my marriage, in thought if not absolutely by deed. It was only a matter of time.

I remembered his words from the night before: "This is what I want. It's all I want." With the wave of his hand over us, it had almost seemed some sort of benediction, but now I wasn't so sure.

I paused in the last of my packing and sat on the bed, staring at the space where he'd been as though I'd find an answer there.

Did he mean he only wanted us, and what we shared? Or did he mean he only wanted to lie beside me – and that was all he'd *ever* want? Or – and this most likely of all – was I reading too much into it?

I wished I could breathe in his scent again, rued that I hadn't thought to taste his skin one more time before he'd gone.

The ache throbbed again, closer to my heart. I sat with my hand over it, noting the beats, the way they fluttered when I imagined making love with him.

Was it too much to hope for? Was I only setting myself up for disappointment?

"Don't ask too much, Abby," I said to myself. Hearing it helped, if only a little. "See where this goes. Take it for what it is."

My chest tightened when the words came to mind yet again.

Say it. Say this part out loud, too.

"A fling," I said resolutely to the empty room. "This is a *fling*."

Then I swallowed hard and finished packing my bag with shaking hands.

***

The stage went smoothly, but I wasn't the only member of the team to look expectantly around upon our arrival in Altstätten.

Jerzy's absence on the radio hadn't convinced us he wouldn't be at the finish. There was no sign of our team's guiding force in the usual chaos of the finish line or the cycling village. But Michael seemed less preoccupied, which I took to be a good sign.

In spite of the chases and tough climbs, I had no more than my usual, expected fatigue. The difficulties I'd had at the start of the Tour were far behind me. I'd finally found my legs.

And not a moment too soon.

Goosh came into the back of the bus a short while after I'd showered and crashed on the padded bench.

"This hasn't stopped bleeping all afternoon," he said, handing me my mobile. "I guess you've got a message or something."

I reached out for it, suddenly anxious. I'd left it on? And left it where *anyone* could find it?

"Thanks, Goosh. I appreciate it," I said, hoping he couldn't tell I was shaken.

It was ridiculous to worry about anyone seeing Abby's messages; they were numbers, nothing else. But an overactive imagination could turn those numbers into all sorts of things, and I wasn't ready to explain my relationship with her to anyone.

Besides, if Jerzy found out, I'd be off the team. There would be no second chance, no opportunity to appeal, just instant dismissal. I'd sneaked out after curfew to see a woman – in doing so I'd openly broken two of the principal rules of the team.

I reconsidered. Technically, it could be argued Abby and I hadn't actually *had* sex, so... A rule and a half had been, at the very most, fractured.

The only rule I'd yet to bend was the one about doping, and while I had no desire to do *that*, he'd doubtless see things differently. One form of deception was as bad as another.

On the way to St. Gallen, while the others went over the day's highs and lows, I made myself comfortable in my seat and read over Abby's messages.

I *liked* having these innocuous little reminders of her. I *liked* the fact she was keeping in touch with me. In a way, I enjoyed sneaking out to see her.

There was certainly a thrill in the element of danger – it was no different than being in the breakaway group, minutes away from the finish, with the group rushing up behind you gaining second by second.

I considered the metaphor in greater detail. Getting out of the hotel without being spotted was the breakaway. There was the same rush of energy, the same wondering if *this* is when they'll catch me, when it'll all be for naught?

Reaching her hotel and finding her in her room was the long, pain-and-pleasure thrill of the pursuit. Knowing your time is limited, and having to stay alert and aware, because any little problem – sudden fatigue, a flat tire, a broken chain – all of these things will give the group the chance to catch you or leave you behind.

Coming back was reaching the home stretch – the final kilometres where you have to give every last ounce of your energy and hope there's no-one else with that little bit extra to leave you behind.

Getting back into my room, safe and sound, was crossing the finish with my arms held high. But more than one victory has been claimed by a hundredth of a second.

Any cyclist can tell you that.

When dinner was finished and the meetings were over, Rom and I returned to our room. I showered and then shaved, waiting for Rom to fall asleep as usual.

Tonight was different. He stayed up, listening to his MP3 player and reading over his road book, scribbling in a little notebook from time to time. A flash of paranoia had me itching to see what his notes were, although I couldn't read Polish at all, certainly not in his chicken-scratch handwriting.

Finally, he switched off his light. I feigned sleep atop the bedclothes, still dressed, with my own copy of the road book on my chest. When his light went out, I opened my eyes and read the time on the alarm clock: 23:45.

Merde. I should have been on my way to Abby's by now.

I had to wait for him to fall asleep. Sound asleep.

It seemed to take a lifetime before his snores were regular, every breath deep and long. I eased out of bed and checked my pockets – wallet, room key, mobile phone, all present and accounted for. I put on my shoes and made my way out the door, checking the corridor to be sure no-one was out and about.

The coast was clear.

I made my breakaway.

*

I knocked softly, not wanting to draw attention to myself in the quiet corridor. I was unsure what to do with myself. My hands and feet were suddenly too large and unmanageable. Any posture I assumed was too posed, too unnatural. I forced myself to stop fidgeting so she wouldn't find me shuffling in some kind of bizarre dance should she look out the peephole in the door.

There was no movement inside the room. I took out my mobile and checked it. It was the right room number, the one she'd sent me a few hours ago. Could I be at the wrong hotel?

I have her number here; I'll call her.

As I raised the phone to dial, I finally heard something.

I stood in the corridor and looked around. Should I knock again or wait?

Knock. If it's the wrong room or something, I'll apologize and hope the occupant doesn't recognize me.

My knuckles only grazed the surface of the door as it opened, so my hand hung limp at my side while I stared dumbly at her.

She must have been sleeping – which made sense because it was shortly past midnight. Her hair was tousled from sleep but her eyes were bright and awake. She was still pulling on a long, pale grey robe which shimmered here and there in the ambient light. It looked like silk or maybe satin, and I almost reached out to her, wanting to touch the fabric to find out what it was.

"Chicco." There was mild surprise in the way she said my name. "Come in." I entered the room, watching her continue to adjust the collar of her robe while she closed the door. I caught a glimpse of her nightgown beneath it – in the light from bedside table it looked to be the same colour and fabric. My desire to touch it intensified.

My desire to touch *her* was even stronger than that.

"Abby, I'm sorry I'm so late – it really couldn't be helped. The meeting dragged on after dinner, and then Rom wouldn't go to sleep, and..."

When her eyes met mine again, what I wanted to say vanished. I imagined it all: removing her robe, pulling her gown over her head, sliding my hands over her body and feeling her warmth against my palms, my lips...

I tried to shake the images, but they'd grown claws and dug deep into my brain. Want was slipping precariously close to need –

would I ever be able to think clearly again if I didn't have her as soon as possible?

My mouth was on hers before I knew it, before I was aware I'd gathered her to myself in the middle of the room, my hands under her robe grasping at her hips to hold her to me.

Mon dieu, we'd barely had anything like a conversation first.

I'm never going to make it. I'll never resist her long enough.

Her hands were in my hair, her mouth opened to mine, her tongue stroking and parrying with mine as though we'd been doing this for a lifetime.

Never going to make it...

My hands moved up to her waist, out of the robe to untie the sash and then underneath again. I savoured the way her breasts filled my hands, the slippery surface of her gown pooling and sliding out from under my touch.

I drew her to me again and bumped the edge of the bed with the back of my legs before sitting down. She stood in front of me, her face and neck flushed, until I took her hands in mine and pulled her down on top of me.

She let out a startled little yelp and laughed. I laughed too, grateful I hadn't actually frightened her. I'd caught her easily and brought her astride me, and now I looked up at the desire written in her eyes.

Childishly insistent, a voice raged in the back of my mind: *Want!*

It would be so easy, too. She was willing, there was no denying it. I was here, with her, with only a few thin layers of fabric between us. That same insistent brainwave was already calculating how many moves were required to see things through to completion – the answer: five.

I was five gestures away from my most primal goal.

And I have to say no? Am I insane?

Yes. Yes, I am.

It was all happening too fast. If we kept on like this, I'd be in *pain* if we didn't see things through.

Not for the first time in my life, I cursed Jerzy and his theories and his methods: damn the whole lot. I'd proven he wasn't the all-knowing, all-seeing figure countless riders had come to believe he was, hadn't I? So didn't it stand to reason he wasn't infallible on this subject, too?

No. Goddamn it, it doesn't.

I couldn't take the chance.

***

While I gazed down at him, something shifted in his expression. It was subtle; a change in the angle of his eyebrow, or maybe in the tilt of his head, as though he were listening to a voice I couldn't hear.

With a light touch, he pushed my robe off my shoulders. I let it fall to the floor beside the bed. His hands slid down over me to push my nightgown up my legs, then stroked my hips, lingering to trace the outline of my panties.

He gently rolled us over so I lay beneath him, nestling him between my thighs. More kisses followed, longer and slower than before with his arousal undeniable.

I eased my hands under his shirt, tracing my fingertips slowly down along his spine, stopping only when I reached his cargo shorts. When I trailed them upward again he shuddered gently against me. He reached back and tugged the shirt over his head with one hand, then awkwardly pulled his arms out of the sleeves before flinging the garment onto the floor.

Now I was free to explore him, as I had begun to that night in his room, with no fear of interruption this time.

"Chicco?" I murmured his nickname into the curve of his neck, loving the heat of his skin beneath my lips.

"*Sì?*" He'd breathed the word more than he'd said it, and I couldn't help shivering as he traced his tongue lightly out to my shoulder and back to my throat again.

"Do you want..." I drifted off, pleasantly distracted by his kisses along the side of my neck.

"What...?"

"Do you want to make love?" I winced, grateful he wasn't able to see my face as I asked. Maybe 'make love' wasn't the right phrase? Maybe it was too loaded with implication and would convince him I believed this was more than it was?

He laughed gently, his breath warm and ticklish against my neck.

"Do I *want* to make love?" The disbelief in his voice, coupled with that quiet laughter, was reassuring. "Do you honestly mean to say you can't *tell*?"

"Well, I...you know." I laughed too, amazed at how natural it felt.

"*Amore*, I think it's pretty clear how I feel on the subject." He drew back to look down at me, still smiling.

While I'm sure he intended no irony in the words, I couldn't help blushing at the double entendre. How he *felt* was undeniable, pressed against me as he was.

"So, then...you *want* to." I tried to make it a statement, not a question. I wasn't sure how well I succeeded. My heart sank when a clear expression of doubt stole across his face.

"There's no question of that. Of course I *want* to, Abby, it's just... Um..." He moved away and lay on his side, facing me. "I want to, but I can't."

Puzzled by this, I rolled over to face him and spared the briefest possible glance to his body's obvious testimony to the contrary. "I'm not sure I understand. You *can't* make love?"

Now it was his turn to be puzzled. His brow knitted in confusion before his eyes widened with alarm.

"What? No! I mean I can – I *can* – but I'm not able. I mean, *allowed*. I'm not allowed to."

Federico was blushing furiously by the time he'd finished speaking, and he moved to lie on his back to stare at the ceiling, mortified.

"'Not allowed'? Now I *really* don't understand."

He sighed, closed his eyes and fell quiet for a few beats. "It's an old sports superstition. It's also one of the rules of the team. While we're riding a race, we're not supposed to, ah, *fraternize* with the opposite sex."

I had the feeling he was euphemising as delicately as possible. But I pushed him anyway. "And by 'fraternize', you mean..."

"Sex. We're not supposed to have sex."

I tried my best not to react. *What the hell? So what is all this about, then?*

"No sex. At *all*?"

He shrugged and looked at me again. "That's the tricky part. I mean, I know some of the guys have done some... *stuff*, you know, with their girlfriends or wives or whatever, but it's not what I want to do with *you*." The expression of alarm leapt into his face again. "I mean to say, that, uh... I *want* to do that stuff with you, but I couldn't *ask* you – I'm not asking you now, either, but I..."

He stopped short and another sigh, deeper and clearly heartfelt, followed. "Fuck," he muttered, passing one hand over his face, and I had to resist grinning.

"Chicco, please… I think I get it now." I sat up, looking around the room as if some sort of answer were hidden somewhere there. "No sex, then." I looked down at him and found his dark eyes watching me intently. "None at all?"

He shook his head and my heart dropped slowly into my stomach as the reality hit home.

This is the most ridiculous 'fling' there ever was.

Stage Fifteen

(170 km – St. Gallen, Swizterland – Freiburg im Breisgau,
Germany)

Rom was still snoring steadily in his bed when I woke to the grey light seeping through the curtains. I went to the window, pulled back the curtain and blearily looked out at St. Gallen, the colours of the town muted and subdued by the misty drizzle falling on the still-quiet streets.

Yawning, I closed the curtain and slunk back to my bed. Jerzy hadn't returned yet, and Michael wouldn't employ the bucket in his bid to wake us for the day, so I opted to chance a few more precious minutes sleeping.

That didn't happen. My thoughts turned toward Abby yet again, and I wasn't sure I was comfortable with that. It was beginning to feel like some sort of obsession. I was living for the end of every stage, hoping for her text message soon thereafter.

I'd been engaged to another woman a couple of weeks ago and I'd been willing to spend the rest of my life with Solange.

Was Abby a rebound and nothing more?

Dammit. I hadn't worried about this until Adrie had opened his mouth.

But if she's not a rebound, what is *she? Is this a short-term thing? What? Am I in* love *with her? So quickly? Impossible.*

I got out of bed again. I was awake; I might as well get ready for the day.

I'd wondered what Abby's reaction might be when I told her we couldn't consummate our relationship, at least for a while. She seemed to take the news well.

Of all Jerzy's rules, that was probably the one I was the most leery of challenging, in spite of Adrie's reassurances to the contrary. I didn't want to consider any of the alternatives he'd mentioned. If I started thinking about it, I'd begin the morning even more frustrated than I'd ended the night before.

***

Three e-mails. The first one I'd anticipated last night before Federico had arrived. It was from Derek, my publisher, asking for more of photos of the recent stages. Since I'd already sent some, I went on to the next message, also from Derek.

"Very good stuff, Abby – exceeding expectations on all counts so far. The shots you're getting on the road are great, too – as good as your finish line pics. Are you keeping a diary as well? Would you consider writing a blog of your experiences?"

I smiled to myself, relieved. At least Derek liked what he saw, which was proof that the extra effort of shooting en route to the finish line was worth it. I considered forwarding the message to Charles, proof that I was doing something of interest to others. Instead, before going on to the final new message, I wrote Derek and told him I'd be happy to do as he asked.

The final message made my hand tremble over the touchpad of my computer.

"Speak of the devil," I murmured, reading Charles' name in the 'from' field.

"I'm home with the 'flu," he wrote. *"Can't find the Lemsip. Didn't you buy any more?"*

My heartbeat steadied and my shaking ceased. "For pity's sake…" I sighed, and then typed: *"It's on the third shelf in the medicine chest. Where it always is. Where you never find it on the first look."*

I clicked *send*. I'd expected more guilt when I got my first message from him. What I felt instead was a strange sort of indulgence, almost a fondness for him.

Leave it to him to get the 'flu in July, and not to be able to find the bloody

Lemsip packets.

A new source of irritation emerged when I let my thoughts drift to Federico. Was I supposed to mother every man in my life? Was that my destiny with him, too?

Of course not. The one thing he hasn't asked of me is mothering, *that's for sure.*

I shut off the computer and considered further.

He hasn't asked for mothering, and he hasn't asked for sex. At least, not all-the-way sex.

Even though there was no-one to see, a quick blush heated my cheeks. Was I so repressed? "All-the-way sex?" I said aloud, disbelieving, resisting the urge to laugh, or maybe to cry. Or both.

Frankly, it was getting hard to tell which was which any more.

It was all so *frustrating.* Even in my own head the answers weren't as clear as I'd have liked. His explanation was simple, and clear. The team rules forbade him from sexual intimacy during a race. It wasn't unusual, if what I'd found online was any indication. I supposed it made sense. Expending energy in sex before a race probably wasn't the smartest thing for an athlete to do.

So, if I wanted to be with him I'd have to resign myself to that, even if it was torture to do so. When we were together, there was so much tension between us I barely rested until after he'd gone.

Frankly, his ability to rest, to sleep so peacefully and wake looking so refreshed, was rather annoying. I'd thought men couldn't be so at ease *not* having sex. Yet when he left each time he'd been happy as a lark. When we met again he was full of passion, ready to frustrate me nearly to tears all over again.

The least he could do was show a little more *suffering* on his part.

I drew a deep breath and exhaled slowly, laughing a little. I packed my computer away, stewing all the while.

Men. They always complain about trying to understand the female mind, but have they ever bothered to take a good look at themselves?

I took out my hobby camera and looked at the photo I'd taken of Federico in the pub. He looked relaxed, confident, at ease with himself and the world. I had taken the photo only – what? – a week ago, give or take a day?

Looking at that simple snapshot filled me with such longing I could hardly breathe. I wanted him beyond rational thought or reason. I wanted him more than I'd ever wanted Charles.

Even if nothing ever happened with Federico, this much was certain: I couldn't go back.

Not from here.

***

The press crush after the race was the usual mess, but the only topic of interest was rehashing the accident from five years ago. All the morbid and depressing details were explored anew, played for drama as though they hadn't already been discussed *ad nauseum* before.

Brunn went silent and continued brooding all the way from Freiburg im Breisgau to Colmar.

None of us were happy with how the interviews had gone. The insistence that Jerzy's health was at a tipping point – that he surely wouldn't be back, that he was much more gravely ill than any of us knew – was enough to make me give my own curt response:

"Well, good thing you're around! I'm quite happy it was you to tell us he's on the way out."

That was when Michael had called a halt to everything and ushered us onto the bus.

At our hotel, the road was so narrow the bus nearly blocked the other lane. The hotel was absurdly small, painted in a sugary pastel blue which looked like cake frosting. Or maybe I was still hungry. We still hadn't had a proper meal.

Michael bounded off the bus and went inside while we collected our things and filed onto the pavement. We found him standing by the door, next to the pretty blonde handing off keys to each member of the team as they entered.

"Take your bags up, lads, then come back down for dinner," he called, indicating the doors to the meeting room across from the stairwell. There was no elevator.

"So who am I rooming with, then?" James held his key up so Michael could see. "Phil's got a different room this time."

"You're all on your own tonight." Michael said. "This place has pretty small rooms, too. Sorry if it's a bit cramped, but I'm assured it's clean and comfortable, and we're the only ones staying here. Go up and get settled in."

I went to the stairs with Rom following close behind. I was already planning my night out – how much easier would sneaking out be if I didn't have a roommate to worry about? – when I noticed Rom was looking less than pleased. My pleasure at the unexpected assist of a private room must have showed, because the disappointment in his face deepened when I glanced back at him.

At the landing of the second floor I paused, checking for my room. Rom continued on his way to the third floor, throwing me another disappointed glance on his way.

"*Ahi*, Rom," I called, and he turned to look down at me from the half-landing. "*Qual è il problema?*"

He blinked in incomprehension, shrugged and then shook his head. "*Niente*, Ciccio. Nothing."

"*Dai, dimmi.*" I gestured for him to stop and talk but he shook his head.

"*Nie musisz się tak cieszyć ze jesteś sam.*" He muttered this to himself, then looked at me again before saying in English, "You have not to be so *happy* for being alone."

With that, hauling his carry-on bag behind him, his larger duffel bag slung over his shoulder by the strap, he trudged up the stairs and out of my view.

Shaking my head I went down the hall and found my room around the corner, at one end of a t-junction.

Michael wasn't kidding. The room *was* small. Calling it a room was pretty generous; it was more like a monk's cell. Square, spare and clean with was a single bed, a simple bedside table with a small lamp on top, and a desk with a chair which I didn't trust to hold my weight if I tried it. At least there was a private bath, which meant I wouldn't have to deal with James' twisted sense of 'personal space' in a communal bathroom.

The room was perfect, particularly since I had no intention of being here for the whole night.

I opened the curtains and looked outside. I counted five different pastel colours on as many façades of the half-timbered houses lining the cobbled street. The wooden beams tracing designs on the outsides of the buildings gave the place a distinctly German atmosphere, though the top-heavy designs of many houses made them look as though they might topple over at the slightest provocation.

I looked at the uneven, overlapping roofs across the street, and I wondered whether Abby found the sights in the old town charming or not.

Okay, first things first; a massage, a shower, change, and get downstairs for dinner. Then I'll sort out how to get to Abby tonight.

***

Federico draped his long legs over the arm of the sofa next to the window after dropping onto the cushions hard enough to make the air *whoosh* out of them. I laughed a little as I crossed the room to sit down on the edge of the bed facing him.

"This *was* a long day for you, wasn't it?"

He nodded and closed his eyes, rubbing them wearily. "Yes, it was." His accent was thicker than usual, and when he opened them, his eyes seemed unfocused. "Not the ride. Just the interviews, and the questions about Jerzy, and all the rest of it. The *best* part of the day is always when I'm on the bike."

He turned to face me, his eyes gaining focus at last.

"And when I'm with you."

He swung his legs off the arm of the sofa and sat up to lean toward me and look me in the eye. I didn't realize I was mimicking his posture until he reached across to take my hands in his.

"Abby?"

I swallowed hard, suddenly apprehensive. "Yes?"

"I think I'm happiest when I get your texts."

I couldn't resist smiling. "Thank you."

Still holding my hands, he moved to sit beside me. I turned to him so he wouldn't release me, then realized he didn't intend to.

"Would you be upset if we lay down now?"

I shook my head. "Well, no."

He leaned closer to me, brushing his lips lightly over mine, a barely-there kiss maddening in its softness. I could smell his shampoo, his soap – even a trace of the shaving cream he must have used a couple of hours before.

I tried not to follow when he drew away, feeling foolish for seeking more. There was no denying that was what I wanted.

He slid his fingers back to stroke my hair away from my face as he kissed me again. His kiss had the same gentle, delicate touch. It was all I could do to keep from returning the kiss more forcefully than he gave it.

"You're shaking," he murmured when we parted. "Are you okay?"

"I'm fine. Really."

He wasn't convinced. His gaze was too inquisitive, too sharp, before his features relaxed into the weary expression he'd worn a few moments ago.

"Please, Chicco," I gestured toward the pillows, temptingly plumped at the head of the bed. "Let's relax for a while."

He sighed and drew away from me before going to lie down, nodding all the while. The way he sank into the pillow, face-first, the rest of his body following piece by piece, said much of his fatigue.

"I guess now it's my turn to ask." I joined him after he got comfortable. His process involved a bit of flailing about, his limbs seeming almost out of his control before he settled on his side, facing me. "Are *you* okay? You seem much too tired."

"Like I said, there was a lot to do tonight."

"All right." I faced him, bunched a pillow up in the crook of my arm and watched as he did the same.

"Abby?"

"Yes?"

"Will this…?" He leaned toward me, sweeping his hand over the space between us on the king-size bed. "*Can* this be enough for you?"

The anxiety behind his eyes pulled at my heart. His gaze shifted as though trying to read my own, and I could feel the twitching of the muscle in his arm when I reached out to lightly brush it with my fingertips.

"It is, and it will be, as long as necessary."

"*Grazie*, Abby."

I nodded and nestled down into my pillow, still watching him. He nestled down too, his eyelids fluttering.

"I'm going to close my eyes, Abby," he whispered. "Just for a little while."

"Okay," I whispered back.

He smiled, half his face obscured from my view by his pillow, bringing me a surge of tenderness. I'd said it to placate him, so he wouldn't feel pushed or pressured, but now I realized I meant it: I *was* content with things the way they were.

I was satisfied having him there with me, knowing there was no need to taunt or tease or lure him, knowing that all he wanted was to *be* with me. We shared a bed, we kissed, we touched and that was all.

And it was enough.

Sure, *more* would happen – it was bound to, with two adults who were attracted to one another, who had already explored each other's boundaries in so many ways – but there was no blind rush into doing so.

Knowing this was enough to give every brief touch, every tiny caress a greater weight than it might have held. When he reached out to trace my cheek with his fingertips, the heat of his touch went deeper than I'd thought possible. I closed my eyes to savour it, rising up to be closer to his touch.

There was no hurry, and that made me want him more than ever.

"We will make love, *amore*," he said softly, closing his eyes again. "I promise."

***

Abby looked so relaxed when she slept, I envied her. It wasn't possible for me to have such a divinely peaceful expression as she did.

I had awakened promptly – as always – when the three hours I'd allowed myself had passed. As soon as I opened my eyes to the soft yellow lamplight, I found her lying opposite me, her face peaceful in sleep.

She was beautiful. There was no one thing about her, no particular combination of her features in the right mix or measure. She simply *was*, and I was as drawn to her as ever.

Her cheeks were soft and round, practically begging for someone to kiss them. The tender, pink pout of her lips was equally beguiling, even as she slept. She shifted position and her dark hair fell over her cheek. A quiet ache stirred deep inside me. I longed to touch her, to wake her with a kiss, but I didn't dare.

Not yet.

It hadn't been like this with Solange. I'd known she was interested when I'd noted how her kisses had lingered too long, how she'd grasped my arm when handing me the flowers or stuffed toy prize on the podium. We'd met each time I stood there, and we'd met a few other times, too. Eventually I asked if she'd like to go out when the race was finished. She'd declined – officially it wasn't permitted – but once the Tour was over she found me and said 'yes'.

She'd never questioned if the offer still stood. She assumed I still wanted her. Of course I did.

Solange's interest encouraged my interest. She was beautiful, which helped. If I'd been asked what made her beautiful, I had a long list of attributes to tick off: her eyes; her hair; those long, shapely legs which never seemed to end...

Abby was completely different. One look in her eyes was all it had taken. I was snared and didn't want to be free.

Which made it all the more difficult to pull myself away from her side to go back to my tiny room several blocks away.

I brushed her hair back, leaned in close and kissed her cheek lightly, trying not to wake her. The ache to stay with her subsided, but only a little. Her eyelids fluttered open and she squinted sleepily up at me.

I moved to shade her eyes from the light. Guilt gnawed at my stomach, intensifying the longer I watched her.

You deserve better, Abby.

"I have to go."

She nodded, still sleepy but more alert. "Okay."

I kissed her cheek again, dipping lower to brush her lips with mine, fearful of giving too full a kiss, convinced I'd never leave if I did.

"I'll see you tomorrow," I whispered, and she nodded silently.

I drew away from her, too slowly, losing my will to go. I paused at the door, refusing to say the words I longed to.

It was too soon, even if the words were proof of my feelings. It wasn't fair to say them now, not when I was leaving her again. Not when she wasn't mine and mine alone.

The street outside her hotel was quiet, save for the idling engine of the taxi I'd arranged for on my way there. I shivered, wishing I'd thought to bring my windbreaker with me. The air was surprisingly cold for mid-summer.

I slid my key card through the slot next to the front door of the hotel. The lobby was empty, but that was no surprise at nearly four a.m. The night desk clerk wasn't there. I figured he was probably lounging elsewhere.

Climbing the stairs, I considered the stage to come that morning. Leaving from Colmar, it would be long but mostly flat –

the kind of stage I could do in my sleep. If not for having to work for Brunn, it might have been a pleasurable ride.

No matter. My chance would come soon.

I paused at the landing of my floor, listening keenly for any sign of life. There was nothing, and so I padded my way along the corridor, down to the t-junction where I turned left.

I should have looked right.

I froze, feeling a gaze focused upon my back. I didn't have to look to know – it had only been a matter of time before this would happen. Besides, I was later than usual, thanks to my false sense of security in coming back to a private room. He was always up early. Our paths were bound to cross.

A thousand excuses went through my mind, each and every one of them something I'd rehearsed a thousand times en route to one encounter with Abby or another. Of those thousand, I knew none of them would stand up to the scrutiny of Jerzy's interrogation.

Shame and defiance struggled for the upper hand as I turned to face him, my shoulders slouched, my head lowered. My muscles thrummed with tension, waiting for the verbal blows – if not physical ones – to follow.

Silence.

I raised my head enough to meet his eyes and found only disappointment. We regarded each other for what seemed an eternity. The only sounds in the hotel corridor were my breathing and the rustling of his windbreaker jacket when he folded his arms across his chest.

When he sighed, I flinched.

I opened my mouth and he raised one hand swiftly in a demand for silence. The other hand held a sample collection cup.

"I don't want excuses. When you get on the bus, you give a sample. After the race, too. Now get to bed. You have a stage to ride, in…" he checked his watch and shook his head before continuing, "…six hours. If you don't do well today, don't worry about the piss test. Just start packing."

"It's not that." My pride demanded at least some protest.

"No? Why else would you be coming in to your room at four a.m., Ciccio? Where do you have to be in the middle of the night?" He spread his hands, a strangely benevolent gesture, as though he were about to bless me and the corridor and everything in it. "Your woman broke things off, didn't she? Or did she change her mind and come running back to you?"

"It's not Sunny." The words felt ineffective and pointless on my lips.

"Enlighten me, then."

I froze.

"The truth," he cautioned, and I folded my arms over my stomach, feeling sick.

I lowered my head again and closed my eyes. My reason was still one of the worst possibilities there were.

"A woman," I murmured, lost. "I went to see a woman."

He sighed again, the sound heavy with dismay. "Oh, Ciccio, no... A prostitute?"

"*Ma, va...* No!" It came out louder than I'd intended, and I bit the inside of my cheek in frustration. "Someone I met a while ago. *After* Sunny." Why I'd needed to clarify this, I had no idea. "We didn't *do* anything."

"So why go there? If you aren't going to fuck her, what's the point?"

"I..." I shrugged and fell silent.

"Who is she? One of the podium girls?"

I shook my head.

"Who, then?"

Again, I shook my head.

"It's important for me to know. If you turn up sick in the next few days –"

"She's not like that! She's –" I stopped short, amazed at how easily he'd drawn me out.

"She's what? A fan? A camp follower? What?"

I shook my head, more fervently this time.

"I know these girls, Ciccio; I know them better than you do." He clenched one fist and raised it, not in a threatening gesture, but in one of frustration. "This is the worst fucking sport in the world – and you fuckers are the most fucking difficult to get to understand this – but you can't run off with these girls whenever you like. They don't like *you*, they like *all* of you, and they have a different one of you every night. Do you have any idea what kind of filth–"

"She's not like that," I repeated, trying to keep calm. "I know she's not. This is different, this is–"

"What, are you *in love*?"

"I didn't say that—"

"What kind of whore is worth sneaking out? What kind of tramp convinces you that it's worth losing your place on the team? She'd better be a damned good lay, Ciccio."

"She's not – we don't –"

"The truth, I said, remember that? The *truth* is what I want to hear from you next, and nothing else."

He met my eyes and I couldn't look away. I'd never felt so threatened or exposed in my life – at least, not since I'd left home. My heart was beating too fast, too hard, making me dizzy and nauseous.

"We don't fuck. We don't do *anything*. Well, we talk. We sleep." My face burned, acid filled my stomach and cold sweat broke on the back of my neck. Was I ashamed because I *didn't* have sex with her?

"You're joking. You really expect me to believe that?"

"I can't prove it, but yes, I do."

He stepped closer to me, his gaze intense. "Is she under-age? Be honest, because if I find out you're –"

"No… No. She's not *under-age*," I hissed in spite of myself. *Mon dieu, what kind of sick bastard does he take me for?* "She's older, actually."

"Older than who?" he asked, taking a step back.

"Me. She's married."

Jerzy regarded me for a long while, chewing his lower lip and scowling as he did so.

"Wait here. Don't move."

He disappeared down the hall and I leaned against the wall, my strength draining through my feet. A multitude of bad scenarios rushed through my head before he returned with a small plastic sample collection cup in hand.

"Let's go," he said, gesturing toward my room. I stood as straight as I possibly could and walked on unsteady legs, feeling like a condemned man facing his doom. I unlocked my door and Jerzy shoved the cup into my hand. "Fill this."

He stood in the doorway while I did my best to produce a sample, my resentment growing every moment. I'd told him the fucking *truth*, hadn't I?

I closed the lid on the cup and sealed it before handing it over. Jerzy's level gaze met mine as he took it from me, his expression grim as ever.

"Don't do this – whatever it is – again. Wake-up call is seven a.m."

He turned on his heel and marched out of my room and down the corridor to disappear around the corner.

I closed the door and barely managed to make it across the tiny room before my legs turned to jelly and I collapsed onto the bed. Now someone knew everything. He didn't seem to believe it, but he knew.

At least I was still on the team.

Stage Sixteen

(200 km – Colmar, France – Heidelberg, Germany)

"Right. Now we're in the flats, things should settle down a bit." Jerzy stood in his customary place between the prongs of the "U" the tables made, and the team sat in theirs. With Brunn one side of me and Rom on the other, plus the frequent sharp glances Jerzy sent my way, I'd never felt so trapped.

He must have kept our encounter to himself; no one gave me as much as a sideways look. Well, almost no one. From time to time Brunn's cool, appraising gaze slid over me, and he arched one eyebrow with a hint of curiosity, but that was all.

It was enough to make me wonder if he and Jerzy had talked.

Today's stage would be long but probably not too difficult. The biggest problem was likely to be the heat: temperatures were expected to be high.

There was nothing extraordinary about the day, except for the fact I'd have to give another sample that morning.

"I don't want any showboating today," Jerzy continued. "No showing off. No impulsive riding. This stage calls for workmanship. Be practical. Our only real concerns are Schlessinger and Legarreta. If anyone else breaks away, let him burn himself out unless I say otherwise."

Like the rest of the team, I nodded agreement, but he was stating the obvious. It wasn't like we'd be distracted by Legarreta –

an astounding climber who had, let's be honest, gotten lucky and wasn't any real threat. No, this race was really down to three riders: Schlessinger, Brunn, and me.

The only consequence I'd anticipated for defying the curfew was that of being thrown off the team. I'd never considered anything else – and testing was a natural reaction to a cyclist sneaking around.

Or, rather, it *would* be, had I been performing absurdly well for the last two weeks. As much as it pained me to admit, I knew I wasn't doing that well. I hadn't flown up and over the mountains or burned up the flats more than I had before. I was riding better than ever, but not enough to make anyone believe I was doping.

It was a stain marring the whole sport, painting us all with the same sticky brush. Whether we rode clean or dirty didn't matter. In the eyes of many casual sport fans, we're all the same. If one does it, the others must do it too.

Having never had a positive test result on your record was one of the things Jerzy watched for when considering new riders. If there was even a whiff of suspicion, Jerzy steered clear of him.

Those safeguards served the team well. *Alta VeloCidad* had the cleanest record in the sport, on every level. We were the envy of many teams, and countless cyclists were desperate sign on at the end of every season.

We got results without chemical assistance. Scientific assistance, yes, but our abilities were down to diet and training. No funny business of any kind.

So it was galling to have to march onto the bus and contribute a sample beyond those required by any governing body. The team would have no idea why I'd been singled out. It would appear totally random since no-one else had been asked to do the same in previous days, and no-one would be asked later on.

No, it wasn't galling: it was *humiliating*.

Jerzy knew it. That's why he demanded it in spite of my explanation, which I still wasn't sure he believed.

I regretted telling him about Abby, but at the time I hadn't been able to stop myself. I *wanted* someone to know, but why had I gone to the worst possible person to share my secret?

He wouldn't care about her being married – thank God we didn't have any 'morals clause' in the team contracts – but now he had something extra to hold over my head, and he'd never hesitate to use it if he needed to.

Finally the team meeting wrapped up and we filed out of the conference room, heading for the bus. In spite of everything, I felt good. I looked forward to warming up, to getting moving, to starting the day for real.

But first, I'd have to piss in that fucking cup.

***

I trudged along the pavement, feeling slightly sick, the weight of my camera bag dragging me down. At nine a.m., the day was already muggy. The heat radiated off the concrete and seemed to wrap itself around me to cling, humid and close, to any bare skin it found. Even my lightweight trousers and my blouse beneath my bright, Tour-issue vest felt heavy after I'd walked nearly half a mile from where I'd parked my car.

While I didn't like leaving my suitcase in the boot of the car, it was the most practical solution to the problem of getting to Heidelberg early enough to check in and be ready before the end of the stage.

I pushed through the crowd, trying to avoid bumping anyone unnecessarily with the equipment I carried, but not hesitating to do so when they pretended obliviousness at my need to pass by. My temper was already frayed and I hated feeling so testy.

I was about to have words with a particularly obtuse group blocking the sidewalk when someone touched my shoulder. I turned sharply, resenting the violation – however mild – to find Pascal smiling at me.

He looked remarkably fresh in spite of the beads of sweat on his forehead, and he reached up to palm them away from beneath his pale brown fringe before he greeted me.

"*Bonjour*, Abigail. May I offer you some help?" He gestured toward my bags.

I sure hope I don't regret this.

"Um, okay. Are you sure you don't mind? Don't you have to carry your own things?"

"No, I'm already set up. My assistant is keeping an eye on things, right over there," he added, pointing past the inflatable archway and across the street. "Why don't *you* join us? There is plenty of room."

"Well, I — okay," I finished stupidly; he was already on his way, forging a path through the crowd so I could follow in his wake.

Once we'd reached the other side of the street, he began preparing his equipment. I busied myself with my camera bag, feeling self-consciously aware of his pretty assistant, a young blonde girl of about twenty or so.

"Abigail." Pascal indicated the girl with a tilt of his head. "This is my daughter, Justine. She is my assistant today."

"Only for today?" I asked, and the girl dipped her head becomingly, a faint blush under the sun-kissed skin of her cheeks.

"*Aujourd'hui, seuls, oui,*" she answered and I looked to Pascal for a translation.

"She says 'yes, for today only'. Justine understands English, but she is shy of using it." Taking my camera from me and giving it a quick, appreciative examination, he shook his head. "I tell her to try more often, but what can I do?"

When he faced me again, a cheery smile spread across his lips and he flipped his fringe back out of his eyes.

"And so? Where is your husband this morning?"

"At the hotel," I answered automatically, while he turned toward Justine and gave her some money. He spoke to her in rapid French and, nodding, she disappeared into the crowd behind us.

"He is at the hotel *again*? Does he ever leave?"

"Sometimes," I said, and Pascal laughed like it was the funniest thing he'd ever heard.

"So he is a man of leisure? We should all be so lucky, eh? Then I could take photos for a hobby instead of a living."

He laughed again and I couldn't help laughing too, even though I wasn't sure what was so funny. His laughter was infectious.

Justine returned with a few bottles of water in hand and gave me one of them. The others she gave to Pascal or stashed away in a small cooler next to his camera bag on the pavement at his feet.

"*Merci,*" I said, twisting the cap. "You'll let me pay you back, of course."

"*Non,*" Pascal answered, and erupted into laughter again. "Chivalry is not yet dead, *madame*; at least, not for me."

I drank some of the water and laughed. "That's good to hear." I plucked at my blouse and vest, trying to get some cooler air on my skin and failing miserably at it. "I really appreciate your help, by the way. This heat is exhausting."

He nodded and knelt to fiddle with his camera, then looked up at me. Before I understood what he was doing, he'd turned the camera toward me and pressed the shutter button.

"Oh, come on! Didn't you say chivalry wasn't dead?"

"I did. How is that not chivalrous? I took a photo of a pretty lady standing in the sun."

"A *sweaty* lady," I corrected with a smile, "who wasn't ready to be photographed." I shook my head and took another drink of my water. "I wish you'd let me pay you back."

He laughed again. "I'm telling you, please, do not worry. The cost of a bottle of water won't break me. And what is more, a lady doesn't *sweat*," he said the word as though it were the most vulgar thing he could think of. "She 'perspires', *non*?"

Justine mumbled something incomprehensible in French and Pascal laughed harder. I smiled in spite of myself, still with no idea what was so funny.

The announcement came over the PA system to call the riders to the line. Pascal nudged me as the teams rolled in to stand in front of us. The Tour officials' car was parked a short distance away.

"Here, take this. I can't have you passing on in front of me."

Befuddled, I turned toward him and found him proffering another bottle of water before I understood what he'd meant.

"I think you mean 'passing *out*' in front of you," I said. "Not 'passing on'."

He looked confused as he considered this correction, and then he burst out laughing once again – this time loud enough to draw the attention of other spectators and even a few of the riders.

"Ah, *pardon*, you are right. Although the alternative is much, much worse."

***

Heat hung over the peloton while we stood waiting for the roll out. I was tempted to spray myself with a blast of water from one of my bottles in an attempt to cool off. Before long the bottles would be warm too. Relief, of a sort, might come once the group got moving and kicked up a breeze.

Chatter amongst the riders was high-spirited as ever. Most of us were glad for the long, flat stage today. There was less pressure today, just a need to be careful, to avoid any mishaps that would have us left behind.

Attilio had the job of chasing. He'd jump onto the breakaway group, should one form, and do his best to stay out for the duration. Our sprinters were hopeful for another chance at points glory now we were riding in the plains.

Even with a hundred different conversations going on immediately within the group, a loud guffaw rose above the din. I wasn't the only one to turn toward the sound, curious to see if there was some particularly amusing activity taking place among the spectators. In the travelling-circus atmosphere which engulfed the race it wouldn't be unusual.

I was startled to spot Abby chatting with a laughing man. Another loud burst of mirth proved he was the one I'd heard before.

Jealousy surged through me. She'd said her husband had gone home, so who was *he*? I watched her, forgetting myself, where I was, and why.

Her hair was pulled away from her face in a high ponytail which shifted and swayed as she chatted with the laughing man. From time to time she cast a cursory glance over my way, her gaze sliding over the peloton and passing me by without hesitation. I watched her until someone bumped me with his elbow, and I turned to find Rom looking at her, too.

His face was full of sympathy, and I looked away, returning my attention to the start line. The officials were in the car and looking back at the riders, getting ready for the roll out.

Never mind. I'll ask her about him tonight.

With that, I put my thoughts of Abby away, determined to focus on the ride. I had a stage to complete before I could see her, anyway.

***

After the roll-out, Pascal insisted on buying me a coffee. When I protested, thinking I had the perfect excuse – a coffee? In this heat? – he overrode me and selected a café with iced coffees on offer. We chatted for a while. I had to resist the urge to look at my watch in an obvious way throughout our discussion. I didn't want to be rude, but I *did* have to drive to Heidelberg to be ready for the stage's finish, and I'd harboured some hopes of getting more shots along the way, as well.

After seemingly endless idle chatter, I worked up my nerve to make my excuses: I needed to get back to the hotel, to collect my husband, to leave for Heidelberg.

"Would you like me to walk you back to your hotel, Abigail?"

Oh, shit.

"Well, I —"

"Papa," Justine interrupted, resting one hand on Pascal's arm. "*Nous avons à faire, aussi.*"

Even if I didn't understand what she'd said, it was clear she'd understood my dilemma on some level.

Pascal nodded and patted her hand. "My daughter is right. We need to get ready for the drive to Heidelberg. Perhaps we'll see you there?"

"It's quite likely." I stood and offered my hand for a farewell shake, but Pascal stood and gave me a swift kiss on each cheek, his hands resting lightly on my shoulders.

I looked down at Justine, still seated at the tiny café table. "Is he always like this?" I asked, chuckling.

She grinned and gave me a small shrug. "*Oui.*"

Oh, good; it's not me, then.

"*Au revoir*, Abigail. We'll see you this afternoon."

I gave a little goodbye wave and picked up my bags, heading for the door. Pascal and Justine waved in return, but Pascal added a quick wink.

I made my way back to my car, glad I hadn't wound up too far behind schedule, after all.

I stopped the car along the race route, outside Bruchsal, and waited with a handful of spectators for the peloton to pass. After the last riders and the final vehicle in the caravan rolled by, I hurried to my car. I aimed for the nearest back road that could get me ahead of the race, knowing I had to leapfrog the race again.

A giddy sense of excitement crept up as I followed another photographer's car to the next possible stop, tempered only with the hope Pascal wouldn't catch me out.

When I arrived in Heidelberg and parked the car in front of the hotel, a sudden realization struck me. I'd had to turn down the music before stopping the car; I'd been singing along as I drove.

How long had it been since I'd done that? How long had it been since I'd been free enough to belt out a tune while driving?

Despite everything that had happened in the last few days, despite the fact that Charles and I were, for all concerns, finished – I was happy.

Happy! Free! I thought giddily, and a glimpse at the genuine smile on my face in the rear-view mirror confirmed things.

I checked in and got my parking pass, then went about settling in. After a shower at the speed of light, I allowed myself to ponder the evening to come.

My cheeks ached from smiling. Picturing Federico asleep next to me on the bed caused a flurry of pleasant warmth in my stomach.

Anticipation welled up in me until I trembled from it. I lay down on the neatly-made bed, closed my eyes and willed myself to be still. I didn't sleep, there wasn't time for that, but soon enough I was on my way to the finish line to wait for the arrivals.

I hadn't been so excited about anything in years.

***

Jerzy looked up as I approached the team bus, his surly expression a harbinger of certain doom. We'd lost the sprint after an unexpected attack from Moravec, the same neo-pro who'd taken the ninth stage. He'd swung out after riding Alvaro's back wheel nearly all the way to the finish and left him half a bike length behind.

"Another, Ciccio," he said, tapping me on the shoulder with the empty specimen cup. I reached back to take it without looking at him.

"I just did this," I said, keeping my voice low. "I can't make again, not so soon."

"Same old song, Ciccio. Hell, throw in a couple of expletives and you've got a musical. Whenever you can, then. Provided it's *before* you leave this bus."

I turned to meet his level gaze. A vision of flipping the cup in his face, collecting my things and leaving came to me.

Maybe after the Tour. Maybe not even then.

Instead, I slouched my way back to the toilet and did my best to produce a sample.

When I came out he was waiting next to the door in a casual

pose so patently contrived it was insulting. I bit my tongue and carefully put the sealed cup in his hand before I went to sit down.

I picked up my mobile and turned it on, waiting to see if he would say anything. He didn't; he went to his own chair at the front of the bus and waited for the others to come up.

Nonetheless, his gaze remained on me as I scrolled to the message list on my phone. I knew I should get used to the feeling, too. As expected, Abby's message was waiting:

3. 0. 3.

At first glimpse I read it as 'S.O.S.'. I slumped in my seat, considering my options. I could try to sneak out again, but chances were Jerzy would have everyone watching out. He wouldn't specify watching for *me*, but I'd get caught if I tried.

I could try to see her at dinner, but I suspected that plan wouldn't work, either. What if he followed me or, more likely, had me followed? Compromising Abby wasn't something I was willing to do.

There was only one option I could take.

'Can't come tonight. Maybe tomorrow.'

I hit *send* with my thumb and put the phone away. A little voice murmured in the back of my mind, and I tried unsuccessfully to ignore it.

This is how it ended with Sunny.

***

I took out my computer and plugged it in. No sooner had I sorted the other contents of the computer bag out on the bed than my mobile began its sing-song chirping.

A message.

Already smiling, I turned to the bedside table where my phone rested within easy reach. It had taken him a little longer than usual to respond, but I could forgive a small delay.

As I read Federico's message, my spirits deflated. I hadn't realized how much I'd come to count on seeing him, on having him come to stay a while with me each night. It had happened so quickly, so easily, I hadn't really taken note of it. I'd begun to take it for granted.

Until now, when I understood how fragile our arrangement actually was. He'd gone back so late last night, had he been caught coming in? I read his message again:

'Can't come tonight. Maybe tomorrow.'

That was all he'd written. There was no further explanation, no more detail. I closed the message and sat down on the bed, turning my phone over and over in my hands. Try as I might, I couldn't 'hear' his voice in those words. They were too abrupt, too terse. Though he wasn't the most verbose person I knew, he had never been so curt with me.

Don't read too much into it.

I turned on my computer and balanced it on my lap, then started flicking through my photos for the day. I paused on one of the shots of Federico and smiled, considering how handsome he was. How handsome they *all* were.

Of course, when you're young enough, you're attractive by default.

I opened the browser and went to my 'favourites' list to click on the *Alta VeloCidad* page. I read his biography there and sighed to myself. *Who am I trying to fool here? He's a kid, for Heaven's sake. He won't be interested in me once we've had sex anyway. He'll get bored and move on in no time.*

I double-checked his birth date on the page, a petty, masochistic act. At twenty-nine he was ten full years younger than me. Why would a young, famous athlete ever be interested in a married woman ten years his senior? It was ludicrous to think this was anything more than a momentary distraction for him.

But he promised we'd make love. At least there's that.

Then again, what good was a promise when it took risking one's career to make it come true? He wasn't crazy enough to do that.

A new email arrived in my inbox. I stiffened, seeing it was from Charles. "What now?" I muttered before opening it.

"Miss you," it said, and my heart gave a little twist before I read the rest. *"When are you getting back from Leeds?"*

He'd sent it to the wrong email address.

I put the computer down on the bed and curled up next to it. Had I really felt so carefree earlier in the day? Had I really been so at ease with what Charles had done?

I wasn't now. That little reminder of what had set all this in motion hurt.

It hurt like hell.

***

I couldn't sleep. I kept thinking about her, about how good it felt to be beside her, to reach out and find her there. I pictured her asleep, her dark lashes on her cheek, the way her hair fell across her face, the soft sound of her breathing.

This was all so unfair to her. Maybe she was better off trying to patch things up with her husband. Surely they could work things out and then she could have a real relationship.

Not one like *this*.

Now that I'd seen how tough it could be, I understood why Solange had got fed up and moved on. What good was a lover you never saw? What was the point in a relationship when you couldn't be with the one you loved?

Sure, Adrie managed things; he'd had a family with his wife who seemed to adore him. But he was firmly in the minority. None of the rest of us had had any real success in our personal lives. For us, it was all about the team – about winning, about pushing ourselves to be the best around. It was all we needed, all we worked for.

And all of a sudden, it wasn't enough. It wasn't even *close* to being enough.

The temptation to get out of bed and go to her was surprisingly strong. I sat up, pushed the blankets aside and put my feet on the floor. I began to visualize the journey to Abby's door, every step of the way, but the image I wanted didn't come to mind.

All I could see was stepping out my door and Jerzy – or Michael, or even Horst or someone else – spotting me right away. There wouldn't be another pardon if it happened again. Without a trace of doubt, Jerzy would never let it slide again.

But he let it go today, and he's never done that, *either.*

I couldn't count on that happening again, though. The risk was too great, and I was too close.

I was too close to the fucking Royal to blow it so casually. This was my dream, and this year was my year. I knew it. I could feel it.

This was it.

Gritting my teeth I got back into bed and pulled the covers over me. Rom continued snoring, not disturbed in the least. I wished I could do that. I wished I could sleep. I wished I could *let* myself sleep.

Finally, I did. I had no choice, since I had to ride in the

morning.

I dreamed of her all night.

Stage Seventeen

(170 km - Mannheim - Bonn, Germany)

My dreams about Abby that night were disturbing. I'd repeatedly awakened and gone back to sleep, only to begin the dream again. We tried to make love, but kept stopping. The frustration was unbearable. Then, suddenly, she was with the man from the start of the stage that morning, letting him put his hands all over her in public.

When I asked who he was, she shook her head and put her back to me, permitting him to do still more intimate things to her, allowing everyone else to see except me. Not that I wanted to see. I wanted them to stop. I demanded as much but she continued to ignore me until my demands became pleas, stopping shy of outright begging.

That was when I saw red – literally, my vision in the dream went scarlet – and I put my hand on her shoulder and spun her around –

And I woke up to find myself in a hotel room with Rom snoring peacefully on the other bed.

I lay on my bed, staring up at the ceiling, panting and shaking like I'd ridden ten kilometres over the roughest pavé imaginable. The trembling in my limbs ran counterpoint to the pounding of my heart. Suddenly sick, I raised my hand to my forehead to see whether I was feverish.

235

My hand came away slick with sweat, and I wiped it on the bedclothes absent-mindedly, trying to forget the image of Abby with the mystery man's face planted between her legs. Nevertheless, it came anyway, bringing another rush of jealousy. It was a dream but I envied the man for being the one she'd chosen, for his being able to do what *I* wanted to do with her.

"This is fucking ridiculous," I muttered, slinging my legs over the side of the bed and sitting up. "I've got to talk to her."

My mobile was on the bedside table, and I considered picking it up to call her. I could take it out in the corridor for privacy, if I needed to. Not that a phone conversation would wake Rom. *Nothing* woke Rom.

But, what if I call and he's *there?*

I shook my head. *No. That won't happen.*

After forcing myself to my feet, I went to the window and drew back the curtain to peer out at the waking city. The sky was starting to lighten. I thought of my mobile again.

No, I want to see her. The phone is too cold, too distant.

At the sound of Jerzy banging on doors farther down the corridor, I turned away from the window and headed for the bathroom. I'd get my shower and get ready before he got here if I could. As much as I hated trying to curry favour, and as much as I disliked trying to finagle a few brownie points, I needed to do it.

The water in the shower took forever to warm up. While I waited, I stripped down and heard the door of the room bang open. Jerzy's shouting filled the short silence which followed. The sloshing of the bucket seemed ominous, even from the other side of the bathroom door.

"Ciccio? *Dov'è sei?*" he barked.

"*Sono qui!*" I barked back through the closed door.

The door swung open instantly – *I should have fucking locked it* – and Jerzy confirmed that I was the person who had spoken.

"You expected someone else?" I asked, spreading my hands and raising them on either side of myself. The steam from the shower swirled and eddied in the cooler air from the room while he raised an eyebrow.

"You'd be surprised, Ciccio." His tone was curt, yet resigned.

There was a hint of sadness in his eyes, and I regretted being sarcastic. He closed the door and I got into the shower at last, making quick work of it.

But not quick enough. Someone started banging on the bathroom door and I poked my head around the shower curtain, fully annoyed.

"It's fucking *open!*"

The door opened and Rom's alarmed expression greeted me. "Ciccio! *Vieni! Vieni!*" He gestured at me frantically. "Come! Come!" and for the first time I was aware of a commotion in the corridor outside our room.

What the hell?

I rinsed off and hurried out, wrapping a towel around my waist as I went.

The little room I shared with Rom was full of our teammates. Attilio, James, Phil and even Goosh had crammed themselves inside and sat hip-to-hip at the foot of the bed nearest the television.

The old TV screen wasn't clear, but the static-filled images were familiar enough: scenes from last year's Tour, intercut with a few other races – Paris-Roubaix, the Giro d'Italia and the World Championships among them – all of them with one frequently victorious rider in common.

'*Doping equipment found in* Speed Zone Italia *vehicles after Marco Lombardi tests positive...*' read the crawl running beneath the scenes of his victories.

I glanced at my teammates, all of them enthralled by the story unfolding on the screen. I couldn't believe it: Marco was one of the riders who'd made the most noise in recent years about riding clean.

"Other riders are involved," the reporter said, and as the camera panned out, I recognized the start line of the day's stage behind her. "Riders of note include another, unnamed rider from the *MassMiler* team. Further details are pending."

"I knew he was riding too well," Adrie said from the doorway, shaking his head as he entered the room. "But I honestly never had him pegged for a doper."

"Christ," Phil muttered. "Are they sure? Who are the others?"

Adrie glanced at Rom before speaking. "A couple of Poles, a bunch from *Speed Zone* and I heard the *MassMiler* rider is Hendrick. But I'm not sure."

Behind me, James sighed wistfully. "I suppose Coleridge is too much to hope for, then."

"Afraid so. Last I heard, he was clean."

"Fuck." James dropped back on the bed with a bounce.

I looked at Rom, who was still watching the screen with great intensity. They hadn't mentioned the Polish riders on TV, and I hoped there wasn't any truth to the rumour.

I turned my attention back to the television, a new tightness in my chest. I'd have to be very, very careful tonight. I'd be subject to extra attention, if not additional suspicion.

Fine. Whatever. I'd piss in as many cups as I had to – until my bladder went dry, if necessary – if I could get a little more time with Abby. I couldn't risk losing her like I'd lost Solange.

***

From the little desk in the corner of my room, I switched off the TV with the remote and turned back to my computer. This news would be huge, and Derek would want to know if I had photos of Marco Lombardi.

I did, but I wanted to be sure they were especially good shots. Lombardi might not have cared much about his own professional reputation, but I'd be damned if I'd let him ruin mine.

I smiled at the arrogance of that while my computer powered up. In spite of how hard I was working on this project and how much effort I was putting into getting my shots of each stage, it was likely to be a one-off and nothing more. Derek had fancied the idea of producing a book about the Tour, so it had been a particularly fortunate coincidence when I'd made my proposal last summer. I would never have done that if Charles hadn't arranged this trip for us in the first place.

But he had, and I had, and so here I was.

So many little things had come together to make this happen. It really was mind-boggling to consider the countless coincidences which had occurred in order for everything to come together this way.

I clicked through the photos on my computer and found a few likely candidates to send Derek. That done, I checked my e-mail and found a new message, as I'd expected.

'I want to use pics of urs with news feed… What do u have on Lombardi? You'll get photog credit.'

"Just this," I said aloud, attaching the photos and emailing back.

I shivered a little with giddiness. At last, a genuine photo credit! So what if it was only in one of his little columns in the online version of his magazine? It was something official, and that's what counted.

Opting to wait a few minutes to see whether he'd reply, I clicked through more photos, pausing as usual over some of my favourites of Federico.

I'm going to have to ask him to pose for me properly. I'd love to have some nice portraits of him, if only just for me.

It didn't seem terribly likely I'd see him anytime soon. With this unexpected furore over Lombardi and the others, it was doubtful he'd find a way to see me.

But what if we met somewhere? For dinner and nothing else?

No, that wouldn't work either. Suppose someone saw us together? Suppose a photographer got it in his head that I was Federico's new flame?

I imagined Charles seeing a photo me with Federico. Part of me recoiled and part of me felt a little thrill at the thought. Even if it looked perfectly innocent, I knew Charles would suspect more was going on. And if he did, he'd naturally ask questions. The questioning would become an interrogation. How well did I think I could stand up against that?

I really didn't want to find out. He was remarkably vindictive when he thought he'd been wronged. The irony was that he'd wanted me to 'get involved' with someone in the first place. Now I had, and I knew he'd be angry. I wasn't sharing the details with him, which meant I hadn't fulfilled my part of the bargain.

Never mind Charles had a girlfriend in London or that I hadn't gone looking for this thing with Federico. Never mind I'd meant what I said: I wouldn't be returning to Charles, one way or the other.

I'd always thought I'd have to be in love with someone else before I could leave. *Is that what's happened, here? Am I in love with Federico?*

I honestly wasn't sure.

After checking my e-mails again, I resumed looking at my photos of Federico, like a teenager mooning over images of a boy I'd never have for my own, daydreaming of a future with him even though I knew it was hopeless.

My crush was growing into something much stronger and I was tired of holding back.

I didn't stand a chance, but I had to keep reminding myself of that. I wanted to enjoy to the fantasy for a little while; I wanted to enjoy the thought of him being mine for good.

I wanted to give in, if only Federico would too.

***

We all filed onto the bus, worn out and distracted. Alvaro was particularly disgruntled, and who could blame him? He'd had a stunning finish – the sprint train had done a fantastic job, giving him a flawless lead-out, yet the only questions the press had for any of us were about Lombardi's doping.

James tried to lift our spirits throughout the drive to Bonn, but it wasn't easy. Halfway through the trip, I finally began to relax. My mobile vibrated in my pocket.

I took it out and opened Abby's message.

'5. 1. 4.'

I read and re-read it, a tiny bell ringing in the back of my mind. Something was off here.

I got my duffel down from the overhead and sorted through it to find my copy of Abby's itinerary at the bottom. The team had been to Bonn several times, but I didn't recognize the name of the street of her hotel. I took out my laptop and switched it on before I tucked the papers away again.

Michael passed by and I tapped his arm.

"What's up, Ciccio?" he asked distractedly, one eye on the stage finish video on the TV at the front of the bus.

"What's the name of the hotel we're staying in tonight?"

"Um… It's the Hotel Lehrer, I think. Why?"

"Is that where we stayed last time?"

Michael laughed, as I'd known he would. "No, that was the Bonn Residence Rooms." He lowered his voice and cast a glance in Jerzy's direction. "Jesus, Ciccio – you know we can't go back *there* again."

I did, indeed.

"I know, but for some reason I thought it was the same place."

Michael continued up to the front and I entered the hotel name in the search engine, I was soon confronted with a fact I couldn't deny: there was no way I could get from the team's hotel to hers on foot. We had half of Bonn between us.

Would I be able to get a cab in the early morning if I didn't book it in advance? I was doubtful. Public transport wasn't an option. If I intended to see Abby, I'd need a bit of luck at the very least.

I got my mobile out again.

'*I will try,*' I wrote, then put the mobile away as the bus pulled alongside our hotel.

As I stepped off the bus, I caught a glimpse of a sign next to the hotel entrance and smiled. I had an epiphany of sorts, a revelation I hadn't anticipated. Abby's hotel was a little over a mile away, yes, but it wasn't impossible to get there quickly.

Not when I had the option of *alternate* transportation.

"Hey, guys!" Phil called, pointing to the 'Rental Bikes Available' sign I'd seen. "Who wants to go for a ride?"

A chorus of groans and laughter greeted his question, and I smiled.

Since the gods were smiling on *me*, it was only fair.

*

Before dinner was over, I told Jerzy I was going up to the room to rest a bit before the evening meeting. He nodded and went back to talking with Brunn, and I made my way out of the dining room and out to the lobby, feeling invincible again.

The feeling expanded when I approached the pretty blonde was still at the desk. I'd made the right decision.

"*Guten Abend,*" I said. She fluttered her eyelashes becomingly as I approached.

"*Bonsoir,*" she replied with a knowing, flirtatious smile, and I couldn't believe my luck.

I folded my arms along the top of the tall desk, trying not to lose myself in the giddy energy swirling inside me. "Ah... *Parlez-vous français...?* Wonderful."

"*Oui, oui, d'accord...* How may I help you?"

"You know, this is going to sound very strange, I'm sure, but... I'd very much like..." I paused to give her a sly smile of my own, reassuring myself it was just this once. I'd do anything to get back to Abby tonight. "I'd like to rent a bicycle."

She giggled, thinking I was flirting with her. To a point, I was.

"Really? I should think you have at least *one* already." She leaned forward, allowing me a generous glimpse of her cleavage.

"One or two, yes. But those are for work, you know? I need something here, for the city. Do you have something which might suit me?"

"I'm sure I do." She stood and sidled around the far end of the desk, making her way down the hall off the lobby. "Come with me."

Ten minutes – and one phone number – later, I retired to my room for a shower and a change of clothes, with the key to a rental bike's lock in my pocket. She'd promised me I could return the bike anytime – I only had to leave the key on the desk after locking the bike in the reserved stand on the side of the building.

It couldn't have been more perfect.

*

The team meeting was mercifully brief, and I lingered to chat with Adrie and Goosh afterwards, with no sense of anxiety or hurry. I felt serene, all my troubles put to rest.

Jerzy was in especially good spirits as well, and no wonder: the team had maintained our standings and it looked like the Royal would stay in our possession for at least a while longer. Rom and Brunn chatted with Jerzy, all of them laughing from time to time, a bottle of wine slowly dwindling amongst the three of them.

Oh, this is too good. But I'll take it, thanks.

After a while, we drifted back to our rooms. I cleaned myself up and then went to rest and wait.

Rom didn't disappoint me. It wasn't long before he drifted off, his MP3 player still switched on beside him on the bed. I lay in the dark and listened for any signs of life in the corridor while the minutes ticked past.

When all was silent, I got up and gathered a few things: mobile phone, wallet, room key, and last but not least, the key for the rental bike's lock. It came with a little elastic key holder to wear on my wrist, but I tucked it into my pocket instead. I had my 'I'm popping down to the bus for something' excuse at the ready if I needed it.

I eased out of the room, not bothering with the bathroom ruse. If Rom woke up and found me missing, it wouldn't matter either way. The corridor was quiet and I walked quietly toward the stairwell, feeling like I was walking on air.

Why worry? As long as I was back before four a.m., everything would be fine.

Using the side door of the hotel, I came out next to the bike rack where the rentals were. I unlocked the bike I'd reserved and rode off into the night.

***

At the knock on the door, I sat up in bed, my heart pounding. I pulled on my robe and went to peer out of the peephole.

It *was* him. I took a deep breath and exhaled slowly, then unlocked and opened the door.

"Hi," I said, and he gave me a slight smile as he stepped inside.

"Hi," he echoed as I closed the door. As soon as I turned toward him again, he raised his hands to frame my face, holding me still for a long, soft kiss. "I'm sorry I'm so late –"

"It's not a problem at all." I wrapped my arms around his neck, and his arms folded around my waist in turn.

"I couldn't get away yesterday," he murmured against my neck as he held me tight.

"I know. It's okay."

"I missed you."

"I missed you, too." The words brought a lump to my throat. We stood together, silent, holding each other until a soft breeze through the open window by the bed gave me a chill.

Federico chuckled quietly and stroked my hair. "Are you cold?"

"Not really."

"Could we...?" He indicated the bed with a tilt of his head.

"Of course." As we stretched out beside each other atop the bedclothes, I wondered at the serious expression on his face.

"Abby?"

"Yes?"

He fell quiet and looked away, then took a deep breath before he faced me again. "Who...?"

I waited until it was clear he wasn't going to finish the question. "'Who'... what, Chicco?" I shook my head to show my confusion.

He cupped the back of my head in his palm and pulled me closer to kiss me.

Startled, I stiffened in surprise, but I didn't mean to resist.

He kissed me harder, and my lips parted beneath his, his tongue sliding past in rough pursuit of my own.

I returned his kisses the way he gave them, my heart pounding hard enough to scare me, my whole body trembling with the force of it. Then his mouth was on my throat, my neck; the heat of his lips left trails I was sure were visible to the naked eye.

His hands moved over me; restless, seeking. He drew my leg up over his hip, his hand moving up my thigh and sliding under my nightgown as he did, pushing the fabric until it bunched up between us.

He pushed his thigh between mine. His cargo shorts stretched taut over his erection, pressed urgently against me as he sighed my name anxiously into the curve of my neck.

With a delicate touch, he drew my nightgown down to expose my breast and cup it in his hand. The warmth of his breath mixed with the cool air drifting in the open window before he pursed his lips around my nipple and sucked gently. His tongue flickered and danced until I ached, never wanting it to end. I wanted more of him, all of him, all at once.

Then his hand slipped between us, stroking me lightly through my panties as his mouth met mine again in another forceful kiss. His tongue and his fingers worked in concert, going deeper with each stroke until I had to pull my mouth away, gasping while I shuddered under his touch.

He pursued me again, his mouth taking mine, his hand withdrawing only to ease under the cloth to touch me directly. Already too sensitive, I couldn't help flinching away this time. His caress gentled, finding a less direct path to follow.

His low, pleased groan rose from deep in his chest where he was pressed against me. It seemed to move through my own body before I realized it *was* me, echoing him.

His caresses continued, slick and seeking, until I clenched my thighs around his hand and shuddered, my breath shaking. My head was spinning. I feared I might hyperventilate if I couldn't regain control.

Federico drew away to pull his shirt over his head. He tossed the garment to the floor without a glance and returned to me, his kisses more impassioned than ever.

If we stop now, I'll explode. Literally. Or I'll burst into flame or something.

"Abby..."

"Yes...?"

No further words followed. Instead, his eyes met mine and held my gaze for what seemed like an eternity. He kissed me again, and then his lips traced down from my lips, lingered over my breasts and then progressed slowly over my belly, their touch softened by my nightgown between us.

Kneeling beside me, he hooked his fingers at the waistband of my panties and tugged, urging them down my hips. Smiling with a tender eagerness I'd never seen before, he put the garment aside and parted my legs to kneel between them.

Oh, God... this is it – we're finally going to –

And then I realized he had something else in mind.

My limbs went numb, I stiffened and I willed myself to reach out for him. "Chicco, I – please, no."

His eagerness faded to bemusement in a heartbeat. He moved to lie with me again, his gaze holding mine, filled with puzzlement. "What's the matter? Why do you want me to stop?"

"I'm, uh... I'm not comfortable with, uh... that."

He shook his head. "I don't understand. Have I done something wrong?"

"No, no... I'm not used to..." I searched frantically for the words I needed so I wouldn't sound prudish. I touched his cheek and he pressed his hand over mine. His stubble tickled my palm. "I'm not sure I like that."

"How are you 'not sure'?" he asked, and then laughed softly. "Either you do, or you don't."

"It's just that I've never –" I stopped short, blushing. Did it need to be so difficult? Why was it so embarrassing to admit? "He never liked to, and –"

"*He* didn't like to? You're joking!" Federico laughed aloud, and my blush intensified. His manner changed abruptly, attentive once again. "You're *not* joking?"

I shook my head in response.

He glanced around the room, clearly confused. "What kind of straight man doesn't like to eat *pussy*?" he muttered.

"Besides," I asserted, desperate to quell my embarrassment, "I don't want you to feel like you, you know, *have* to."

"*Have* to?" Federico looked me in the eye again, breaking into a huge, boyish grin. "*Mon dieu*, I've never heard such a –" He shook his head, meeting my eyes. "Abby, I *want* to do this. I want to make *you* happy, and honestly, it is something I enjoy, too."

I said nothing.

He leaned in and kissed me, long and soft, and my tension ebbed away. His hand moved along my side, pushing my nightgown up again. A fresh ache throbbed where his fingers now caressed and teased between my thighs.

"If you really want me to stop," he whispered, his breath warm, his lips tickling my throat. "I will. I promise."

I couldn't speak.

I closed my eyes, and nodded.

Time stopped until his mouth touched me, a gentle kiss. Then another, and then another. Kiss after kiss, the tender pull of his firm lips and the warmth of his breath sending shivers through me. There were only his kisses and his hands, coaxing and encouraging me with gentle persistence until I surrendered.

And then his tongue was sliding over me, slipping deeper before stroking insistently, not stopping even when I whimpered, helplessly, beneath his ministrations. He continued while I shuddered around him, when I cried out wordlessly and gasped for breath. When I clutched at him and my hips rose up, seeking more, his kisses delved deeper, his tongue danced over me until I cried out again.

Only then did he stop, pausing to trace kisses along my thighs and belly, and then he moved to lie with me, his mouth finding mine, still perfumed with my scent. The hard length of him sought where his mouth had just been, heavy khaki separating us even as he moved insistently against me, heedless of any barrier.

I reached to unfasten his shorts and he stopped me, pushing my hands away before doing the job himself. Impatient, I pushed at his waistband with the soles of my feet, my hands grasping at his back all the while.

I couldn't think, I could only feel. Hopelessly empty, I ached for him to be inside me at last. Anticipating his skin against mine, I was surprised to feel warm fabric instead of skin. He hadn't undressed completely, but still had on his underwear.

Oh, no, no...

Still, my hips rose to meet his as he moved against me, aligning with me perfectly, striking the right spot over and over. The pendant on his necklace swayed above me, flashing in the lamplight. I closed my eyes as his efforts left me with no choice but to bury my face in his chest and cry out in a mix of frustration and satisfaction. His rhythm faltered and then he increased his pace until I was trying to match him, grinding against him in search of that *just so* moment.

We found it within a breath or so of one another. His rhythm stuttered and then slowed to a halt, an eager pulse like our heartbeats between us.

He sank down onto me, exhaling a low, long sigh, and I wrapped myself around him, loving the feel of his warmth, his spent exertion in my arms.

It wasn't exactly what I'd wanted, but it was close.

***

At first, there was only the loss of coherence, the utter absence of anything else except the pleasure of release. Then came complete and total exhaustion, and I sank down onto her while my heart slowed and my breathing steadied, and I vowed to stay with her like that forever.

Forever lasted about ten whole seconds.

What the hell did I do?

Even before the thought had fully formed in my head, I had moved away from her, snatched up my shorts from the floor and rushed to the bathroom, mortified.

Once inside with the door safely closed behind me, I stripped down and tried to fight back the shame building inside me.

Gesu... What am I? Some horny teenager or something?

I balled up my underwear and stuffed them in the wastebasket under the vanity. Sure, I could rinse them clean, but I wouldn't be here long enough to dry them, so what was the use?

I had a quick wash in the bidet and pondered my course of action.

First, I had to apologize to Abby.

Second, I had to head back to the team's hotel – soon, if not immediately.

And third...? I wasn't sure, but there had to be something else.

Sighing, I dried off and pulled on my shorts, taking extra care as I zipped up. I still couldn't believe I'd done it. A dry hump? At my age? At hers?

The rush of humiliation seemed never-ending. At last I stepped out of the bathroom, trying to compose myself so she wouldn't have further cause to be upset.

I turned the corner and found her sitting up, her nightgown demurely arranged over her legs, her inquisitive gaze awaiting me.

"Is everything okay?" she asked.

I stopped short and folded my arms over my chest. "Abby, I am so, so sorry."

"For what?"

"This." I gestured around the room, meaning, 'for what I did to you'.

"'This', what? Did I do something wrong?"

"No! God, no. *I* did."

"You're not making sense."

"I used my girlfriend as a masturbatory aid," I said, shaking my head.

Abby burst out laughing. "You *what*?" She waved me over, still laughing, and patted the bed beside her. "Come here, please."

Her voice was tender and sweet, and I crossed the room, anxious to be at her side. She was all I wanted in the world, all I could ever ask for. That she wasn't offended by what I'd done was a shock.

"Chicco," she began so softly I had to lean closer to hear her. "You've done more to make me feel good tonight than anyone else ever has."

"Yes, but then I –"

"That too." She laughed again, falling back onto her pillow with a distinctly happy sigh. "God, I haven't had a dry hump since high school! I'd forgotten how much fun that could be."

"You thought it was *fun*?"

Her expression grew somewhat more serious. "Considering what limitations you have placed on you, I have to admit it's even more flattering than it might otherwise be."

I lay down beside her. The lamplight made her skin look like velvet. I still tasted her on my lips, recalled how slick she'd been beneath my tongue; I forced the images away in spite of wanting to do it all again.

"We *will* be together. I promise."

"I know we will. When the Tour is over, and you don't need your energies for the race. I'm looking forward to that." She smiled again, and I had to look away because it made her too beautiful. I wanted her too much.

"I am too," I said, and reached out for her.

**

With that, he curled against my back, his long, lean frame moulding to mine, his arm around my waist, his cheek nestled in my hair. I closed my eyes and concentrated on his warmth and the feel of him breathing, a hypnotic rhythm which lulled me to rest.

It was a wonderful way to fall asleep.

.

Rest Day Three

(Bonn, Germany)

It was an incredible way to wake up.

I sensed the light growing brighter and the air had a particular coolness to it which told me the day was just starting. The first notes of birdsong drifted in on the breeze which blew through the open window, raising gooseflesh on my back.

Curled against my front, Abby's softness drew me closer, seeking more of her warmth. I breathed in the subtle perfume of her hair and the clean salt and musk of the skin at the nape of her neck, felt the weight of her breast in my palm. A low, pleasant stirring in my groin rose in response to her closeness.

She shifted closer to me and sent another rush of warmth below my belly. I pressed against her, savouring the way we fit perfectly together. I gave her a light kiss on the curve of her neck and she shivered and nestled down into her pillow with a pleased sound as I finally opened my eyes.

I had no idea where I was.

My heart pounded once, twice, and then seemed to stop while my blood went cold. I scanned the room for a clock, hardly daring to breathe. When I read the one on the nightstand, my heartbeat went into triple-time, my mouth dry but filled with a nauseating, metallic taste.

Merde!

It was almost five-thirty in the morning, and I was still in Abby's room.

I flung myself off the bed to snatch up my shirt and shoes from the floor. Knowing I was never going to make it to the team's hotel in time, a part of me wondered why I was bothering to rush. I was off the team for sure, regardless of having held the Royal for a few stages. Jerzy had all the reason he needed, now and he'd already warned me before.

Still, here I was, dressing on the run with Abby blinking in confusion atop the counterpane I reached the door, turned and looked at her and I knew that I'd remember her like that forever: sleepy eyes uncomprehending, hair in a tousled mess, nightgown hitched up over her thighs and hanging at an angle off one shoulder.

Dear God in Heaven, help me; I want her.

I went back to give her the deepest, longest kiss I dared. "At least there's this, *amore*," I murmured as we parted. "We'll have more time to spend together soon."

I'd barely closed the door to her room before I was fumbling in my pocket for the key to the lock of the rental bike. I ran down the corridor, giving no thought to how much noise I made, not worried that I might fall over some poor housekeeper doing her job in the early hours of the morning, because I really didn't care.

My heart was screaming at me to go back and curl up with Abby, damn the consequences, but I hurried to the bike rack in front of the hotel and fumbled the lock open. After orientating myself, I took off for the team's hotel.

The only vehicles on the road were the city trams and the service vans for the hotels and restaurants, all of them trundling along from one delivery to the next.

I pedalled frantically, my chest tight like I was suffocating. I sped past one vehicle after another, narrowly dodging a couple of unexpected open doors and a few drivers returning to their parked cars or trucks in the process. At a traffic light, I hopped the curb onto an empty sidewalk and shot past a café worker putting out tables and chairs. His co-worker was spraying down the sidewalk in front of the café, leaving a length of hosepipe curled up in my path.

I braked too hard and my rear wheel locked, sending me into the gutter. I recovered easily enough. The subsequent near-miss with the delivery van turning the corner was a bit too close for my comfort.

I ignored all the complaining shouts and protests, leaving them behind me as fast as I could. The team hotel was in sight.

I hopped off before I'd even stopped the bike, running alongside to slap it into the rentals rack next to the side door. I fastened the lock, winced when I realized I'd knocked the tire out of true, and bounded into the lobby, aiming for the elevators and hoping for a miracle.

The gods weren't smiling on me anymore.

All of the team management, crew, and every last rider stood in the meeting room off one side of the lobby. Last but most certainly not least, Jerzy stood there seething, bucket in hand.

The hum of conversation came to a halt as I stopped short. I hoped I didn't look as ashamed as I suddenly felt. Silence filled the lobby – even the hotel's desk workers went quiet – and Jerzy crossed the faux-Turkish carpet over to where I stood on the ceramic-tile floor.

The bucket arced with surprising grace, the rim shining as the ice water spilled out of it, the metal striking the tiles with a sound like a breaking dish. Small chips of the tile flooring skittered away from me while the bucket rolled lopsidedly and then rocked to and fro on its dented side. He'd thrown it too hard to get me very wet, only from the knees down, but I did my best not to shiver from the freezing cold on my bare legs or the water that filled my shoes.

"*Skurwielu!*" he shouted, and it seemed like everyone in hearing range ducked down a bit, except for me.

I'd known it was coming.

After his outburst, Jerzy stood silent and scowling in front of me. I met his eyes and said nothing.

I wondered whether the silence would ever be broken, and by whom. To my surprise, Rom was the one who first broke from the group.

"*Daj mu spokoj, zostaw go-*"

"*Trzymaj się swojego fiuta,*" Jerzy growled, and I knew that phrase moderately well, Polish or not. It was one of his stock phrases: "Hold your own dick." All the while he never took his eyes off me.

Rom lingered a dangerous second or two longer, then gave me a sympathetic look and retreated to the safety of numbers.

"Go get your things. You're done. Go away," Jerzy said, his eyes still meeting mine.

"*Hören wir seine Erklärung. Es ist vielleicht nicht so schlimm, wie Sie denken,*" Brunn said.

Jerzy twitched ever-so-slightly. "All right, then," he answered with an air of exasperation and looked at me. "Explain. Make it good. Where were you last night?"

He knew. He *knew*, but he wanted me to say it in front of everyone. I'd broken one of his rules, and my punishment would not only be expulsion from the team, but humiliation in front of my soon-to-be-former teammates.

I swallowed dryly and took a deep breath.

"I'm sorry I'm late, Jerzy."

That was all I gave him before I turned to go upstairs.

*

Back in the room, I towelled my legs dry and changed my socks and shoes, throwing the wet pair into the plastic laundry bag the hotel provided before stuffing them into my duffel. Packing my things didn't take long. Almost everything I had with me was already in one of my two bags. I tossed my toiletries into my shaving kit and dropped it into one bag, double-checked that everything else was in the other, and took one last look around the room before I made to leave.

I had no idea where I might go. It made sense to go back to Abby, but if she were following the Tour, then I'd still be following the Tour too, like some dimwit who couldn't get the hint after having been shoved out the door. How pathetic would *that* look?

When I opened the door, I found Brunn stepping up, hand raised, ready to knock. I considered telling him everything I'd kept to myself from the start of the Tour but thought better of it. What was the point?

I'd leave quietly with some dignity intact. Jerzy hadn't been able to take that from me, so why throw it away?

"Listen, Chicco." Brunn blocked me from passing through the doorway, and I adjusted the duffel's strap on my shoulder while I waited for him to move. "Maybe I could come in? We could talk privately?"

I shrugged and stepped aside so he could enter. He closed the door behind him and, when he sat on Rom's rumpled bed, I turned to face him.

"What is it?" I asked, not bothering to hide my impatience. "I thought I'd beat a hasty retreat before Jerzy lobs more buckets at me."

"Don't worry about that. I spoke with him. You're not leaving."

My head swam at his unexpected news. I leaned against the wall so I wouldn't fall over.

"What? How-?"

"Never mind that. Just tell me something."

I said nothing, but Brunn shrugged off my silence to pause and regard me in his calm, calculating way. "Do you still want to get the Royal back?"

"That's probably the dumbest question anyone ever asked. Of course I do."

"Then do what I'm telling you." A ghost of genuine concern crept into his face. "Let me put it this way: whatever you were doing last night, I don't care. But *don't* do it again. I won't speak up for you again if you do."

I thought of Abby, now alone in her hotel room, wondering what had happened to me. I needed to speak to her. I needed to see her again.

"I appreciate that, but I can't make any promises." I looked down at the carpet, following the woven pattern, noting how a dirty path had been worn into it.

Brunn sighed and I raised my eyes to see him shaking his head. "Then do whatever the hell you want. It's your loss. Put that stuff away, get into your kit and come down to the bus for the recon ride. All the excitement this morning doesn't change that."

I didn't answer. He stood and walked past me, his arm brushing mine as he went by.

"Don't you want to keep it?" I asked when he'd reached the door.

"What?"

"The Royal." I turned to face him. "Isn't that why you're here?"

He eyed me coolly, his expression shifting back to stone-cold indifference.

"Whether we're on the bike or in the team car, Chicco, it makes no difference. It's why we're *all* here."

The door closed behind him and I sat down on my bed. The Royal *was* the reason we all were here. In all the confusion and rush, in my desire to be with Abby, I'd almost forgotten about it.

I'd never have believed that was possible.

I still wanted it, and by some miracle I was still close enough to get it – with a little luck.

But my luck looked like it was running out. I'd carelessly squandered my chances, and if I didn't stop acting impulsively, I'd screw myself out of any chance I had left.

Last night – all of it – had been one foolish impulse after another, and I'd probably done more damage than good with Abby as well.

I rested my head in my hands while cold fingers clutched tight around my heart. I'd thoroughly fucked up this time, and the price I was going to pay was something I'd never considered.

Abby.

I changed into my kit as quickly as I could before grabbing my mobile and getting ready to leave. I paused, my thumb over the key for my contacts list, and stepped away from the door, my heartbeat heavy in my chest.

Just one quick call, to tell her – what? That Jerzy hadn't killed me?

I dialled her number, hoping I wouldn't wake her – that her phone would be off or the battery dead – whatever might work to put off the conversation we had to have.

She picked up immediately, and her soft "Hello?" drove a spike into my heart.

That single word brought with it the sensation of her breath on my skin, her arms wrapped tight around me, her skin warm and smooth under my hands.

I couldn't speak; the words wouldn't come. All I needed was her name; if I could say that, the rest would follow, but I didn't want it to.

"Chicco?" she said, and the spike grew cold, an icicle through my core. "Is everything okay? Are you all right?"

"*Sì*, Abby, I'm okay." The words seemed to come from someone else's lips; they felt too foreign to be mine.

"What happened? Did you get in okay?"

I struggled through the sensation of sleepwalking, biting my lower lip so I could feel something – anything.

"Chicco? Are you still there?"

"*Sì, sì*... Jerzy caught me –"

"Oh, no."

"Brunn convinced him not to throw me out – I don't know

how, but he did – so I'm still here."

"Thank God. Oh, thank God. I am so glad to hear it!" She laughed, the sound full of genuine joy, and the spike grew even longer and keener. "Maybe tonight you can tell me about what –"

"Abby, *amore…*"

"Did you ever notice," she continued, her voice taking on a brittle tone, "that you slip into Italian whenever we talk? Mostly, I mean. You're French, but then you almost always speak Italian –" There was a frantic edge to her voice.

"Abby," I repeated, fighting for calm.

"Yes." It was a statement, not a question.

"After what's happened today…" I trailed off; the very thought of the words created a bitter taste in my mouth. "I'm afraid I'm not going to be able to see you for a while."

A long silence followed.

"I know," she said at last. More silence, and then; "Don't hate me, Chicco, but… I'd almost hoped you *would* be thrown off the team, if it meant I could see you. I'm sorry, but I did."

I couldn't help smiling. "I don't hate you, *amore.* I understand it – I felt the same way."

She sighed – a watery sound close to tears.

"I should have made love with you," I said, the words out before I realized I'd spoken.

"I was thinking the same thing."

"I *will*, though. I promise."

"*After* the Tour." She didn't sound convinced.

"*Oui*, after the Tour."

"Ah," she said, going quiet. I listened hard, aware I needed to get downstairs to the bus very soon, but the sound of her breathing held me captive. "We're back to business, now, eh?"

"What do you mean?"

"You just spoke French. *Au revoir,*" she said, and hung up the phone without waiting for my reply.

*

All eyes were on me as I boarded the bus. Some of my teammates regarded me with open wonder – *How is he still here?* – while others looked at me with something like resentment.

Jerzy said nothing, not even bothering to look my way. I waited for a sarcastic comment at the very least, something about me being the last to arrive, but no comment came. I understood why when Alvaro got on board, one hand held high.

"I know, I know," he said, waving a pair of cycling shoes over his head. "I found mine in the room. I'm ready now."

Jerzy signalled abruptly to the driver, and the bus doors closed. The atmosphere amongst my teammates was subdued as the bus rolled out to take us out of town for our reconnaissance ride.

A sly grin playing across his face, Adrie sank onto the seat next to mine. Though Brunn and Jerzy sat at the front of the bus, well out of earshot, I was hesitant to speak. Every breath I drew felt like it could tumble the house of cards currently shielding me from the wrath of our *directeur sportif.*

"One of us has a guardian angel, Chicco," Adrie muttered, "and it sure as hell isn't me."

Jesus, that's all I need: Brunn as my guardian angel. The Teutonic Avenger.

All the old resentment rushed and roiled inside me. If I were in his debt, did that mean my bid for the Royal was null and void?

No. If I can't have Abby, then by God, I'll have the Royal.

Even the brief thought of her brought a new surge of pain. *No, that's not over yet, either. I refuse to think of her in that way.* I'd find a way to see her, even if it meant carting Rom along with me as a chaperone.

"All the same," Adrie continued, "I'm glad you're still with us, kid."

I looked up at Adrie to find him smiling pleasantly at me. My own smile rose in instinctive response. "'Kid'?" I echoed. "Have you been watching American movies again?"

He laughed and shook his head. "No; sometimes you're really fucking immature."

My face fell and his expression sobered.

"It took real guts to stand up to Jerzy like that this morning. I admire that." He nodded to himself, as though considering some sage wisdom he ought to share. "Remember one thing, Chicco," he said, lowering his voice so I had to lean in to hear him.

"What's that?"

"If you undermine his authority again, you might find that you've done more than stand up for yourself. You might find that you're standing alone."

I stiffened, ready to protest, and he raised one hand to quiet me.

"Chicco, this team *needs* him to be invincible; his word has to be *law*. Otherwise, why the fuck are we here? If they," he tilted his head toward Goosh and Teodoro and a few of the other younger team members, "get the sense that they don't have to pay attention to what he says, what do you think happens next?"

Adrie paused, letting his question hang in the air between us. I could almost see his words suspended over the armrests of our seats, hovering darkly before they faded away.

"Remember what I told you before, *Ciccio*: as a team, we can help you, or we can abandon you. Which do you prefer?"

That he'd switched to my team nickname didn't go unnoticed. Nor did the thinly veiled threat his words contained.

"*You* stand up to him all the time," I said, and Adrie made a *-tch-* sound, shaking his head. "It's *true*. Nothing ever happens to you, though. He gets pissed off, but he never threatens to toss *you* out on your ass. Why is that? Do you have something to hold over his head?"

I tried to make it sound light-hearted, but my anger showed. Adrie regarded me out of the corner of his eye before speaking again.

"I'm thirty-seven fucking years old. How much longer do you reckon I'll be riding?" He looked at me, waiting for my response.

I didn't answer.

"Exactly. I can mouth off all I want and it won't make one fucking bit of difference. I'm a rouler, a super-domestique. But he doesn't want to risk losing me for real. Sure, I've had my day, but he knows – and I know – that he can send me off on suicide missions every now and then. I'm also one of his best lines of defence for keeping powerful little fuckers like you from getting too far out of line."

I started to open my mouth to protest, but the words didn't come. Adrie glanced toward the front of the bus and then sank back down into his seat, leaning in close once again.

"You lack focus lately, Ciccio. Get your shit together and you'll go far for a good long while yet. You're a goddamned *champion*, you stupid little fuck. The sooner you figure that out, the better off you'll be. Quit fucking around already and *get to it*."

With that, he stood abruptly and went to the front of the bus.

Any smart response I'd prepared at the start of his little speech had evaporated by the time he'd finished.

I sat and stared at the back of the seat in front of me, my spirits lower than ever. Leave it to Adrie to insult me and praise me in the same breath.

Champion. People threw that word around so easily nowadays it had lost all meaning. So why was it when *he* said it, it carried so much weight? I didn't doubt for a second that he meant it, but it almost seemed like too much to live up to.

The bus slowed to enter a parking lot outside an empty shopping centre. A few other buses were already there, some with riders milling around prepping their gear, some empty, waiting for the team to return. Mechanics and soigneurs milled around, chatting and double-checking spare gear.

As we disembarked, the cyclists still waiting to depart waved or catcalled to us, and everyone mingled and talked for a while. Now that I was among people who knew nothing about my misadventures of the morning, I relaxed a little for the first time that day.

That lasted until I noticed Rom ghosting my every step from a respectful distance.

For fuck's sake.

"I'm not going to disappear, Rom."

"I thought so before," he grumbled, not bothering to lower his voice.

I stopped and waited for him to catch up to me. "What do you mean?" I asked quietly, and he took my cue.

"*Non fidi di me.*" he said softly. "You don't trust me," he repeated, his scowl deepening. The expression looked strange on his face.

"*Cosa?* What are you talking about?"

He folded his arms across his chest, an air of determination surrounding him. "I take you up mountains," he continued in laboured Italian. "I make sure you reach the goals, yes? I keep secrets, but you still don't trust me."

Oh, right, I had Abby in the room.

"I *do* trust you —"

"No, you don't. If you did, you'd have told me where you go out at night. I know you were going, but I say nothing – not even when Jerzy thought something was going on."

Fuck.

"You mean-?"

Rom nodded. "I told him I was sleeping, that I never saw you leave. He believes me, I think."

"But you knew?"

"Your bed was empty, the bathroom too. Motherfuck... I'm not stupid."

Thinking back, Rom had been the first to step forward, presumably to defend me. It hadn't been a small risk to take, especially with Jerzy already having quizzed him about me.

"I *never* thought you were stupid, Rom."

"You never call me *Robaczku*," he said. "Why not?"

I couldn't help smiling. "I can't pronounce it."

He laughed loudly, two sharp barks which did much to reassure me. "Bullshit!" he chortled and I had to laugh too.

"When you two are finished with your little *tête-à-tête*, there's a recon ride to do," Adrie called before disappearing around the far side of the bus.

I faced Rom again. "I'm really sorry about everything."

He waved me off, walking around and past me, and I understood that, almost in spite of myself, my domestique had actually become my friend.

Stage Eighteen

(157 km – Bonn, Germany – Maastricht, Netherlands)

Standing at the start line that morning, I didn't see Pascal in the crowd. Granted, I wasn't looking especially hard, but he did have a tendency to stand out. After a while I realized I was *hoping* I wouldn't see him at all. I'd passed the rest day in a distracted and uneasy mood after Federico's call. I was too tired to keep up the charade of the happily-married photog on holiday in order to fend off Pascal's flirtations and advances.

In spite of my frustration at being unable to see Federico, I wanted him so much it hurt. He was the reason I hadn't slept well last night, and why I'd been so distracted the day before. With little or nothing to photograph, I'd been at loose ends the whole day, checking my e-mails and reviewing my photographs compulsively.

I'd gone to a bookshop in search of something to read in English because I was bored with the satellite television in my room. The reports on the TV news about the Tour were preoccupied with *Speed Zone Italia*'s ousting from the race. A few of the talking heads were even speculating about the Tour leaders – if Lombardi was doping, what did that say about the riders doing better than him?

It was almost enough to shake my faith.

My thoughts turned back to Federico. It wasn't *his* decision not to see me. I knew he wanted to be with me as much as I wanted to

263

be with him. He'd messed up, been caught out, and the penalty was a forced separation for the both of us.

Not for the first time, I wished I'd woken up earlier, that I'd roused him and sent him on his way in time to avoid being caught. I regretted being so short with him on the phone. I also wished I weren't *still* angry with him. It was pointless and made no sense at all, but some bitter, uncharitable part of me wanted to blame him, so I did.

Now the teams were gathering at the start line. I moved through the crowd of spectators, camera in hand, snapping candid shots as I went. When I found Federico I could hardly breathe.

He turned in my direction, his eyes seeming to find mine through the camera lens. I froze in place, waiting while a drop of sweat trickled down my back. There was such an expression of longing and apology on his face, it hurt to see it. I wanted to wrap my arms around him to shield him from everyone and everything in the world, if only I could.

Yet my resentment lingered.

I snapped the photo, noting as I did that Rom was watching me, too. He was frankly interested, making no pretence of looking elsewhere. I liked the boy immensely for that.

I smiled and Federico smiled in return. I raised my camera to take another picture of him with Rom before I turned to other cyclists nearby. I could still feel his eyes on me as I moved down the line.

The urge to turn and call out to him, in front of everyone, came so swiftly I barely stopped myself. The words were there, impossible to believe, impossible to admit, but nonetheless *there*.

And if I said them, the spectators would take me for some lonely, middle-aged woman acting like a foolish fangirl. I would appear no different from the youngsters who clustered together in the cycling village with their signs reading 'Marry me, Foxy Fede!' or 'I love you, Ciccio!'

Declaring my love for a man I hardly knew wasn't something I was quite ready to do.

Not yet, anyway.

***

Shortly after we emerged from the hills outside Bonn, the

headwind picked up, bringing dark clouds. The short, easy ride into Maastricht wasn't looking so comfortable anymore.

The humidity clung to me while the come-and-go sunlight made the temperature seem cooler. Still, it brought no relief from the heat. Soon the sun disappeared altogether and the threat of rain became a promise.

Beneath my wheels, the road undulated smooth and easy, the tarmac clean and level. From overhead a sprinkling of rain fell but it seemed to evaporate as soon as it hit my helmet, my jersey or my skin.

The wind strengthened, forcing the peloton to break into smaller groups. The groups broke down further, forming echelons to cut through the strengthening wind.

A low rumble of thunder drowned out the sound of the helicopter filming us from a distance. Both the thunder and the helicopter were scarcely noticeable above the *whap* of the wind in my face. The sounds rose and fell like waves, accompanied in our earpieces by Michael's frequent commentary on the race and Jerzy's intermittent instructions.

I moved to the head of my echelon, dug in and braced against the wind. Another spray of rainfall lanced my face like fine needles. The sun suddenly emerged, making the road surface glitter brilliantly and then disappeared, plunging the world into semi-darkness. My eyes watered from all the changes in light, and I blinked to clear my vision.

There was a *clack* of changing gears and the sounds of sudden effort which indicated a breakaway. Led by Schlessinger and Motta, they went charging off the bunch ahead, leaving the rest of us shaking our heads at such a foolish move.

If the darkness up the road was any sign, they would be rushing into the rain in a few kilometres. Making a breakaway now was pointless – especially for someone as highly placed in the GC as Schlessinger.

That was, unless none of us went after them. If there *wasn't* any rainfall on the road ahead, Schlessinger stood a good chance of gaining back some of his time and snagging the Royal from Brunn.

A chase group formed from the remainder of the bunch the two *Maxxout* riders had broken from. Jerzy's command came an instant later, before I could even consider rising out of my seat to give chase.

"Major, J.B.: go with the chasers. The rest of you: stay where you are."

I hung back and watched, frustrated, as Adrie and James shot out of the bunch in pursuit of the breakaway. Part of me rushed away with them. I gritted my teeth, biting back curses I longed to shout. It was ironic – if I weren't already so close to the Royal, I'd actually have had a *chance* at it.

A glance in Brunn's direction confirmed he was thinking the same thing. The slight, smug crease in his cheek was proof enough. He knew I was gagging for a chance, on the alert to seize any opportunity afforded me. Whether it came as the result of someone else's tactical error or simple luck, I'd take it.

For now, there was nothing I could do. I swallowed my frustration, took another turn at the head of the group and kept smoothly stroking the pedals. I maintained the ambitious tempo even when complaints rose behind me.

Schlessinger would be caught and pulled back by the chase group. Brunn would keep his lead. Soon enough, someone somewhere would go wrong and I'd have to grab the chance. We had two more days in the mountains before the Tour was over, and I was sure I'd ride better than ever there.

I could feel it.

After the mountains, there was the final time trial on the flats to Paris. *That* would be my moment.

When it was all over, one way or another I'd have the Royal. And then, God willing, I'd have Abby, too.

A short while later, Michael's voice in my ear confirmed Adrie and James had caught the breakaway with the chase group. We were gaining ground, bridging what little distance there was in-between.

More thunder rumbled, the helicopter passed far overhead, and Michael's voice came over the radio.

"We need a volunteer to come back for the gear, lads. Who's it going to be?"

"I'll do it," I said, grateful for the change of pace.

I slowed and drifted back to the team car. I permitted myself the briefest possible respite by grasping the rain gear as Michael paused in handing it over, pushing me along with the car. I kept pedalling, lest it look like I was taking advantage of serving as domestique for a while.

"How's it going, Ciccio?" Michael asked.

"So far, so good – but if this weather keeps up, it's going to get messy."

"Keep to the front, stay out of trouble." Jerzy's instruction from the passenger seat was automatic, mechanical.

I nodded to show I'd understood. I glanced inside the car to find him staring straight out the windscreen.

The crew in the car kept handing the rain gear up to me, helping me stuff the tightly folded ultra-lightweight jackets and nylon sleeves into my pockets and under my jersey to carry them up to the team.

"*Robaczku, wracaj po wodę!*" Jerzy bellowed into the radio, and I took it as my cue to depart.

I advanced through the peloton, finding my teammates and giving them their gear as I went. Rom went backwards, going to the team car as I had done, this time for water. He gave me a look somewhere between resignation and boredom as he went. He abhorred flat stages at the best of times, but before long the weather would make it miserable going.

Once I'd distributed everything, I sat up and rode hands-free to unfurl my own jacket and put it on. All around me other riders did the same. The bright colours of the peloton became more uniform as we sheltered beneath black, white or silver-grey rain jackets. The sky had darkened considerably and the first heavy drops of rain struck the tarmac in the near distance. I got covered up and relaxed a little, breathing the humid air as we approached yet another small town.

Thunder rumbled around us as we swept around a curve where the wet and metallic smell of rain rushed into our faces, carried on a stiff wind. Not long afterward the rain came down. It wasn't as fine as before and grew heavier as we plunged into the murky light beneath the clouds.

Everyone slowed. Not dramatically, not all at once, but enough to ensure no-one slid out of control on the oil rising on the wet surface of the road. The peloton broke in two again, but there was no chance of another breakaway.

The spray thrown from the wheels ahead was motivation enough to go forward to the front of the group. It was impossible to see clearly with the road grime splashing into my face.

According to the voice in my ear, we were now nearly caught

up to the breakaway group. Once we got out of the town and into the trees along the road ahead, the peloton would be one large group again.

There were still spectators gathered on the sidewalks along the race route in spite of the rain. Some carried umbrellas, but most wore raincoats and hats or hooded windbreakers to fend off the wet, the better to watch the peloton pass by.

"Sharp left coming up, then a hard right and we're on a straightaway out of town." Michael's voice was intermittent, scratchy, but the reminder came just in time. A couple of riders misjudged the turn and skidded out to bump the kerb – hard. They looked as though they were riding on ice, their wheels shuddering and slipping over the road surface.

Despite my own momentary loss of traction I made it through. Behind me came some surprised shouts and a few catcalls from luckier riders, teasing their mates for their near-misses.

The final curve out of town was less treacherous and we picked up speed as we made for the straight road into the trees. We'd catch the breakaway group soon.

A motorcycle faded back toward us, the driver taking care not to get in anyone's line, staying far enough away to keep from splashing us. The pretty, raincoat-clad girl astride the back of the bike held up a chalkboard, angling it to keep the rain off and show us we were twenty seconds behind the break.

Knowing Adrie and James were working to slow them down, the pack increased speed – nothing too dangerous for the wet roads, but enough to cut the break's lead by a few more seconds – and then we were in the trees.

A whole new set of difficulties arose. While the rain was weakened by the height of the trees and their proximity to the road, there was an increase in the amount of debris to avoid. There were small branches – little more than twigs, really – on the sides of the road. Leaves and pine needles were scattered over the wet tarmac, making the slick surface bumpy as well.

The breakaway group were now in sight, slowed by the same debris we'd encountered. We were nearly on top of them before they disappeared around a bend in the road.

Before we took the curve I caught the sounds of brakes squealing, metal scraping across tarmac and the heavier *thud* of bodies doing the same.

Someone shouted a warning and we all slowed, doing our best to avoid riding over the unfortunates who had hit the deck ahead of us. Thanks to the anonymity of the rain jackets we wore, it was hard to know who was who. Swinging wide, I narrowly missed locking up with one rider, who raised a hand to fend me off and promptly knocked into someone else instead.

By chance I avoided the same fate and managed to skirt the shoulder on hard-packed ground before unclipping from the bike. I carried it up to a clear spot on the road and mounted again, taking a quick look back over my shoulder at the carnage. Schlessinger glared at me as he got up from where he'd landed amongst the gravel and dirt before he hobbled over to his bike and checked to see if there was any serious damage.

With that, I rode on, carrying Brunn along behind me as the rain started to fall in earnest.

***

After dinner, still thinking of the photos I'd taken in the afternoon, I climbed the stairs to my room of the B&B. I propped open the window to let in some fresh air and, thanks to the short rainstorm, the breezes were cool and comforting, sweeping away the heat of the day.

I lay down on the bed and watched the curtains sway back and forth in front of the window. The hypnotic movement lulled me into a post-dinner doze. Each cool caress of the breeze inside the room made me think of Federico's touch; light and careful, gently provocative.

I rolled up into a ball, facing the window so the breeze would keep touching my cheek. I wanted the fantasy to continue. I *needed* it to.

I thought of his kisses, his lips so firm and strong on my own, and the way they parted and pressed against mine. I shivered, remembering our first kiss; the brief, slick touch of his tongue on mine before he'd drawn away.

It was torture, pure and simple, but I couldn't help myself. Watching him arrive at the finish today, I'd imagined finding him in his room afterwards and lying beside him to share a few kisses. Nothing more than that – just enough to sustain me until the next time we were alone.

A fantasy was all it was or could be. He'd disappeared into the care of his chaperone and the team staff, hustled away to clean up, eat and recover after a long day in the saddle.

But what if...?

What if the end of the Tour *wasn't* the end of us? What if we were able to make this work? Then what?

Could I be content with stealing a few moments here and there with Federico? If we were an actual couple, would it make a difference? If Jerzy's rules meant anything, then the answer was no. Obviously the team was held to a higher standard than many others, even if the demands seemed unreasonable.

Federico had said that Jerzy got results. It was the reason they were willing to live their almost monastic existences in the first place. As for the wives and girlfriends, how did *they* deal with being forced away from their partners for so many months of the year?

I couldn't even imagine it.

What I *could* imagine was frustrating enough: more days – and nights – like this one.

I took a deep breath and sighed. While I wouldn't be able to spend the nights with him, I'd at least be able to spend *some* time with him. Wouldn't I? That would be better than what I had now.

Right now, I had... nothing, except memories of the time we'd stolen to be together.

I drifted, turning my thoughts to his kisses, sinking back down into the doze which offered to take me away from the world for a little while. The room washed out from around me, the last light of the day dimmed and darkened, and soon my memories gained clarity, bringing Federico's face close to mine again.

The sharp trill of the hotel phone jolted me back to the real world, and I found myself sitting up on the bed, my hand already resting on the receiver.

I permitted myself a small hope that it was Federico calling, though I doubted it.

"Hello?"

"Abby?" Charles' voice was full of apparent concern. "Is everything okay?"

"Of course it is. Why? What's going on?"

"I should ask you the same. I've been calling your mobile for the last hour, and you haven't picked up once. I was afraid perhaps something had happened to you."

I cursed under my breath and fished my mobile out of my handbag. The battery was dead – I'd forgotten to charge it during the drive in to Brussels.

"My phone's dead," I explained, trying to keep calm. *What if Federico tried to call? Would he think to call the hotel?* I stood and put the phone on the bed so I could get to my bags. "I didn't realize it wasn't on."

Keeping the receiver wedged between my ear and my shoulder, I unzipped the front pocket of my suitcase and dug out the mobile's charger.

"Well, thank goodness for that." The genuine relief in Charles' voice stopped me in my tracks.

I paused, surprised, seeking the words for a response.

"Is everything okay with *you*?" I finally ventured.

"Well, uh... Yes, yes it is."

"You're feeling better?"

"Indeed. I went back to work today."

"That's good."

"Yes. Abby?"

"Yes?"

"When are you coming home?"

Closing my eyes, I sank down onto the bed, feeling as though I were falling through a dream. Hadn't he written to *her* a couple of days ago? Or rather, hadn't he *meant* to, but instead sent the e-mail to me? Hadn't he realized his mistake?

"I'll be home when the race is over. That's a little over a week from now."

I wanted to ask him about her – *Is she back from Leeds yet? Do you know about the e-mail error?* – but at the same time, it felt good to pretend that maybe he missed me.

'Too'. That he missed me, too.

"I thought maybe you were ready to come home, that's all."

"Why?"

"Maybe you're done making your point by now."

"'Making my point'?"

"I know why you stayed there without me."

I considered the possibility that he really might know. A horrified thrill shivered through me.

"You do?"

"You're only doing this to spite me." He added a weary sigh as though I were an obstinate child, being pointlessly wilful. "I wish you would come home."

"Why? Do you need me there for something?"

God help me, I wanted him to say 'yes'.

"Of course I do. You know that."

"Really?"

"Abby, you know I don't have all the details of the household available. I need your help with –"

My heart went cold and I lay down again, curling up without a thought. Naturally. It had been too much to hope for.

"Send me an e-mail," I said, hearing the distance in my own voice. "I can do most of it from here, if I must."

"I'll do that later," he said, suddenly conciliatory. A long pause followed, then slowly, almost reluctantly: "I miss you."

"I miss you, too," I parroted with numb lips, meaning the words and somehow *not* meaning them at the same time.

There was a distant fumble and *click* on his end of the line before I let the receiver drop onto the cradle from fingers which had gone cold.

"Fucker," I muttered, willing away the burning behind my eyelids as I got up and closed the window to the night.

***

There weren't any messages from Abby. We hadn't communicated at all since I'd called her from the hotel in Bonn, and I didn't expect to hear from her anytime soon. I'd been trying not to think about her too much – trying instead to focus on the race and what I needed to do there. She had a way of sneaking into my head when I least expected it.

The downtime, like now, was the absolute worst. As the bus rolled out of Maastricht toward Antwerp, my thoughts kept straying to her, and the temptation to call her grew stronger and stronger in spite of my teammates' antics.

No matter how loud and thumping the music on the sound system, no matter how manic the guys became, Abby lingered in my mind. I joined in, joking with the guys, and hoped it wasn't too obvious that my mind was elsewhere.

Thanks to the inclement weather I'd gained two precious seconds on Schlessinger and Legarreta. It was enough to make the pair of them nervous, and that was satisfying indeed.

Adrie sat in front of me and took out his road book, and I turned to watch the scenery pass outside the bus window. The next song started – yet another techno-dance-funk choice of Goosh's, I guessed – and then Phil and Teodoro started whooping in time to the beat. Not long after, Alvaro and Attilio joined in, hooting laughter.

"Rock out wi' yer cocks out, gents!" James shouted, and Adrie glanced up, only to roll his eyes and go back to the road book with a slight smirk on his face. James was dancing up the aisle clad only in a towel, flapping the edges upward while he gyrated obscenely to the music.

I was curious what Jerzy's reaction would be, but he was too engrossed in conversation with Michael to pay attention to the lads. When I faced the back of the bus again, I spotted Brunn in the crash pad with Rom. My stomach turned at the sight. Rom's English wasn't good enough for a heavy conversation, but Brunn spoke Polish pretty well.

Worse still, Rom looked nervous, ill at ease. He shook his head and shrugged, not looking Brunn in the eye, and when he looked up and met my eyes, he ducked his head. Brunn, in turn, sat up straighter, nodding, and something about the gesture sent a rush of ice down my spine.

I sank back into my seat, sliding down as if I could hide from the apprehension which made my heart race harder than it ever had on a bike.

Stage Nineteen

(171 km – Antwerp – Amsterdam)

By the time Jerzy came round to wake us, I'd been lying in bed staring at the ceiling for an hour or so. I wasn't tired, just slightly ill. I kept remembering Rom's guilty look and how he'd avoided looking me in the eye.

I hoped to keep my breakfast down; I wasn't ready to abandon the race for illness. I wasn't ready to abandon at *all*, but if my roommate had ratted me out, I wouldn't have any choice. My clandestine activities in recent weeks had been brought to light in Bonn, sure, but no-one besides Rom knew exactly how long they'd been going on.

And if Jerzy found *that* out, I was beyond fucked. This wasn't an infraction that would get me kicked off the team riding the Tour; it would get me kicked off the team – permanently.

I had no-one else to blame. My sneaking out and staying out as long as I could to see Abby hadn't affected my riding, but there was always the chance Jerzy would say it *had*, that if I'd been more responsible, the Royal would be mine now. If I'd resisted the temptation to see Abby, I might have ridden better and maintained a higher place in the standings.

I'd never thought about that before. Was it true? Had I been sabotaging myself all along?

Fuck.

There was no way to know, except to avoid seeing her for the remainder of the Tour.

BAM! WHAM!

Doors started banging open along the corridor, a sure sign Jerzy was getting closer. At once, I was able to shift gears and think about the race again. I got out of bed and went to the window, opening the curtains to find dark grey clouds hanging low over the city. It seemed they might snag on the jagged rooftops, which looked like black slate atop the chalk-and-charcoal facades. All the colours were muted in the early morning mist, and I finally felt tired enough to go back to bed.

Too late.

The door slammed open and I turned to face Jerzy, who was already calling our names. He paused, gave me a curt nod, gestured in Rom's direction and then disappeared from the doorway to wake the others.

Rom stirred and rolled over, preceded by his customary lead-out man. I headed for the bathroom.

It was business as usual – at least for now.

***

When the hotel phone rang, I jumped. I set my computer aside and reached for the phone, bracing for a conversation with Charles. Would he launch into whatever statement he'd prepared, call me by name, or start demanding to know when I'd be home – as if he didn't already know?

"Hello?" I took a breath and waited for the barrage.

"Is this Mrs. Abigail White?"

I paused before answering the unfamiliar voice. Was this Pascal, perhaps? No, it couldn't be. I hadn't told him where I was staying.

Besides that, the accent was wrong.

Someone from the hotel, then?

"Yes, this is she. How can I help you?"

"Mrs. White, this is Heinrich Brunn. I'm a teammate of Federico Renard."

"I know who you are," I said, the world slipping away from me to become distant and surreal. Brunn had called *me*? What the hell? "Why are you calling me? Where did you get this number? How –"

"I'll explain, Mrs. White, if you give me a chance."

It was amazing; his tone never wavered, not in the least. I couldn't think of anyone else who could be so brazen – calling someone he'd never met, and then taking such an approach? – and stay so calm.

"Go ahead, then. Explain how you knew where to find me. Explain how you even know *who* I am."

Surely Federico hadn't told him – or anyone else – what hotel I was in?

"I will, over dinner."

"Excuse me?"

"If you come to dinner, we can talk."

Oh, God... He must think I'm one of... "I'm sorry, but I'd rather not."

"Mrs. White –"

I cringed, hating him calling me that, hating the guilt which rose so easily at the implication behind the name. "Abigail," I said, resigned. "At least call me Abigail."

For a wonder, he paused. "Abigail," he repeated before continuing. "I'll be in your hotel's restaurant in half an hour. Please come downstairs so we can talk." He expected me to do it.

I got the feeling people rarely said 'no' to him.

"I told you, I'd rather not."

"I want to talk to you about Federico. It's important."

"What about him?" I had trouble keeping my voice steady, and I resented it. I wanted to stand up to this man; even more, I wanted to *defy* him. I certainly didn't want to give him the satisfaction of ordering me around.

"I'd prefer to discuss the matter with you at dinner."

"*Mister* Brunn," I began, my heart still beating far away from my body, "I think you might have misunderstood something about my *friendship* with Federico." I put an emphasis on the word and hoped it would clarify things for him.

An interminable silence followed.

"Half an hour." That was all he said.

I found my curiosity was piqued in spite of myself.

"Fine. I'll be there."

*

I waited in my room for precisely thirty-eight minutes before I went down to the restaurant. I peered around the corner, wondering if I would recognize him without his cycling kit, in his street clothes. Thinking hard, I couldn't remember ever seeing Heinrich Brunn in civilian clothing – not even when he'd had the car accident some years back. Every report had shown him in his team gear, usually racing across the finish with a grimace etched into his face so deep one would be forgiven for thinking it was a permanent feature, or standing atop the podium of the Tour d'Europa with his arms held aloft in a victorious pose.

At first I looked right past him. He was seated at a table in the corner, dressed in a tennis shirt and faded jeans, one scuffed purple-and-white trainer jutting out from under the beige tablecloth.

My first impression was unexpected: a fangirlish thrill ran through me when those piercing ice-blue eyes found me in the dining room entryway. His expression didn't change, not even while he stood.

He didn't try to hide the fact he was assessing me as I crossed the room to join him. With every step I took, I found myself increasingly angry, defensive and determined to get through this with my dignity intact.

"Mrs. White," he said quietly, the words turning up slightly in a questioning tone, his German accent putting a faint 'v' in place of the 'w' in my name. I nodded and he reached out to take my hand in his, though only by the fingertips – a surprisingly disarming and graceful greeting – before gesturing to the chair opposite his.

"Mr. Brunn," I said by way of acknowledgement, his name feeling strange on my lips. I'd heard Federico call him 'Brunn' so many times it had taken a personality of its own in my mind.

I hesitated before sitting down, and saw a corner of his mouth crease, a brief quirk of what looked like amusement before he pulled out my chair and helped me to sit.

After he took his seat, we regarded each other in silence over the place settings. He wasn't as handsome as I'd expected, nor was he unattractive. His eyes crinkled in the corners, and the tan lines from his sunglasses contrasted with his ruddy complexion. The lines around his mouth were set deep enough that there were light tan lines there, too.

At last a server joined us, handed us menus and recited the evening specials both in Dutch and French before he retreated to allow us to make our choices.

Brunn watched me carefully for a short while longer, then opened his menu and gave it a quick once-over. "Do you speak Dutch, Mrs. White?"

"No. And I told you before: you might as well call me Abigail."

"That's right. Do you speak French, then?"

"No." I continued reading, wishing he would get to why he'd asked to meet.

"I could order for you, if —"

"This isn't a date," I said abruptly. "You don't have to do that. Besides, the listings are in English as well." I half-turned the menu toward him to make my point, and he nodded. We went back to reading in silence.

The server came and took our orders — I chose a lamb dish, Brunn selected a fish stew — and we resumed our mutual assessment across the table. Even with the tension in the air, it was a more pleasant night out than the last evening I'd spent with Charles.

My hand drifted to my pocket and my mobile phone tucked away there in case Federico should try to call. He wouldn't, but part of me still hoped.

My dinner companion was clearly no fan of small talk. For the duration of the meal, neither of us spoke. When the bill arrived, he deftly reached out and took it, speaking to the server in rapid Dutch before the man departed with Brunn's credit card in hand.

"How long have you known him?" Brunn asked. After so much silence, I suspected he'd hoped to take me by surprise, to startle me into confessing something. My throat tightened and I sipped some water to relax it.

"Not long." I brought my gaze up from the table to meet his and those sharp blue eyes fixed me in place as though they had pinned me to my chair. The rush of heat to my face and neck an instant later made me feel flustered, foolish. "Since the Tour started."

"How did you meet him?"

"He checked on me after the crash in Lorca. Remember?"

A silent eternity passed.

"That was you?" Brunn asked, with the slightest hint of astonishment. "He took you up to his room after that crash? That doesn't sound right."

"No." My face grew hotter and I wondered if the low lighting in the restaurant would cover the evidence of my rising distress. "That was later. We met a few times, after Lorca. Just by chance, nothing planned."

He must think I'm some sort of stalker or something.

"We met again in Andorra, on the rest day," I continued. "He came into a pub where I was having dinner, and he stayed for a while." I still felt defensive, but Brunn's impassive gaze somehow compelled me to continue. "After that we kept bumping into each other – it's all perfectly innocent."

"Andorra." Brunn's forehead creased, then smoothed again. "Did you know that was when he found out his fiancée left him?"

It was my turn to be surprised. "No. He didn't mention it, either. Not until later, anyway."

Brunn pursed his lips.

"You really didn't know he had to sneak out in order to see you?"

I shook my head. "I didn't know about the rules. He only told me after the fact. By the time I understood how much trouble he could get into, it was too late."

"'Too late'?"

"Nothing happened." I tried not to think of the last time I'd seen Federico. *Something* had happened that night, indeed, but not quite what Brunn likely expected.

"What did he get from you?"

"What do you mean?" He didn't answer but I understood his implication soon enough. "Give me a break; I'm not a *pusher* or something."

"That's not what I meant." Nevertheless, there was a hint of relief in his expression. He seemed to slip into deep thought. "*Why* did he come to see you? What did he *get* from you?"

"I don't know." I shrugged helplessly. "We talked. We slept. That was it."

He arched an eyebrow.

"Okay; we kissed. We held each other. That's *all*. It never went farther than that."

An almost overwhelming need to confess swept over me and I forced myself to hold back. There wasn't anyone I could talk to – and the man sitting in front of me right now was about as far as was possible from being a perfect confessor.

Brunn shook his head, clearly puzzled. "He's risking so much, for..." He took a drink and tilted his head to one side, regarding me as though I were an exhibit in a zoo. "What do you talk about?"

It was too much.

"None of your business." A much-belated rush of strength returned to my limbs and I moved to push my chair away from the table. "I've told you more than you have any right to know, as it is." I paused, still seated. "Why don't you ask *him*, anyway? Why call me? For that matter, how did you know who I am, or where to find me? How do you know *any* of this?"

"I found out. That's all."

Another pause. I sensed the frustration beneath his placid façade. It was clear he was trying to sort everything out, but nothing was coming together for him.

In the meantime, I considered his last statement. Federico had sworn that Rom knew nothing about us, save for the near-miss in the conference room in Courmayeur. Aside from that almost-meeting and a smile in my direction the other day, Rom and I had never actually *met*. Could he have said something to Brunn?

"Nothing happened," I repeated. The words sifted like powder on my tongue. I took a drink to wash them away.

"That doesn't matter. It's enough he defied Jerzy one too many times. I've done all I can for him. He fucks up again, he's done."

"There won't be any more problems. He's already told me we can't see each other anymore."

The faintest glimmer of surprise lit his eyes. Grim satisfaction stirred in me to see it.

"He did?"

"Yes. He called me on the rest day and said he couldn't meet me again until the Tour is over. I agreed. End of story."

After a lengthy pause, Brunn nodded, almost seeming satisfied for the first time.

"I can see why he likes you."

"Why?"

"You're smart, calm. Not high-strung like his last girlfriend. If he can get himself together, you'd be good for him – when the Tour is *finished*. He's a good kid, but that's the problem. He's still a kid."

"No," I said, offended on Federico's behalf. "No, he's not. *That's* the problem right there. He's a man, an *adult*, but you've known him so long, you can't see him as anything but some snot-nosed kid in spite of what he's done – of what he's achieved."

"You can't understand." He shook his head, an infuriatingly dismissive gesture. "He's been raised in a sheltered way – within the team – since he was a teenager. Cycling has been his life since he *was* a kid."

"He's told me all about life on the road with Jerzy in charge. How you're only allowed a little time with your families during the stage races, and how you socialize mostly with each other until the off-season – all that stuff." I shrugged and raised my hands off the tabletop. "So what? How does that make him some sort of idiot savant on a bike?"

"You're twisting my words."

"Then clarify things for me, please. I honestly don't understand what you mean."

"Didn't you notice that his family weren't there for the French stages? Didn't you wonder where they were? No? If he hasn't explained why during your *talks*," he almost sneered the word, "it's not for me to tell you. He's taking too many chances right now. Too many stupid risks off the bike – but *you* can't see *that*. You're too busy seeing him as—" Brunn cut himself short, a flare of colour rising in his face, an unexpected crack in the frosty façade.

"Go on," I said, as coolly as I could.

He looked at me and blinked slowly.

"It's not like that." I rested my fingers along the stem of my wine glass and idly turned it round and round.

"What *is* it like, then, *Mrs.* White? What is he to you?"

It was precisely the question which lurked in the darker corners of my mind. What, exactly, was Federico to me? A fling? A friend? A partner?

I shook my head, still turning my glass, the round crease in the tablecloth deepening with every revolution. *I don't know,* I wanted to say, but didn't dare.

"I'll tell you what he is to *me*," Brunn said, his tone suddenly softening. "He's my teammate. He used to be my friend. Now he's someone I'm depending on in order to win this race."

"You want to know what we talk about?" I asked quietly.

He exhaled softly before he spoke. "Yes, I do."

"We talk about the team. About what he wants to do when he can't ride anymore." I made a point of meeting Brunn's eyes as steadily as I could. "Sometimes, we talk about *you*."

"Me?" He seemed genuinely surprised, which surprised me, in turn.

"Of course." Silence hung between us a while before I continued. "You know he's angry. I'm inclined to agree with him."

"Of course you are."

"You don't think Jerzy handled things poorly? He waited until the last minute to bring you back onto the team for the Tour – really pushed the limits, from what I've read in the trades – then didn't make a decision about who would be leading the team until the Tour was well underway. He'd all but promised that to Federico this time around – then *you* came back. Can you really blame the guy for being pissed off?"

"Ciccio needs to control his temper better. It's affecting his riding."

"No doubt about that. He's improved, though. He's found his focus again."

Brunn folded his arms across his chest and nodded. "Perhaps."

"If he hadn't been so distracted with the politics at the start, he'd be riding better than you are, I'm willing to bet."

He raised one eyebrow. "Unlikely," he said. "He still has to beat Schlessinger."

I shook my head and stood up, ready to go. "He thinks you stole his chance."

To my amazement, Brunn laughed – a truly pleasant sound.

"He still has his chance," he said. "He's just got to take it."

***

The sturdy sofas and loveseats scattered about the lobby of the team's hotel in Amsterdam had seen better days. The reporter interviewing me on behalf of a French sports magazine didn't seem to mind, however, and we settled there to finish the interview. I got the feeling his employers hadn't sprung for much of a meals budget, since we'd begun our chat between mouthfuls at the team dinner.

A team dinner minus Brunn, who was still nowhere to be seen. While I did my best to concentrate on giving politic responses to the questions asked of me, I kept wondering where my teammate was.

At the same time, I was dying to call Abby, if only for a few minutes, to see how she was. I sneaked glances at my phone, half-expecting to find her room number there, or a text message to let me know she wanted to talk.

I knew she was frustrated. We never should have allowed ourselves to grow so accustomed to seeing each other; had I known how dependent I would become on seeing her, I'd never have let things go so far.

When I was riding, I focused on the race without a problem. The hardest times came before, and after – nights were especially tough – but when I was on the bike, I forgot almost everything else.

"Okay, one final question," my companion said and I tried not to sigh with relief. "How do you feel about Heinrich Brunn being team captain? There was a general consensus, wasn't there, that *you* were supposed to be leading the squad?"

"Obviously not." I hoped my laugh was convincing.

"It doesn't trouble you to have Brunn in charge?"

"No, it doesn't. Jerzy feels Brunn's the strongest rider, and that's enough. There's no point in carrying a grudge. He has the best chance of winning the Tour."

"But you aren't far behind. It's unusual, isn't it, to have two riders from the same team so closely ranked in the top of the GC – much less in contention for the Royal?"

"I suppose so. But that's a sign of how good this team is. That's all."

"If you had a chance to go after the Royal, would you? You're in an advantageous position now – barring any exceptional moves by Brunn or Schlessinger – so is that something you're considering?"

There was movement by the front doors. I glanced over as Brunn came in, watching me carefully as he passed by. We nodded to each other and he went into the conference room where Jerzy was waiting with Michael and a few others.

"I think I have to give you the most honest answer I possibly can, Rene," I paused to consider my words.

"Yes?" he asked, holding the little microphone closer to me. "Yes?" he prodded again, a little anxiously, when I stayed quiet a little too long for his liking.

I gave him the biggest, most sincere smile I could.

"No comment," I said, stood up, and walked away.

Stage Twenty

(140 km – Amsterdam – Eindhoven)

I was going crazy. I don't know how the image could be so persistent in the midst of warming up but it was there and refused to budge: Abby, sitting dishevelled atop her bedclothes, her lips parted beneath mine as I kissed her goodbye.

Linked to that memory were others, a Gordian knot of images and impressions: Abby's skin, warm and smooth, bearing a hint of some scent I couldn't identify but smelled every time I was with her; her lips pressed firmly to mine, resisting yet yielding; the soft, wet flick of her tongue on mine; the slick, humid touch of her lips and tongue on my throat; her hands caressing me; her warmth beneath me, beckoning; the silent entreaty in her eyes, refusing to beg but nevertheless pleading for more from me.

And why hadn't I given her what she wanted – what *we* wanted? Why hadn't I seen things through? Because of some stupid superstition of Jerzy's?

I shook my head – hard – trying to dispel my doubts along with my memories of her. It didn't work.

My trainer's hands touched my sides, guiding me on the bike and forcing my train of thought back to the present. Around the perimeter of the training area outside the team bus, spectators and fans were taking pictures on all manner of cameras: mobile phones, digital pocket cameras, professional-grade equipment. I ignored

287

them, giving an occasional acknowledgement whenever I shifted the focus of my warm-up.

They called my name, Brunn's name; some fans even called out to Jerzy or Michael when they emerged from the bus. Not hearing our names was excusable since we all wore earphones to listen to music or motivational podcasts or whatever else we might have chosen.

In my peripheral vision were a cluster of girls – at best, they could be called 'young women' – standing at the ready, prepared to squeal or shout or chant my name if I should happen to glance their way. A few of them had made t-shirts with my cover of *Grand Tours* on them, and I wished for the millionth time that I hadn't agreed to that photo shoot, or that article.

'The Face of the Tour'. I groaned. It was as though a weight tugged at my neck, dragging me lower on the bike. I sat up and took my MP3 player out of the pocket on the back of my jersey, shuffled to a new song and resumed my position on the bike while the fast electronic beat pounded in my ears.

I was suddenly aware of something large and white on the perimeter around the team bus, something catching the sunlight brightly enough to make me squint. With the least little tilt of my head, I was able to see it clearly.

The 'Foxy Fede' banner was back. *Merde.*

The attention should have been flattering. However, it only served two purposes: to provide an inordinate amount of distraction and to enhance my reputation as a lightweight in the sport. I had a hard enough time being taken seriously without screaming fangirls jumping up and down whenever I appeared.

On the bus I grabbed a quick shower and put on clean kit for the race. I focused on the ride ahead from Amsterdam to Eindhoven. The only problems would be the wind or inclement weather, and there wasn't much rain in the forecast.

Finally, the team sat for the last meeting of the morning. Michael paced at the front of the bus, reciting the usual litany of reminders and goals while we feigned interest or our need to know. Silent as ever, Jerzy stood to one side, watching as though waiting for someone to contradict the carefully-laid plans for the stage. Then we were out, signing autographs or posing for quick photos with the fans on the way to the sign-in stage near the start line.

I tried not to think of Abby amidst the flashes of the cameras surrounding the start line. Magnified by hundreds in the hazy mid-morning light, the impression of the come-and-go brightness was unsettling. I went deeper into myself until my only thoughts were of the road ahead and what I needed to do there.

It was a normal day.

*

Once we left Amsterdam it started raining, scarcely more than a mist which fogged my glasses and clung to my skin, chilling me as I rode. When the wind blew harder, that mist began to sting – not just cold, but a biting cold – and I was forced to don my rain jacket.

By the time the peloton passed Utrecht, the wind died down and the rain became a dreary drizzle. After so many accidents earlier in the week, no one took a chance on crashing out. Everyone rode cautiously, biding their time and energy for the final circuit around Eindhoven and the inevitable sprint finish.

Teodoro placed fifth in the stage, boxed in by the violent battle for first which raged at the front of the bunch. The riders who placed first and second had done so cleanly – their lead-out men, not so much. Instead of dropping back and out of the way as expected, they'd caused more chaos by swerving toward one another and blocking other riders – Teodoro among them. He'd held back from plunging into the melee and arrived safely at the finish.

However, beyond the finish line, fisticuffs broke out between the competitors, resulting in disqualifications for the two riders involved.

On the record, we'd managed a third place finish, but Teodoro wasn't satisfied with that.

"I was still fifth across the line," he grumbled while we watched the video of the finish on the bus en route to the hotel. "That's all that matters."

"Yeah, well, I'd prefer all of you avoided fistfights anyway," Michael said, passing on his way to the back of the bus. He switched off the video and turned the TV to the news.

"Speaking of fistfights..." Adrie stood in the aisle, watching a replay of the fight on the TV screen.

Phil shook his head, half-grinning, and James laughed out loud.

"Jaysus, there's nothing more pathetic than a scrawny bloke in cleats trying to throw a punch!"

"I reckon you could do better, then?" Phil challenged, smirking, and James threw a soft, open-handed slap his way.

"You know it, big boy," he simpered. "Let me put my shoes on, and I'll show you how much better I –"

Michael waved a hand in their direction, silencing them, his attention focused on the television. I sat up straighter in my seat and Adrie leaned on the backrest of my chair as the bus turned a sharp corner.

"Shit..." James grumbled when the image on the screen cleared long enough for us to read the tickertape scroll along the bottom edge:

"BANHOF TESTS POSITIVE: REMOVED FROM TOUR D'EUROPA..."

"Figures," Phil said, now studying the stitching of the armrest of his seat. Banhof's team, *Zuverlässige Branchen*, had been working with us throughout the Tour so far. If one member of the team had tested positive, then it was likely the whole team would be under extra scrutiny.

"That's one less ally for us, I'd wager." Adrie made his way to his seat, his expression inscrutable.

"We'll do fine," I said, surprising myself and, judging by their faces, a few of the others. "We've got ourselves, and we're all we need to take this. We're nearly there, right?"

James smiled and Adrie nodded, but Teodoro continued staring out the window.

***

While I wouldn't want to change a single second I'd spent with Federico, the events of the last few days had left me at a loss for what to do with my down time.

It was only while eating a dinner consisting of coffee and a sandwich in a coffee shop near my hotel in Eindhoven I realized the time had come to admit the truth: I was lonely.

This feeling was unexpected, since I was no stranger to keeping my own company. At home, I was alone while Charles worked in London. I spent time with friends – people who were more acquaintances than friends, in some cases – but I was generally fine by myself. I occupied my time with projects and plans, and I didn't find talking to myself anything out of the ordinary (though I was seldom caught in the act).

But this was different. Wandering in cities I'd never seen before, unable to share my experiences with anyone had me feeling a bit lost. It had been tolerable when I'd shared the stories about my day with Federico. Now, however...it was unsettling, discomfiting. It was as though everyone knew I was alone, that my marriage was ending, that I'd been conducting an affair with a younger man only to have it quashed before it could start, that I was one of *those women* who sneak around and do things behind other people's backs.

I felt like a failure.

Some of this tumult was the result of my dinner with Brunn the night before. I hadn't told Federico about it – how could I? We hadn't talked on the phone since that disastrous rest day in Bonn. Besides, this felt like face-to-face information, not something to reveal in a text message or phone call.

My loneliness persisted while I sat in a quiet Eindhoven coffee shop, one with an English menu outside. I watched couples come and go; some sat outside at the little café tables, others canoodled over their cups in various nooks and corners.

I ached for company. I yearned for Federico to stroll through the door and join me, even though I knew it'd never happen. I wanted to sit across from him in a public place and not worry that we'd be seen.

Instead, my salvation from solitude took a different, yet familiar form strolling in through the front door.

"Abby! I *thought* that was you," he said, stepping up to my table.

"Pascal; how nice to see you. How are things?"

He shrugged dismissively and grinned. "*Bon, bon...* And how are *you?*"

"I'm well, thanks." I gestured to the empty seat across from me and he pulled it out but didn't sit.

"Don't tell me – the husband is not here?" He glanced around and then gave me a sly look.

"He went home," I said. I gave a *what-can-you-do* gesture with one hand. "Work – you know how it is."

"Of course. Excuse me, I'll join you in a moment."

As soon as he'd walked away, I wondered if telling him the truth about Charles had been a mistake. When he joined me again, he had an air of expectation.

"Get any good shots today?" I asked, hoping to keep the conversation from getting too personal.

"I think so. I'll know tonight when I take another look. I wish I'd been on the motorbike, though – there were some remarkable crashes out on the course today. At least four riders are out of the race now."

"I saw that. It's the rain, I guess."

"At least it's not like Rotterdam a few years ago. What year was that? I've forgotten now – oh, yes, in 2003. Terrible, terrible rains, but that was only for one day. I'm still surprised they held the stage."

I nodded, knowing the stage he meant: a time trial which had been raced in a downpour – almost a *deluge*, really. I didn't think a single rider racing that day cared to recall his time at the end – nearly everyone had turned in the worst ride of their career. Many hit the deck and their seasons had come to premature ends.

Only a few riders managed respectable times, and that year Heinrich Brunn had been one of them.

"So when did your husband go away?"

I should have known.

"A couple of days ago. He was called back for an emergency at work," I lied.

Pascal nodded solemnly and took a sip of his coffee.

"He left you here alone," he said, and it wasn't a question.

"I can manage on my own," I said, hoping to infuse the words with as much nonchalance as possible.

"That's good. But just in case, may I offer you my mobile number? If you should need any assistance, you could call me."

Without warning, my heart sped into overdrive. Was it wise to accept his number? Would he expect something from me if I did?

"Pascal, that's very kind of you, but like I said: I can manage on my own."

He shook his head, negating what I'd said.

"I insist, Abigail." There was a distinctly paternal tone in his voice which shook me. "Here." He took a pen from his breast pocket and scribbled on a paper napkin. "I'm not going to ask for your number, but I must insist that you take mine. In case of need." He slid the napkin toward me but I didn't reach for it. I did read it, scanning from right to left, the numbers upside-down in my view.

Pascal turned his attention out the window to the people strolling past in the early evening shadows. We sat in silence for a while before he turned to face me again.

"You should keep your head up, Abby," he said, his tone softening now. "There are all sorts of opportunities for freelancers here, you know?" He extended his arms outward in a gesture so ridiculously grand I had to smile. "Take me, for example. I'm doing photos for a friend who interviews the riders. Would you like to come along?"

I laughed, shaking my head. "Another time, perhaps? I'm looking forward to relaxing, tonight. Today was harder than I expected – that rain at the midpoint of the drive took me by surprise."

"It took everyone by surprise, my dear." He hoisted himself out of his chair with feigned difficulty and tipped me a wink. "Well, I'll see you at the start line. Better, join me at the sign-in. There are some great shots to be had there."

"I'll keep that in mind. Thanks."

He nodded and left. I sat, considering the possibilities and then reached out to snag the napkin with his number on it.

Just in case.

***

Once off the bus, we were herded *en masse* to a conference room for a more settled team strategy meeting. The place had already been set up for dinner: another buffet-style arrangement overseen by our team chefs and dieticians.

We mingled and mixed freely until the meeting was called. It was, in essence, a recap of the day's ride and the unfortunate events afterward. Michael started us off, commending Teodoro and the rest of the lead-out train for their prudent assessment of the situation at the finish and for their skill in avoiding what could have become a messy finish to the day.

When Jerzy came to his usual place between the tables, he stood there until all murmurs or whispers faded completely away.

"Tomorrow should be an easy ride," he said, turning his gaze to each one of us in turn. "But that doesn't mean you can slack off. I

293

saw some of that today. I expect you – all of you – to ride to the best of your abilities. I will accept nothing less."

He remained a while longer, once again regarding us one by one before he turned and left the room. The door hissed shut on its pneumatic hinge and silence filled the air.

Conversation slowly bubbled up amongst us.

"What the hell was that about?"

"What's going on?"

"Michael, what's up, mate?"

Rom looked at me questioningly and I shrugged, as confused as everyone else. That was the meeting, over and done.

Now I sat in the hotel on one of the leather sofas by the lobby window, watching the people passing by. The sun had come out and the pavements were drying, taking on a patchwork-repair look while they did, some splotches of damp slower to evaporate than others.

More rain was imminent, with dark clouds hanging moodily over the city. While I pondered whether the concrete in front of the hotel would dry completely before the next rain could fall, I saw her.

Abby strolled past the tinted window and the determined scowl of concentration on her face made me smile. Filled with sudden longing, I barely resisted the impulse to get up and follow her down the street, wherever she might be going.

If not for my interview scheduled five minutes from then, I'd have done it without a second thought.

I never learn.

Instead, my hand went into my pocket, and I took out my personal mobile. I scrolled down to her number to read and re-read it before hitting 'send'. All of this took – maybe – a couple of seconds.

No, I couldn't *see* her, but there was no reason I couldn't *talk* to her.

***

The unexpected *chirp* of my mobile gave me a slight start as I crossed the street and headed toward my hotel. Without looking, I dug around in my handbag, extracted the still chirping phone and flipped it open. Expecting Charles calling from work or from an associate's office, I didn't bother checking the caller ID.

"Hello?"

"You look amazing."

Confused, I had to sort out who my caller was, and then the smile spread easily across my lips. "Chicco," I said, glancing around.

"Don't bother looking for me," he said, and a spooky little shiver ran through me. "I'm in the hotel you passed now. I saw you go by." He exhaled softly into the mouthpiece, then: "You've got gorgeous legs."

I laughed a little and he did, too. "Thanks."

"Those walking shorts you insist on wearing don't hide the fact, you know."

"Maybe I don't want them to."

He laughed again and we fell into a comfortable silence while I continued walking to my hotel.

"I miss you, Abby. I want to be with you." There was an inexplicably *dangerous* pause on the line while I passed through the lobby. "I want to lick those legs, right up to the top." His voice was soft, gentle, akin to the implied caress. Another little shiver hit me, my legs momentarily weak while I climbed the stairs to my room. I paused on the landing until the wobbly-jelly feeling receded.

"I miss you too, Chicco, but should you really say such things if you're in a public place?" I tried to make it a joke, to sound light-hearted, but I couldn't tell if he'd heard it that way.

"I don't care who hears me," he said, his voice strengthening, and I imagined him sitting straighter on his chair or sofa or whatever, looking around the room. "I don't care who knows, not anymore."

"Shush." I put my key in the lock and turned it, the tumblers making a noise loud enough to echo in my phone.

"I really don't, Abby." He said my name with a small emphasis, a little stronger, a little louder than the rest of the sentence.

"Chicco…" I scolded and slipped into my room, shaking all over as I closed the door.

"Ab-*by*…" He chuckled again. "I'm alone, don't worry. I'm waiting for someone."

"Okay. I mean, that's fine – but stop with the dirty talk." I sat carefully on my bed, the jelly-legs feeling back in full force.

"'Dirty talk'?" You think this is 'dirty talk'?"

"Don't start."

Don't stop.

"I won't. We stand enough chance of getting kicked out of here thanks to Jerzy's wake-up calls, so why make things worse by making obscene phone calls from the lobby?"

I had to smile at that. "So, are you calling to try and embarrass me, then?"

"Maybe."

His tone made me feel warm all over, heat pooling deliciously low inside me.

"A week and a half, Abigail. Then we'll be together, yes?"

"Yes. Yes, we will."

"*Bon, bon, mais —*"

He sounded distracted. I listened closely, trying to decipher the jumble of noise on the other end of the line. It finally occurred to me that someone was speaking to Federico and he'd put his hand over the phone.

The voices became clearer; they were speaking French. I listened and, not for the first time, I found myself wishing I understood the language. What little I remembered from school indicated there were introductions being made, names exchanged.

Another rush of warmth swept over me as I recalled the words he'd breathed against my skin when our kisses had grown particularly heated. French... or had it been Italian?

"Abby? I should go now. My inquisitor – I mean, interviewer – and his photographer are here."

"Okay," I said, hoping his slip was the joke it seemed to be. "We'll talk soon."

"Definitely. *Au revoir, mon amour. Tu vas me manquer jusque-là.*"

He hung up the phone. I hadn't understood the last part of what he'd said, and this time I was sure it was all in French. Perhaps I was reading too much into it, but I missed when he'd addressed me in Italian.

Then again, we weren't alone, were we?

The next realization tickled anxiously at the back of my mind for a while before it emerged fully:

When he'd exchanged greetings on the other end of the line, he'd spoken French with two men: a reporter and a photographer – one of whom was named Pascal.

Stage Twenty-One

(145 km – Maastricht – Ettelbruck)

The first breakaway group shot off the front as soon as we cleared the neutralized start of the ride. Not that most of us could see it: the rain and gloom of the morning kept all but the front of the bunch from seeing much of anything.

Radio communication was spotty at best. Teams relied instead on the tried-and-true method of sending a rider back to the team cars for updates.

In any case, the only person I had to keep an eye on was Schlessinger. His crash two days before had cost him more time than he could spare.

After we passed through the feed zone midway along the route, the pace slowed further still. Riders ate and chatted in spite of the miserable weather. Along a relatively spectator-free section of the route, riders took quick, discreet 'natural breaks' before returning to the group.

Kilometres passed while the darkening sky pressed lower and lower. The rise and fall of the road was the only thing unpredictable enough to keep me from slipping into total complacency while I rode. There was no rush, no hurry to catch the breakaway or even to regroup.

Rom and I made our way to the front. The wind picked up and Gustafson and Laroche from *Étalon d'or* joined us to help cut through the wind. When I took the lead position, the rain obligingly drove into my face hard enough to make the drops feel like sleet and force the sensation of cold all the way to the bone.

It sure as hell didn't feel like July any more.

The television camera motorcycle sped off ahead and the peloton started up a gentle slope leading into a wooded area. The road narrowed considerably as we crested a rise shortly after entering the trees.

A squelch in my earpiece made me flinch. There was a blast of Jerzy shouting – the urgency in his voice made my flesh crawl – and then the descent began, wet tarmac curving out of sight into the trees while the motorcycles with the photographers dropped back through the pack.

As we took the bend I spotted pieces of metal lying next to the road, and a spray of something glittering not quite like sand on the tarmac. The wobble of my rear wheel was my first indication of trouble. Just a small skid, barely enough to knock me off balance, but enough to make the hair on the back of my neck stand up in alarm. This wasn't normal. Up ahead, Laroche went off the road trying to avoid colliding with Gustafson.

I made a futile attempt to stop when my tires skidded across the tarmac but ended up in the ditch. I lay there for a few moments, fighting the grey haze over my vision which accompanied the pounding in my skull. I hauled myself stiffly to my feet, my kit soaked through from the muddy ditchwater. I took a quick inventory of any possible injuries and found none. My hands, shaking with adrenaline, roved over my bike to check it wasn't badly damaged.

The front wheel clearly was: it was bent damn near in half.

Obscenities streamed out of my mouth in counterpoint to another chorus of curses behind me. Laroche stood next to the ditch, pulling broken branches out of his spokes and flinging them back into the woods.

"Fuck!" He dragged his bike out of the muck of the verge and limped along the edge of the road. "What the hell was that?" he called to Gustafson, who had pulled off to wait for his teammate to assess the damage from his fall while a handful of other riders passed us by.

Rom was a few yards ahead, looking back at me, his eyes wide and alarmed while he stared at my front wheel. I scraped muck off my arm and caught a glimpse of bright red mixed in with the shit-brown earth and leaves clinging to my fingertips. Everything was intact as far as I could tell, but my shoulder throbbed like a bitch. Another swipe of my hand over my leg revealed another cut and several scrapes – felt more than seen beneath a layer of mud – and both my rain jacket and kit were trashed.

Another squelch burst into my earpiece. I flinched again and considered pulling the damned thing out.

Then came the shriek of countless brakes locking, wheels skidding and the wet *whump* of bodies hitting the deck on the too-slick tarmac. The air around us filled with shouting and complaint, startled voices expressing surprise and frustration and cursing in a dozen different languages and dialects.

Sharp, pained cries were lost in the woods, some of which were chilling to hear, meaning fractured or broken bones, Tour-ending injuries of all sorts.

To make matters worse, the road was too narrow for the medics or the team cars to get through with so many men scattered across the tarmac. Everything came to a halt.

"Motherfuck – there's something on the road back there!" Laroche shouted, livid.

"Wh--- --ing on? -re you throu— th--- -et?" Michael's concern came through on my radio, even if his words didn't.

I bent to grapple with the mangled wheel, my muddy fingers slipping over the lever of the skewer in the hub as I tried to release it. "Give me your wheel," I said, but Rom was already scrambling to remove the front wheel from his own bike.

I switched the wheel out and hesitated. Brunn emerged from the chaos, picking his steps awkwardly in his cleats and looking considerably worse for wear. His leg was covered in road rash, one side of his kit shredded to the point of covering little more than his dignity.

He waved a hand at me and I got back on my bike, wincing at the pain in my shoulder. Rom gave me a look of encouragement as I passed him by, and then I focused on the task of getting Brunn out of there.

We turned another curve in the road and the scene of incredible carnage was lost behind us. I had never seen anything quite like it before. Brunn was still riding slowly and I was obliged to carry him, in spite of my reluctance to leave our other teammates behind.

Joined by a couple of riders from the fledgling *Ligne Infinie* team, we rode out of the trees into the marginally brighter daylight of the open air.

The downward slope ahead of us was wet too; the road darkened to a pitch black under the grey sky, but it was clean and clear. Brunn slowed still further, trying to communicate with the team car.

I wasn't the only rider casting wary glances over his shoulder, but I was the only one having difficulty doing so. The adrenaline rush from before had faded, and the pain was rising. The metallic taste had turned bitter and I spat again and again to get rid of it. Without thinking, I reached for my water bottle and realized it was long gone, lost amongst the chaos under the trees.

"Fuck," I muttered and spat again, to no avail. *Why didn't I take Rom's bottle?* He'd get another from the team car when they brought him a new tire.

In spite of our slow pace, we were catching up to the few riders who'd made it out in one piece before. There was no chatter.

The staccato beat of the blades of the helicopter above drowned out any other sound. My earpiece was silent, save for come-and-go bursts of static and indecipherable voices.

***

The first reports were unclear – and thanks to the heavy rain so were the images which came in. I heard Federico and Brunn's names all around but couldn't understand the hastily-spoken French, German or Dutch to determine what had happened. Were they part of the group which had crashed on the narrow road in the forest?

All I understood was that there had been an unimaginably huge crash and that several riders were now out of the race.

Adding to my anxiety were the always-hasty additions of *Brunn* or *Renard* to what sounded like casualty lists. Each time, my heart either sank to my feet or raced to the base of my throat, bringing anxious nausea with it.

I stood with the other spectators, my camera and gear tucked safely away under my rain slicker, and watched the screens. The live feed resumed and the first images were of Brunn and Federico, leading a straggling group of maybe a half-dozen riders up a climb and into a small village.

The picture flickered and froze, jumping forward when the feed connected again. Federico looked over his muddy shoulder, an expression of clear concern etched into his face as he turned forward again. He winced when he reached to take a water bottle from Brunn and he favoured one arm.

More riders came into the picture, many of them looking worse for wear: torn kits and jackets, missing water bottles and damaged bikes hinting at the falls they'd taken. The proof was in the close-ups provided by the television cameras on the motorcycles. A few of the riders not only had damaged kits, but bled from scrapes and wounds they hadn't yet had tended to. One rider was in obvious pain, holding his hand awkwardly and grimacing whenever he grasped the handlebars of his bike.

The aerial views showed little of the scene of the crash. Too many trees obscured the road so only frightening and tantalizing hints reached the spectators at the finish: glimpses of bright colours on the dark tarmac, bikes tangled into graceless heaps of metal, riders lying on the road or alongside it or hobbling around like decrepit, aged men.

The mind filled in the details the eye couldn't quite see. I was relieved to know Federico had come through: muddied and scraped, but apparently intact.

The camera panned back to put Federico and Brunn in frame again. Brunn spoke into his microphone, looking frustrated. The two teammates conversed, holding themselves stiffly, glancing back at the other riders in their wake before leaning in to talk again. Federico kept shaking his head and suddenly looked aghast at something Brunn said.

He gestured behind them fervently before Brunn shouted, pointing at the road ahead of them. The apparent argument continued unabated, raging hard enough to make their bikes wobble worryingly beneath them from time to time.

I wished desperately that I could read lips, to understand what was happening between the two of them.

Finally, Federico moved away from Brunn and shook his head one last time before rising out of his saddle and riding hard, pulling away from the dozen or so riders behind them. Brunn followed immediately but the others looked put out to meet the sudden increase in pace.

They didn't meet it for long. Brunn stayed behind Federico and the two of them put distance between themselves and the others in short order. The reason for the attack was obvious: Schlessinger was unhurt, but the wait for a new bike after the chaos of the crash had put him in the hole, time-wise.

Was this some sort of payback for Schlessinger's attack when Federico flatted out in the early days of the race?

Any way one looked at it, it was an impolitic move, at best. It was unsportsmanlike behaviour at worst.

Another camera, another angle: this time the screens displayed what the motorcycle-bound cameramen had filmed and the crash was worse than I'd imagined. Supporters of various teams and cyclists groaned when they saw their favourites injured or taking to the road too slowly to make up lost time. Team cars threaded their way through the carnage on the road – bike parts and water bottles were scattered across the tarmac like the toys of some petulant child, and riders remained in the midst of it all, with faces twisted into grimaces of pain and frustration. It was difficult to tell one emotion from the other until a team or Tour doctor tended to the injured rider. Then there was no mistaking the pain for anything else.

The camera lingered on one young rider lying in the dirt on the far side of a drainage ditch along the road. He was covered in mud and grime, his rain jacket and jersey in tatters with bright, raw skin and blood shining through. He held his arm awkwardly, supporting it with his other hand.

Someone next to me drew a sharp hiss of breath at the sight and I glimpsed him commenting to his companion while gesturing to his collarbone. "*Einde verhaal,*" he said, shaking his head. "*Zijn tour is voorbij.*"

I didn't need a translator for that. *"His Tour is finished."*

The scenes on the screen changed again. Small groups of riders headed out into the open road again without any enthusiasm. They limped along, gaining speed over time but going nowhere near as fast as they had before the pileup.

More riders emerged, unhurt but having been held up by the confusion and the obstructions on the road. The groups split into their respective teams, uninjured riders attempting to lead their teammates back and make up for lost time.

For some, the whole enterprise was over and done. Some riders pulled off the road, shaking their heads, holding themselves up awkwardly until one of their team cars came up alongside. Some got in the cars with a minimum of fuss, others engaged in heated conversations with their *directeur sportifs*, their hampered gestures visible even from the high vantage point of the helicopter cameras.

The narration of the television commentators was broadcast over the scene, but broke off abruptly when the coverage cut back to Renard and Brunn.

***

By now we knew that the crash had taken out more than a handful of riders. Looking over my shoulder, back to the woods, only a few riders had emerged, looking much the worse for wear.

The only thing we could do was to slow up and wait, to give the others a chance to get rolling again.

In the meantime, only a handful caught up. I glanced around and saw the same dazed, befuddled expression on all of their faces. I reckoned I must look like them: confused, angry, uncertain.

"What are you doing, you dumb motherfuckers? Just fucking RIDE!" Jerzy screamed in my earpiece, loud and clear. My legs were already carrying me forward with Brunn on my wheel before I forced myself to hold back.

"This isn't a simple mechanical," I protested. "Jesus! We can't attack *now*! We haven't even been able to see the race doctor yet –"

"Unless you're ready to go home today, DO IT!"

I looked at Brunn, astounded. "He can't be serious."

"Get going, Ciccio. I'm on your wheel."

"Fuck that – no way."

"Jerzy gave us our orders. Go."

I pointed behind us, shaking my head. "After all that? Are you fucking joking? What the hell is wrong with you two? It's suicide to ride like this! We'll have the whole fucking peloton against us –"

"We need to make our gains where we can! GO!"

I would have sworn I could smell the desperation in Brunn's breath as he bellowed that last word at me.

My stomach was sour with frustration: this *wasn't* right, but I could only follow orders. I cursed loudly and kicked hard, pulling ahead, disgusted with Brunn and Jerzy's deplorable tactics, and disgusted with myself for playing along.

Other stragglers attached themselves to us and we picked up speed, aiming for the drier roads ahead and leaving the carnage further behind.

***

I switched off the television and shut down my computer. Stretching lazily, I considered my options – dinner out, or staying in to enjoy room service.

Or... I *could* soak in a hot bath and turn in for an early night.

I got up from the bed and went to the bathroom, admiring the extra-large Jacuzzi-style bathtub before turning on the water and adjusting it with care.

Steam rose to fog the mirrors over the sink and the vanity while I undressed, and I watched myself fade into nothingness while the tub filled behind me. I wished I could somehow see what Federico saw when he looked at me.

My image didn't impress me. Nothing special: not too skinny but not too fat, straight brown hair, brown eyes, reasonably toned figure since I'd never had kids.

He liked my legs.

He'd made that comment more than once – or had I replayed that phone call in my head so many times it felt that way?

Speaking of phone calls...

I hurried into the bedroom at the sound of my mobile chirping insistently from the nightstand. Shivering from the sudden change of temperature from one room to the next, I fumbled to answer, saying "Hello?" before I'd even brought the phone properly to my ear.

The soft laughter on the other end sent a more pleasant shiver through me.

"*Ciao*, Abby. Is everything all right?"

It is now.

"Yes, I'm fine. How are you, Chicco? You looked pretty roughed up today."

There was a pause before he spoke again. "*Sì, sì*, it was a bit rough."

I went to turn off the taps before the tub could overflow. "But you're okay?"

"I'm fine. A bit banged up, but I was quite lucky, all things considered."

There was something strange in his tone, a sense of distraction lurking behind his words.

"Chicco? What's going on?"

"You saw the news, yes?"

"Yes. I didn't understand all of it though. There's no proper English TV channel here. Why?"

Another pause, this time long enough to make me think the line had fallen. In the silence I noted the sound of a television in the background on his end of the line, then the soft click of a dry swallow.

"They're saying we should have waited."

"What do you mean?"

"The press, first of all; a lot of fans, for another. They're saying Brunn and I acted unfairly, that we should have gone slower into Ettelbruck. They're saying we took advantage of half the peloton being down for the sake of gaining forty seconds on Schlessinger. They're right."

I sat on the edge of the tub, my heartbeat rising in my chest. It was troubling to hear him so upset. "Chicco…"

"Jerzy wouldn't let up. We only did what he told us to do." He took a deep breath and exhaled, the sound a gale blowing into the mouthpiece of the phone. "It's not fair," he said, sounding impossibly, improbably young. "I didn't want to ride that way. I didn't have a say in it. I protested, but they weren't having it. Were we supposed to neutralize the stage? That's an official's decision, not ours."

"No, that would have been a bad idea."

"Hmm…" was his noncommittal response.

"Listen, Chicco – there is no way to win this from a PR standpoint. Ride to victory and you weren't fair to the others. Neutralize the stage and you weren't fair the sprinters – the few who got there, anyway. What's more, you had to do what Jerzy told you, right? People who fault you for that would fault you no matter what."

Yet another silence on the line, filled faintly by the changing channels of the television. Someone who sounded like Rom asked a question, but I couldn't understand what he'd said. Federico's hand rustled over the mouthpiece as he gave a brief response.

"*Grazie*, Abby. Thank you so much."

"For what?"

"For letting me know I'm not crazy. I'm screwed no matter what I did. I knew I'd – we'd – done the wrong thing."

"I'm sorry about that." I wished I had him in front of me so I could offer him more effective solace.

"I did what I could to slow us up, without making it too obvious. No-one's mentioned that. I guess it worked."

He chuckled a little and I smiled, feeling a little better hearing it.

"They'll figure it out, one day."

"I miss you."

My heart constricted around his words. "I miss you too." I trailed my hand along the edge of the tub. "So, what will you do now? Tonight, I mean?"

"Recover. I've had a massage and dinner, and now I'm cooped up here with Rom for the night. We might have an Italian lesson and pack it in. You?"

"Me?"

"What will you do tonight?"

"Sleep, I guess. I'm tired of watching the news, and I don't feel like going out alone."

"It won't be much longer, *amore*. Soon I'll be able to take you out. Dinner, even dancing if you want."

"Dancing? Really? I didn't know you danced."

"I don't. But if you want to, I will."

"And if I want to stay in? Order a takeaway and watch some crap movie instead?"

"I can do that."

I smiled with a dreamy sense of anticipation.

"Or, we could make love all night," he said with a matter-of-fact tone which sent pleasant heat flooding through me. "Not continuously, of course, but whenever we wake and take a notion to."

"That would be wonderful."

"I know you will be. I should go."

"Okay. Good night, Chicco."

"*Buona notte, amore.*"

I listened keenly, trying to hear any sound on his end, and was rewarded with his long, wistful sigh before he switched his phone off.

Stage Twenty-Two

(156 km – Metz, France – Chaumont, France)

The pain came back when I pulled the bed sheets off myself after waking. What had been a slight, dull ache roared back to life with that simple act. Worse yet, the sheets stuck to the dressing where I had bled through and the creams applied had gone tacky.

Before breakfast I had the gauze on my shoulder replaced and the discomfort I'd awakened with was tempered by the physio's officially-sanctioned creams and unguents. Any further hurting would have to be overcome via mind-over-matter.

Nearly everyone had taken a fall on the wet and messy roads yesterday. Every rider has to deal with it at some point; "road rash" is an unpleasant and inevitable part of the job. At breakfast I joked with my team-mates about the smell of the creams and about sticking to the bed sheets while the wounds healed.

Riding hard was the only real antidote to the pain. Everything going on around me, avoiding collisions or distractions and keeping up the pace pushed the pain down. Whenever the hurt resurfaced, I put my head down and got on with riding it out.

The group went full-gas most of the day. It was a relatively easy ride, especially compared to the clusterfuck of the day before. We covered the kilometres much faster than expected or planned, a tailwind pushing us not-so-gently along most of the route. I chatted with other riders, our topics covering everything from the weather to yesterday's crashes to what the teams had planned for dinner after the stage.

So far, there wasn't any open vindictiveness, other than from the usual suspects. I wondered if the oft-repeated footage of my argument with Brunn had something to do with it. I hoped so.

I'd take any break I could get.

Sean Morell from *Big UK* and I slipped back to our team cars to play domestique, collecting extra water bottles and moving through the bunch to deliver them to our respective team-mates. We made our way toward the front where both our teams were controlling the race, trading off the lead. The pack gained speed steadily but slowly, reeling in the breakaway with deceptive patience. Now the end of the stage was nearly in sight and the lead-out riders were preparing for the final attacks.

I distributed the bottles to my teammates before slipping into position near the head of the group. Never mind the hurt. With the finish approaching I was still in great shape.

Alta VeloCidad assumed the lead. I pulled hard to try and fracture the lead-outs for the other teams, until the peloton was strung out behind. A grimace etched itself deeper into my face with every kilometre. I dug deep, then deeper still until the escapees were in my sights.

Reeling them in metre by metre, the bunch swallowed them up, pushing them exhausted out the back as the peloton broke into several smaller groups.

I faded back and the next member of my team took my place. I slipped back into the line when my last teammate passed me by, allowed myself to be pulled along in their slipstream, easing my efforts while I saved my energy. If everything went according to plan, I'd need all my strength for the crucial final kilometres.

***

I stepped into the welcoming coolness of the hotel lobby, glad of the relief from the late summer sun. Pulling my camera bag higher onto my shoulder, I crossed to the desk and waited for the clerk while she dealt with a client. I looked around, taking in the tasteful, understated décor and anticipating the text I would send to Federico when I knew which room I was in. This was still a moment I looked forward to, even though I wouldn't be seeing him.

The clerk's soft greeting caught my attention and I turned to her, itinerary in hand. She typed the reservation number into her computer and took a small envelope out of a drawer, handing it to me along with my key.

"What's this?" I asked, admiring my name written in delicate, feminine handwriting.

"A private message for you," she said with a small shrug. "You had a call before you arrived."

"Oh, okay. Thanks." I considered opening the envelope right then and there but tucked it into my handbag instead and went up to my room. As soon as I set my bags down, I took out the envelope to examine it again.

"Chicco...?" I whispered, a smile tugging at the corners of my mouth. I carefully lifted the edge of the envelope and opened it, sliding out a page of hotel stationery folded small enough to fit neatly in my palm.

I unfolded it to read a short message, written in the same script as my name on the envelope: *Meet and greet tonight at seven at Hotel du Roi. Come see me?*

I had to smile. For once, I'd be the one sneaking in to his territory and not the other way around. I sank down onto the bed with a pleased sigh. At least now I'd see him. My seemingly endless and empty night now had something to fill it.

*

I took care while dressing, choosing a simple brown knee-length skirt, a long-sleeved blue cotton blouse and a pair of comfortable flats. I wanted to be sure I would be comfortable and inconspicuous enough not to call attention to myself.

The sudden image of Brunn's cool gaze sprang to mind and made me hesitate. What if he saw me and decided to say something? Would he call me out and tell Federico that we'd met for dinner a few nights ago?

I sat down at the foot of the bed, my hands shaking. Why had I agreed to meet Brunn in the first place? I should have known better. I should have told Federico right away.

Tonight. I'll tell him tonight.

I stood and crossed to the table where my camera bag rested. I tucked my wallet and mobile phone into one of the side pockets, picked up my room key and took a deep breath. In spite of my newfound anxiety, I was eager to go, eager to see Federico again.

I moved in a sort of underwater silence, everything around me fading back, back, until sounds seemed muffled and the only thing in focus was the way ahead of me. I hardly felt the hotel carpet or the pavements under my feet. The warmth of the day was distant, barely reaching me as I walked. I didn't feel unsteady or afraid now, but excited and slightly fuzzy-headed.

The team bus was flanked by the other team support vehicles in the hotel parking lot. As I stepped into the hotel I wondered how many other guests were staying there and complaining about the inconvenience.

A small sign on an easel directed attendees of the meet-and-greet to one of the conference rooms off to one side of the lobby. I started shaking again when I stepped through the open double doors. The team was seated behind a long table draped with banners with the *Alta VeloCidad* logo on them at the front of the room, all of the riders dressed alike in their sponsor-issued sweats, some of them still with wet hair after showers and massages, some already wearing sleepy, distracted expressions.

Federico's eyes caught mine. I froze to the spot, smiling so hard it hurt. He looked genuinely surprised – had he really not expected me to come? I should have texted to let him know I'd be there.

I sat behind a group of girls whispering excitedly, snapping quick photos and suppressing squeals of delight each time. I adjusted my camera bag slung over my shoulder and blushed.

Federico caught my eye again, gave me a shy, lingering smile, and immediately had to be prompted for a question he'd missed.

***

It was excruciating, sitting in front of a crowd and pretending that Abby wasn't in the room. Fans asked questions, snapped photos and we did our best to be entertaining in spite of our fatigue.

I desperately wanted the dinner to start so I could excuse myself – if possible, of course – and try to talk to her. She could pretend to be another fan and I wouldn't have to sneak around for once. We could chat freely and no-one would think anything of it. It was perfect – I couldn't have planned it better myself.

But it didn't happen that way. Instead, when the fans were dismissed and the team headed to the dining room down the hall, I took advantage of the confusion and went to her. When she saw me coming, Abby pretended interest in a painting, a bland, passionless still life on the wall outside the meeting room. I stopped several times on the way to pose for photos or sign an autograph. Each delay took a lifetime.

She didn't turn to face me, but her hand was extended back to me in a subtle gesture of acceptance. I took it and we crossed the hall and went into the stairwell, the door shutting silently behind us while I led her up to the next landing, halfway between floors in the blessed cool and quiet.

***

He approached from behind, and with every footfall, I saw him in my mind's eye, felt the length of his familiar stride, even knew when to put my hand out so his could capture it. He led me out of the room without a backward glance.

Then we were in a corridor, then in a stairwell like the one I recalled from Courmayeur, all whitewashing and stale concrete dust. His arms went swiftly around me, pulling me to him before I was able to put my arms around his neck. There was an awkward pause while I shifted position, my camera bag bouncing on my hip, and then his mouth was on mine, hungry, seeking, relentless.

There was no point in asking if he was concerned about being caught. This wasn't sneaking out in the middle of the night, or lying about where he'd gone. The 'meet-and-greet' with fans was over but the dinner wasn't. It was a risk – but there'd be no convincing him otherwise.

Not that I wanted to. I wanted to steal away with him, for this reason, for this purpose. I wanted his mouth on mine, his hands beneath my blouse, his body pressed as close as possible.

His lips traced heatedly along the line of my neck, a low, urgent sound rising from deep inside him. I brought my mouth to his throat and the sound rumbled inside him again.

"Abby," he sighed my name more than said it. Before I could answer he had one hand twined in my ponytail, holding me in place. "Give me your mouth."

How could I not? The only option I had, the only one worth

choosing, was giving in.

His mouth found mine and took my kisses greedily, as though I'd denied him. When he drew slowly away, breathing hard while he untangled his fingers from my hair, his grin was infectious. It was impossible not to return it. We laughed quietly together, and he pulled me to him again; this time the gesture was tender and reassuring, the surest sign of the intimacies we'd shared.

"Sorry," he said softly, his breath warming the top of my head.

"For what?"

"For making things worse."

I knew too well what he meant.

"Do you think anyone saw us leave?"

"Probably. I don't care, anyway."

"You don't? What if someone says something to Jerzy?"

"I don't care," he repeated, and his light, careless tone told me he meant it.

I only wished I could feel as strongly about it.

"Abby?"

I looked up at his mouth moving wordlessly before he cupped my face in his palm and bent to give me another kiss.

Each slow stroke of his tongue drew desire rushing through me. I became molten metal, heavy and liquid, seeking form, hoping to be shaped by his touch.

If he'd asked, I'd have agreed — whatever the request might have been.

When we parted this time, the grin was in place, but his eyes were unfocused and foggy, almost dreamy. He caressed my cheek and slowly shook his head as if in response to some question he longed to ask.

"It feels so dangerous, having you here like this." He shook his head again with a soft laugh. "Not that I care. I'm glad you are." He gazed into my eyes silently, moving as though to kiss me before he hesitated. "I should go." Clearing his throat he straightened up, glancing around the empty stairwell.

"All right. I'll go upstairs and leave from there," I said, indicating the stairs to the next level up with a tilt of my head. "It wouldn't do for anyone to see us come out of here together."

"That's true."

"Chicco? There's something I need to tell you."

His expression became wary, one eyebrow rising questioningly.

"Okay. What is it?"

"A few days ago, I... uh..." I hesitated, unsure how to tell him about Brunn. I took a deep breath, inhaling his scent and the cool air of the stairwell, then plunged forward. "I had a phone call from Brunn."

Federico stiffened and drew away from me. "What did he want?"

"He said he wanted to meet me, and I agreed. We had dinner and talked."

"And you talked about...?" He took another step away from me and leaned against the railing.

"You," I answered, trembling and hating the distance between us. "At first, I didn't want to meet him, but –"

He nodded again, his gaze sharp and clear. "I know how he is, don't worry."

"I'm sorry," I said, and now my voice was shaking, too.

"For what?" Federico moved back to me, framed my face in his hands and looked me in the eye.

"For not telling you sooner. I just didn't want to do it over the phone – it didn't feel right."

"I understand, *amore*. Thank you for being honest."

He brought his mouth to mine for a slow, tender kiss, quite different from the ones we'd already exchanged. He pulled away once more and met my eyes again. "Just a few more days," he said, more to himself than to me, then smiled again, raising one hand to his mouth as if to swipe away any traces of lipstick.

My heart sank again even as he gave me a last, swift kiss and moved toward the stairs down to the door to the corridor. I turned, suddenly uneasy, and hurried up to the next level.

***

As soon as Abby was out of view I started back down the stairs, seething. Who the fuck did Brunn think he was, contacting Abby that way? How the hell did he know how to find her in the first place?

The sound of the door opening below forced me back several steps. I started inventing harmless but plausible excuses in case I'd been spotted, panic rising in my blood.

Before I could go into full fight-or-flight, I caught a glimpse of the newcomer: Alvaro. There was barely enough time to for me duck behind a concrete column and wonder what he was doing before the door opened again to admit someone else.

The man stood with his back to the landing where I hid behind a concrete column the stairs circled around. Alvaro focused intensely on his guest, the line of tension in his jaw obvious even from a distance. He folded and re-folded his arms, fists clenched, while they spoke rapidly in Catalan, their words lost to me in the echoes in the stairwell. Alvaro glanced nervously toward the door and seemed about to fold into himself as though he might be sick.

The man extended his hand and Alvaro gave him a handful of Euros in return for a small packet of some sort.

It was inconceivable, but I'd seen it with my own eyes. The man left, then my teammate leaned against the wall and shut his eyes as though in profound pain. Then, suddenly, he stood up straight and went out, slamming the door shut behind him.

I stood rooted to the spot, uncertain what to do. I'd been gone too long. I forced myself to move, descending the steps calmly, taking my time opening the door and then stepping out into the corridor.

Alvaro was only a short way further up the hall, talking on his mobile phone, oblivious to my approach. I went past him without speaking. He followed me, still involved in the call, irritation in his voice before he abruptly closed the call.

We entered the dining room together. Alvaro immediately started joking and laughing with Teodoro in Catalan.

I chatted with the others, keeping up my end of the conversation with the scene I'd witnessed in the stairwell replaying in the back of my mind.

Brunn glanced over at me and hesitated, catching my eye. His usual impassive expression faltered for an instant and he turned back to Jerzy to resume their discussion with an air of nonchalance.

He knew that I knew about his meeting with Abby. Now I had to decide what I was going to do about it.

***

I knew I'd never get to sleep: I was too tense, too shaken to easily relax. After those stolen kisses I hadn't been able to calm at all. I couldn't get him out of my mind.

I got dressed again and went down to the coffee shop wondering what I could drink to settle myself. Alcohol would be a terrible idea. But it certainly had a considerable appeal.

The menu was posted outside. The words swirled and danced in front of my eyes, impossible to understand in my distraction.

"Now *that* is a woman deep in thought."

I turned to find Pascal leaning against the wall, watching me.

"That," he continued, "or this is the most interesting menu in all of Chaumont."

The laugh which escaped me was louder than I expected and even Pascal took a good-humoured step back.

"Sorry." I put up one hand in a 'halt' gesture. "You took me by surprise."

"I hope I didn't startle you."

"Of course not." I looked at the menu again. "I'm having an off day, er, night."

Pascal crossed to the door and opened it, gesturing that I should precede him. Cool air drifted out over the warmth rising from the pavement. "May I buy you a coffee?"

"I'm afraid that'll keep me awake."

"Decaffeinated, then? Or perhaps a tea?" He cocked an eyebrow, still holding the door open for me and earning an annoyed look from the hostess.

"All right." I stepped inside, hoping this conversation wouldn't add to my already agitated state.

I should have known better.

No sooner had we been seated and placed our orders than he produced his opening gambit: "I cannot help but notice that you are still here alone."

I said nothing, preferring to let him continue so I could be more certain where this might be going.

"Are you really married, Abigail?"

My mind leapt – not to Charles, but to Federico.

"Yes, I am."

Pascal regarded me silently and I resisted the urge to speak and fill the silence as the waitress brought our drinks.

"May I be direct with you?" he asked at last.

"When haven't you been?"

Pascal smiled wryly, nodded and slid one fingertip around the handle of his teacup. "So you've noticed this."

"Of course I have. I appreciate that about you, you know."

"*Merci*." He took another slow sip of his tea then set it down to lazily stir in more sugar. "Abigail, you must admit it is a little strange that you are here alone this way. Either your husband is very careless or you are very brave."

I said nothing.

"It is very dangerous, even in these modern, more enlightened times, for a woman to travel alone."

"I disagree."

"I know." He looked beyond me, his gaze focused out the window. "So who protects you? Who takes care of you?"

"I do."

"Your lover doesn't want the job?"

The slight, teasing tone of his words couldn't hide the bite of the sentiment.

"I don't have a lover, Pascal."

"You'll forgive me for not believing you."

"I'll try to, but I can't guarantee it. Why are you so convinced of this, anyway? I'm not French or Italian," I added, trying to tease him in return.

"Why do you suggest only a *Française* or an *Italiana* would take a lover? Why not a Spaniard or a German?" He laughed. "Okay, perhaps not a German."

"What do you mean?" I considered getting my handbag and going away. This was getting much too close for comfort.

"These choices intrigue me. Perhaps you have a French or Italian lover. Maybe both."

"Maybe neither." I shook my head and pushed my own cup of tea away. "Pascal, you are making me uncomfortable."

"I'm sorry. That was not what I wanted."

"Here's an idea: why don't you *tell* me what you want? Come right out and say it."

"You. I thought that was obvious."

To my amazement, the confusion in his face seemed absolutely genuine.

"Aren't you married?"

He shook his head now. "Not that it would make a difference, but no, I'm not."

"Well, that's reassuring. Right now it seems the only person I need protection from is *you*." I stood and picked up my handbag, my throat tightening. "Is this the only reason you've been nice to me?"

"Not at all. You needed a little advice, a little help. But you are an attractive woman, Abigail. Any man would want to be with you." He held his hands out to his sides. "Is that so hard to understand? Or so wrong to want?"

***

My personal phone chirped from my pocket and I took it out, giving the screen a cursory glance. Certain it wasn't Abby, I flipped the phone open and distractedly answered.

"Chicco, *oláááhhh*..."

The breathy delivery was unmistakeable, still carrying enough power to literally stop me in my tracks.

"Sunny."

Ahead of me, Rom stopped short and spun around, his eyes widening. If I hadn't been so surprised myself, I'd have burst out laughing at the look on his face.

"*Sim*," she said, as warmly as though we'd only spoken the day before. "It's me. How are you?"

"How *am* I?" I asked angrily, walking past Rom who was still fixed in place. "Ah, Sunny... I'll tell you how I am."

I closed my phone to end the call and then shut it off, even though I desperately wanted to hear her voice again.

Stage Twenty-Three

(165 km – Chaumont– Chalon-sur-Saone, France)

I woke up angry, with my phone completely out of charge. I'd slept fitfully, repeatedly waking to turn the phone on and look at Solange's new number. I'd even programmed it in, labelled it with her name, and resolved to delete it roughly a thousand times before I'd lost my nerve and left it.

Then I'd tried to forget it – to forget *her*, to forget she'd called – but the sound of her voice had brought everything back. Everything before Andorra, that is. Everything else was like a confusing, half-remembered dream.

And that made me angrier still.

It shouldn't be so easy to forget. Her betrayal couldn't be glossed over or dismissed. I'd already tried to move on. Wasn't that why I'd been killing myself, risking my position on the team in order to see Abby?

Good Christ—Abby.

I wanted to be angry with her, too. It would have made things easier on me if I could write her off, but knowing she'd met Brunn – at his insistence – wasn't something I could dismiss. I trusted her, but why should I? I'd trusted Solange and look where that had gotten me.

I didn't need more complications. I needed focus. I needed to ride and I needed to win. The end was practically in sight, and here

319

I was, worrying about my personal life – of all things – when I needed to be resting for the final stages of this race.

*

Five kilometres away from the finish, I took my place at the head of the peloton and raised the tempo as high as I could. We'd shared the workload with *Etalon d'Or*, and I'd worked my way forward while my team prepared Teodoro's lead-out. Crossing a bridge over the canal, however, something went wrong behind me. In the midst of the jostling and jockeying for position, aiming for the easy turn ahead onto the Avenue de Paris and the final sprint toward the river, there was a collision. The ensuing pile-up of riders and bikes tangled together and blocked most of the road.

I knew this only because Michael informed me over the radio. A glance over my shoulder was enough to know the chaos would take precious time to clear up. Worse yet, it was well outside the three-kilometre limit from the finish, so no-one's time was safe.

Somewhere in that heap of riders and machines were Schlessinger and Brunn. *Alta VeloCidad*'s sprinters were caught up in the mess, too. Only Adrie and Rom, along with a handful of riders from the other teams, were with me. I was the only contender on this side of the crash.

Jerzy shrieked instructions but they weren't necessary. The taste of aluminium filled my mouth as Adrie pulled ahead of me and we both lowered our heads and got on with it.

The ramshackle bunch followed our lead, and we rounded the turn onto Avenue de Paris, cranking the pedals with all we had left. The final sprint was ours to take, and we would.

The only question left was who would be first across the line.

*

I'd fought for the stage win but it had gone to one of *Etalon d'Or*'s riders instead. The sting of that loss was nonexistent, though. The crash outside of Chalon-sur-Saone cost my main rivals enough time to let me leap-frog Brunn and land back in the lead. With no small sense of satisfaction, I stepped out onto the stage, my arms raised high as I scanned the photographers at the foot of the stage for Abby.

Turning to my left, I shook hands with the race official who first presented me with the Royal, helped me put it on and then zipped it up in the back. I collected my stuffed animal trophy from the red-haired podium girl along with her professional kisses on each cheek, but when I turned to collect the flowers from the other girl, I startled and nearly stepped right off the riser in surprise.

Solange gave me a dazzling smile and placed a definitively non-standard kiss on my lips to the shouts and jeers of the crowd.

I forced a smile onto my face and faced the crowd, holding my prizes aloft while I tried to remember the Royal was on my back, and that was why I was there.

Distracted as I was, I made to leave the stage a few beats too soon. All I could think was that I wanted out of there, away from *her*.

My anger lacked real focus. Had the organizers thought this would be a pleasant surprise? Springing my ex-fiancée on me like this was certainly a strange thing to do.

And what of that kiss? Was she really going to pretend nothing had changed between us when she was the one who left? For fuck's sake, she'd screwed someone else and sent back the engagement ring! It wasn't a simple *misunderstanding*.

Out of sight of the cameras in the no-man's-land of the backstage area, I handed the prizes off to one of the team handlers and pushed my way out into the sunlight again.

***

I continued taking photos through my confusion. Shot after shot in rapid succession of Federico raising his hands in the air to greet the cheers of the crowd, receiving the Royal, turning to get his flowers and stuffed mascot – each with a kiss – and then the look of amazement on his face as he understood who had given him that last kiss.

Solange? Here? On the podium, no less?

Strange gave way to surreal and I watched her follow him offstage along with the officials.

Why hadn't he mentioned this to me?

Maybe he didn't know, but how could he *not* know that his (supposedly) ex-fiancée would be a special-occasion podium girl? And what luck – she was here on the day when he won the Royal again.

Shit. It was a fairy-tale, wasn't it?

Jealousy prodded a lance at my heart. Their kiss hadn't seemed particularly 'ex' to me, either.

The ground at my feet seemed made of sand, shifting and spilling into my shoes to weight me in place and drag me down. A thousand possibilities went through my mind at once, from Solange discovering she was pregnant to Federico calling her and begging her to come back.

Of course, *why* he'd do that after what he claimed she'd done was a mystery to me, and how she could keep that a secret was even more puzzling.

Unlikely on both counts, I decided, though I didn't quite believe.

My own self-confidence took a hit each time I recalled their kiss on the podium.

A familiar face popped up in my peripheral vision and I busied myself packing my things away.

"Ah, Abigail. So nice to see you."

"Pascal," I said coolly, leaving it at that.

"Well," he said, seemingly undaunted, "today was certainly interesting, *non?*"

"How do you mean?"

He made a sound of disbelief and gestured toward the now-empty stage. "They broke up, and now she's *here?* Very interesting – though I'm not one for celebrity gossip."

"Me neither."

Funny that I'd never really thought of Federico as a *celebrity* in all the time I'd known him.

"So, what are you doing now?"

"I'm going to drive to Lyon, check into my hotel and rest. Alone," I added, unnecessarily.

He nodded and pulled his camera bag up on his shoulder. "Well, maybe I will see you tomorrow?"

I shrugged and started walking, swallowing my anger as I went, unsure who I was angrier with: Pascal, Federico, or myself.

***

I tore through my press interviews at speed, biting my tongue each time they asked about Solange's surprise appearance.

–No, I didn't know she was going to be there.

–Wasn't it obvious I was surprised?

–Yes, of course it feels great to be in the Royal again.

–No, I didn't think I was home free.

–I'm only here thanks to the team and thanks to Jerzy giving me the chance to take advantage when I could.

–I can't speak about team strategy right now.

–No, I don't plan on seeing her later.

–No, we're not getting back together.

Upon reaching the end of the press line, I felt like I'd ridden another hundred kilometres. Only this time I'd ridden through rain. And mud.

My soigneur, clearly sensing my fatigue, gave me another recovery drink and then saw me to the team bus in haste. I shook his hand at the door, laughed at his slightly-off-colour comment about Solange and dragged myself up into the privacy of the bus.

Once inside the air-conditioned, dimly-lit interior, well away from prying eyes, I flung my baseball cap with the team insignia toward the back of the main compartment of the bus as hard as I could.

"What's going on?"

I spun around to find Goosh regarding me with a confused expression.

"You didn't see?" James asked him, surprised. "Didn't you recognize Solange on the podium?"

Goosh shrugged. "I just thought she was an unusually high-maintenance podium girl."

To my horror, when the others laughed, I wanted to defend her. I went to my seat and took my phone out of my rucksack, hoping desperately for a message from Abby.

Jesus, what if she thinks I knew Solange would be here today?

As if confirming this, my inbox was empty of new messages.

I switched the phone to silent and shoved it back in my bag before I went to the back of the bus to grab a drink. On top of my anxiety over Abby and the adrenaline rush of seeing Solange again, I was exhausted.

I mentally rehearsed explanations for Abby and imagined sharp retorts for Solange while I stood at the sink, my hand wrapped tightly around a bottle of water.

I knocked the water back, then turned and went down to the toilet. I splashed some water on my face before pausing at the sight of myself in the mirror: the elements in the reflection didn't match. Anger and worry battled plainly in my face in spite of the fact I was wearing the Royal.

Even I had to admit things were fucked up. I hoped I could turn it all around.

***

I sat at the table in the hotel room, flipping aimlessly through the photos I'd taken so far. Across the room the television droned, the sound low, newscasters discussing events of the day in French spoken so quickly I'd never understand it. I glanced in that direction to find them showing a clip of the day's stage.

Without looking back, I reached for the remote control next to my computer on the table, meaning to switch off the television. Federico was interviewed before he'd even dismounted his bike, his answers coming haltingly as he struggled to catch his breath.

This cut to a shot of the podium presentation with Solange looking elegant in a standard-issue cocktail dress in the Tour's signature shade of royal blue, imparting the lingering kiss on Federico's lips. The image on the screen cut to Federico once again, speaking to the press while dressed in the Royal he'd won this afternoon.

I ran my hands through my hair, my eyes focusing on the television so hard it hurt.

Solange. On the podium. Just like when they first met.

I should have known it was too good to last. Thank God I hadn't told Charles anything yet.

Had my confession about my dinner with Brunn led to Federico's reunion with Solange? Could that have been the catalyst? Was this somehow his way of getting back at me?

After Federico gave a final smile and turned away from the camera, the interviewer concluded his report and the program shifted to a discussion of business news. At last I picked up the remote and shut the television off, plunging the room into silence.

Tightness gripped my chest and I inhaled a long, slow breath to dispel the discomfort. I closed my eyes and sat up straight, stretching in my chair. I exhaled and tried to centre myself.

It made no difference. Opening my eyes I spotted my mobile in the midst of my things scattered across the table. My fingers twitched with the urge to call him, to ask about her.

Actually, calling *anyone* would have felt nice. Anyone – Charles included – might have taken the edge off the encroaching sense of desperation. At the very least, an argument would provide a welcome distraction.

My encounter with Federico after the meet-and-greet hadn't helped matters. Having him so close, driving me into a frenzy without hope for release only ended with unrelenting, pent-up energy and no outlet for it.

All day I'd done my best to avoid thinking about Pascal and our conversation at the coffee shop, but now I was defenceless against them. After seeing him post-race, the sense of being cheated was almost palpable, a physical thing I could reach out and touch.

Or strangle. Whatever.

Here I'd believed Pascal's flirtations were harmless, of no real consequence at all. Instead, he'd had designs on me all along. Yes, he'd helped me out, had even called in a few favours here and there to assure that I'd have as much access as possible. But now it seemed he'd only done it all in order to curry favour and build up to some kind of encounter.

How ridiculous I'd been. How foolish and egotistical. I'd believed that Federico, a man ten years my junior, found me desirable enough to replace a podium girl/fashion model in his heart – or at least his bed. All the while I'd been oblivious to the real intentions of another man, who, in retrospect, had intended to seduce me all along.

Maybe it was true, then. All men *are* the same. Perhaps I shouldn't be so disappointed in Charles after all.

Not that Pascal had acted on his sentiments last night. He'd made no attempt to stop me when I left following his revelation. Instead, he'd stayed seated at the table while I had tried to hurry away with as much of my dignity intact as possible. He'd shown remarkable restraint this afternoon, and I was reluctantly grateful for that.

My ears burned, my face flushed, and I pressed my cool hands to my cheeks as if to push the warmth away.

The desire to pack everything and go home was strong. Scarily so.

325

I looked at my computer, my cameras and my half-packed suitcase and, incredibly, felt the tightness around my chest ease a little. I couldn't do that, tempting though it might be. I only had a few days left of the Tour. It was best to stick it out and get through it. Otherwise, I would be doing exactly what Charles always said I did: flitting off to find another hobby to fill my days. Again.

I hoped I could sleep that night. I wished I had Federico's skill of being able to drop off to sleep almost at will.

With this came the memory of him sleeping soundly next to me, and the tightness around my chest returned.

The reason I slept at all was thanks to fatigue from following the Tour and working to get my shots. I no longer wondered if the effort was worth it. I'd given up worrying about that – I had given myself this task and I was doing it – but I was more concerned with what would come after the race was over.

***

As we went up to our rooms after dinner, the only thing I wanted was sleep. Ninety minutes on the bus to transfer to Lyon had taken a greater toll than I'd have expected.

Jerzy greeted me when I stepped out of the elevator, and I immediately thought back over the last couple of days, wondering what I'd done, now.

"Ciccio, you have a guest."

Abby! My sleepiness dissipated instantly with the thought of her being brave enough to face Jerzy and come see me. When Solange stepped forward from around the corner and gave a little wave, my disappointment went up in a wave of both anger and surprise.

"*Ei*, Chicco," she said, her voice like silk, her words swaying along with her hips as she approached me. "How have you been?"

I looked at Jerzy, amazed. *This* had to be a first. He feigned disinterest while Solange pressed a kiss to my cheek and then wiped away the lipstick stain with her fingertips.

Suddenly the walls of the corridor were too close, yet I felt exposed. I looked around, wanting to talk to her in private. At the end of the corridor was a room the team had converted into a sort of canteen for the riders, with tables filled with snacks and drinks. It was empty.

"Jerzy, could we...?" I tilted my head toward the canteen.

He shrugged, again pretending indifference.

Solange gave a little chirp of a laugh and started in that direction, leaving me behind. God, but she was a sight to see as she walked away.

"I'm only doing this," Jerzy said, raising one hand, index finger extended, "because I hope talking to her will get you straightened out, Ciccio. Maybe get you back on track, where you should be, yes?"

Heat rose in my cheeks but I said nothing.

"Go on. But don't get up to any foolishness. I want that door unlocked."

Jesus, I wasn't going to fuck *her.*

I nodded and covered the length of the hall in a few quick strides. Now that I had my chance to question her, no real questions came to mind. Here she was, in the flesh, and she clearly wasn't angry with me. Did I really *care* what had gone on?

Hell, yes, I did. But I needed to stay calm, to form my questions carefully and clearly. Confusing the issue by giving her a reason to have gone in the first place wouldn't do me any good.

I closed the door behind me and I stood with my back to it. It seemed if I took one more step, I'd fall into an unimaginable void.

Let's get it over with.

"So. Here we are," I said to fill the silence.

She tilted her head fetchingly, in the way I remembered all-too-well. "*Sim.* Here we are."

I went to one of the tables, selected one of the sport drinks at random and opened it without looking at it. The scent hit me as I took a swig from the bottle, the too-sweet taste nearly ricocheting back up my throat. I winced and swallowed before turning to face her, twisting the bottle cap back into place.

"What brings you here, Sun-, er, Solange?"

"As if you didn't know."

"I don't."

Another smile, another tilt of her head so her hair would spill over her eye. I remembered her perfecting this move in the mirror one evening, shortly after we'd gotten together. I'd watched her for ten or fifteen minutes then sat up on the bed and asked how long she'd do that.

She'd turned to me, smiled and put a hand on her hip. "I'm practicing, like you do when you go for rides."

"I *train* on the bike."

She'd shrugged and gone back to her reflection. "Practice; training; it's all the same thing, *não*?"

Seeing her do that move now did nothing to endear her to me.

"Why are you here?" I asked.

"I wanted to see you."

"Why?"

"I missed you."

Right. I stayed silent, hoping she'd explain herself after all.

"Actually, I came here to give you something."

"What's that?"

Solange eased closer to me, leading with one hip so she stood beside me next to the tables.

"Just a little kiss," she said, breathing the last word against my cheek.

Startled, I turned to face her and found her lips waiting, parted slightly in anticipation.

Just a little kiss...

I had no chance to think before her lips met mine, their warm, wet welcome drawing me in. It was all so natural, so easy, and then my arms were around her. She pressed tightly against me, our kisses going deeper and harder, my hands seeking and finding their favourite places – the softest curves, the firmest flesh.

Her quiet sighs between kisses warmed my skin, her body pressed against mine, the friction between us heating the very air around us.

"Chicco, *meu amor*, is there any chance...?"

"Any chance of what?" I murmured, willing to give her anything she asked as my mouth slid over the curve of her neck.

"That we could..." She shrugged, the gesture somehow managing to draw her whole body up over mine and back down again as she guided my mouth to hers. "You know," she finished at last, and her tongue flicked oh-so-briefly over my lips.

"No, I don't know." I kissed her again, the first curl of frustration tugging at me. "Tell me."

"This is so like you," she giggled. "You always want me to explain everything."

A chill slid down my spine.

"I do?"

She pulled me back for another kiss. "Yes, you do. All the

time."

"Is it my fault you enjoy leaving me in the dark?" I reached back and pulled her arms down from around my neck. I kept her hands in mine, noted the faint trace of lighter skin on her ring finger and took a step away.

"What do you mean?"

The feigned innocence in her voice infuriated me. Dammit, she'd taken me in so easily!

"I *mean* that you disappeared without a word – not even a text message – you ignored my phone calls and now you pop up like nothing's changed."

At least now she had the decency to look slightly shame-faced, even if that pout was as well-rehearsed as her hair flip.

"I know. I'm sorry."

"You're *sorry*." I dropped her hands.

She nodded, avoiding my eyes. "I was so confused, and... I don't know what I was thinking."

"I saw the layouts you did with him. Sunny, what *was* that? It was so unlike you. You lied to me. Why?"

"I thought you'd be jealous."

"When have I ever been jealous?"

"I *wanted* you to be."

Shaking my head I took another step away from her, struggling to make sense of this. "You *wanted* me to be jealous?"

"*Sim*..." She followed me, trying to take my hands in hers. "I get to see you so little, and I thought if you were angry enough, jealous enough, that I'd see you talk about me in the trades, and –"

"You what? Why would I talk about this? It was humiliating enough that the guys knew what was going on!"

"I wanted you to declare your love for me! To say you'd fight for me because you loved me!"

"You sent back the fucking ring! A *fifteen-thousand-euro* ring!"

"I know, I know..." Solange caught my hands again and I let her hold them this time. "I loved that ring—it was beautiful." Her voice had softened, lowered until I could barely hear her.

But I understood her perfectly.

"So it was all..." I searched for the right concept, at a loss. "It was all a *publicity stunt?* You couldn't let me in on it?" She shrugged, and I pulled my hands free to hold hers again. "I tried everything to reach you, Sunny. Phone calls, e-mails, texts – I even tried to call your *mother* and she wouldn't answer me."

She looked up at me through her long false eyelashes, her dark eyes soft and beguiling.

And calculating.

"So... You want the ring back." It wasn't a question, but she clearly thought it was. She shimmied in excitement as though she could scarcely contain herself.

"*Sim, sim* – I want it all back: the ring, you; everything."

A chill accompanied the rigid smile forming on my face.

"Sunny?" I caressed her hand gently, already feeling the distance expanding between us. "You really want that ring back?"

She nodded enthusiastically, squirming in anticipation.

"You're going to need something, then: Abseiling equipment and a metal detector."

"I'm sorry—what?"

"When you sent it back to me, I threw it down a mountainside in Andorra."

Her eyes widened in shock before I kissed her hand on that pale tan line where the ring in question had once been.

"Good luck, my sunshine."

I dropped her hand and walked away.

Stage Twenty-Four

[126 km – Saint-Pierre-d'Albigny, France– Sestriere, Italy]

Before doing anything else that morning, I checked my phone for a message from Abby. The fates didn't oblige. Still, with the whole business with Solange resolved, I was remarkably light-hearted. It still bothered me to think she had hurt me for the sake of publicity, but as I'd reasoned last night: better to find out now than after we'd married.

As for Brunn, well, I'd deal with him later.

While the team walked to the dining room for breakfast, I tried calling Abby. There was no answer, and the line fell. I tapped out a text before I ate.

"Miss you. Only a few days to go."

I hit 'send' and put the phone in my pocket as the conversation around the table grew livelier. Adrie looked at me askance as I joined in the chaotic back-and-forth amongst my teammates and a slow grin spread across his face.

"Welcome back, Ciccio." He grabbed the bowl of rice and spooned a generous helping onto his plate.

"What do you mean?"

"Nothing, really. You haven't been yourself lately. It's about time you lightened up a little."

Phil exchanged a look with James and Attila, and Rom grinned, directing his attention to his plate. All of them chuckled secretively

331

while refusing to meet my gaze. There was no obvious ill will behind it but for the rest of the meal, I kept catching them watching me with stupid grins on their faces.

I decided to ask Rom about it later.

Later came sooner than I expected, when the bus made its way from the hotel in Lyon to the start line in Saint-Pierre-d'Albigny.

Goosh sat next to me, his eyes bright with curiosity and mischief.

"So? Is it true?" His whisper was almost drowned out by the bus' engine.

"Is *what* true?"

"Did you see Solange last night?"

Oh, for...

"This explains breakfast," I grumbled as Phil and James popped their heads up over the backs of the seats in front of me.

"Don't dodge the issue," Phil said sternly, pointing a finger. "Did you or didn't you?"

"And did Jerzy allow it?" James added with a sense of urgency. "I mean, *shit*, man – that's a miracle."

"I heard Jerzy let you go to your room with her," Goosh added.

"No, he didn't. Jesus, you're a bunch of gossiping fishwives."

"But you *did* see her." Phil snapped his fingers, suddenly triumphant. "I *knew* it."

"Did you, eh... *Eh*?" James prodded.

"No."

"No?" Goosh echoed, obviously disappointed.

"No."

"Damn." James slipped out of sight before popping up again. "Nothing at all?"

"No," I affirmed. "Nothing at *all*."

Adrie settled into a seat opposite me on the aisle. "You talked, though."

I nodded. "I said my piece. She answered my questions. We're over. Done."

"I still can't believe he allowed it, after all his talk," Phil grumbled.

"He did it so I could get her off my mind. That's all."

James sighed. "And here I'd dared hope for the occasional reprieve."

"Sorry, mate. Not happening. No change in official policy."

"I bet *Maxxout* doesn't have this rule." Phil busied himself wiping at a smudge on the window.

"You gonna defect?" I asked.

He glanced around making sure Jerzy wasn't listening in. "If they allow conjugal visits and if they'd have me? In a heartbeat."

I laughed. "Not a chance. Everyone knows you two are a package deal. One of you is bad enough."

I watched Jerzy, focused as he was on Alvaro who sat nearby, intensely discussing some matter with Teodoro.

I had no doubt. Whatever was going on between the twins, Jerzy knew.

It was only a matter of time.

*

My ride that day was disappointing, by any standard. Exhausted beyond reason at the finish, I steered the bike through the crowd until I spotted one of the team's handlers waving to me and making his way through the crush. Everyone pushed past me to get to Brunn, reporters with smartphones recording, video cameras of all sizes held aloft by fans and news crews alike and angled to film him. He'd finished well ahead of me but the crowds had been too much for security to hold back.

Now the scene was mostly under control, I was snagged on the outer edges in spite of the best efforts of Dan, one of the team's soigneurs. He put one hand on my back and forged a path with the other arm, sweeping people out of our way.

The jumble of voices and shuffling chaos was left behind, replaced by team vehicles lined up in a cordoned-off area away from the finish line. I caught glimpses of myself in the shiny surfaces of the vans and SUVs along the road, the team logos flashing through my subconscious while Dan directed me to *Alta VeloCidad*'s section. The team doctor appeared from between a couple of vehicles and helped me to sit down in the open hatch of a car.

He asked me question after question and I answered each one through a befuddled daze.

"I don't know what happened there – I was fine and then...?" I shook my head, lowering my gaze to stare at the road beneath my feet. "I didn't bonk, I just... I don't know. I don't even feel that bad

333

right now."

The soigneur handed me a bottle of the usual post-race concoction and I gulped down the beige-brown liquid, my mind churning over every detail of the climb. I'd lost time – an inexplicable and unfathomable loss – but I wasn't too far behind. But, Christ – tomorrow we were climbing again, up Alpe d'Huez, and if I rode again like I had today, I'd be out of contention for good.

I was desperate to get back to Grenoble and our hotel, to rest, to eat. The route was still clogged with spectators; we'd be at least a couple of hours on the road before we could settle in for the night.

Jerzy appeared in my peripheral vision, standing at the end of the bumper, leaning in to look at me under the hatch. He didn't speak but eyed me with a measured, precise gaze.

I leaned back against the boxes of food and gear stored in the back of the car, and looked at him.

"I'm fine."

"You'd better be," he said and stalked away, toward the podium where Brunn was about to receive the Royal.

***

I put down my suitcase and sank into the chair next to the window with a sigh. The view of Lyon was beautiful: the Saone River seemed almost within reach, as though I could dive into it from my room, while the Basilica de Notre Dame de Fourvière stood just within sight on the hill opposite my hotel.

When I finally pulled my gaze away from the window, the subtle details of the room revealed themselves: the brocade of the bedclothes and the curtains; the burnished brass doorknobs; the soft glint of gold-leaf in the paint of the edges of the doorframes. All of these things whispered softly of prior guests who had passed hours here, luxuriating in their lovers' embraces; of long, languid nights with the windows opened to the evening breezes. I could almost picture them, ghostly, passing through the room while I watched and envied them.

Loneliness swept over me and I resented the ease with which it did, carried in on every breath I drew. Aware of a weight in my hand, I looked down and found my phone cradled in my palm, my thumb stroking the keys as though I were about to place a call.

I put it on the table and walked away, my shadow preceding me along the wall as I stepped toward the bathroom door. I reflected on Federico's call a few nights before, on his insecurity over how things had been handled after the crashes outside Ettelbruck. I could almost feel the swirling steam from the bath I'd been drawing when I'd tried to reassure him.

I missed him *too* much. My hand shook with the realization and with my unsteady heartbeat. Small wonder, then, that I jumped when the phone on the bedside table rang, the old-fashioned bell adding to the sensation of timelessness in the room.

After a deep, calming breath, I answered.

"Abby! It's about time you got in." Concern tainted Charles' voice even as he chastened me. "I've been trying to reach you all day."

"Why didn't you call my mobile?" I asked. "It hasn't rung once."

"I've been trying it all afternoon. Have you switched it off?"

"No, I haven't. Hang on." I put the phone on the bed and retrieved my mobile. Unlocking it, I sat down on the bed and picked up the receiver and tucked it against my shoulder. "That's odd... There's no signal: no bars, nothing. It's not even acknowledging I'm in Lyon."

"Must be a problem on their end, then."

"Must be..." I echoed and sat back against the headboard, one leg propped up on the bed. "Is everything all right?"

"Well, yes, everything's fine, I—"

My mobile beeped once, twice, signalling the arrival of several messages at once. "Oh, hey, it's working again."

"Don't interrupt me, please."

"Sorry." I pulled a face and picked up the mobile. I cleared the notices of Charles' calls, one by one. He hadn't exaggerated when he said he'd been trying me all day.

"As I was saying; I wanted to get you up to date on a few things about the house."

"Okay, what's up?"

"There was some damage to the roof this week, apparently. A storm passed through..."

He droned on and on while I made sure to acknowledge him occasionally. I knew him well enough to know he was reading from a paper in front of him, ticking items off as he went. When I got home after the Tour, no doubt that same sheet would be tacked to the corkboard in his office downstairs. Any unfinished tasks would fall to me.

I continued deleting notices, half-listening to Charles, until Federico's number popped in the messages queue. I pressed the key to open it and read:

"Miss you. Only a few days to go."

Unbidden, an image from that night in Bonn came to mind: Federico's pendant of the Madonna del Ghisallo, swaying on a silver chain above me, keeping time with his rhythm.

Low heat crept up my throat to leave light perspiration on my chest and the back of my neck. It was all I could do to keep from fanning myself in order to cool down.

"Abby?" Charles' voice seemed to come from another planet – tinny, distant and so far removed from the image in my mind it was hard to acknowledge it was there at all. "Are you still there?"

I don't know. Am I?

"Yes, I'm here. The line was a little noisy," I lied.

"When are you coming home?"

"I told you: when the race is over. Why do you keep asking?"

"I'm ridiculously optimistic. I want to believe that you'll see you've made your point and do the sensible thing by coming home."

"Do you really want that? Do you really want me there?"

"I can't believe you'd ask that."

"I can't believe it either." I sighed, filled with a sudden desire to put the phone down. "I wish you'd be honest with me. For the once."

A silence followed; this one so long I was certain the line had gone down for good.

"You know I love you." It wasn't a question or a reassurance. Instead, his voice was weary as though he'd been explaining this for ages. "I don't understand why you don't get it."

"That's simple, really. Maybe I'm strange, but I don't see how having affairs is proof of love for your partner."

He exhaled, a slow breeze reaching across the miles to push me away from the phone. I waited for him to speak again and found myself hoping – however faintly – that he'd challenge me on this.

I wanted him to explain it all away, to offer an excuse or two, or three, for me to grab hold of to deny the reality I knew too well.

"We've discussed this," he said finally, in a tone which indicated he wouldn't discuss it any further.

"Tell me what changed."

"I don't understand."

"Tell me what *changed*. What happened in the last ten years which made you think I'd agree to these proposals you've made, or that I'd ever want," I breathed deeply and forged on, saying the words I hated so much, "an open marriage."

There. I said it. I realized I'd never said those words out loud to him before.

"I wanted you to be happy," he said at last. "You've been so unhappy for so long."

"I wasn't unhappy. I wanted more time with *you*."

"*And* a home in Hampshire, and funding for all your little hobbies, and on and on... All of which meant I had to spend more time away at work to give you what you wanted."

"That's not fair. That's not what I *wanted* – not at the start, anyway. I had to do *something* with all that extra time I had alone." I took another deep breath and plunged ahead once again. "And it still doesn't explain your...*girlfriends*," I finished weakly, feeling tired and foolish.

"I've told you before, Abby, there wouldn't be any harm in it if we both agreed—"

"I don't want that! I can't do that." I spared a fleeting thought for Federico before I refocused on the conversation at hand. "I wanted a faithful husband, Charles. I wanted *you*."

"Abigail, I, ah... I—"

"You have a mistress. I know."

"That's not what I was going to say."

"Really?" I knew my disbelief was evident but I couldn't keep it out of my voice.

"I was going to say that I know you're lonely, Abby, and I know the reason you stayed there."

My heart stopped. Why hadn't he said so before now? "You do?"

"This is just another one of your little hobbies that's gone out of control. Once this race is over, you'll come home and then who knows? Maybe you'll see things my way."

Maybe I already have.

"Charles, I know about her. I know you've been with her since you've been back, too. Let's drop the charade, okay? I'm tired of pretending like I don't know, and I'll wager you're tired of acting like nothing's going on."

"We should talk about this when you get home. Not on the phone. Not now."

"Why not? Because it's too hard? Because you can persuade me if I'm there? I won't be; you should know that by now."

"It *is* hard, Abby. To keep on like this—"

"Do you think it's easy for *me*?"

"Don't be so dram—"

"I'm *not* being dramatic!" I cried, for the first time aware of the tears on my cheeks and the tightness of my throat. "I've been swallowing my pride and playing along all this time and I am *sick* of it." It was a struggle to keep my voice steady but I managed. "I'm not doing this anymore."

"Have it your way, then," he sighed, resigned. "I know you'll come to your senses in time, and then you'll come home."

"Why do you think that?"

"Because your whole life is here. Everything – your house, your friends and family – you won't leave that behind."

Before I could answer, the line cut off. Tempted though I was to throw the phone across the room, I resisted. I considered going through the day's shots on the computer, but the task of sorting them suddenly seemed like too much work and not nearly distracting enough, to boot.

No, I needed dinner, and, quite possibly, a drink.

***

Another bus ride, another hotel, another reporter waiting to ask the same questions I'd already answered two hours ago. After getting a thorough massage and then eating, the last thing I wanted was to have to sit down and chat with yet another journalist.

But here I was, doing exactly that in a corner of the lobby of our hotel outside Lyon. This one's name was McCleary, and he had a look I'd come to know too well: the one with a hint of slyness, of conniving, another would-be investigator hoping to dig up some obscure dirt in order to launch himself above the others.

After a few minutes of small talk – a cameraman stood at the ready with a small digital recorder, looking bored – he sat back in his chair and cued the cameraman to start filming.

The discussion was relaxed at first, covering the day's race, his New York accent the only distinctive thing about his questions. They were almost identical to the ones I'd been asked a half-dozen times – or more – after the end of the stage that day.

I kept my answers simple, playing to the team script:

Yes, I was happy Brunn was in the Royal yet again.

Of course I was mildly disappointed not to have the Royal now, but this is a team sport, blah-blah-blah...

Yes, it was remarkable *Alta VeloCidad* had held on so consistently to the lead of this Tour.

No, I wasn't troubled by my difficulties today. These things happen. I hadn't lost too much time.

Yes, I'd like to regain the Royal, but like I said, 'team sport'...

He smiled – a quick grin before he regained his professional demeanour – and I knew he was about to start a new line of questioning.

"So yesterday must have been especially good for you, right?"

I nodded and shrugged. "It was nice to get the Royal back, yes. That's always a good feeling – still, easy come, easy go." I laughed. "That's bike racing."

Another glint in his eye, and then he continued. "Well, you got the Royal, yes. But your fiancée was the one to give it to you."

"Not exactly," I said, ready to switch over to 'dumb jock' mode, if only to make things more complicated for him. Now I knew the direction he was going to go.

He consulted his notes then looked up at me with a strange, false smile. "There are rumours going around—"

It was all I could do not to smirk at him. I knew well what those rumours were.

"—that you were kicked off the team a week ago. Is that true?"

I forced myself to shake my head and laugh in response, although my stomach knotted tight. Had I really thought word about my expulsion – however brief it had been – wouldn't get around?

"No. It's not true. I was never off the team."

"That's not what my sources say."

I shrugged, aware the cameraman had stepped a little closer.

"I was never off the team."

"My sources also say that Heinrich Brunn intervened to keep you on. Is that true?"

My eyes narrowed and I tried, too late, to stop them. I sat up straighter and resisted crossing my arms. I didn't want to look like I was on the defensive, even if I was.

"No, of course not. If I wasn't kicked *off* the team, no-one had to intervene to keep me *on* the team," I explained, slowly, as though I were talking to a dull-witted child.

"But why would anyone say this if it wasn't true?"

"People like to talk," I said as airily as I could, and a hand landed heavily on my shoulder.

"I'm sorry to interrupt, gentlemen," Michael said, his tone light, "but Ciccio needs to get to the team meeting."

At this, I shrugged again, stood, and offered my hand. "Pleasure talking to you."

"Thanks for your time, Federico."

Michael steered me away, out of the lobby and toward the elevators around the corner.

"I didn't know about a meeting."

"There isn't one," Michael said, pressing the call button. "I overheard what he was saying to you." He glanced back toward the lobby as the doors slid open. "Asshole," he mumbled under his breath as I stepped inside. "Like we don't have enough trouble already."

"What's that?" I asked, though I understood him plainly enough, and pressed the button for my floor.

"Huh? Oh, nothing. Management stuff. Never mind." He waved me off distractedly and the doors closed, leaving me alone with the soft hum of the rising elevator.

***

There was no rational explanation for it, but I'd done it anyway. Now I stood outside the restaurant adjacent to my hotel, waiting in the fading evening light for him to show up. I spotted him some distance away, strolling casually along the sidewalk as though he'd expected this to happen.

It was strangely flattering when he checked his reflection in a window and patted his hair into place in a nervous gesture. The fringe over his forehead refused to behave and flopped into his eyes.

When he stepped up to me he extended one hand cautiously

and I reached automatically to shake it, only to have him bring my hand to his lips for a swift, gentle kiss.

"Abigail," he said, giving me a wink.

"Pascal," I said and nodded, withdrawing my hand. I couldn't help smiling.

We entered the restaurant and were seated, menus in hand, before either of us spoke again.

"I appreciate you giving me this chance." He set his menu aside after only a cursory glance and focused his attention fully on me. I hadn't anticipated the sincerity I found in his eyes, and it unsettled me.

"It was only fair. Besides, I wanted to apologise."

"You? For...what?"

"I'm afraid I overreacted before. I'm sorry about that."

"You were being careful. I was too forward."

I shook my head. "No; I was being oblivious. And I was a little hurt, to be perfectly honest."

We paused while the waiter brought our drinks: water and a carafe of white wine.

"Hurt?" Pascal asked after we placed our orders and we were alone again.

"I wanted your friendship to be genuine."

"It *is*," he laughed, already shaking his head. "We *are* friends."

"Is that possible?"

"Why shouldn't it be? Just because I find you attractive doesn't mean we can't be friends. I do have *some* measure of self-control."

"Why did you help me out that first day? Was it because...?" I asked leadingly, and he smiled and shook his head.

"*Non, non...* You looked out of your element and I wished to help. That's all. I did what I would want someone to do if, say, Justine needed assistance. When I kept seeing you, well... Never mind that. The point is that I wished for success for you. You have talent, Abigail. Who am I to stand in the way of that?"

The waiter approached the table again, bringing our meals. We ate in near-silence while I considered what he'd said.

I was surprised at how comfortable this felt, quietly sharing a meal with minimal conversation. We exchanged smiles amidst small talk regarding the food or the wine.

Finally, Pascal picked at the remains of his dinner, his eyes trained on the plate. "I hope you aren't still offended."

"I'm not, I guess. It's just that I... Pascal, I'm sorry. I simply don't feel the same way."

He licked his lips and looked chagrined as he toyed with the edge of the tablecloth. "I will ask you this one last time: are you *certain?*"

"Yes, I'm certain." I got some money out of my bag and put it on the table, only to have him wave it away.

"I told you, I'm paying for this. It doesn't mean we're on a date, though." His smile that followed was warm and gentle as always.

"*Merci.*" I took this as my cue and stood up, handbag at the ready. "I should be going. Thank you for the dinner and for the rather...interesting conversation."

"It's my pleasure, of course." He stood with me, leaving the money for the bill behind as he moved to join me. "May I escort you to your hotel?"

"*This* is my hotel," I said quietly as he held the restaurant door open for me. "But thanks anyway."

"May I walk you to your room?"

"No, I don't think so."

"Why not?"

He was standing too close. It wasn't threatening, but still made me uneasy. And yet I didn't really want him to leave.

"Pascal, I, ah... I don't think that'd be a good idea."

"Because...?"

"Good night," I said, hoping the finality in my voice was clear.

He took my hand and shook it gently, then raised it to his lips and kissed the air above it, as he had when he'd arrived. The light brushing of his lips over my fingers gave me a sweet shiver and I was slow to pull away.

"*Bon soir*, Abigail. I'll see you at the start line tomorrow?"

"Really? You're not upset with me?"

"Don't be silly, *ma chérie*," he winked at me as he spoke the endearment. "We're still friends, *non?*"

"I suppose so. See you in the morning."

A truck rumbled past, almost but not quite drowning out his final comment:

"Friends for now."

Stage Twenty-Five

(81 km – Grenoble, France – Le Bourg d'Oisans, France)

Rom and Attila worked hard, pulling at the front of the group, doing their damnedest to get both Brunn and me up the climbs. Schlessinger was still in sight – the gradient was steep enough to slow him and keep him from getting too far ahead.

The switchbacks ended and the slope gentled enough to allow us an all-too-brief respite, and I settled back into my saddle. Tomorrow would be a rest day – there was that to look forward to once we'd got this final climb behind us.

The descent would be murderous for the pack. Sharp switchbacks, low walls and sheer drops into ravines or off the side of the mountain lay in wait. I'd overheard the *directeur sportif* of one of the other teams discussing it after they'd done a reconnaissance that morning:

"I was in the *car* and I nearly shit myself."

I grinned, remembering. I'd gone over the route map, studied the recon photos and video. I knew what it was going to be like and I couldn't wait.

As I've said before, I can ride the hell out of the descents.

I'd have Brunn behind me, which sucked the fun right out of things. This was my day to shine and I fully intended to, even if Brunn was attached to my arse like a saddle sore.

The ascent resumed in earnest and we launched our final assault

343

with Attila in the lead followed by Rom, me, and Brunn. Attila would pull until he couldn't go any further at that pace, then Rom would take over, and then it was up to me get Brunn up and over. It was standard procedure – since I was the strongest descender, the guys got me to the top where I would pull Brunn along in my wake. Once we were over the summit and down the descent, there was a short, mostly flat run into the city and the finish. I'd have to do my best to get Brunn launched over the line, since all the sprinters – ours included – would still be dragging themselves up the mountain.

As long as we held Schlessinger in check, there was no problem. As it was, we were nearly on top of him. The crowds of fans were growing along either side of the road. What had started out as isolated clusters of spectators along the sloping roads became longer lines of cheering, encouraging participants in the circus-like atmosphere.

Spectators gathered anywhere there was space to stand: straddling ditches along the road with one foot braced against the side of the mountain or with their feet placed in the grass on the verge like a tightrope walker's so they wouldn't stray onto the tarmac. Some brave souls even stood shouting on the brickwork of the low support walls on the open side of the road, with nothing to keep them from falling down to the valley or switchback below.

Other fans ran with us as we rode past, shouting encouragement or epithets in our faces, offering a helping hand on our backs to push us along before they doubled back to do it again with the next group of riders. Most of them did it for the benefit of the television cameras on the motorcycles which wove their way back and forth ahead of the riders. The majority of the futile attention-whoring efforts would never survive to make the edited footage on the evening news broadcast or race replays.

Still we climbed, our pace little more than a fast walk or jog thanks to the gradient sending us skyward.

The road twisted and turned to follow the ridgeline, leaving little space for fans on either side, and the chaos and confusion intensified. Schlessinger looked over his shoulder, his grim expression darkening when he saw us gaining on him. He dug in deeper still in an effort to power away.

None of the other riders in our small group would come forward for a pull. Brunn hectored and harassed another team's rider, trying to goad him into taking a turn at the front. A weary shake of the head and renewed focus on the road directly ahead was the only response.

Rom was still struggling to pull me along, gnashing his teeth and casting his own dark glances backwards. His desire to break away was clear in his expression. I longed to do the same before Attila dropped back, fading through our group, unable to keep the necessary momentum to bring Brunn along.

Rom shouted something which was lost in the air horns and exuberance of the spectators around us. Jerzy continued bellowing in my earpiece, and soon I was aware of someone cursing emphatically nearby.

It took time to realize the person swearing was Brunn. I looked back and found him struggling with his bike. A jammed gear? Some other sort of mechanical issue? Before I could comprehend what I'd seen, I glanced back again, distracted by an expression I'd never seen in Brunn's eyes before:

Panic.

The temperature shifted downward ten degrees, the air turned foggy around my field of vision. I was the nearest member of our team to him, and our team car was behind the bulk of the pack somewhere down the mountain. He was the team leader – I'd have to give him my bike so he could continue.

The movements were ingrained, automatic: my numb fingers closed on the brakes and I moved to unclip from the pedal and dismount. Then, striking me with almost physical force – a single command, hurled from lungs as powerful as a furnace bellows:

"*VAS-Y!!!*"

I didn't think, I followed Brunn's command and moved. With the taste of aluminium in my mouth and my skin crawling off my bones, I moved. Rom poured it on and shot away, the road fell away under our wheels while the summit came ever closer. Before Schlessinger crested the top and slipped out of view, I knew without a doubt I had him.

I had to get to the *bottom* of the mountain first.

Radio silence while Brunn dealt with his own problems behind me meant Jerzy wasn't shrieking in my ear. The crowds currently shouting so loudly I could feel it in my guts would soon be behind me, too.

I unzipped my jersey about halfway and then snagged a page of the newspaper from one of the team crew waiting with an armful of them in front of the barriers. Moving swiftly, I stuffed the newspaper beneath my jersey and zipped up as I rode across the line marking the summit. The shadow of the banner overhead slipped past and, as the road sloped downwards, I settled in for what promised to be a heavily technical descent.

Schlessinger was ahead of me, no doubt riding as hard and as fast as he could in hopes of gaining time. He knew that I knew he'd never outpace me on this descent. I only had to catch him up.

We both knew I *would*. Then he'd have to try and keep up with *me*, which wasn't as easy as he'd like.

I sped downhill, leaving Rom behind and taking the switchback curves at speed, slaloming as though on skis. Cold air whipped past my face, numbing my legs and forearms. It was as though I'd gone deaf. After the screaming chaos of the climb and my heart pounding in my head, I now heard nothing at all. The wind buffeted my ears, drowning out all but the *schirr* of the bike beneath me and the percussive drone of the helicopter overhead.

Time ceased to exist. The road unfurled ahead of me, limitless, and I was flying.

***

My heart in my throat, I stood near the grandstand and watched the screen across the road. Federico was catching up to Schlessinger, gaining precious seconds I'd thought lost. Brunn's mechanical issue had taken much too long to resolve, and he'd only now reached the summit of the mountain. There was no chance he'd make it now; the Royal was up for grabs between Schlessinger and Renard, and the two of them were riding hell for leather for it.

All around me the spectators leaned forward as though they'd be able to see the action on the screens more clearly. I could hardly bear to watch and, shaking, I tried to make sure I had my camera equipment ready for the first arrivals, due any time now.

On the screens Federico caught up to Schlessinger and said something to him. The response was an angry, almost flailing wave of a hand. When the next switchback hooked downward ahead of them, Federico gave way and let Schlessinger go through the curve first, only to resume his post on his opponent's rear wheel.

More talk, more gestures – a psychological battle woven into the fabric of the physical one? Then Federico shot ahead, cutting perilously close as they took the next curve and resumed speed on the straight.

It was all so dramatic: the sheer drops alongside the road, the panorama spread out behind them. I wondered if they saw any of it in the midst of their competition, or if it was lost in the adrenaline rush of the ride.

As Federico pulled clear from his rival to take another curve at a speed so high I cringed, a single, morbid thought flashed through my mind, too terrible to contemplate. I pushed it away before it could get a deep hold, but it lingered at the edges of my awareness.

What if he falls?

***

Schlessinger already looked wobbly. He'd spurned my efforts at diplomacy and truce-making, so I put my head down and went full gas. Hurtling ahead with everything I had, I was determined to put him as far behind me as I could. I took the curves at top speed, knowing he'd never keep up the pace I was setting.

I could hardly contain my excitement.

I swept down the next-to-last switchback curve, aware as I entered the outer sweep that I'd nearly overcooked this one by several inches. The tell-tale skid of my wheel and my slide toward the low wall along the ravine, where I lost traction on the crumbled tarmac lining the gap between the road and the stonework, tamped down my previous high spirits in a hurry.

And then I was back on track, still gunning for the next curve and the straight road leading back down to the valley beyond. I almost laughed: I'd barely broken stride.

***

I couldn't believe my eyes. The images on the screen drew a collective gasp from the crowd at the finish line, and my throat closed over the taste of panic even as I swallowed my own worried cry.

Instant replays didn't make it any less terrifying, either. I watched again and again as Federico slid, his rear wheel skittering and shimmying toward the low wall, and just as that wheel started slipping out from under him, the miraculous catch and forward propulsion which delivered him onto the clean road surface.

Worst of all was knowing what could have happened if he hadn't recovered so quickly – that he shouldn't have evaded that fall so easily, that he'd cheated fate somehow. His cavalier wave toward the helicopter was only slightly reassuring.

My relief which followed, however, was short-lived.

***

I tucked myself in tight, folding my body between the handlebars and the saddle to become as aerodynamic as was physically possible when the road straightened for the final descent. The whole world rushed past me, no sound but the wind roaring by my ears – and even *that* was nearly drowned out by my heartbeat.

A quick glance over my shoulder proved Schlessinger was nowhere in sight. I couldn't help grinning – I'd shaken him off at last. I moved back into the saddle again, still pedalling for speed on this final straightaway.

I had no reason to doubt, anymore. The Royal was mine.

There was no chance he'd catch up now – nor would Brunn, for that matter. Tomorrow was a flat stage, and it was unlikely anyone would snatch it away then. The last stage was a time trial, and if I felt half as good that morning as I did right now...

I ignored the thought, putting my focus on the road ahead.

No point in jinxing myself.

***

The footage of the ambulance and the paramedics waiting for the medical helicopter to extract him from the ravine was gut-wrenching. The sight of him, bloodied and battered and in obvious excruciating pain made me ill.

I still couldn't believe what I'd seen, and so I continued casting my gaze down along the road to the finish. The handful of riders in the breakaway had already crossed the line and I'd taken my photos of them distractedly, my attention diverted by the images on the screen until I'd made a point of positioning myself where I couldn't see them anymore.

After his impressive descent, Federico's lead was considerable;

he would still arrive ahead of any of the other contenders. I wondered if he had any idea of what had happened on the mountain behind him. When he finally rolled across the finish line to the crowd's modest cheers, he looked somewhat puzzled.

"I don't think he knows about Schlessinger," someone said close to me, and I turned to find an official talking to one of the Americans. "I'm sure no-one's told him. I heard Jankowski said to keep mum for now because Renard didn't see it himself."

"How is that possible?"

"He doesn't even know what happened to *him*, much less to Schlessinger."

My desire to try to get to him right away fell to the wayside. Give him time to recover – for Jerzy to fill him in, for him to absorb what had happened – and then he would feel how he would feel. I'd find him later if I could.

Although it had been a while ago, knowing I'd sent Chicco my room number made me feel terrible. I continued taking photos of the peloton's arrival, determined to let him know not to worry about trying to see me tonight.

Brunn passed the cluster of photographers where I stood and went swiftly to the team handlers awaiting him.

A relieved murmur passed through the crowd. There would be no podium presentation that afternoon. I moved to watch the screen one more time and saw footage of Schlessinger being loaded onto the air ambulance. The images cut to the area behind the podium stage even as the helicopter flew overhead, bound for the hospital in Grenoble. The dazed, befuddled expression on Federico's face – along with the relief and gratitude on his team director's and teammates' faces – said everything about how close he'd come to being that passenger.

***

Hours passed. I was numb with surprise and shock. I wasn't sure what had happened; if not for the fact it was all caught on camera, I wouldn't have known anything *had* happened.

The fact remained: I had quite literally skirted the edge of death on the side of that mountain and come out all right on the other side.

I watched the replay of my near-miss again and again, the

images on the television stubbornly refusing to connect to my memories of the events. The footage of Schlessinger being extracted from the ravine and assessed by the medical team was more surreal.

But it *had* happened. All of it.

There were no interviews or outside intrusions (Jerzy's orders), but there'd been someone from the team with me the whole time. Once I was left alone, I finally stitched it all together. The shudder of the bike frame beneath me, the skitter of the wheels over the broken pavement, the sinking give of my rear wheel as it went into the gap and smacked the low wall at an angle that was somehow *wrong*.

The recovery wasn't as clear. The next few yards were a blur. The ravine below, the trees and rocks and the sheer face of the mountain falling away? Those were sharp and detailed as they hadn't been before.

Every channel on the television showed the same scenes, reported on Schlessinger's condition – grave – and noted that the day's results had been neutralized. It was surreal, watching myself ride like a man possessed, oblivious to what I'd scarcely avoided.

I couldn't help some resentment at this: I'd nearly killed myself and another rider, and it didn't even count for a day's work.

There was no thought, no conscious decision. She'd given me her room number so I could call her and nothing more – she'd said as much in her second text message. Yet I was getting off the bed and putting on my shoes, giving myself a cursory glance in the mirror before turning to go.

It was crazy but nothing about this had been sane, had it? The only clear thought I had was of being with her, of making damned certain no matter what that I wouldn't lose another chance.

No matter the cost.

I stepped out and started down the hall, grateful that Rom wasn't in the room yet. Not that it would have changed anything.

For the first time I moved without extra care or caution. I'd made up my mind and I would see this through. I'd waited too long, needlessly, and I'd nearly lost any chance I'd ever have.

Before I turned the last corner before the side door, I knew.

Jerzy stood to one side of the corridor, his arms folded across his chest, his gaze focused on the frayed carpet on the tiled floor.

I barely slowed. I didn't care.

"You go, you're done." There was none of his usual bluster or menace – not in his stance, not in his voice.

I paused with my hand on the door handle, the metal bar cool against my feverish palm.

"I mean it. You'll finish the Tour, but that's it. You don't ride for me again."

Taking a deep breath, I closed my eyes and opened them again.

I'd made up my mind.

***

His hands caught in my hair as the door swung shut behind us, and the sound of his back hitting the door echoed down the hall beyond. I clung to him, memorizing how he felt in my arms, all-too-aware that I'd nearly lost any chance of feeling him against me like this again.

My hands moved over him in fleeting, worried caresses, touching his face, his shoulders and back, his chest, his waist. He shook – or was that me? – while I reassured myself he was okay. At last satisfied with his well-being, I pressed my cheek to his chest and swallowed the tears that threatened.

He tilted my face up to his and kissed me. It was not a tender kiss by any means. Where his kisses had contained an underlying passion before, this one was filled with a hunger he'd never shown.

I sought more, wanted to draw more from him in my own selfish desire to know him better. But this wasn't the time, the atmosphere was all wrong, and the hint of desperation tainted the touch of his lips on mine.

Besides, he still had a race to finish.

"You can't be here," I managed between kisses. "Chicco, this is a bad idea."

He drew away and pressed his lips to my temple.

"No, it doesn't matter," he whispered, the words nearly lost in the rustle of my hair over my ear. "I needed to see you." He kissed me again, his hands sliding over me, seeking, finding. There was nothing more for me to do but give him what we wanted.

***

She tensed at my touch, her whole body stiff with expectation and anxiety under the sheen of slippery grey silk. The warm give of her flesh under my hands, the silk sliding and folding in my grasp, her sighs breathed against my lips between kisses – all conspired to drive me forward into her room, the night's conclusion emerging between us.

There would be no more half-measures now. There was no point. The press of her body against mine, yielding when I sought, voluptuously soft where I was hard, beckoned my hands beneath her nightdress. I gathered the fabric in my fingers, bunched it into my palms, lifted it up even as we stepped toward her bed, her subtle dizzying scent in the air between us.

As I pulled the garment over her head, any final lingering doubts whether she wanted this too were also discarded. I stepped back to take in the sight of her.

Never mind our previous intimacies, never mind the intensity of those encounters – this was the first time I'd ever seen her completely nude, and she tried bravely to meet my gaze.

I tore at my own shirt, pulled at it in fistfuls to get it over my head and then flung it to a corner of the room. I fumbled out of my jeans, shoes, underwear – desperate to be as naked and exposed as she was.

Desperate to be with her, because she was all I had.

Her lips parted, her tongue sweet and firm, seeking and challenging mine. Her body so soft, her hands sliding over me when we lay together, there was nothing else – no other place or time existed or ever would.

I didn't want her any more – I *needed* her. As much as breath or food or sleep, I needed her.

"Chicco," she murmured, her breath warm on my neck, her arms tight around me as she raised her hips and urged me closer.

As I slipped inside her, she sighed. Her whole body thrummed with the sound, sending a small tremor through me.

***

It was like falling, a sensation which made me wrap myself around him and hold tight. I wanted to fall. I wanted to fall further, faster than I ever had before, and I wanted to take him with me to whatever depths might take me.

He was right there with me, I knew; I could feel it when his control slipped and he moved with an urgent, frantic energy, his breathing ragged. When he slowed or paused and kissed me with an almost frightening intensity, I knew he was close and struggling not to fall first.

I couldn't stop kissing him – his lips, his throat, his chest – and I urged him forward, knowing I couldn't keep from falling again. I clutched at him, my hands grasping at him in wordless pleading until he understood and gave in.

I cried out, unable, unwilling to stop this time. His efforts continued but it wasn't long before he exhaled into my hair, his whole body shuddering against me, inside me. He tried to pull away afterward but I held him in place, not wanting him to go.

I didn't want him to leave me while I cried. He would surely see the few silent tears which slipped from the corners of my eyes to wet my temples and tickle my earlobes. I wasn't ready to see his face, to let him know that I'd finally betrayed my husband in every possible way, and what hurt me was the fact it didn't hurt to have done so.

***

When I started to move away she held me closer, and I sank gratefully into her embrace. I'd been operating on the remnants of one adrenaline rush or another for the entire day.

Her warmth and softness were hypnotic, lulling me into a hazy half-sleep. I reached to secure the condom when I withdrew, and my half-sleep vanished as I moved away from her, heart racing.

She startled too, her eyes wide with surprise. "What is it? What's wrong?"

I met her eyes, a flash of guilt burning my stomach as I did. An eternity passed before I could speak.

"I didn't – I forgot –"

Anxiety filled her expression.

I'm such an idiot. How could I do this?

"Chicco," she began, her voice soft, shaky. "Is there anything else you should tell me?"

"What do you mean?"

"You're...ah..." She covered her face with her hand and shook her head. "You're, you know, *clean*, right?"

Understanding clicked into place in spite of the chaos in my head. "Oh, right. Yes, I'm fine, I'm..." I had to laugh a little at the next thought. "Jerzy tests us for *everything* before the season starts to be sure nothing will affect our performance."

To my amazement, Abby laughed too. She rubbed her eyes with the heels of her palms and swiped her hands back to pull her hair away from her face. Her eyes were a little red, her face flushed pink.

She was beautiful.

"I'm sorry, Abby. I wasn't thinking—"

"Neither was I. It's okay, though."

"It is?" I asked. She smiled, then switched off the bedside lamp and lay down again. I lay down beside her. "You're sure?"

"Absolutely."

I drew her to me, kissed her and closed my eyes. There was so much more I needed to say, to do. I was exhausted. I was exhilarated. I resolved to tell her what I'd been thinking since I'd arrived at the hotel that afternoon, once things had settled down again.

Just six words, but I knew they could change my life.

***

We lay facing one another, foreheads touching, our arms draped loosely over each other. His breath brushed my face, gentle warmth which came and went with a reassuring rhythm. Lulled into a near-doze myself, I almost didn't understand when he spoke, his voice so soft it faded into the darkness.

"I want to abandon the Tour."

I gaped at him, disbelieving. "Why?" I managed at last.

"Because of today, because I didn't know what happened to Schlessinger, and because..." His fingers alighted on my cheek, finding me unerringly in the dark. "Because of you."

"Me?"

His nod shifted the pillow as his forehead rubbed mine.

"I want to be with you."

"You *are* with me."

"I want to *stay* with you. There's no point in anything else."

"Yes, there is, Chicco. You have a shot at winning this – at winning the whole thing."

"Perhaps, but after today..."

"You still can."

"I don't want it."

"You *do*. You know you do. If you give it up now, you'll regret it. You know that, too."

Silence stretched out between us, infinite in the night.

"I want you."

The helplessness in his voice tore at my heart.

"I want you, too," I said. "But I don't want to be part of your regrets."

His intake of breath anticipated another protest.

"That's what I'll be if you abandon," I continued, speaking before he could. "When you look back and see you *could* have had it, and you realize you gave up for nerves and, well...you'll never forgive yourself – or me."

"I'll never regret any of this."

"I hope you don't. I really do."

Another silence passed between us.

"Abby..." he began, but didn't complete the thought.

He didn't have to.

The truth was simple. I never wanted him to leave but I was afraid of what might happen if he stayed. I wasn't worried for myself, but for him – how many chances would he take? He'd already been caught and forgiven once; it didn't seem likely he'd find such lenience from Jerzy again.

But oh, how good it felt to have him there with me. After the initial post-coital awkwardness, he now seemed content to rest with me, his arms around me as we calmed and dozed together.

My head on his chest, I listened to his heartbeat and his breathing while tracing my fingers lightly through the hair on his chest. I could still taste his kisses; the salt of his skin lingered on my lips.

I closed my eyes and hoped to fall asleep, not wanting to think about him leaving or how I'd feel when I was alone this time tomorrow. For the first time came a glimmer of dread for the end of the Tour. In spite of everything, I couldn't see a real future beyond it.

At least, not for *us*.

***

The weight of her arm across my chest, her breasts pressed against my side, the heat of her inner thigh on mine – I knew I'd be able to trace where they'd been for days afterward.

I was too aware of every passing second, knowing that each one took me further past the point of no return.

Not that it mattered. Jerzy had made it clear enough and I had chosen this.

My eyelids drooped while I listened to Abby's breathing. Giving in, I closed my eyes and listened even more closely. She shifted position, moving her hand so it rested over my heart.

She sighed quietly and I recalled when I'd slipped inside her. The recollection was too much – too intense, too vivid – and I reluctantly blocked it out.

Satisfied, at ease with her beside me, the first doubt began to worm its way into my head.

Was she worth this sacrifice? My first response was *yes*, followed closely by a faint voice crying *'Too soon to know!'*

It wasn't Jerzy's voice, it wasn't Sunny's voice – which I would have expected to hear – but it was certainly a familiar one:

It was my own.

I opened my eyes and found her sleeping sweetly, her face nestled against my chest. I let my head fall back onto the pillow again, her hand over my heart now much too heavy, pushing me down and holding me there.

I must be out of my mind. What have I got myself into?

She shifted, making another soft sound like a cat's purr, and the familiar pull of desire stirred deep inside me.

This was no impulsive act. I'd known Jerzy was serious when he'd given his ultimatum, and I'd left the hotel anyway. I'd needed her beyond any sort of common sense or clear reason and I'd followed through.

There was no-one else to blame for my actions. The sacrifice had been mine to make, and I had.

In a few days, I'd know if I'd made the right decision.

Rest Day Four

(Grenoble, France)

The timing was uncanny. No sooner had I stepped back into my room and started to undress for bed, than there was a knock at the door.

I hesitated, trying to recall if I'd noticed anyone in the corridor when I'd come in, or if I'd passed any familiar faces in the lobby on my way through.

Another knock, louder this time. I'd already stripped to my undershorts before going to look through the peephole.

Jerzy stood there with two familiar men: the vampires. Anxiety knotted my stomach. There was no point in getting dressed, considering that one of these men would be seeing quite a bit more of me as I gave my samples.

I unlocked and opened the door as Jerzy reached for his master key. He seemed surprised to find me there, but that swiftly shifted into his trademark scowl.

"Took you long enough." He pushed me aside with one hand and switched on the light with the other. In spite of everything, Rom continued sleeping, his soft uninterrupted snores drawing curious glances from the two newcomers.

Jerzy slapped Rom's bare foot where it stuck out from under the covers, raising his voice to give an ominous-sounding command in Polish.

Rom's eyes snapped open and he sat up, looking lost and

confused. Another barked command from Jerzy had the boy out of bed, the sheets clutched around his waist in a bid for modesty.

"Let's get this over with," I grumbled, heading for the bathroom, one hand extended for the sample collection cup. "I'd like to get some sleep, you know."

Jerzy raised an eyebrow but gave no other sign anything unusual was going on. One of the agents handed me a cup and followed me into the bathroom, discreetly positioning himself to spot any potential trickery on my part.

With effort I filled the cup, trying to ignore the brief sidelong glance the agent gave me. Self-consciousness hit me – my imagination ran wild along with my guilt, and I could have sworn I smelled Abby's scent on me. I wished I had taken the time to shower before I'd left her hotel.

Next, the agent took a blood sample while we stood at the sink. In spite of my fatigue, I was grateful that he took his time about it. While I held the rubbing alcohol-soaked cotton ball to my arm afterward, he labelled the samples with neat, efficient strokes of his pen.

"Five a.m.," I said, reading my watch as we stepped back into the room. "This couldn't have waited another couple of hours?"

"You know the rules, Renard," the other agent replied, taking out reams of paperwork and sitting at the small table in the corner.

I shook my head and joined him, signing in the usual places while Rom stepped into the bathroom for his turn.

"Yeah, I know," I said resignedly. "I suppose I should count myself lucky that it's a rest day, instead?"

I signed, initialled, and signed again, more from habit than any real comprehension of what was written on the pages in front of me.

"If it makes you feel any better, the whole team's getting the same treatment today. We're not singling you out." The agent gathered the paperwork and scanned the pages quickly, then tucked it into a folder without looking at me.

"It just seems excessive."

"Everybody says that."

The bathroom door creaked open again and Rom appeared back in the room, still wrapped in his sheet. His minder followed behind with an expression on his face somewhere between wonder and envy.

Rom seated himself at the table next to me and reached for the paperwork handed to him. Jerzy mumbled instructions to the boy, who nodded sleepily as he signed and initialled. He yawned, a huge effort which seemed to swallow half his face, and both agents appeared to stifle echoing yawns of their own.

The two men double-checked their paperwork and the samples, and Rom slouched back to his bed, asleep before he hit the mattress.

Fatigue hit me out of nowhere, slamming into me hard enough to knock me sideways. All the events of the day – the ride, Schlessinger's crash, my own near-miss, the time I'd stolen with Abby and what we'd done – set upon me.

A hand on my shoulder guided me to stand up and go to my bed, the blackness of sleep and relief hovering overhead. I lay down, the sheets cold and smooth beneath me, bringing back the sharp memory of Abby a short while ago. However, that memory didn't follow me into sleep.

But the guilt did.

***

The rush of being with Federico lasted even in his absence, the excitement of the act exhilarating even in retrospect. Yet, in the silence of my hotel room, I knew I'd gone too far.

The tears gathered behind my eyes until the ache was almost unbearable, and the realization of what I'd done sank in. I had a vague sense of nausea as I pondered having broken my marriage vows. I could no longer justify my anger or frustration with Charles. I'd surrendered all rights to any last traces of moral superiority.

Part of me insisted, defiantly, that I'd been driven to it. Charles' cheating, his insinuations that I should take a lover, a gut instinct to level the playing field – all had played a part. There was more to it, though, and I knew it. From the first time I'd spoken at length with Federico, I'd wanted to be with him.

How to go forward from here?

I lay in the middle of the bed and cried silently, breathing in Federico's scent from the sheets and his pillow. I hated that he'd gone. I hated that we'd had to meet this way. I even hated, with a sudden and unexpected passion, the race that had brought us together, that had made me go so far beyond my own boundaries.

Just two more stages.

Just three more days and it would all be over.

Or... I could pack up and go. Right now.

Fresh anger flared at the thought.

Oh, sure. I *could* go home. I could go home and lie about what I'd done tonight, letting Charles think he was right about me all along. I could do that, and then face his snide remarks about my inability to finish anything, and then finally spend my days (and almost as frequently, my nights) alone in my house in Hampshire, waiting for him to come home and leave his girlfriend for me. Again.

Only this time I'd have to call it what it was: a delusion, a lie I'd made up to comfort myself when I was lonely or too afraid to make a move one way or another.

No.

I wiped my palms across my cheeks to dry them and shook my head. I couldn't do that again. Not after this.

Christ, the *idea* of the pitying looks on my neighbours' faces when I went down to the shops, knowing that they knew my husband and I were apart made me crazy. I couldn't do that. I had to find a *purpose* this time. I had to see this job through and then see what came of it.

And what about Federico? Was there a future with him, or no?

Thinking about it realistically, as much as I hated to, I had to say it wasn't likely. After all, I'd be as lonely as I'd been before. His job would take him away from me most of the year, so I'd still be sitting alone at home waiting for his return.

I wasn't sure about starting a family at this late date, either – and surely he'd want that? So many cyclists married young and started families right away, but wasn't I too old to start down that road?

A dull throb started at the base of my skull, slowly rising until my whole head ached. I pressed my fingertips to my eyelids and waited for the pain to fade. It didn't. I rolled out of bed to get some aspirin out of my handbag and felt surprisingly exposed, somehow more naked than naked.

I stood in the middle of the room, my heart beating so fast it made me dizzy.

This wasn't how I was supposed to feel. I was *supposed* to be happy, excited, walking on air. I'd made love with –

Scratch that. 'Made love with'? How could I call it that when I wasn't even sure I'd hear from him again?

No, that wasn't fair, either. He hadn't been in any real rush to leave, had he? Hell, I'd nearly had to force him to go.

The cool, conditioned air made me shiver and I picked up my nightgown from where he had left it at the foot of the bed and put it on.

I didn't want him to get into any trouble. If he'd stayed any longer, the odds of him getting caught were increased. What was the use in that?

***

I made my way down to the dining room of the hotel fairly early and found few of my teammates there. Several had chosen to sleep in – Rom, for one, was still snoring away upstairs, and Adrie had taken advantage of the chance to visit with his family.

I sat down with my breakfast at a table by a window in the corner. I'd tried to sleep but failed. I'd replayed the events of the day before – Schlessinger's fall, my night with Abigail – and grown more and more troubled as the hours passed.

He wouldn't have fallen if he hadn't been so determined to keep up with me – he'd *never* been able to keep up with me on descents. He knew that. He hadn't improved his skills that much since we'd ridden on the same team.

The clink of my spoon in my bowl told me there was nothing left. I needed more to eat but my stomach rebelled at the thought. I pushed my empty plate away.

Michael came in and started in my direction. His face was full of quiet concern, making me even more ill at ease. For fuck's sake, Schlessinger hadn't died, had he?

Had he?

I didn't want to know, but my breakfast sat uneasily in my stomach as Michael approached. If there were any changes, any turns for the worse, I was about to find out. The morning news had been full of details, replaying the footage of the rescue – he'd fallen into a ravine and been surprisingly lucky not to be killed, they said – and showing me arriving at the finish, still oblivious to what had happened.

"Morning, Ciccio." Michael sat across from me and smiled

tiredly. I nodded in greeting. Speaking suddenly seemed like too much trouble. "Schlessinger's in hospital across town," he continued. "If you want to go see him, we'll get you there."

"Let's go." The words came without hesitation, without any real thought. I suppose I'd been considering that possibility all along.

*

Schlessinger couldn't talk yet – a broken rib had punctured a lung – but he could nod or indicate with the hand on his uninjured arm. Not that he'd respond to anything I said. He faced away from me, turning his head as soon as I came in the room.

The nurse advised me not to ask any complicated questions, to keep to simple 'yes' or 'no' inquiries. With this in mind, my opening conversational gambit was direct and to the point.

"You dumb fuck."

I stood next to the bed, trying to ignore the sting of antiseptic in the air.

He pretended ignorance of my presence, his attention focused on the closed curtains of his window. He'd been knocked out since he'd arrived in hospital the day before, but now he was as awake as his pain medications would allow.

It was enough to allow him to make a point of ignoring me.

I was alone with him, as the nurse had promised, and I was grateful for the drawn curtains. The paparazzi outside wouldn't get a shot of this pathetic reunion. I pulled up the chair from the corner and sat down, leaning forward to rest my forearms on the bed.

"You stupid...dumb fuck," I repeated, knowing he couldn't say anything to me but half-wishing he'd react in some way.

"What the hell were you thinking? You've never – not once – been able to keep up with me on a descent. Especially not one like that." I shook my head and shuddered in spite of myself, glad he was facing away from me. "You're luckier than you realize, *Scheisskopf*; you nearly killed yourself yesterday. Surely even *you* know that by now."

He turned back toward me, his eyes closed, his bruised jaw set with defiance. A few quiet moments passed while I watched his eyes twitching beneath his eyelids, the blond lashes flickering restlessly as though he were about to open them and look at me. I knew better. He'd always been one of the most stubborn people I'd ever known.

"When you're on your feet again I'll come see you. But I'm going to give you a punch in the face when I do. Trust me, you deserve it."

His eyes flicked open for an instant, then resolutely shut. It seemed that the corners of his mouth twitched upward before pressing down again. A smile resisted, though barely.

I stood and put the chair back before I faced the bed again.

"Dumb fuck," I said one last time, swallowed hard and left.

Michael stood in the corridor, leaning against the wall near the nurses' station. He arched one eyebrow at my approach.

"How'd it go?"

I shrugged. "He's pretending to sleep," I said as we walked to the elevator. "He can't talk anyway, not that there's a lot to chat about."

"It'll take some time, but he'll be okay." Michael pressed the call button and we waited in silence until the doors slid open and we stepped on. "He might even be back on the bike next season."

I glanced at Michael. He didn't look any more convinced than I must have.

"I keep feeling like this is somehow my fault; like I pushed him too hard or something. I didn't think he'd do that – chase so hard, I mean."

"That's bike racing. You knew his weakness and you tried to exploit it – like he did on the climb with you. It's no different."

"I don't climb at 80 kilometres an hour, though."

"Would that you could, though – am I right?"

The elevator doors opened and we stepped out, making our way to the side entrance where we'd come in earlier. I caught a glimpse of a handful of photographers and reporters in front of the main entrance at the end of the corridor as we passed.

Schlessinger's accident would be news for another day or so, and then something else would snatch the headlines away. It would have been the same if it were me upstairs, attached to tubes and wires, unable to talk and so medicated I couldn't feel much of anything.

"When he fell, we thought about telling you right away."

"You did?"

"Yeah, we opted not to because you were riding so well. With

Brunn haemorrhaging time, it seemed the better choice."

"I'd expect nothing less from Jerzy," I said, trying not to sneer. "Bless his mercenary heart."

"That's the thing, Ciccio. *I* pushed him not to."

I stopped short and Michael belatedly stopped, too. "You?"

He nodded. "After we'd seen how well you were descending, all the time you were gaining on the pack, we didn't want to throw your ride. You had that near-miss and we *really* didn't want to risk fucking up your ride. You recovered so quickly that when the first call came through that he'd gone down... We didn't know how bad it was, at first. Once we knew, we had decisions to make.

"I pushed for radio silence. I was sure that if you knew... " He shook his head. "To have that on top of Brunn's losses, well, we couldn't afford that. Of course, if we'd known they'd neutralize the stage..." He shrugged and looked me in the eye. "I'm sorry."

I started walking again. When I opened the door I spotted a few journos between us and the team car and immediately felt a sense of dread.

I pushed my way through the small, frenzied group, ignoring the cameras and microphones thrust in my face as questions were fired at me from all sides at once.

Their voices overlapped, blending together into an incoherent mess as more reporters rushed over from the front of the building to join in. Even if I'd been paying attention, I doubt I'd have been able to understand anything they were saying to me.

It wasn't until I was inside the car with the door closed against the cacophony that I really had a chance to consider what Michael had said. I'd assumed it had been Jerzy's call to keep the news from me.

Sure, it was true that I'd have lost focus if I'd known about the incident – not to mention how bad it actually was. But, for Michael to keep it quiet and Jerzy – of all people – to be persuaded not to tell me?

Considering the likely outcome, why would Jerzy have *wanted* to tell me?

As the car pulled out of the hospital parking area, I grabbed the bottle of water I'd left on the back seat and gulped it down even though it was lukewarm, then closed my eyes and pressed the back of my head against the headrest.

Fuck me. It was too much to think about. Too many

machinations, too many conflicting possibilities – more than merely playing favourites, it seemed like a positively Machiavellian scheme with me as an unwitting pawn, all to get Brunn the win. I'd been right all along: on some level, I was being set up to fail, and I'd managed to avoid it almost in spite of myself.

Abby, too, had made a good call. Abandoning the Tour would have been a mistake. I was now more determined than ever to win this thing.

I wouldn't be able to tell her face-to-face, but a phone call was certainly in order. At the very least, I should be able to see her on the last day of the Tour.

If I had my way, after that, I'd never be without her again.

*

Back at the hotel, I was shepherded into a cordoned-off area beside the team bus. Our bikes were already on the rollers for a stationary warm-up spin before we'd take short ride. The crew had done a good job of arranging things to keep the press at bay, and I was grateful. I made a mental note to do something especially nice for them no matter what my position was at the end of the Tour.

Sometime later, as we drifted toward the equipment truck to gather our things for the ride, Michael came out of the bus and made his way over to Alvaro and Teodoro.

"Guys, guys – hold up," he called, his tone cool.

Alvaro looked up at Michael and then glanced toward the hotel door. Jerzy stood there with his arms folded across his chest, his face impassive. Teodoro was already loping in that direction before Alvaro drew a deep sigh and removed his helmet. He followed slowly in his brother's wake, eyes downcast, shoulders slouched, clearly resigned to his fate.

Next to me, bent over his bike and fussing with his bottle cage, was Adrie. He straightened up and watched Alvaro enter the hotel, then exhaled a long, slow breath.

"Shit," he muttered, shaking his head.

I gave him a sidelong glance. "What's up?"

"Jerzy must have found out about Teo. It was really a matter of time."

I shook my head, uncomprehending. This didn't go with what I'd seen a couple of days ago. *Teodoro* was up to something too?

"What are you talking about?"

"I guess there's no harm in telling you now." Adrie looked around us before leaning in closer. "Alvaro told me the other day that he was having a problem with a control officer from back home." He tilted his head toward the door and pretended to fuss with the straps of the helmet in his hands. "He said he'd been paying off some leech for years who's been threatening to reveal some dirty secret from their junior career."

"No joke?"

Adrie shook his head. "Based on what he told me, Teo tested positive around the time Jerzy was ready to pick them up, and this guy suppressed the results so they'd make the team. Once they were pro and doing well, he turned up and told Alvaro to pay or he'd produce the documentation. It's been going on for years – Al's practically skint, now – and the guy turned up asking for more cash than usual." He glanced around again to be sure no-one was listening in, then continued. "Al told him to fuck off, 'cause he didn't have anything else to give the guy anyway. I guess the shit's hit the fan."

Thinking back to the night in the stairwell and the evident payoff I'd witnessed, my stomach lurched.

"Jesus Christ," I muttered. "I had no idea."

"No-one did. Not even Teo."

"I don't suppose there's any chance they're just talking in there?"

Adrie shook his head again. Something in the gesture seemed utterly final. "You know the rules, Ciccio. They're the same for everyone."

Michael exited the hotel and went straight to the DS's car, nodding at Brunn as he passed. Brunn called out and clapped his hands together once, twice, the sound reverberating off the walls of the hotel and the side of the equipment truck with a metallic echo.

"Enough talk, ladies! Let's get moving!"

Already mounting his bike, Phil glanced around and rolled toward Brunn. "What about Al and Teo?" he asked as the group gathered at the edge of the parking lot.

"Don't worry about them. Let's go."

Stage Twenty-Six

(135 km – Loches, France – Le Mans, France)

Still hearing Charles' voice in my head, I woke with a splitting headache. Feeling ill, I dreaded the day working under full sunshine. After what had turned out to be a nearly nine-hour drive the day before – the result of both my own distraction and the GPS sending me the long way around every chance it got – I'd collapsed into my bed at the hotel and struggled to sleep.

My dreams hadn't allowed me much rest, either. They were filled with replays of my nearly-endless drive and scenes where Charles appeared unexpectedly at my hotel, demanding that I break things off with Federico. Such images had become the stuff of quasi-nightmares.

I pulled myself out of bed and rummaged around in my handbag for my bottle of aspirin. I downed three pills with a full glass of water before getting into the shower. While the water flowed over me and the reputedly 'invigorating' scent of my shower gel filled the shower cubicle, I considered the logistical challenges ahead of me for the day.

I had to go to the sign-in and get some photos, then get to the start line to grab a few more shots of the riders. After that, I'd push through the crowd and get to my car – which I'd have packed beforehand – and drive to Le Mans with a few leap-frog stops on the way to photograph the peloton as it passed. If I had time, I'd check in to my hotel before going to the finish line and the podium for the final shots of the day. With that, the twenty-sixth stage would be over and done.

The funny thing was that I was practically on autopilot as far as the work went. Only two days left. It was hard to believe, but it was true and the thought lightened my mood.

If only I knew what to expect afterwards. Originally, Charles and I had planned to stay in Paris for a couple of days after the race. I'd called last night to be sure the room was still on reserve and everything was fine. So why was this worry digging around in the back of my head?

My mobile phone beeped. I wrapped up in the hotel-supplied robe and went to check it.

'Bonjour, Abby. Two days.'

I sat down on the edge of the bed with a sigh, pleased and melancholy all at once.

During the drive up to Loches, I'd thought about Federico. I didn't want to dismiss what had happened – that was impossible – but I didn't want to build it into something more than it was. Now I'd had time to think about it, I knew he'd been in a particularly vulnerable state that night. He'd needed our connection; so had I, and we'd seized our chance when we'd found it.

There was something not quite right about the whole situation, and I couldn't help feeling as though he had grabbed hold of me for all the wrong reasons. He'd been ready to marry Solange a few weeks ago – so was I his rebound?

For that matter, was he *my* rebound? I didn't plan to go back to Charles, so my marriage was over. Where did that put Federico in my life? Hell, where did it leave me?

I got up and put my phone away. I was wasting too much time. There were too many things I needed to get done.

"Right," I said, my voice was too loud even though my headache was subsiding. "Get dressed. Eat breakfast. Pack the car and go."

From the hallway I faintly overheard a male voice bidding someone "*Bonjour.*" A sudden, intense wish to hear it from Federico's lips burned through me.

Two more days.

It was a lifetime and no time at all.

My head gave a single, huge throb at the thought. I tried to let myself slip back into autopilot again. I'd need to do that to get through the day.

A gallon of coffee probably wouldn't hurt, either.

***

As we drove to Loches for the stage's start the mood on the bus was grim. I kept waiting to see if Phil or James would try to joke and lighten things up. Instead, everyone regarded Teodoro and Alvaro's empty seats with expressions of remorse or surprise that they weren't there.

There were no farewells. They were gone before we got back from the ride in Grenoble. We'd arrived at the train station with our personal black cloud hanging over us as we made our way to the platform. The final stages of the race were upon us, and although there were still chances to be taken on the road, this year's Tour was all but decided.

Fans in the train station had snapped photos and asked for autographs, and the team had obliged. Questions about the twins' whereabouts were glossed over – we honestly didn't know – although by that time they were surely heading home.

The ride afterward from Grenoble to Chateauroux on the *Train Grande Vitesse* had been disquieting. The French heartland slipped past our windows at high speed. An ever-changing landscape which normally drew awestruck comments from even the most jaded riders failed to elicit a reaction from anyone riding in our carriage.

I was sure they'd find a new team. They were too good not to. But I still had a lingering doubt that they'd ever be as good as they were with us. Once riders left the team, very few continued to perform as well as they had under Jerzy's watchful eye.

"You know the rules."

Adrie's words on the subject sat uneasily with me, the sentiment a cold weight in my stomach. I knew the rules as well as anyone else did, but seeing them applied so thoroughly when I'd had so much leeway wasn't right.

Yes, I was off the team as soon as the Tour was over, but I'd managed to get by with so much for the duration of this race, it felt unfair.

Maybe Schlessinger had been right all along. Maybe Jerzy had been playing favourites with me over the years. He'd worked more closely with me than with many of the other riders, to be sure, and I'd seen the interviews with Schlessinger and other riders where they'd slagged me off as Jerzy's "Golden Boy".

I'd won my races fairly. Everything I'd achieved I'd done with my own hard work. With Jerzy's guidance, true – but that was also true of everyone on this team. Our successes were the reasons why riders were desperate to ride with this team: he made winners.

But maybe... No.

I took a deep breath and exhaled hard, shaking my head to clear it. The only sounds on the bus were those of the wheels, the engine, and the murmur of conversations scattered around the cabin. Music played, too low for the melody to be easily distinguished against the other noises, an almost hypnotic drone.

We'd had the television on for a while, but it was switched off when it was clear the only real race-related news would be about the twins' expulsion. Rumours were flying thick and fast – speculation raged that they'd been caught doping, they'd argued with Jerzy and he'd booted them out, or even that they'd paid off riders on other teams to help them to win. Disturbingly, it seemed that every one of the rumours had some tiny fragment of truth in them.

In a couple of days, with the race over and my contract dissolved, I'd be in their shoes.

I got up and went back to the kitchenette to grab a bottle of water. The ride today would be fairly easy by the looks of it, so I was already mentally preparing for tomorrow's time trial.

I returned to my seat feeling edgy, vaguely tempted to do something crazy – shout or scream, throw something, maybe? – to break the tension and the silence.

Instead, I took out the well-worn copy I'd made of Abby's itinerary and scanned it, noting the name of her hotel in Le Mans before I tucked it away in my bag. I got my phone and thought about what I wanted to say before I started tapping a message onto the screen.

Once finished, I hit *send* and sat back with a sigh. I put my phone away and got my mp3 player out, stuffing the earbuds into my ears as I switched it on. I rolled my shoulders, trying to will the tension out of my muscles. Then, ignoring the glance Brunn sent my way, I closed my eyes and tried to zone out for a while.

In two more days, it would all be over.

In two more days, something else would begin.

I wasn't sure what it would be.

***

A familiar voice called my name as soon as the peloton rolled out of view on the road out of Chateauroux and the crowd had begun to disperse. Pascal crossed the street to join me, all smiles under the already remarkable heat of the day. My headache lurked in the pulse-points of my temples, threatening to bloom again in spite of the aspirin I'd taken.

"*Bonjour*," he said, his voice carrying a slight lilt.

His grin was decidedly infectious and I couldn't help returning it. "*Bonjour*," I replied, and his face lit up even more.

"Ah, *magnifique*! She speaks the language now." He said this to a few members of the crowd as they passed by us, earning several puzzled looks in response.

I rolled my eyes before putting my equipment away. "I'm afraid French still is some distance away from being my second language."

"What *is* your second language, then?"

An inexplicable heat crept into my cheeks before I could answer. "I don't have one. I'm strictly monolingual, I'm afraid."

His expression turned suddenly serious. "I must advise you to work on that, Abby. Honestly, you would benefit a great deal knowing another language. Especially in this line of work."

"I guess so." I shrugged and started walking to the photographers' parking. "I hadn't really thought about it before."

"You should. Think about it, I mean. A second language – preferably French – could make the difference between this being a hobby or a career for you."

I half-laughed in spite of myself. "Nice of you to say."

"What do you mean?"

"A 'career'? That's being a bit generous – I'm only somewhere halfway between hobby and career, at best."

"Exactly. You can either rise to your potential or fall back among the other *fangirls*." He sneered the last word and I looked at him.

371

"'Fangirls'?"

He held his hands up as if to ward off a blow, his camera bags sliding to and fro across his chest like oversized medals. "Ah, *pardonnez-moi*, I didn't mean any offense. You really are better than the young girls or the lonely housewives who come here and take photos of the riders."

I continued to my car without speaking. The 'lonely housewives' comment had hurt. I unlocked the car on the kerb side and loaded my equipment into a box behind the front seat, then stood to face him once again.

"I have 'put my foot in it'?" he asked.

I nodded. "Maybe a little."

He sighed, looked around at the other departing photographers' cars. "I've seen your work, Abby. You're good. You've got a good eye."

"Thanks. But I reckon being a pro takes more than a 'good eye'?"

"*Oui, oui...* You've got that too."

"Oh, come on." I folded my arms across my chest and slouched, trying not to think of the minutes slipping past, already contemplating how fast I'd need to drive to get to Le Mans ahead of the peloton if I stopped along the race route in the interim. I hoped the GPS wouldn't lead me astray like it had yesterday.

"You *do*. I've seen you climb up lampposts and push big men out of your way for a shot."

"I've never pushed –"

"I've seen you *work* for a shot, and I've seen what you come up with."

"You've seen–?" I stood up straight, intrigued.

"Online, *oui*. Your posts about the Tour. Your shots show you've got talent. You need to work on that."

"You're very kind to say that." I shook my head, strangely emotional all at once. I'd never told him where my photos could be found – but he'd sought them out.

"Well, it's just a thought." He glanced at his watch with an air of irritation. "We'd better go – we've got a schedule to keep, *non*?"

He hurried off, leaving me with the sensation there was something more he'd meant to say. I got in the car and sat for a few minutes with the engine idling while the AC cooled the interior. Once again, a wave of sentiment came from out of the blue and I tried to pin it down to one distinct emotion.

It took a while, but when it came to me, my eyes stung with unshed tears.

Gratitude.

***

The ride to Le Mans was exactly what I'd expected. The closest GC riders to myself and Brunn weren't pushing too hard, possibly saving their energy for a final go in the last kilometres. I kept myself safely in the group, riding in the wheels to conserve as much of my own strength as I could for tomorrow.

The breakaway was allowed to go off without any trouble; no-one in that group was a threat to the top ten riders – much less to the top *three*. In fact, now that Schlessinger was out of the picture, as far as I was concerned I had only one real competitor left: Brunn.

Still, it wouldn't do to lay claim to any titles yet. Anything could happen, and I knew well that my teammate would be keen to gain any time he could.

I started feeling twitchy as the kilometres passed, unable to keep from noting each and every time Brunn drifted back to the team car for a chat. I didn't want to let it get to me, but it was hard to resist that creeping doubt worming its way into my subconscious.

I was also aware of the other GC riders watching me. It felt better in some ways – being the watched and not the watcher – but being the focus of attention had its own pitfalls.

All things considered, whatever happened today I was looking forward to tomorrow's time trial. God alone knew how well I'd do, but since everyone else was as tired as I was after a month of riding, the odds were still in my favour. Even though it was hard to believe, I felt good.

How long it would last, I had no idea.

***

As I waited at the desk while checking in to my hotel, the clerk gave me two envelopes along with my room keys. "These arrived for you a short while ago," she said, a small Mona Lisa smile creasing her mouth at my evident surprise.

"*Merci,*" I said, hoping I had the accent right. I tucked the envelopes into my handbag and kept my hands busy checking my mobile for any messages while waiting for the elevator.

Once out of sight of the desk clerk with the doors closed, I punched the button for my floor and withdrew the envelopes from my bag. A quick glance told me nothing other than my name was written in neat, precise script on the outside. One envelope had a stiff feel to it. The other seemed to contain a single folded sheet of paper.

I put them away and managed to hold off opening them until I was somewhat settled in my room. Camera bags ready, I pulled the lanyard with my photography pass attached to it over my head and put on the light green vest with my Tour ID number written across the back. I'd have a look at the messages and then bolt for the finish line in short order.

I opened the lighter envelope first, to find a message from Charles:

"*Call me.*"

I crumpled it up and tossed it onto the bedspread. "When I'm good and ready," I muttered, picking up the other envelope and tearing it open.

A laminated press pass similar to the one looped around my neck slid out onto my hand. I pulled a sheet of paper out and read it.

"*For tomorrow, for Paris,*" was scrawled in unfamiliar, barely legible handwriting.

I paused and read it again, as though somewhere in those four words was some clue as to what it meant or who had sent it. It didn't look like Federico's handwriting, and besides, when would he have sent it? He was on the bike, right now.

The thought of him riding snapped me back into the present. I had to go. I snatched up my camera bags and room key, paused to look at the press pass and the note and then hurried out of the room.

***

The banner marking the final three kilometres passed overhead and the pace kicked up. *Alta VeloCidad* had no-one in contention for the sprint win anymore, but Phil, James and Adrie were riding all-out with Brunn tucked in behind.

"What the fuck's going on?" I shouted into my microphone. No answer. I yanked the earphone out and let it dangle over the collar of my jersey, riding harder to get into the line behind Brunn.

It was exactly as I'd suspected; Jerzy was skewing things to give Brunn a chance to gain more time on me. What was next? Sabotaging my bike? Throwing a musette into my spokes to take me out?

Motherfuckers.

I gritted my teeth and hung on as we flew past the two kilometre marker. The ever-changing team formations took on something that – if one stretched their imagination considerably – could almost be considered order. Adrie pulled off the line and sat up to drift backwards, the sprint trains parting for him like a raging river around a rock in its midst. I scarcely glanced his way.

The carefully-prepared sprint trains disintegrated as the pack slowed suddenly on a hook to the left. A few riders toward the back went down, blocking the rest behind them, while others swung wide and sought their teammates in vain hopes of re-aligning themselves for a proper lead-out.

The churning chaos had taken over and those in the lead were even more solidly placed than before. In the aftermath I gave up marking Brunn. I had other things to concern myself with – keeping the wheel ahead of me and staying upright in the constant shifting and panic of the peloton all around were chief among them.

It all came down to this. The riders around me hammered on the pedals and made their way toward the finish, bobbing, weaving, shouting and shouldering one another out of the way while at top speed.

The shouldering grew still more aggressive, every man fighting for the right wheel, the best place. Expended riders faded back. They appeared to roll backwards, heads low, energy spent, jobs done. The remaining riders in the bunch moved to avoid them.

The group streamed to the right, the numbers winnowing down to the last men, preparing to launch their sprinters. A gap opened as the rider in front of me followed a different line and I kicked hard, surging forward. My vision tunnelled. All I saw was the line across the asphalt ahead, marking the finish.

I didn't look back. Nothing was happening anywhere but

straight ahead. Digging in one last time, the finish seemed to rush toward me. I crossed the line, thrusting the bike forward with an involuntary cry from somewhere deep inside me.

A concussive burst made my insides shake. The noise of the crowd ratcheted up to a higher register, their shouting and cheering rising to a hysterical pitch. It was too much and, thanks in part to my heart pounding in my ears, it quickly ceased to register any more.

*

Hands came out from all directions to touch me, to give congratulatory slaps on my back, and finally, to physically support me. My soigneur cleared a path through the photographers and reporters and lead me back behind the podium, an assistant rushing alongside me while they steered me along on my bike. I was still clipped in, merely holding on to the handlebars and trusting them.

When the confusion cleared, I finally managed to dismount from the bike and someone guided me to a chair in the shade of a marquee behind the podium. I slumped wearily, my eyes shut to the handful of press allowed in the area. Goosh was there to take my helmet and give me a bottle of water, which I opened and poured over my head, relishing the cool stream in the afternoon heat.

I tried to relax, to catch my breath and then drink the water and the can of soda the soigneur brought me. The press were escorted out of the marquee to give the stage winners and myself a bit of privacy while we stripped down and changed into clean kits for the presentations.

One more day.

If it all went as I planned, if I rode as well as I needed to...

Don't think about it. Don't jinx it.

I was only three seconds ahead of Brunn – he could still take the Royal from me.

In the meantime, however, I still had the Royal on my back and reality was finally sinking in: if I rode well tomorrow, I would keep it. The Royal was mine.

Stage Twenty-Seven

(25 km – Versailles, France – Paris, France)

The light from the window slid and distorted along the plastic surface of the laminated press pass as I turned it over in my hand. A cup of coffee cooled in front of me on the breakfast table, my stomach too nervous for me to be properly hungry.

I was sure I'd figured out the source of the pass. The team's press agent had issued it, which meant I could go "backstage" – behind the barriers where the team would gather immediately after the stage.

Federico must have pulled strings to arrange this. Somehow, this single, simple act made everything that much more real. Our lovemaking in Grenoble had already begun to feel dreamlike, as if it were a distant memory instead of something which had happened a few days ago.

At the sound of a soft, melodic chime, I put down the pass and rooted through my purse for my phone. I hadn't bothered to call Charles the night before, and he hadn't called me, either.

I paused when I saw it wasn't his number on the screen but Federico's. I pressed the green button at the top of the keypad and I brought the phone up in what felt like slow motion.

"Hello?"

Shouldn't he be getting ready to ride or doing something – anything – besides calling me?

"Abby." His voice was low, furtive, and it felt like a stolen caress.

"Hi, Chicco. What's going on?"

"Did you get it?" He sounded distracted. I pictured him with one hand cupped around the mouthpiece of his phone.

"Yes, I did —"

"Good, good. You'll be there, yes? In Paris?"

His accent had become more pronounced, giving me a slight shiver in the way it turned common words into something more exotic to my ears.

"Of course I will."

"At the finish, I mean. Use the pass to come there. I'll need..." He drifted off, distracted again. "I'll need to see you then. Please. Just," another pause, "just be there."

"I will, Chicco. Barring any —"

"Be there, Abby," he repeated, and the sudden edge of urgency in his voice grasped my heart, twisting it somewhat unpleasantly.

"I will," I said, trying to put as much reassurance into the words as I could. "I'll be there."

"I have to go, but... I'm not sure how much time I'll have with you tonight."

The breeze from the overhead fan, though the paddles were turning lazily, seemed too cold. I tried to hold back the first emerging thought, and failed.

This won't be the last time.

"We'll play it by ear, then."

Indistinct voices on his end of the line were followed by the sound of his hand muffling the mouthpiece, then scratching and static, and then he returned.

"I'll see you. Soon. When the race is over."

"Okay. I'll see you in Paris."

"Paris," he repeated, and the line closed.

***

I was grateful to get on the stationary bike that afternoon. Warming up, concentrating on my form and thinking ahead to the ride I had to do in a few hours was the best way to shake any distractions.

The morale of the others was fairly high, in spite of recent events. When the guys arrived in Paris, they'd be able to relax until I crossed the line. Regardless of the outcome of my ride, we'd share a final lap along the Champs-Elysees, then meet up for the team dinner – where we'd have all the alcohol we wanted and hearty servings of literally *anything* we'd missed during the Tour. Our chance to cut loose had finally come, and we would take full advantage of it, with Jerzy's blessing.

There was a holiday mood as a result. In twenty-four hours, we'd be scattered across the continent, resting up and waiting for the next race.

Or, rather, *they* would be. I wouldn't be joining them for any more races.

But they didn't know that yet.

For me, this would be the longest day of the entire Tour. As the leader of the race, I'd be the last to start, and so I'd wait while rider after rider from our team departed for the start line to make their ride to Paris.

Once or twice I caught myself thinking of Abby and pushed the thought aside. She was a distraction I could do without. The less I thought about her, the better.

When I saw her tonight, I'd start making up for lost time.

*

Time slowed to a crawl. I checked and re-checked my bike to be sure everything was ready to go. I left the bike in the care of the mechanics and took a moment for myself to sit alone in the subdued quiet of the team bus.

I rolled my shoulders, flexing away the tension gathering there. I stepped out of the bus one last time, looking up at the canopy pulled out over the warm-up area in front of it.

I tested my radio and Michael's voice came through my earpiece, loud and clear. He was already in the front passenger seat of the team car which would follow me all the way into Paris. Jerzy would be in the car following Brunn.

I mounted my bike and rode to the start area at the end of the team village. I rode in slow circles in an area fenced off from the public while Brunn prepared in the start house ahead of me. A race official in a suit and tie, silhouetted against the afternoon light, stood at the open end at the top of the ramp with a clipboard in his hand. Brunn was hidden from view by another official standing behind him, holding the bike upright while my teammate remained clipped into the pedals.

Electronic chimes started counting down and the first official held his hand out, counting off from the five-second mark. When the final chime sounded, he snapped his hand back and Brunn pushed off.

A Tour rep waved to catch my attention and signalled that I should go up to the start house. I got off my bike and walked awkwardly up the steps in my cycling cleats, allowing the other officials time for their own last-minute inspection of the machine.

Then I clipped in, supported by the same stout official in the same manner every other rider today had been. My heartbeat quickened in anticipation while I waited.

Below the forward ramp, the road stretched out ahead between the barriers holding back the crowd. Flags waved and spectators leaned forward for a better look, their camera lenses flashing in the sun. A cool breeze blew as clouds cast a shadow over the course.

My name rang out in a multitude of accents, sometimes followed by wordless shouts, sometimes by catcalls.

I went deeper inside myself, drew long, steady breaths and listened keenly for any sign of trouble. The race today wasn't about the three seconds remaining between Brunn and me. It wasn't even about winning the overall. It was me against the clock.

The official held up his hand and counted along with the electronic chimes for the last time that day.

'Cinq…'
Breathe in.
'Quatre…'
Breathe out.
'Trois…'
Breathe in.
'Deux…'
Breathe out.
'Un…'
Breathe in.

The final chime beeped, the official's hand twisted away from my view and I pushed hard, rolled down the ramp and began my ride to Paris, twenty-five kilometres away.

***

It was with some anxiety that I took my place with the other photographers behind the painted white stripe after the finish line. My camera felt absurdly heavy around my neck and in my hands. I hadn't felt this nervous since arriving in Lisbon a month ago.

As each rider crossed the line, I snapped the best shots I could, trying not to flinch when riders shot by me so close I could have literally reached out and touched them if I'd chosen to. The memories of the fourth stage's finish hadn't quite faded after all.

Once they were past, I would turn to watch the video screen and the time ticking away on the clock. Federico was making excellent time, but Brunn led him by four seconds at the second checkpoint.

I didn't want to think it, but I could hardly keep the thought away. If he didn't make significant gains, Federico could lose the entire race by mere *seconds*. To Brunn.

I wasn't sure which part of this equation would prove more painful for him. From the start he'd been unhappy in the role of lieutenant to Brunn's captain; to lose by such a close margin would be the hardest kick when he'd already be down.

But why was I thinking he might *lose?* It could easily go the other way, with Brunn missing out on the top podium.

My anxiety rose inside me. I stilled my shaking hands long enough to capture a shot of the next rider across the line, held that position and caught the next rider a few seconds behind him.

With a few seconds to spare, I took a quick look at the shots I'd taken. I reset and prepared for the next shot: one of Federico's teammates, with one of the worst times for the day.

Ouch.

When he passed the cadre of photographers he was already shaking his head in self-disgust and – it seemed clear to me, at least – some measure of relief. His race was over.

Federico's ride wasn't, though. I checked my watch and did some quick mental math. It wouldn't be much longer now.

***

The kilometres rolled past, lost in the hum of the tyres on the road and the wind rushing over the rear disc wheel. My heart rate was right where it needed to be. I rode smoothly.

Michael's voice in my ear gave constant encouragement and kept me up to date on my time as I approached the second checkpoint. Brunn had been the fastest through not long before.

A short flutter of panic rose and fell in my chest. This wasn't a long ride, and there was too much to lose if I fucked up by even a fraction of a second – not to mention a few seconds.

The road curved and I glanced at the road sign as I passed it: Pont du Garigliano.

"That's your halfway mark, Ciccio, keep it up!"

I gave a small nod though he wouldn't see the gesture, adjusted my position and took the turn onto the bridge. Spectators lined the road, applauding as I passed.

Pouring on a little more effort, I glanced up and spotted the time on the display next to the screen at the time check. I put my head down again and renewed my efforts, grimly satisfied with the knowledge I was neck-and-neck with Brunn now.

Twelve kilometres to go.

***

My gestures were automatic, cued in by the efforts of the photographers around me: raise the camera, aim, focus, shoot. In between riders I watched on the screens mounted alongside the finish line archway.

The seconds ticked away in slow motion, interminably dragging out the minutes. When Brunn passed the third checkpoint the graphic on the screen named him as the "virtual leader" of the Tour by nearly five seconds.

My trembling increased until I was sure it was visible to anyone who looked at me. I fumbled for my bottle of water and drank the lukewarm contents, then shifted position and picked up the promotional flyer that I'd been resting my bare leg on so I wouldn't feel the heat and grit of the tarmac on my skin. Glad I'd remembered to put on sweat-proof sunscreen that afternoon, I fanned myself with the flyer and waited for the next riders to come in.

The crowd erupted, cheering and jostling in place, and I turned to look at the screen again. Federico had gone through the third checkpoint; he was now two seconds behind Brunn.

"Oh, please, oh-please-oh-please-oh-please..." I murmured, unable to hear myself over the noise of the crowd.

The image on the screen shifted to the small cluster riding in with enough speed to maintain the required distance from one another. I raised my camera and grabbed a few more shots, wincing when one of the riders from *Ligne Infinie* swept past too close for comfort. I smelled his sweat in the wake of his passing and wished desperately that the race were over.

Now the screen showed Brunn, then Federico and then finally went to a split-screen. I didn't want to look – I could hardly bear to watch.

And then, finally, I refused to believe. My heart pounded so hard I couldn't breathe, and I forced myself to raise my camera and take a shot of the screen. A glance at the image on the back of my camera said it all. The revelation in the pixels left me lightheaded while I grappled with my bottle of water again and prepared to photograph Brunn as he approached the finish line.

***

The crowd noise drowned out everything – even my own thoughts – and pounded in time with my heartbeat, creating a vibration which throbbed down to my fingertips. The sound moved over my skin, dripping off along with my sweat. Before I'd stopped, one of the team doctors was at my side, his hand on my back keeping me steady while the soigneur guided the bike through the gap in the barriers.

I didn't look up. I couldn't. I didn't have the strength left.

The doctor spoke to me but I barely understood in the chaos of reporters, photographers and spectators surrounding me. Everyone shouted my name or reached out for me, snapping photos as my makeshift entourage passed by en route to relative privacy.

Photos. Photographers.

Abby.

I tried to raise my eyes to look for her, but I couldn't see through the handlers leading me along. I let my head loll forward. Of course she wasn't there – if she'd been with the other photographers, she'd have to fight the crowds too.

The doc rubbed my shoulder, patting my back with the flat of his hand now and then before handing me something to drink. It did nothing to quench the thirst which seemed to start in the marrow of my bones, but it cleared my head a little. When we'd moved farther away from the finish line I could hear and follow the doctor's questions. I nodded or shook my head in response as we slowly rolled along.

The power of speech left me as reality sank in: I'd done it.

I struggled to think straight in the confusion around me. The press of the crowd eased up considerably after we passed through another set of barriers to go to the riders' paddock behind the podium. Brunn was already there, exhausted and destroyed, and Jerzy was with him.

They stood off to one side, Jerzy's arm around Brunn's shoulders in a victorious hug. His podium standing was secure, then. Goosh appeared next to me and obligingly poured a cool bottle of water over my neck before helping me dismount my bike. Brunn settled into a plastic chair nearby and a handler started a cursory clean-up of his charge while Jerzy started toward me, wearing an expression of sheer elation.

"Two on the podium," he said to the reporters who gathered around him, though I had to read his lips to understand. "We've got two on the podium!"

I took off my helmet and Goosh reached out to exchange it for the bottle of water he was holding out to me, a delirious smile on his face. I kept scanning the crowd for Abby. My leg muscles were watery, screaming in pain from the effort it took to keep me standing upright. Congratulatory slaps on the back felt as though they were only light taps, each landed in a sleepwalk daze, yet each one threatened to topple me. The jubilant shouting and cheering seemed to have nothing at all to do with me or what I'd done.

I'd won the Tour. I'd made a place for myself among the greats, my name was now destined for the history books and sports annals.

Yet my heart was sinking to my feet, my stomach churning with anxiety with each second that passed without sighting her.

I continued searching the crowd. She had to be there by now: she'd promised. Or was that wishful thinking on my part? Maybe she hadn't actually said she'd be waiting at the finish. Maybe she hadn't even said she'd stay with me. Maybe I'd misremembered everything.

For all I knew, she was on her way home.

Across the press barrier reporters fired questions my way. The select few permitted into the small expanse of grass and dirt crowded closer and cameras were now aimed my way from a short distance, blocking my search.

Abby. Oh, Abby, no...

Goosh took the empty water bottle from me and handed me a soda, suddenly looking concerned. I gulped it down, too distracted to answer any questions no matter how many times they were repeated at varying volumes, too agitated to sit in spite of my fatigue.

Jerzy threw his arms around me in a bear hug which threatened to squeeze the air out of my lungs and leave me limp on the earth beneath my feet. "You did it, boy!" he cried, and I wondered if I'd be able to hear when we got back on the team bus. "You did it! I'm so proud of you! I knew you would do it."

With that, the air *wooshed* out of my lungs and I was filled with a sense of gratitude like I'd never felt before. Jerzy hugged me again, squeezing me hard enough to force the tears out of my eyes and onto his shoulder, and I hugged him back, giving in to the urge to weep openly. I wept with joy for what I'd achieved, with fatigue and relief that the race was over, and for what I was about to lose. Jerzy was a man of his word and nothing would change his mind.

In spite of everything, I would miss him.

He grasped my shoulders and shoved me away, looking me up and down like a proud father assessing his son on his graduation day before pulling me to him in another bone-crushing embrace.

I finally sank down onto the chair provided for me and my team handler swooped in to clean the road grime off my face, arms and legs while I struggled not to go limp. Workers for the race organization came in and set up a screen between us and the press while my soigneur handed me fresh clothing for the podium presentations.

My hands shook as I stripped out of my grimy, sweat-stained skinsuit and cleaned myself up. When I'd managed to get half-dressed, I gulped down the protein drink Goosh handed me and then slipped into a fresh *Alta VeloCidad* jersey.

Once all the riders were dressed, the screens came down. Right on cue the press moved in, waving microphones and pointing cameras, asking questions and jostling for the best position in the crowd.

I heard none of it. I saw little of it. All I saw was Abby, dressed in jean shorts and a royal blue t-shirt, pushing through the crowd toward me. Jerzy released me and I turned to face her as she reached the innermost circle of the news crews.

Ignoring the microphones thrust in my face, I pushed toward her and gathered her into my arms, laughing and holding her tight while we turned in a circle. Her smile was the brightest thing I'd ever seen and I couldn't take my eyes off her. I lowered my mouth to hers and kissed her deeply, still turning round and round on the spot, my heart racing as hard as it had out on the *parcours*.

This was winning.

This was victory.

Final Podium

(Paris, France)

The last kiss Federico gave me was tinged with weariness and a hint of the passion he still held in reserve. He mouthed one word to me before the tumult of the crowd and his departure for the final podium presentations separated us:

Tonight.

I turned away and fought through the crowd in order to get to the press area in front of the podium. After he'd been zipped into his final jersey, when they gave him the bouquet of flowers and the cut crystal trophy, he held them aloft with tears in his eyes, the epitome of a man whose greatest dream has come true.

My throat tightened and tears stung my eyes. Though I'd had nothing to do with his success, I was proud enough to burst.

Bottles of champagne were opened and duly sprayed out over the nearest spectators, the foamy streams sparkling under the late afternoon sun. This final ritual completed, he stepped down from the top post of the podium. Federico paused at the edge of the stage to scan the crowd and wave, eliciting excited cheers from his most devoted (and mostly female) fans. I continued taking pictures, lowering my camera after capturing a shot of him wearing a huge smile as he tossed the flowers in my direction.

I didn't manage a picture of his laughter because I was struggling with my awkwardly-caught prize, trying to keep it from falling apart or hitting the ground. A rush of self-consciousness swept over me an instant later along with the realization I was being photographed.

Again, whispered a voice in the recesses of my mind.

I made my way out after Federico was gone. I was still determined to get a few more photos before going back to my hotel.

I stood along the barriers at one end of the course while the teams did their final laps along the Champs-Elysees. They waved to their fans as they went, stopping now and then to sign autographs or to be photographed with especially persuasive fans. Every team paused for a group photograph in front of the Arc de Triomphe, to mark the occasion as though they were typical tourists.

That afternoon, I was rewarded with what were surely some of the best candid photos I'd taken during the Tour. Now all the public events were over, I took a few final photos of the somehow sad and dejected aftermath as the festivities wound down.

The walk to the hotel took forever. After that brief moment, being held in Federico's arms, kissing him in front of God knows how many onlookers, everything felt distant and unreal. The thought gave me a shiver as I walked along the city streets beneath the late afternoon sunshine. My hand rose to my lips, touching lightly there in pale imitation of his kisses and with anticipation of more to come.

I hardly felt the pavement beneath my feet, or the soft breeze pushing past me as I walked up Avenue de Wagram in the late afternoon shade.

Tonight.

We'd only known each other a couple of weeks but it felt like a lifetime had been leading up to this.

All at once, a sensation of being watched swept over me. I slowed my pace and glanced over my shoulder but saw nothing out of the ordinary. I crossed the street to stand in front of my hotel and glanced back.

This time I saw him.

Pascal.

My relief was tempered by the camera around his neck. I froze in place while he crossed the street to join me.

That was when the full realization struck: a short while ago I'd been in Federico's arms, surrounded by his team carers, news crews and photographers.

Even more to the point: I'd been in the arms of the winner of the Tour d'Europa, surrounded by press recording it all.

If Charles hadn't seen the images yet, he soon would.

I suppressed a shiver before Pascal joined me. As I met his eyes a wave of guilt washed over me. All the lies and half-truths I'd told him prickled on my skin and I folded my arms across my chest.

"So," he began, his tone gentle. "You are married to a cyclist?"

I bit my lip and didn't answer the facetious question. He stood without speaking, his hand straying to the camera strap before dropping to his side.

"Why didn't you tell me you weren't married?"

"Because I *am*." I looked him in the eye and held my ground.

"Abigail, I am sorry I doubted you." His smile was unexpectedly sweet. He reached and drew out my hand from the crook of my elbow, then raised it to his lips to give it a gentle kiss.

"Why did you follow me here?" I asked.

His expression turned wry as he released me. "I was going to ask to meet your husband, but..." When his words trailed off, he shook his head and sighed. "I tell a lie. I was going to take your photo, Abby, but now I cannot."

"You were —"

"But now, no."

I blinked back tears. "Pascal, I don't know... Honestly, I don't know what to say."

"I know. I can't believe I'm doing this." He took my hand again and kissed it, then moved to give me a kiss on both cheeks. He lingered, still holding my hand, his lips close to mine before he sighed and stepped away.

"You're sure?" I adjusted the strap of my own camera bag and stood up straight to meet his gaze. "If you want to, go ahead."

He shook his head. "*Non*," he said with a sudden weariness. "The next days will be difficult for you, you know? They will be looking for 'Renard's Mystery Woman'." He crooked his fingers in the air as he said this last. "The tabloids will be very curious, and the paparazzi can be merciless." His mouth quirked. "Unlike me."

"All the more reason for you to get the first photo and steal the wind from their sails," I offered. Yet again, he shook his head.

"I can't be the one to put you through that. I value our friendship far more than the money." Pascal drew a deep breath and turned to go. "I wish you all the best, Abby, in all things. *Bon courage*."

"*Merci*, Pascal."

He walked away, giving me a small wave over his shoulder without looking back.

***

I don't know how it's possible for time to pass in both a blur and a crawl at the same time, but after the podium presentations that's what happened. I caught the merest impressions of people asking – no, *shouting* – questions, with me trying to understand and answer in whatever language the questions were in. Then I finally found the relative quiet and privacy of the team bus.

Only *relative* quiet, because the party had already begun. Techno music blared from the sound system, while a video of the race highlights played on the television screen at the front of the bus. Some of the lads had changed into their civilian gear and others were still dressing and packing their bags.

I picked through my clothes, thinking of the hotel where Abby would be that night and wondering when she'd be there. When I picked up my phone at last I found plenty of missed calls. I scrolled through the list, checking for Abby's number.

She hadn't called.

A flare of guilt ignited when my mother's number showed up in the list, along with that of my agent and several friends' or acquaintances' names. My texts were much the same: numerous brief congratulatory messages, one after another, including one from Solange (one word: *congrats*), and one from my agent, Marcel (*OFFERS COMING IN! CALL ME*).

I didn't bother with the voice messages awaiting my response. Calling to check them would be pointless anyway in the din currently surrounding me.

Later, I promised myself. *I'll make the calls later.*

"The team soiree is at *Maison Fête* tonight. As the guest of honour, I'm assuming you'll be there." Michael leaned against the seatback and gave me a wan smile. He looked exhausted, but happy, and I wondered if I looked the same.

"I suppose so," I said, zipping my duffel closed. "It'd be pretty strange if I weren't, *non*?"

"Exactly."

"Besides, I'd like to say my goodbyes."

The confusion on Michael's face was surprising. "You're being awfully dramatic, aren't you?"

"What do you mean?"

"We'll be meeting up in a few weeks for some training before the Vuelta. You make it sound like you're not riding anymore."

I shrugged. Hadn't Jerzy told him yet I was off the team?

"Of course, if you want to sit it out, that's your choice. Why not wait and see how you feel, eh? Give yourself a chance to recover and see how you feel then."

I nodded, dazed. "All right. Good point."

"That was a fantastic ride today, Ciccio. Well done." He gave me a solid slap on the shoulder and turned to make his way off the bus. I watched him go, hope rising stubbornly inside me. Had Jerzy's bluster in Grenoble been a bluff? Or had he changed his mind as soon as I'd crossed the finish line today?

It would be *insanity* to kick the winner of the Tour d'Europa off the team. The sponsors would never forgive him.

But why couldn't I imagine him going against his word?

*

The evening passed in noisy, wine-and-alcohol-fuelled celebration, with the team and all the crew (and their families and/or partners) gathered in the ballroom *Alta VeloCidad* had rented out for the occasion. It felt like a wedding, what with the DJ playing music over speakers set up haphazardly around the room and wildly mismatched couples dancing amidst the tables.

I spotted Rom sitting off to one side with the daughter of one of the soigneurs. He concentrated hard on what she was saying while she leaned close enough to kiss his ear if she chose. I suspected he wouldn't object if she did; he looked more focused than I'd seen him in the race.

More proof of the celebratory mood was Brunn's uncharacteristic grin while he chatted with one of the photographers commemorating the evening. That Brunn would seem satisfied with second place was something I'd never dreamed possible, but he clearly was.

Throughout the night I laughed and joked, ate and drank and

posed for photo after photo with various members of the team's crew. It was a struggle to keep from checking my watch too obviously, to keep my agitation and desire to leave at bay while waiting for the party to wind down. Marcel even put in an appearance long enough to tell me I had several obligatory interviews the next morning starting at eleven a.m., and where to meet the journos doing them.

I hated this, knowing it meant yet more time away from Abby, but there was no avoiding it: it was part and parcel of being the winner of the race. Citing fatigue from the race, I asked him to reschedule as many as he could and he nodded and darted out the door.

That's when I realized what winning this race meant to everyone else: he'd never jumped so fast to do *anything* in all the time I'd known him. This was a fringe benefit I'd have to get used to.

The volume of the music dipped considerably and I sipped the champagne in my glass, anticipating yet another smile-and-wave-for-the-crowd moment. There had been several already tonight, and I'd only recovered from the blindness from the dozens of ill-timed camera flashes from the last one.

Instead, Jerzy and Michael stood next to the DJ, talking with him before Michael appropriated the microphone to be better heard over the din of conversation and laughter.

A momentary whine of feedback drew attention to Jerzy, who fussed with the collar of his sport coat until the silence was absolute. He looked out at the partygoers with a mild, crooked smile, then raised the microphone.

"Ladies and gentlemen," he began, his English unusually heavily accented, his voice thick. He cleared his throat and continued, "Thank you for coming tonight to celebrate *Alta VeloCidad*'s win of the *Tour d'Europa*."

A burst of applause and cheerful shouts filled the room and quieted down quickly.

"I don't wish to detract from the festivities, but there *is* some news which I feel must be shared this evening."

The alcohol I'd consumed that night threatened to boil up out of me as heat rushed to my face. Was he mad? Surely he wouldn't break the news of my expulsion from the team *now*?

"As you all know, I've worked with Federico Renard for many,

many years. I could even argue that I discovered Ciccio when he was just a pudgy fourteen-year-old competing in amateur races right here in Paris."

A small ripple of laughter moved through the room at this and I bit my lip and forced a smile at the same time.

"My career has been – how do you say? – 'hitched to Ciccio's star', for some time. Well, seeing that he's reached this goal today, now that he's accomplished so much, it seems..." He paused and cleared his throat again and swiped one hand over his forehead, giving a half-laugh as he did so. "Well, it seems it is the time for the partnership to end."

A low murmur threaded through the crowd, and I could feel gazes shifting back and forth between Jerzy and me.

Fuck. I gulped down the contents of my glass and set it back on the table with an unsteady hand. When I looked up again Jerzy was looking directly at me, his crooked smile wavering.

"Tonight, I must tell you that I have been forced to make a very, very difficult decision. This is probably the hardest decision I've ever had to make, but events during this race have forced my hand."

His eyes never left mine, not once, while he spoke.

"Ladies and gentlemen, this is not only a victory party," Jerzy said, picking up a glass of champagne. "It's also a farewell party."

Another murmur in the crowd, this time more insistent. I tensed, debating whether I should get up and leave or wait for him to actually say it. Why on earth would he do it this way? Wasn't a press release good enough?

"I'm leaving my post as general manager and DS of *Alta VeloCidad*, effective immediately." Jerzy waited for the reaction of the crowd to die down, then looked at me. "I thought I should go out when we were on top. Thanks to you, Federico, I can do that."

My legs refused to follow orders at first, but I gripped the edge of the table and got to my feet as someone – I think it was Adrie – got a freshly-filled glass in my other hand in time for me to raise it in acknowledgement of Jerzy's toast.

***

I managed to send one text to Federico. My room number, as usual, plus a short message: *pick up key at desk*. I then called the front desk and told them I was expecting a guest, so would they mind giving him the key when he came in?

The battery of my mobile could hardly withstand the onslaught of calls from home. During a quiet period, when the phone wasn't vibrating or ringing, I checked to see how many messages I had: too many. Too many to deal with, even with hours to go before Federico would join me.

There was one call in particular I dreaded receiving. It didn't come until nearly midnight, and he rang through on the phone in the suite instead of my mobile. His voice was distant on the line, so I knew he was calling from his office in London. When he called using that phone I always struggled to hear him.

"I saw," he said, and I listened hard, hoping to hear some semblance of an emotion.

There wasn't.

"You saw," I said. It wasn't a question. I'd known he'd watch, particularly when it was clear Renard – my "favourite," my "boyfriend" – would be the winner. What I hadn't known was Federico would hold me in the middle of the crowd for what felt like an eternity before giving me a kiss which would be captured at a thousand different angles, photographed, broadcast and tweeted around the world.

I also hadn't known I wouldn't mind, or that I'd bear the subsequent barrage of texts, calls and emails from my family and friends, with their questions and/or accusations, with something like ease.

I flinched at hearing his voice so soon. I suppose he'd never expected my betrayal to be so public, had never anticipated that I'd been telling him the truth all along: if I were with someone else, it would only be if I were gone for good.

"So," he began after a lengthy pause, "*this* was how you chose to tell me?"

"Don't play high and mighty with me. It's what you wanted, isn't it?"

"Not exactly, but I don't know if it's worth fussing over small details."

The barb wasn't quite sharp enough to draw blood, but maybe it would bruise. I didn't know how to tell him that was the best he could hope for.

That was when I realized that hearts don't always break all at once, or for the reasons we expect. Heartbreaks can take time to happen – years, in some cases, days or hours in others – yet the final fracturing instant can overwhelm or even disappoint. This was the case for me.

The disappointment, I mean.

Because I felt nothing for him; not anymore.

The sound of a key in the lock caught my attention and I turned that way as the door slowly opened and Federico peered around it. "Abby," he said, my name turning into a question on his lips as he realized I was on the phone.

"Abby!" Charles shouted down the line, and I recoiled a little, surprised I still had the phone in my hand. "I can't believe this!"

"What? What can't you believe?" I asked, though I knew already. Trying to focus on Charles' voice I turned away from Federico as he closed the door.

"You have him *there*? Now?"

"He just got here –"

"Tell him to go."

I laughed in spite of myself. "I'll do no such thing! How dare you? How *dare* you think, even for an instant, that you could give me an order like that?"

I sighed, shaking my head. It was too much. I didn't want to do this anymore.

"I'm not paying for a room so you two can—"

"Then *don't*," I interrupted, suddenly shaking all over. "Don't pay for it. I'll pay—"

Now Charles gave the laugh I'd come to know too well over the years, the one which told me my interests were piffling, unimportant things. The one which reassured me he had no doubt I'd fail, that I'd never see my latest endeavour through to the end.

I gripped the phone harder and heard the plastic casing of the handset creak as I closed my eyes.

"Abigail, *darling*, you couldn't possibly afford it. Don't get ahead of yourself."

"You might be surprised," I muttered, unwilling to raise my voice. "I'm anything but ahead of myself right now."

"Tell him to leave, or I'll notify the hotel I'm not going to pay for the room. They'll kick you out."

"I don't care. I want him here, he's staying, and that's that."

"Goddammit, woman! Do –"

The silence which followed was broken by the soft *click* of the switch hook being released. I turned toward the telephone table to find Federico lifting his hand from the phone's base. He extended his other hand without a word.

***

I waited, still reaching out to her, trying to gauge her reaction to what I'd done. Even though I'd only been there a short while, I'd heard enough to convince me to do it. I hoped her shaking was from anger and not fear.

Finally, Abby handed me the receiver and I dialled the number for the front desk.

"*Réception*," answered the solicitous voice of the slender blonde I'd spoken to on my way in.

"*Allô*; this is room 615 requesting that you hold any calls until further notice."

"*Certainement*. No calls to 615."

"*Merci beaucoup*." I put the phone down and turned to Abby, waiting to see her reaction before I remembered she didn't understand French.

"I'm sorry about that," Abby said, gesturing vaguely toward the phone.

She didn't seem too troubled by my having interrupted her husband in mid-rant.

"Don't worry," I said, trying not to spook her any more than she already had been.

Her eyes met mine, shining, filled with emotions I couldn't read. *A married woman. Are you really ready for this?*

I wanted to ask if she was okay, but the question seemed to imply perhaps she shouldn't be, and it was somehow expected. She rubbed her eyes with one hand. The tumult of emotions was still in her gaze, but also something else: resolve.

This made me smile, and to my considerable relief, she did too. Just like earlier that afternoon, her smile was the brightest thing I'd ever seen.

I reached for her again and she stepped into my arms, wrapping her arms around my neck as we kissed, soft and slow. We drifted out of the entryway and into the living room of her suite to settle on the sofa without parting.

"You taste like champagne," she said quietly and I shrugged, grinning.

I slipped one hand under the back of her t-shirt, relishing her smooth skin beneath my palm. She moved to put her arms around my neck again and then slowly slid over me until she was nestled in my lap, her legs resting on the sofa cushions.

We sat that way for a while, curled up together in the corner of the sofa, kissing heatedly but not pressing for more.

It was killing me.

There was no way she didn't know it, either. Every so often she would shift just so and her bottom would press against me in the most exquisite way, until I finally grasped her hip and held her in place.

She made a soft sound, somewhere between a whimper and a sigh, and kissed me harder this time. I fumbled with the button of her jean shorts and she reached to help me, shimmying out of them without leaving my lap.

Which only made things worse.

"If we keep on like this, *amore mio*, I'm not going to last much longer," I confessed against the curve of her neck, and she laughed softly.

"Italian again," she noted with a quiet laugh. "Anyway, I might beat you to it," she whispered, drawing back to kiss me again. She guided my hand between her thighs, an action which would have seemed almost unthinkable not long ago. I curved my fingers over the soft cotton covering her, felt her heat through the fabric and closed my eyes.

I really *wasn't* going to make it at this rate.

"There's something in my suitcase we'll need," I said, gesturing vaguely toward the object in question with my free hand.

She twisted away from me to look at my carry-on suitcase where it stood near the sofa. "I'll get it – I can reach it from here."

I held her steady as she stretched out and grasped the handle of the bag and dragged it over to us. Clearly, she didn't want to waste time any more than I did.

"Where is it?" she asked, already reaching to unzip the top pocket.

"Right inside there – see?"

"No, but..." Abby looked at me, her hand exploring blindly behind her. "Wait a second, what's this?" She pulled out a different package I'd stashed inside, wrapped in blue and silver paper.

"That's for you. I meant to give it to you later, though."

Mischief lit her eyes. "Later?"

"Well, now's a good time too, I suppose."

She tore into the packaging eagerly, a childlike expression of delight on her face until she discovered the contents.

"Chicco? Is this… Is this really…?"

"It's the Royal I was wearing when we met, yes."

"But…" She unfurled the jersey and it made a soft, whispering sound as the bottom hem pooled in her lap. "Jesus, Chicco. I can't accept this."

"Of course you can. I've got plenty of 'em."

"Really? Really-really?"

"Yes," I laughed and she examined the Royal once more. "It's yours. You can even try it on if you want to."

"Oh, I don't know…" She stared amazed at the jersey in her hands. "*Can* I?"

"Go ahead."

She ran her hand over the material, and moved to put it on. Her hesitation surprised me before she pulled her t-shirt over her head and flung it to one side. Wearing only her bra and underwear, and taking care not to elbow me carelessly, she twisted and turned to draw the jersey up over her arms, then let me zip it up for her.

I lingered there, my fingers straying over her breast where the fabric stretched a little tighter before I let my hand drop to trace the zipper down to the hem. I stroked her upper thigh lightly until she shivered, pressing her bottom against me in the same tantalizing way she had before.

When I pulled at the waistband of her panties, she reached to help me again. She flung them in the same direction as the t-shirt she'd discarded a few minutes ago before guiding my hand once more. With nothing between us her heat warmed my palm and I slid one finger closer to the source as she trembled beneath my touch.

I kissed her again, holding her to me as I parted her lips and teased her tongue with mine. She squirmed in my arms, one hand over mine to urge me on, until she pulled her mouth away to draw deep, shaky breaths. I slowed my caresses and she shook her head, burying her face against my neck.

"Please don't stop," she whispered, showing me how she

wanted me to continue.

I did my best, distracted as I was with my own excitement, and she grabbed hold of my shoulder, gasping as she shuddered around me. She raised her shaking hand to my cheek to hold me in place while she kissed me, hard.

Then she was unfastening my trousers and urging them off me while I struggled out of my shirt. I couldn't think. I was lost in her soft curves and she was still clad in the now-unzipped Royal, with her bra undone and pushed out of the way. Then her sweet, delicious heat was wrapped around me and taking me in.

Christ, I couldn't even speak. I could only point deliriously toward the suitcase again and again until she got the message and dug out the silver foil packets in the top pocket. We separated long enough for me to wonder what the point was in this part when we'd already foregone the precautions the last time, and then I was ready and she took me in once again and it didn't matter anymore.

Post Race: Day One

(Paris, France)

I didn't recognize the sound of the telephone when it rang. The quiet, *chirrup*ing tone didn't register at first. Then I remembered I'd arranged a wake-up call in case I failed to rouse myself for my eleven a.m. interview.

I fumbled for the receiver in the curtained darkness and brought it to my ear slowly, feeling the efforts of the last month in every fibre of my body as I did so. The chirpy voice of the morning shift worker rattled out a cheerful "*Bonjour, ceci est votre réveil par téléphone.*"

Now awake, I had to prepare to face the next obstacle of the morning: leaving Abby. The sight of her dark hair spread out over the white glow of her pillow, one tanned shoulder peeking out of the tangle of sheets, was impossible to ignore.

When I pulled the covers back up over myself and slid closer to her, she shifted position slightly, burying her face in the pillow. I kissed her shoulder and then brushed her hair back from her face.

She opened one eye slowly and squinted up at me. "Who was that?" Her words were muffled between us in the bedclothes.

"My wake up call. It's nine. I'm going to order breakfast – what would you like?"

With a shrug she burrowed under the covers again. "Fruit would be good. Or some pastry. And coffee, please. *Lots* of coffee."

I picked up the phone again and placed the order with room service. Abby peeked out from the rumpled bedclothes, watching me with unusual interest until I hung up. I couldn't help laughing at the way her dark eyes blinked up at me.

"What is it?"

"I'm sorry. I find it fascinating when you speak French."

"Really?" I laughed again. "Why is that?"

"Your voice is deeper than when you speak English."

"No..."

But she nodded and I rolled over to gather her in my arms, breathing in the scent of her hair as I kissed the soft skin next to her ear. "I've never noticed this," I insisted.

"Why would you? When you're speaking you're not listening..." She paused, clutching my shoulder with a small shiver. "You're not listening objectively to yourself."

"Good point." I drew back to kiss her mouth, my hands straying over her warm curves under the covers.

If only I didn't have that damned interview... The temptation was strong, but the threat of the room service cart arriving while we were in the middle of things was enough to deter me.

"I should get ready," I said with a sigh, and she nodded, reluctantly releasing me.

I loved her for that.

***

He rolled out of bed in the languid, relaxed manner I'd come to think of as particularly *his*, filled with his natural grace of movement. He was captivating, even when he was only crossing the room to open the floor-length curtain and peek outside.

My breath hitched in my throat at the way the light struck him: he shone against the low light in the rest of the room, shadows and highlights playing over his skin in a manner somehow provocative and matter-of-fact at the same time.

"Abby? Is something wrong?"

"Definitely not."

"So, what is it?"

"Nothing, I just... I wished I could take your picture."

"Why didn't you?" He closed the curtain and my eyes had to

adjust.

"I can't photograph you like that."

"Like what? Nude?"

His accent twisted the word in a way that made me blush. I hoped he couldn't tell. "Well, yes...I mean, *no*, I couldn't."

"Why not?"

Without thinking I glanced at the dresser on the opposite wall where my camera bag rested. Federico crossed the room again and opened the bag with swift, sure movements. A small part of me wanted to protest, growing more insistent as he drew the camera out, removed the lens cap, and then aimed the camera at the mirror in front of him.

He pressed the shutter button and it *click*ed softly in the silence before he turned and aimed the camera at me for another shot.

"Don't," I said quietly, raising one hand as if I could hide from the lens.

"Doesn't anyone ever take *your* picture?" he asked, sitting next to me and raising the camera yet again. I shook my head, thinking of Pascal the afternoon before.

"Not usually; no, they don't."

"That's a pity," he said and carelessly pressed the shutter button again. The *click* sounded so much louder up close. "You didn't answer my question. Why couldn't you photograph me now?"

"It doesn't feel right," I said with a shrug. "It's an imposition. It's...opportunistic."

"I don't understand." He placed the camera gently in my hands. As soon as he did this I felt a little better, but still not as *complete* as I did when I was working.

I blushed again, recalling the wholeness when I'd been with him a few hours ago, as though a lost part of me had been found somewhere unexpected.

"If I took a picture of you now, here, like this...I'd have to keep it to myself." I bit my lip, considering whether the light would have changed too much in the last few minutes to try to recapture the shot of him from before.

"Why?"

"You're not serious. I don't want to talk about this if you're going to joke around."

"I *am* serious. Why couldn't you publish it? Get some publicity?"

403

"Then I'd be like Sol-" I stopped myself from saying her name, unsure of how he'd react. "I'd just be like *her*, taking advantage and using you. I don't want to do that."

"You wouldn't be. This is different: I'm giving you permission." He leaned forward to look me in the eye. "I'm saying you can do it. I ask only that you keep me in the loop."

I shook my head again and he took the camera out of my hands, examining it more closely. He adjusted something and then held the camera at arm's length, pointed toward his face. He was framed crookedly in the screen on the back before I realized it was recording video.

"I, Federico Renard, give my permission to Abigail White to take photos of me at *any* time, and to do whatever she wishes to do with those photos, including selling them to magazines or publishing them in a book of her own. I say this of my own free will, because I love her and want her to be happy."

I gaped at him as he stopped the recording.

"There," he said, handing the camera over again. "If you keep that, you have all the proof you need on the matter." He leaned closer, cupped the back of my head in his palm and gave me a long, soft kiss. "I have to get ready. Room service should be here soon."

I nodded, still dumbfounded and unable to respond.

When he disappeared into the bathroom, I waited for the sound of the shower to start running before I reviewed the video he'd made. Surely I'd imagined it. Surely he hadn't said he *loved* me and recorded it for posterity.

I played the video several times, start to finish, the voice of the backlit Federico on the screen competing timidly with the slightly-off-key rendition of some unfamiliar French pop song ringing out from behind the bathroom door.

I barely heard the knock on the door in the living room.

Shit, room service!

I fumbled out of bed and grabbed the plush bathrobe off the chair where I'd draped it the night before. Stepping out of the darkness of the bedroom, the bright light of the living room nearly blinded me. I squinted as I wrapped myself in the robe as demurely as I could while hurrying to the door. After quickly pulling my hair back to make a messy ponytail, I opened the door at last.

"*Madame*," the porter said, and tilted his head toward the dining table at the other end of the room in an elegant gesture. His comportment was purely professional as he wheeled the cart through the suite. Without another word he transferred the dishes to the table and put the napkins and silverware in their places as precisely as though we were in a restaurant. Once everything was in perfect order, he breezed out of the room, bidding me "*Bonjour!*" as he went, closing the door softly behind him.

I sat on the sofa and pulled my robe more tightly around myself. I should have been elated, but surely it was too soon for Federico to say something like that? Perhaps I was reading too much into it. If I were lucky, couldn't this be a case of something being lost in translation?

But no, it didn't seem to be. After less than three weeks of clandestine meetings and never having spent twenty-four consecutive hours together, he was saying he *loved* me?

Never mind that he'd been ready to marry Solange before her true nature emerged. Either he meant this – and was too immature to realize how hastily he'd fallen – or he said the same thing to every woman he was with.

I could have handled the situation with no problem – fling, not a fling, whatever – if he hadn't said he loved me. This, now; *this* was a game-changer, and I had to figure out where I stood.

***

"So, Federico, who was that lovely lady you were celebrating with yesterday?"

"I'm sorry?" Now that all the usual and technical questions were out of the way, the personal ones had come to the fore. I had no interest in answering this one no matter how pleasant my interviewer, Stéphane, might be.

"Please, don't play coy. The whole world saw you two – there's never been a bigger post-win kiss in the history of the Tour! So who is she? Obviously Solange is out of the picture?"

"Obviously," I said, allowing myself a grin in spite of his gossipy tone. It was the *Grand Tours Magazine* fiasco all over again. "But I'd rather not talk about her right now. All in good time, you know how it is."

"For a kiss like that, I wish I *did* know," Stéphane enthused, arching one blond eyebrow. I held my silence until he spoke again. "Of course, the rumour mill is already in full swing."

"Is it, now?"

"*Oui, oui* – in fact, there are some saying she is a married woman, some are saying she was seen with Heinrich Brunn; you know how rumours are, though."

Brunn's name nearly made me flinch. "But what has any of this got to do with the race? Or my win?"

"Nothing at all; it is merely a more *human* aspect, isn't it? 'The great love behind the winner'?" He held up his hands as he said it, as though framing a marquee.

I shook my head. "I understand what you mean, but we're not ready to talk about our relationship."

He nodded in response. Something in the gesture seemed like a challenge. "I see, but then, it must be very…*new*, yes? You were engaged to Solange some weeks ago, but now you're with another woman? When would you have time to meet anyone during a race like this?" He gave me a wink, loaded with innuendo. "No, no, this cannot be a *new* relationship. You're only human after all!" His laugh boomed out and I forced the corners of my mouth to twist into what I hoped was an approximation of a smile.

"Let's say it's complicated and leave it at that."

Another booming laugh and eager nod, and Stéphane extended his hand to me. "Just as I suspected," he said and we stood together. "It was a good win, Federico. Congratulations – and hey, off the record," he leaned in and pulled my hand to draw me closer, "we were all eager for you to beat the German, you know."

Which one? I wondered, and nodded in response, withdrawing my hand and resisting the urge to wipe it on my trouser leg. "*Merci,*" I said, and then he was gone, leaving me alone in the room. I took out my phone and scrolled through my messages in an effort to distract myself until Marcel came to collect me for the press conference.

Unable to focus, my mind kept wandering to what Stéphane had said about the "rumour mill" and the implications this held for Abby. I'd been so stupid, insisting on her being there. Now she was the subject of gossip and who knew what else.

When the door opened and Marcel stepped in I startled, dropping my phone onto the table with a clatter.

"*Mon Dieu*, Chicco – are you okay?"

"Yeah, sure. Why?"

"You look like you're going to be sick."

"Nah, I'm fine. Really. Fine." I stood up and he gave me a wary once-over before I stuffed my phone in my pocket and folded my arms across my chest. "Let's get this over with, okay?"

"Sure, sure – of course. But *are* you okay?"

I looked at him, tired all the way to my bones. "I've got a lot on my mind, Marcel. I need to rest as soon as I can."

He moved to one side and gestured for me to go before him. "Right down the hall in the conference room around the corner," he said, still looking concerned.

I cleared my throat and stood up straight, then forced myself to walk down the hall to the room full of reporters, knowing without a doubt what at least *one* of the questions would be.

***

My hands shook with agitation as soon as Federico left the hotel. I didn't want to watch television; after what Pascal had told me the day before, I was afraid of what I might see.

When I checked my email, it was as though a bomb went off inside me. I started shaking, hot and cold all over, my hand trembling when I raised my chilly fingers to wipe the sweat away from my forehead.

My eyes refused to focus beyond the first dozen unread messages, struggling to take in the names of people I hadn't spoken to in years alongside those of my best friend, my brother, and, oh dear Lord, my mother as well.

I picked up my mobile and switched it on, listening to it *ping* and vibrate against the sofa cushion next to where I sat. I knew it was downloading voice and text messages from most of the people who had written to me, plus others – including former co-workers and acquaintances from town I'd volunteered with at the library or craft shows.

With the phone on loudspeaker, I forced myself to listen to the beginning of most of the voice mails before deleting them. I listened to a few, saved some for later and then deleted the rest.

Most of the calls, naturally, were from women. Several were unable to keep the thrill of being close to the heart of a scandal from showing in their voices. The only men in the mix were my boss/editor Derek, my brother (again) and, of course, Charles. His messages were the briefest of all: he'd left one short, sharp "Call me" after another.

I'd finished the voice messages and was thumbing through the texts when the mobile chimed in my hand for an incoming call. I checked the screen warily, unsure if I would answer if it was Charles.

Blessedly, it wasn't, but I was still nervous about answering.

"Sweetie, what on *earth* is going on?"

I hadn't expected to hear such tenderness in her voice. My anxiety faded away into relief and I curled up into a foetal position on the sofa, with my head cradled on the armrest and the phone pressed to my ear.

"Hello, mum," I said, and was met with a momentary silence on the line.

"I'd wondered why you hadn't come back with Charles, but I guess I've my answer now, eh?"

"Uh-huh. Well, there's more to it, of course. When did you find out?"

"Last night. Marcia called to tell me to watch the report on the sports news. I thought she was excited because you'd managed to get on camera. I had no idea."

"Sorry."

"Still, it begs the question, doesn't it? Honestly, what *is* going on? I thought you and Charles had gone on this trip to rekindle things between you two."

"I'd thought the same, funnily enough." I sniffled, wiping my nose on the back of my hand. "Turns out Charles has been seeing someone. He called her all the time, kept telling me it was about 'work', but I overheard him making plans to meet her. Then he went home."

"And...what? You ran out and grabbed the first boy you saw?"

Amazingly, there was a hint of teasing in her voice. I froze in place before moving to sit curled against the armrest.

"You're not angry?"

"Why would I be? It's your decision to make, and it's not really for me to judge. Besides, I know you too well. You wouldn't do something like this lightly. *Would* you?"

"No, of course not."

"And, also knowing you, I'm sure there's a fascinating story behind all this."

To say the least. I cleared my throat, unsure of what to say in response.

"If you need representation," she continued, "let me know. I'll start vetting the lads in the office. I'm sure someone will be happy to step up for you. Or do you have someone?"

Even though she couldn't see me, I cringed. "Yeah, I'll need someone. Charles got our lawyer."

"Ah. That's not good. Are you worried that he'll have intimate knowledge of your case?"

"So to speak."

"What do you mean?"

"I mean, that's who he's been seeing. Jennifer Goodrich was our lawyer."

Mum sighed, a sound of pure resignation. "Not good," she repeated. "Still, he surely wouldn't be foolish enough to use her in this capacity. Abby, may I give you some advice? Do whatever you want with it, of course."

"I could sure use it."

"Come home as soon as you can. You need to hit the ground running – if Charles files for divorce, it could go badly for you. You need to strike the first blow."

"I know." I curled up tighter, the phone cradled between my ear and the armrest once again. "I just feel, I don't know, sort of *frozen.*"

"Thaw out, darling. Now is the time for action."

I couldn't help smiling. This was my mother in a nutshell.

"I will. Thanks, Mum."

"It's what I'm here for. Ring me when you get home."

"Okay."

No need to say goodbye; she'd already rang off. As I packed up my computer and switched off my phone, I toyed with the idea of calling Charles but pushed it away. I didn't want to muddy my thinking any more than it was. The sound of the key in the lock assured me my thinking would soon be muddled in other ways.

***

The sight of Abby sitting on the sofa made me feel like I'd come home. The quiet room and the soft late afternoon light gave everything a sense of peacefulness the rest of my day had lacked.

Every time we'd met during the Tour, through all of those

secret stolen moments, lying next to one another on her bed, there had been the feeling of being in the eye of the storm around us.

She stood up as I crossed the room, and a rush of relief flooded through me when she was in my arms again. I'd never had this with Solange; never, not once.

And then there had been the press conference – all the questions about her, the assumptions they were already making about us – and felt ill. If she hadn't watched that on TV, I hoped to at least be able to prepare her for what might be coming.

I meant to explain, to tell her what to expect, but instead I ended up kissing her. I lost myself in her softness, the smooth curves beneath her clothes which filled my hands so perfectly, the wet slide of her lips over mine.

With the curtains still closed, the bedroom was semi-dark, the only light coming through the still-open door. She pushed the door closed but it didn't latch. There was only enough light to illuminate her as she undressed, her skin glowing pale in the half-light.

We lay together on the still-made bed, exploring one another at our leisure until I couldn't stand it anymore and pulled her on top of me. She smiled when I whispered her name, understanding what I needed and reaching into the drawer of the bedside table.

Christ, she even made *opening* a condom packet sexy, never mind the slow, teasing way she put it on me. When she finished I was so worked up I was afraid if she stroked me like that one more time, there'd be no need for it.

Then she settled astride me, riding me for all she was worth, and I desperately tried to hold out for her to climax before me. Every roll of her hips, every low sigh she made which showed her pleasure and her effort brought me closer to the edge. Desperate, I urged her to sit up and slipped my hand between us to stroke her clit.

A sharp, sudden buck of her hips as she cried out and the tight clenching of her heat around me was proof enough I'd succeeded. She slowly lowered herself to rest with me while she caught her breath. I closed my eyes and tried to relax, delaying the inevitable.

We kissed, slowly at first, then with greater urgency as I rolled us over so I was on top. We moved together, her soft sounds growing louder as she held me closer, tighter, rocking to meet my thrusts.

Her eager gasps filled my ears as I arrived at the point of no return. I couldn't help calling out when I came. I kept thrusting until she clutched at my back, her fingers digging the flesh along my spine while she wrapped herself around me even tighter.

With a final, soft shudder and sigh, Abby relaxed. Still inside her, I sank into her waiting embrace, grateful, exhausted and satisfied.

This was how I'd wanted things to be with Solange. But no matter how many promises we'd made, no matter how much I'd worked to make myself believe in her, we hadn't been like this.

It never was. Not once.

We parted and lay together in a loose embrace in the growing darkness. The shadows deepened, softening as the light from the street seeped around the curtains. My eyelids grew heavy with contentment and I drifted off with the softness of her hair against my cheek, her breath warm and ticklish on my chest.

Every single thing in my life was perfect.

Post Race: Day Two

(Paris, France)

My eyes opened to darkness, with only the glow of the light from the streets to see by. Abby and I were still atop the bedclothes, lying tangled together in much the same position we'd drifted off. The only sound was her gentle breathing next to me.

I lay silent, savouring everything, loving her softness and the heat of her body, amazed at how right everything felt. I'd won the race, kept my place on the team, racked up several lucrative endorsement deals – hell; I'd even got the girl! 'On top of the world' didn't even begin to describe it.

She stirred next to me; I pulled her closer. She draped her arm over me lazily and made a purring sound as she stretched and curled up with me again.

"Abby." I said her name for no reason other than how it felt to say it. The next words came naturally, gently, and they felt good, too. "I love you," I murmured into the curve of her neck, breathing in the scent of her hair and the salt of her skin.

She tensed. "What?"

"It's true, Abby: I love you."

I shifted position and smiled down at her. The way she looked up at me was enough to dishearten even the most confident man, which until then, I had been.

Until *that* look.

Surely it was a trick of the light. I pulled away to switch on the lamp on the bedside table. When I turned to face her again, she had pushed up onto her elbows to face me. We looked at each other for an eternity, neither of us speaking while the implication of her silence sank in. I wanted to look away, preferring that she not see my disappointment.

"It's only been a couple of weeks," she said quietly.

I half-laughed, caught in disbelief. "You honestly can say you didn't – that you haven't –" I cut myself short and shook my head, looking away. "It's not just been me," I asserted. "I know that."

"I didn't say it *was* just you. It's – it's not enough time, is it?"

When I looked at her again, her wide, earnest eyes met mine.

"I mean," she continued, "this has been the most incredible, most wonderful time of my entire life, but is it enough for...for that?"

"For what?"

"For falling in love."

I studied her face closely, seeking any sign that she was joking. She couldn't mean what she was saying. Hadn't I offered her enough proof of my feelings?

In the meantime I gripped the bedclothes in both hands and fought the vertigo as my whole world tilted out from under me.

***

Federico's eyes bored into mine with such intensity I longed to look away, but couldn't. His dark gaze transfixed me.

Still, confusion boiled inside me. Making love with him had brought every conflicting emotion to the surface. Not long ago I'd wondered if it was possible I might be falling in love with him, and that was *before* Charles had left me behind, *before* I'd made my decision to let whatever happened, happen.

So why was I fighting it now? Now that he had declared it, why was I sitting here waiting and hoping desperately for something – anything – that could prove what started weeks ago was real and not mere infatuation?

And then his intensity was tempered by hurt, and I wished I could take back what I'd said.

"Chicco –" I began, and he sighed, his hand rising to touch my cheek.

He leaned in and brought his mouth to mine for a slow, soft kiss. When we parted and I tried again to speak, he silenced me with another kiss, this one harder than the last, his hand still holding me in place.

He pressed closer as his kisses grew stronger and more determined. Still, he paused before he pushed between my thighs and softly whispered my name. The quiet, questioning lilt in his voice made it clear that he really *was* asking for permission.

I nodded, still aching with empathy and desire when he slipped inside me with a low sound of satisfaction. Something about that uncertainty and hesitation each time we'd joined, that respectful request for permission stirred something in me I couldn't explain.

I wanted him too much. Longing for him like this made me afraid that *this* was all I wanted from him. What if there wasn't anything more than physical attraction between us?

The thought rang false.

Then I was swept up and lost in him again – his kisses, his caresses pursued me until I was out of my head and in a world that only existed between the two of us. The only world I wanted to be in.

***

I'd first moved on impulse and then on simple need. I'd expected another, more definite rejection from her, but met none.

The most troubling part was how easy it was to disappear into her. Every time we were together she became all there was in the world, soft and warm and salty-sweet, taking me in and holding me tight. Her hands and her mouth left traces on my skin, hot and wet, cooling in the darkness and leaving me gooseflesh and eager for more.

Every sound she made – of pleasure, of frustration, of need – told me what to do. I only wanted to make her happy, to give her what she wanted or needed most. Suddenly, I was ready and struggling to hold back until I was sure she was satisfied.

And then I was coming, and she felt it, and it was enough for her to join me.

As we parted, I was aware of two very different things: we hadn't used a condom, and there was someone knocking at the front door of the suite. I didn't want to call her attention to either thing because I didn't want this to end. It seemed as though we'd reached an understanding at last and I didn't want that to change.

I also had a bad feeling about who might be knocking at a hotel room door at six a.m.

***

I jumped a little at the sound of a knock at the door.

Federico lay next to me, breathing hard, staring at the ceiling as though reading something written there and showing no sign of responding to our unexpected guest. He sat up, moved to the foot of the bed and snatched his jeans off the floor to put them on, muttering to himself in French all the while. His face was still flushed with exertion as he pulled his shirt on.

"Okay, then; when you're ready, you call him and let him know you won't be back, and –"

"What?" It took a moment to understand what he was talking about. "Just like that, eh?" I asked, strangely slighted.

Federico paused and looked at me, puzzled. "What do you mean? The race was over three days ago, and he has to know you're not coming back. You'll be confirming that."

"I will?"

"It's been plenty of time for *that* at least, *non?*"

"Time for what? Preparing my statement?"

Still seated on the end of the bed, he blushed deeper in confusion and I felt a fleeting pity for him. He looked so, so young, and that made me feel worse than ever.

Did he really think it would be so easy for me to leave Charles? Emotionally speaking I was already gone, but the actual separation and departure wouldn't be accomplished in a day.

"I thought you wanted..." He trailed off uncertainly, seemed about to speak again then turned his attention back to getting dressed.

"You thought I wanted *what?*"

"Me," he said, not looking my way.

"I *do*. You've no idea how much." I had a brief urge to laugh.

"It must not be enough if you won't stay with me."

"Please, don't–"

"No, don't worry about it. Go *home*. Go back to a man who doesn't love you the way you want and who you claim *you* don't love. At least the two of you are well-matched."

"It's not like that. And you have no idea how difficult this is, how hard it is to know you want someone so much it's actually frightening, and not be able to be with him."

"But what's keeping you away? What's holding you back? Just *leave* him."

"I *will* – but it's not that simple."

"No? Why not?"

"I can't explain. You wouldn't understand."

"Why wouldn't I?" A hint of desperation crept into his voice.

Another knock at the door, louder, and his mobile on the bedside table began to ring at the same time.

"*Jé-zzzus*..." he groaned, grabbing his phone and smacking the screen to answer the call as he moved to the living room of the suite. "*Allô*," he grunted into the phone, his footfalls stamping mutedly across the thick carpeting in the other room.

The door opened, and muffled laughter followed almost immediately. I caught a bit of conversation in French, and then Federico poked his head around the door of the bedroom and gestured for me to stay in bed.

"Don't worry, okay? It's the vamp—I mean, it's the doping control. I have to give a sample. They'll be gone in a little while."

"How did they know you were here?"

"I told them yesterday. They needed to know, so they could find me."

"Oh, okay."

He nodded and closed the door, but I pulled the covers more tightly over myself anyway. During the Tour, when he'd said he and his teammates had very little freedom to do as they wished, I'd thought he'd meant that *Jerzy's* rules were restrictive. Now I understood a little better what he'd meant.

Six o'clock in the morning, in a hotel not on his itineraries, and they'd still found him? There was something disturbing about that, and something sad, too.

***

It was the same routine as always: the agent followed me into the bathroom while I produced the sample, and then sat down with me at the dining table to fill out the paperwork. He glanced toward the bedroom door and arched an eyebrow meaningfully at me. And then I remembered – he was the one who'd come to my room in Grenoble.

In spite of myself, I wanted to laugh. Undoubtedly he thought I had a woman in every hotel I stayed in.

He leaned closer to me, tilting his head toward the bedroom door."Is that *her*?" he whispered as I handed the sheaf of papers back to him. He put them away carefully, casting glances my way to show he was waiting for my answer.

My urge to laugh faded at once. I folded my arms across my chest and said nothing, and the sly smile on his face disappeared. He'd crossed a line and he knew it.

"Well, that's everything, then. I'll be on my way."

"Yes, you will," I said, and stood to let him know the sooner he left, the better. I walked him to the door and waited while he stepped out into the quiet corridor.

"I'm sorry about that," he said, offering his hand and taking me off-guard. I hadn't expected an apology. "Best of luck to the two of you," he added, then made his way to the elevators around the corner.

I closed the door and walked quietly toward the bedroom, detouring to get a glass of water at the wet bar next to the dining area. My mood darkened again as I thought about my conversation with Abby.

None of this made any sense. How could she want to be with me and still be so adamant about leaving? What was it about me that drove women away like this? After all we'd done to be together, after all the risks I'd taken, *this* was the end result?

No. Unacceptable.

I'd been kept in the dark by Solange, and I'd be damned before anyone would toy with me like that again. I'd been honest with Abby and I had nothing to hide. If she didn't love me, then that was fine. It would hurt like hell to let her go, but I wouldn't let her fool herself into going back to *him* for anything in the world.

***

"Is everything okay?" I asked when Federico stepped back into the bedroom.

"Everything's fine." His voice was strained, as though he were trying to keep his temper. He watched me, his expression unreadable. "Nobody else knows I'm here, Abby. Don't worry — they won't say anything."

Shit. I hadn't even thought of *that*.

"There's so much to learn, isn't there?" I sighed, folding my arms across my raised knees and resting my head on them.

"What do you mean?" He undressed and got back into bed.

"About dating a famous person, I mean." I shook my head and sat up to face him. He draped his arm around my shoulders and waited for me to speak. "In all this time, and I know this will seem hard to believe, but... I haven't often thought of you as a *celebrity*. You've just been 'Chicco' to me." Federico smiled as I said this, but didn't interrupt. "Once in a while it would hit me that other people would be interested in what's happening between us, but then it would sort of, I don't know, fade. It didn't seem important, but now I'm seeing it's more complicated than I expected."

He made a small, almost involuntary sound at this but said nothing. His brow creased, then he withdrew his arm and lay down. I lay down with him in the silence which followed.

I rested my hand on his chest, his heartbeat steady under my palm. His rhythm was a bit slower than mine, and I slowed my breathing, the better to feel it as I closed my eyes.

He tucked my head under his chin and wrapped his arms around me, making me feel small and protected. He stroked my hair with one hand and exhaled softly, and I smiled at the gentle rise and fall of his belly.

It was perfect. No husband, no team demands, no race to ride, no return trip to take; just the two of us, alone, in our own little world.

But these sorts of moments can't last and this was no exception. Neither of us wanted to acknowledge the end, so we both tightened our embraces as though doing so could slow time and keep us together.

"Stay," he murmured, so quietly I barely understood him.

"If I could..." I answered ruefully.

He drew away a little and turned my face up to his. At last the world seemed to freeze in place while I let myself get lost in his dark eyes.

"Stay," he whispered. He brought his mouth to mine. "Stay," he repeated, but gave me no chance to answer. Instead, he kissed me harder than before.

The fierceness of the kisses which followed left me gasping before they strayed down my throat to my shoulder and then to my breasts. His hands slid roughly over me, raising gooseflesh as the heat of his touch cooled.

This time he didn't ask permission.

*

Late morning light filled the room when Federico opened the curtains with the remote control he'd found in the nightstand. We lay side-by-side, barely touching, in a silence that almost hurt.

"I still don't understand why it's so important for you to go back to him," he said, turning the remote end over end in his hands.

"I'm not going back to *him*."

"Haven't I shown you how I feel? Hasn't anything I've done in all this time been proof enough for you?"

He pulled away abruptly, kicked off the covers and sat up to put his back against the padded headboard of the bed. He wasn't pouting, but the expression on his face wasn't far from that. He tossed the remote onto the table. I watched the flat plastic box totter at the edge before it fell with a quiet *thump* onto the floor.

"You don't understand, Chicco. My husband is not terribly fond of losing."

"Neither am I."

"I mean losing to *me*."

He looked surprised at this and I sat up next to him.

"*That's* why I have to go home. I can't stay here and give him even more ammunition against me. As it is, I can't prove he did anything with her, but he has plenty of proof about you and me. I'm bound to lose the house and everything else."

Federico moved closer. I could feel the heat of his skin.

"Why not let it go, then? Come with me. Give him everything and come with me."

"Are you seriously asking me to give up everything in my life for you?"

"What? No, no – I didn't mean it like that. I meant, I –" He shook his head as though trying to clear it. "Abby, I'm only trying to say I want you with me. That is all."

Overcome, I nodded and lay down. He stayed where he was. In spite of my annoyance at his previous statement, and only slightly mollified by his explanation, my eyes strayed over him while he sat beside me.

Although we'd made love many times, I still couldn't believe that he was there with me. I needed to stop seeing him as a celebrity and see him as 'Chicco' again. I needed us to just be *us* again. I needed time to *think* without distraction.

I had to find a way to tell him, but I didn't know how.

And then it occurred to me how to explain.

***

Abby sat up again to face me, a peculiar expression on her face. If not for the conversation we'd already been having, I'd have thought it looked like hope. She pulled the covers over herself modestly before speaking.

"Here's the thing: neither one of us has had a chance to *think* since this started. Every day has been too full to do that. You've travelled and trained and raced and recovered—"

"*And* done everything in my power to be with you when I could," I snorted, angry in spite of myself. If she only knew what I'd willingly given up for her, maybe she'd understand. No, considering how things were playing out, maybe it was more likely she'd probably panic and run away.

Ignoring my outburst, she forged ahead:

"*I've* been taking photos and driving from city to city in countries I've never visited before, stressing myself out in the process. I've been meeting deadlines and dealing with being alone and...finding out my husband's been cheating on me and planning to go back to his lover whether I was with him or not. On top of all this, I was involved with you and feeling things I couldn't even begin to understand."

She took a deep breath, wiped one hand across her face and continued.

"The point is, everything has been so jumbled up and out of control – even the last couple of days – that neither of us has had a chance to stop and think about *any* of it."

"I know what I *feel*, Abby. Doesn't that matter?"

"But how do you know what you feel is the real thing? How do you know if you're fooling yourself?"

"You *know*. I can't put it any clearer than that."

"But you were engaged to her, weren't you? Didn't you 'know' with her, too?"

I shook my head, felt a rush of heat to my face. "No – I never did. That's what I'm trying to explain: I never felt anything like this, and I can't doubt it for a second."

Her hands trembled atop the blanket and I reached to put my hand over both of hers. "What did you feel with *him*, then? Do you feel the same way about him now?"

"That's not the point."

"It's the *only* point, Abby."

"I don't feel what I used to feel for him, no." Her shaking worsened and I held her hands more tightly. Her whole body seemed to thrum with a barely contained energy. "I never felt like I do now, either. But I can't believe it's good for us to jump into something with our eyes closed." She shivered and her teeth chattered.

It was almost as though she were contagious: it took all my will not to shiver, too.

A quiet *tap-tap-tap* of teardrops hitting the covers over her lap caught my attention and I reached to wipe the next tears away. She leaned against me, her head in the hollow of my shoulder, and a few more of her tears fell onto my chest. I left them there in spite of the way they tickled, cooling as they dried.

"Chicco, we need to do this like adults. We need to go forward slowly. I know that's not romantic or anything like that, and it's the opposite of what we've done so far, but I think it's the right way to go about it. Honestly, we hardly know each other. If we rush into this, don't we stand a bigger chance of one or both of us getting hurt?"

Mon Dieu, this wasn't how I'd pictured this going at all.

"If I stay here," she continued, and the tremor in her voice made my heart hurt, "If I do that, it's taking the easy way out. Charles will be able to say our marriage was just one more thing I lost interest in and let fall to the wayside, one more casualty of my short attention span.

"If I don't go back, it's like I'm leaving it all up to him – to file for divorce if he wants, or to stay married if he prefers that. And if he *does* file, it'll be his chance to be the wronged husband, abandoned by his flighty wife for a younger man. Everyone in the world knows about you and me now, and he'll play that up to his advantage. But that's not what bothers me the most, and it's not what tells me I have to go home again – at least for a while.

"I *have* to see this through. I *have* to be the one to say 'I'm finished with all of this, and here's why.' I've got to show him that this decision was mine and mine alone, and I've got to stand up for that. I don't know if it makes any sense to you or not, but I can't stand my ground from another country – I have to do it there, face to face, or it's meaningless."

"But if you stay here, maybe..."

"Maybe *what*?" She sniffled and grabbed a tissue from the box on the bedside table to wipe her eyes and nose delicately.

"Maybe I could find a way for this not to hurt you so much."

***

A fresh surge of tears welled up in my eyes at the sincerity of his words. "I wish it were that simple," I said, and he looked away, toward the farthest corner of the room.

"Why isn't it so simple? Why can't it be?"

"Chicco, no matter what, the fact that I'm leaving him is going to hurt. Having my marriage end is going to hurt. It hurts because I believed, and because of how much I *wanted* to believe. It hurts because I made myself believe even when I know I shouldn't have done. I need time to get past that before I can trust myself to trust someone else again."

The silence spooled out endlessly and I began to second-guess every word I'd said. *What if he misunderstands? What if I said the wrong thing? What if -?*

"How long do you need?" he asked.

"What?"

"How long do you need?" he repeated.

"I don't know. I looked online the other day, and it'd be..." I sighed, not wanting to say it. To put a number, a time limit to it was surely asking for trouble. "It looks like anywhere from four to six months. That depends on whether he fights it, or if he's already filed, or a million other things."

I wiped away the tears as soon as they started to fall, and then Federico tightened his arms around me and placed a kiss on my temple.

"Four months it is, then."

He sounded resigned but not angry, and my heart fluttered anxiously. I could feel him shaking, too, suppressed emotions churning under the surface.

"I can't guarantee anything, though," he said, and I nodded, not looking at him.

"You're right, of course," I said. "It's not fair for me to ask you to wait —"

"No, no. I mean I'll try to wait that long, but I can't guarantee I will."

I couldn't look up at him. At least he was being honest. That was good, even if it hurt too much to even think of what that really meant. He must be furious, or hurt, or—

"Abby, look at me."

I shook my head.

"*Abby*." His hand cupped my chin and turned my face up to his and I tried closed my eyes, trying not to wince in anticipation of what I would see when I opened them. "I can't guarantee I'll wait because I might have to come for you *before* then."

I opened my eyes.

Caught fast in his gaze I trembled, anxious, until the voices of doubt faded and I was able to see what he was seeing in me. The barriers I'd built between us – whether for self-defence or in moments of disbelief – fell away, razed by the intensity I found in his eyes.

This was what I'd wanted all along.

ACKNOWLEDGMENTS

First and foremost, I must thank my husband, Alessandro, for all the encouragement and help he has given me since I first suggested, in 2009, that I would like to write a novel set in the world of road cycling. He didn't laugh, and he helped me to design the initial route of the Tour d'Europa, using a slightly out-of-date atlas and our fingers to measure distances from the beginning to the end of each stage. Luckily, we found better methods (thank goodness for Google Maps) along the way. His assistance in keeping different aspects of the stages straight in my head cannot be undervalued.

Next, I must thank the folks who assisted me with the languages contained in this story. When I tweeted for help, they were there to assist immediately and I am grateful to Hande Leimer of vinoroma.com and Jonathan Sachse for their help with German; to Gisela R. and José Been for giving me some authentic Dutch phrases; and to Michael Dean and the Kirschenbaum family for their much-needed assistance with the Polish phrases in the story. Any mistakes, misuses or other errors with any languages in this story are mine and mine alone. I'd also like to thank photographer Roz Jones for her time, Edward Pickering of Cycle Sport UK (he knows why), and Nimani Fernando for the line of dialogue she gave me after an exchange on Twitter. (I'm still laughing about the snails, Nim!)

I must thank my critique partners, Nell Dixon and Jason Horger, who helped guide me along through the first draft and kept pushing me to finish in the first place, when things got tough. Thanks also to Derek Duggan for his suggestions and advice, as well as the pieces of cycling "colour" he's shared along the way. I'd also like to thank Oliver Ross for contributing the team name of *Alta VeloCidad.*

More thanks go to the members of both Famous Five Plus and

Romance Divas for all of their support and advice along the way. Also, I say "Thank you!" to all of my "Beta Readers" who slogged through the nearly-final manuscript, caught errors/typos and gave me their honest opinions on the story: Kitty Fondue (of VeloVoices.com), Georgie Francis, Jill Pennington and Kimberley Troutte all gave up time from their busy schedules to give me a better idea of what was working – and what wasn't. I've done my best to live up to their expectations since. Extra thanks go to Georgie Francis for her kind and generous permission to use her photo in the cover art for the ebook version of the book.

And last, but certainly not least – Thanks, Mom! – for getting the word out about my books and gently goading me to get this one done, too.

If there's anyone out there I haven't mentioned, I promise, the slight is unintentional.

ABOUT THE AUTHOR

An aspiring writer from the age of eight, Kimberly Menozzi began writing her first stories instead of paying attention in school. While her grades might have suffered, her imagination seldom did. She managed to keep most of her stories together for years, then lost them after a move when she left a trunk full of papers behind. (She meant to go back and get them, but circumstances prevented her from doing so.)

So, she started over again. And lost those, too.

After a trip to England in 2002, she began work on *A Marginal Life (Well-Lived)*, inspired by the music of Jarvis Cocker and Pulp. The novel was completed in 2003, and is undergoing rewrites with hopes of future publication.

Also in 2003, she met and fell in love with an Italian accountant named Alessandro. She married him in 2004. This necessitated her arrival in Italy and she has lived there ever since. After several months of working for language schools and writing blog entries for her family in the US to read, new story ideas began to develop.

Finally, in 2007, she began work on a new project, inspired by her love/hate relationship with her new home. The novel *Ask Me if I'm Happy* was completed in 2009 and was released November 15th, 2010.

On April 28th, 2011, Kimberly published a novella, a prequel to *Ask Me if I'm Happy*, titled "Alternate Rialto".

In 2009, while watching the Tour de France, Kimberly began work on the novel which would one day become *27 Stages*.

Kimberly presently has two novellas in the works: *None So Blind*, a second prequel to *Ask Me if I'm Happy*, and *Milan, NC*, a stand-alone love story set in a fictional North Carolina city.